Trouble
with Boys

Also by

Tangled Up In You

The Trouble with Boys

GEMMA ENGLISH

POOLBEG

This novel is entirely a work of fiction. The names,
characters and incidents portrayed in it are the work of the
author's imagination. Any resemblance to actual persons,
living or dead, events or localities is entirely coincidental.

Published 2005
by Poolbeg Press Ltd
123 Grange Hill, Baldoyle
Dublin 13, Ireland
E-mail: poolbeg@poolbeg.com

© Gemma English 2005

The moral right of the author has been asserted.

Typesetting, layout, design © Poolbeg Press

1 3 5 7 9 10 8 6 4 2

A catalogue record for this book is available from the British Library.

ISBN 1-84223-189-8

Typeset by Magpie Designs in Goudy 10.5/14 pt
Printed by Nørhaven Paperback A/S, Viborg,
Denmark

www.poolbeg.com

ABOUT THE AUTHOR

Gemma English lives in Swords, County
Dublin, with her husband Mark and their
son Jack. They still all live as peacefully as
possible with Harvey the Cat.

Gemma works in the Bank of Ireland
Mortgage Services Centre in the IFSC.
Her first novel, *Tangled Up In You*, was
published by Poolbeg in 2004.

ACKNOWLEDGEMENTS

My thanks, as always, go to Paula and all at Poolbeg for their hard work in promoting and encouraging me from the start.

Thanks also go to Gaye Shortland for correcting all my grammar and spelling mistakes. (How I ever completed Third Level Education is a mystery to me!)

A very special thank-you goes to my parents, family and friends. I feel I must mention Elaine O'Leary at this point, a girl who never ceases to amaze and amuse us with her tales of loves lost and loves that should never have been encouraged to begin with!

And, of course, my heartfelt thanks go to my boys: my husband Mark, who buys me trashy magazines and chocolate when I need inspiration, and our son Jack, a baby who helps to heal my heart a little more each day.

My final mention, as always, is for our baby Matthew, watching all the excitement from heaven. I miss you.

Dedication

To the boys in my life,
Mark, Matthew and Jack

– no trouble at all!

1

If my mother is to be believed, my interest in the opposite sex began at about age five. The story goes that I was in high babies when I sent a boy sitting close to me a note. The note was short and to the point. It politely requested that the boy in question "Kiss Amelia". I am Amelia and I handed him the note. The boy took the note, read it and started to cry. He then told on me to the teacher, and the teacher told my mother when she came to collect me. Sean Baker, this was the boy's name, never kissed me, and I never asked him again. Also, just for the record, I'm not ugly.

I started this by saying, "If my mother is to be believed". The fact is, I have no memory of actually writing or handing over the note to Sean. But I do know what went on after the note was sent – my parents have told that story at every family gathering we have had for coming up on twenty-two years. You'd think they'd get bored telling the damn story again and again, but apparently not.

At the time this story begins, I was a lot older, in fact I was closing in on that big three-zero at a gallop. I had grown up a lot and no longer sent small boys lewd notes. In fact, I was a veritable pillar of society.

I owned a small apartment in Clontarf and lived there very happily, if feeling a little lonely at times. I had a car and a full driving licence. I had three goldfish, named Breakfast, Dinner and Tea. I had a skinny but incredibly lazy cat called Ghandi who sat beside the goldfish bowl all day and stared in at them. The only tell-tale sign that Ghandi was alive was that his tail wagged when you rubbed him and he bit your hand when it got too close. I used to wish he had a nicer personality, like one of those cats on TV, who sit on laps and purr, but I did grow to love the bad-tempered furhead!

In fact, I still own all the things listed above, including Ghandi who still sits at the goldfish bowl. Nevertheless, there have been a few significant changes in my life.

Also, at that time, I had a job working in a recruitment agency in the city centre. It was a well-paying but dead-end job, and both boring and stressful – a deadly combination. I was good at my job; I had the diplomas on my wall and letters of thanks to prove it.

The day I started there were fifteen people in the office; I was the sixteenth person in the door. Three years later all the same people were doing all the same things and telling all the same stories they were telling then. It was as if I'd entered the *Twilight Zone* or *Groundhog Day* and couldn't find my way back out. You'd think that in the course of getting everyone else around me jobs, I'd have found a good one for myself. I hadn't though and there were times when I really did think I would die there.

Of course, there was another reason why I couldn't or wouldn't leave. His name was Ray Donnelly.

2

Ray was absolutely gorgeous. He recruited PA's and secretaries for short-term contracts around the city. Millions of pretty young things fawned over him all day – OK, millions may be an exaggeration – about ten, maybe twenty – and I hated it. The masochist in me would sit and watch it every day. I knew he was only being polite and professional, but did he always have to take their phone numbers and promise to call them as soon as something "special" came in?

Ray was perfect, and not in that perfect-teeth, tanned-skin, blond-hair type of way. He had dark brown hair for starters with pale blue eyes that sparkled with just a hint of trouble, the kind of trouble girls like me can't help falling for. He was always dressed to kill and everywhere he went there was just a hint of aftershave hanging in the air behind him. He was wonderful and I was not the only one around who thought so. There were quite a number

4

of girls in the office who hovered around the water-cooler hoping to catch his eye. So far none of us had succeeded in catching his fancy, but that didn't have to stop us dreaming, did it? It didn't stop me dreaming anyway. I dreamt about Ray a lot.

One Wednesday I was spending a few hours contentedly watching him work. It was about 10:30 in the morning. I was being no trouble at all to anyone, just ignoring the pile of paperwork in front of me, having decided instead to watch Ray work through his. I'd been happily watching him for about twenty minutes when Ruth appeared at my desk. She stood directly between "the vision" and me – the look on her face confirmed that had been a deliberate tactic.

"Yes," I said, not moving my gaze, now staring at her midriff.

"Where do you want to go for lunch?"

Food. My attention was diverted. "Will we try out the new place on the corner?" A small café had just opened and the smells were wonderful.

"Right so. Are you going to do that work at all today?" Ruth eyed the bundle in front of me.

"Yes. I'll get it done after lunch."

Just as she was leaving she muttered that Jack would be joining us.

"Fine," I lied.

She knew I was lying. Everybody knew I could just as easily have kicked Jack as look at him. That sounds dreadful and I am not a violent person. Jack just irritated me. For starters, he was so quiet and he watched everyone. He claimed it was a very interesting pastime. He said he "people-watched" and that it gave him "a feel for the person before actually speaking to them". I thought it was odd and I couldn't help but feel a little bit analyzed anytime we got together. And as anyone who's ever felt analysed will know, you never actually feel a "little bit analysed". It's usually an all-or-nothing kind of situation. But please don't get me wrong. I could see that Jack was a nice guy; he seemed clever and Ruth thought he was very funny. In fact Ruth liked him a lot. I liked Ruth a lot and I respected her judgment, but I just couldn't feel anything much more than irritation when I was faced with Jack. I'd read a piece in Cosmo – they were judging people's personalities and giving them a colour. I was something ridiculous: mango or violet or something. This got me thinking that if Ray were a colour he'd be lime green or canary yellow. Something noticeable, unmistakable. And if Jack were a colour he'd be beige. Most women like beige. I have a few beige tops, and it can be a very flattering colour. But it's bland. Beige is a nothing kind of colour. I decided Jack was the human equivalent of a beige top.

Of course, Ruth couldn't see what I was talking about. She really liked him and had always found him to be great company. She had on occasion conceded that he became quiet when there were lots of people around, but supposedly when they got together he was a riot. I always doubted it, but Ruth liked him and we were getting lunch together, just the three of us. It was going to be fun; I could just sense it. We gathered our coats and bags and left the office at 12:50. Our intention was to get to the café before the lunch-time rush. Everyone in the Dublin 2 area code and some from the area codes 1 and 4 had had the same idea. We all waited and eyed the last few free seats in the window of the café.

Then came the awful words from Ruth: "Amelia, you go and grab that seat. I'll get your sandwich."

Horror filled me. I hate that — sitting at an empty table, reading the no-smoking sign with great interest as paying customers carry their trays around looking for a seat.

"Do I have to?" I whined. "I hate taking up the seats with no food. It's embarrassing."

"I'll sit with you," came Jack's voice from behind me.

I'd forgotten he was there. I swear to you, he was that quiet. Thank God I hadn't said how great Ray looked — only Ruth knew about the infatuation.

"What?" I said.

"I'll grab a seat with you. I know how you feel. I hate grabbing seats with no food too. But this is a drastic situation. We need to take action." Then he laughed so I took it he had made a joke.

I smiled weakly at him. "All right then," I said, giving my money and order to Ruth.

Jack did the same and took a seat with me. We looked at one another, then out the window. I was aware that perhaps I should make some small talk, but to be honest my mind was a blank and, anyway, why was it me always making the conversation with him? Why did he never think of anything to ask me? I could feel myself getting

7

annoyed with him for no real reason. So I carried on looking out the window. Then without realising it, I yawned.

"Are you tired?" he asked.

"What? No."

"Oh." There was a pause while he looked at me. "It's just, you yawned. I assumed you were tired."

I looked at him. God, he was the most boring man alive! "To be honest I hadn't noticed. I yawn from time to time during the day – it really has nothing much to do with the fact that I'm tired – more bored, I think."

Perhaps I was being mean to him, but honestly I was not in much of a mood for pandering to him at that moment.

Thankfully Ruth arrived with our sandwiches just in time. Another few minutes alone with Jack and I would have left the table, perhaps the restaurant.

She dished out the goodies. I say goodies but what I mean is gruel. Not that the café had anything to do with it – Ruth and I were in WeightWatchers and neither of us was enjoying it.

I sat choking down a tuna sandwich on brown with a tiny bit of butter, lettuce and onion. In actual fact I'd have really liked a ham and cheese toasted sandwich with Pringles and a side salad smothered in whatever relish that was adorning the plates of the people dining beside us. I sat over my Diet Coke and tuna, damning my hips to the seventh level of hell.

Jack was eating a cheese baguette with all the trimmings, a full-fat Coke and Pringles. If I needed another reason to be irritated with him, I had it.

Ruth and Jack chatted and, to be fair to him, he was a bit chattier with her than he was with me. I still thought "a riot" was overemphasising it.

3

Ruth and I became friends almost as soon as I walked in the office door that fateful Monday morning three years ago. I think our main bond was the fact that we were both a good stone overweight. Put it this way: if a doctor had weighed me, he'd probably have fainted and when he came round he'd most likely have told me I was clinically obese. To put it another way, I was sure that when I died it would take a few more pall-bearers than normal to carry me out of the church. Ruth and I had joined WeightWatchers about four months before this. In that time we'd lost a total of five pounds between us. We hated WeightWatchers or WW as we called it – and not just WW – we hated any kind of forced exercise or diet regime. As soon as I hear the word "diet" I get hungry. It was becoming a huge problem. I was getting a huge bum among other things.

Anyway, Ruth and I were walking home from Weight

Watchers. It was a twenty-minute walk from my apartment and we should have done it more often. As it stood we did it only twice a week, going to and coming from WeightWatchers at the school hall. Maybe if we did it more often we'd have lost more than 2lbs between us that week. Every Wednesday night we would walk to the local national school in fear and dread; we'd hardly speak with anxiety. Fifteen minutes later we'd walk home again, blood boiling with anger, swearing black and blue that that week we would keep to our points and lose at least 7lbs.

Then without fail we would stop at the off-licence, buy a large bottle of wine and drink it in my apartment. We would then talk crap at length and solve all the world's problems. I often thought about using a Dictaphone and sending the tape off to the Taoiseach. To date we had the health system all sorted out and we were working on infrastructure. Infrastructure, as well as being a bitch of a word to say when you're tipsy, was proving to be more complicated than we'd thought. Teen pregnancies would just have to wait, perhaps another month or so, before we could get round to sorting them out.

As usual, after our "weigh in" we were headed for the off-licence when a small disaster occurred. My bag fell off my shoulder as I was walking. It landed on the ground. I bent to pick it up and noticed it had fallen in a puddle.

"Would you look at that?" I complained. "Only bloody puddle in the street and my bag falls in it." I sniffed my bag. "I hope it's not dog pee."

Ruth tutted, nodding in half-hearted agreement. She

was not overly concerned with the fate of my bag, and I couldn't blame her. So we walked on in silence, her looking around and taking in the beauty of the sea front, me muttering to myself about the wet patch on my bag. We headed to the off-licence, trying our best to ignore a group of fifteen-year-olds in badly fitted jeans, skateboards in hand, waving money at us and begging us to get drink for them.

They had made a number of mistakes – their first was dressing like that, then there was the irritating flick of their fringes. I must be old – their constant flicking made me want to cut their hair or at very least clip it on one side. Then they made the fatal mistake of addressing me as "Hey, Missus". Did I look like an old married? Forget what I just said about their fringes before you answer that.

As if that wasn't bad enough, they then called "Fat cows!" after us when we ignored them.

I was prepared to ignore them. After all, we may have been overweight, but we were the ones who would soon be leaving the off-licence with a bottle of wine tucked under our arms. Ruth was not. She turned on her heel and told the gang leader that he should take the tenner he was currently waving in our faces and go to the nearest clothes shop and buy either a pair of trousers that fitted or a belt. Childish as it may sound, the look of shock on the teenager's face was worth the embarrassment of being an adult involved in a slanging match with a child. He actually blushed and pulled his jeans up.

We walked into the off-licence and chose our bottle of wine. As I got to the till and delved into my bag for my purse, the full extent of the disaster became apparent. The smell of perfume was overwhelming and all my things were drenched in an orange-coloured liquid. I paid for the wine with a wet twenty-euro note and smiled at the assistant as he took in the puddle that was forming on the counter under my purse.

Outside the shop I showed the evidence to Ruth and together we found the offending bottle, or half of it to be exact. The "puddle" was my nice perfume and now there was none left. I was raging about it. We didn't solve the world's problems that night – we just complained bitterly about the shoddy packaging that expensive perfume comes in.

The following day I was on the phone to my mother, still bemoaning the fate of my new and very expensive perfume. She cooed sympathetically to me down the phone. Mothers are wonderful for this type of thing.

Jack appeared at my desk. I looked at him, expecting the usual handful of faxes, but he began to mouth something at me. I put my mother on hold.

"What's wrong?" I asked him.

"I heard you fell quite badly last night. Are you all right?"

"I didn't fall," I replied.

"Ruth told us. She said you fell very heavily on your shoulder, that you landed on your bag and broke your nice perfume. I heard you were upset." He looked concerned.

"Jack, I didn't fall. My bag fell off my shoulder. Anyway, I'm on the phone, but don't worry – I didn't

13

fall." I went back to my mother.

Just as my finger hovered over the hold button, Ray appeared at Jack's shoulder.

"Amelia, scarlet! We all heard about the fall." He laughed. "Bummer!"

I smiled, mortified. "Look, I don't know what Ruth told you but I did not fall over last night. My bag fell – there seems to be some mix-up in the story here."

Ray smirked. "Amelia, there is no shame in taking a tumble; it happens my granny all the time. Were you mortified?"

"Look, get Ruth. I didn't fall last night or any other night. Where's Ruth?"

"She's outside smoking," Jack replied.

"Well, get her in here, will you?" Then I remembered my mother was still on hold. I turned back to the phone. "Mum, I have to go. I'll ring you later."

Ruth was summoned and appeared at my desk flanked by Jack, Ray and Louise. She was looking at me with that giddy expression that told me she was enjoying herself and was taking nothing back.

"Ruth, take it back," I said. "I didn't fall, heavily or otherwise, last night."

"I wasn't looking at you all the time! All I know is this: I looked around to find you close to the ground with a broken bottle of perfume in your bag."

"Ruth, you know full well I didn't fall. I dropped my bag and the perfume smashed!"

"Is that what happened? I couldn't say for sure," Ruth smirked.

14

"You know that's what happened!"

"Is that really what happened? Her bag fell off her bloody shoulder?" Ray was incensed.

"Yes, it is," I confirmed.

"That's crap." Ray sounded deflated as he slid off my desk and returned to his own.

That broke up the crowd and they dispersed around the room, back to their own desks.

"Well, you're not hurt. That's good to hear." Jack smiled as he walked away.

Ruth grinned at me and about three seconds later she emailed me to say, "*At least it got Ray over to your desk for ten minutes. Will you ever again wash the part he leaned against?*"

I had to laugh, because I had just been looking at the corner of my desk where the wonderful Ray had rested his derrière and was just considering the merits of leaving it as a place of worship from now on.

Again, Jack came for lunch with us the following Friday. He was becoming a regular fixture, but he was no easier to talk to, so for the most part he just sat and talked to Ruth while I battled with "tuna on brown" and hunger pangs. Jack asked how the WeightWatchers was going for us.

"I hate it," I said with venom.

"I'm not loving it," Ruth agreed.

"Why are you all trying to be so skinny? I think you look fine. Both of you," Jack advised us, while eating a mouthful of cheese.

"Thanks, Jack!" Ruth beamed at him.

"We want to look like Audrey Hepburn," I told him.

"Audrey Hepburn was pretty, but she wasn't perfect," Jack said.

"She was damn near it," I sniped.

"Marilyn Monroe was a size 16, I'm told," Jack said, "and she was gorgeous."

"She committed suicide," I sniped again.

"Not because she was a size 16!" Jack laughed.

"How do you know?" I asked.

"The human skull weighs 8lbs," Ruth announced.

Confusion reigned, and we both looked at her.

"What's that got to do with anything?" Jack asked.

"Well, we should be allowed to take that into account when we're being weighed," Ruth said. "They should take those 8lbs off your overall weight. There's nothing at all you can do about that 8lbs, is there?"

"Commit suicide according to Amelia," Jack grinned. "Or cut your head off."

"Ha fucking ha, Jack. That's not funny!" I tutted.

Ruth and Jack both sniggered.

"It is funny actually," Ruth giggled.

4

The DART was running late. The mock exams had just started and every student in Dublin seemed to be getting the train from Clontarf station. When it did show up it was packed, and people actually fell out the door when it opened. They pushed back in as new commuters tried to get in too. Again I wondered about the safety of Irish Rail. That thought and India came to mind together. Why was that, I wonder?

I finally got a later train and reached the office at 9:45. Very late. Luckily a few other people had their own commuter horror stories. It seemed every method of public transport was having an off-day.

It appeared that Ray had been the only person in the office on time, and he was making full use of the facilities when I got in. He was having a very animated conversation with someone on the phone. He glanced at me as I passed his desk, then lowered his voice and carried on.

He seemed to be defending himself from some verbal abuse. I wondered if it was a personal call. I know you shouldn't do it but I was bored and fed up after the nightmare journey. I went to make a cup of tea, which operation took me closer to his desk, and while I was making it I listened hard to the call. What I could make out was this: he was talking to a girl and he seemed to be explaining some remark that was made over the weekend. I couldn't make out what he'd said exactly. It was bad though – he kept apologising to her. The tea was made and I really had to sit down – this type of loitering was not a good idea. Anyway, Ray had noticed me. He knew I could hear every word. I had to go back to my desk.

He hung up and looked straight at me. Oh God, he was going to ask me if I'd heard enough! I'd be mortified. This was awful. Then to my surprise he winked at me.

"What is it with you women?" he laughed.

"What's wrong with us?" I asked, trying not to sound as surprised as I felt.

"Why is everything a hanging offence with you guys?"

"Not everything is a hanging offence. What did you do?"

"Oh, I can't bloody remember. I said something about the size of her arse, I think."

"Well, Ray, that is a hanging offence! Or was it complimentary?"

"She didn't think so."

"That's it, you're blown out. Sorry, but you deserved it." I smiled at him.

"Oh well, I'll just have to turn all my charming

18

attention on you then. You don't mind, do you?"

"Well, if you must turn your attention on someone it might as well be me." I kept my tone level, though inside I was screaming. I looked over at Ruth's desk, but she and Jack were outside smoking. No one was here to witness this momentous occasion. And I was going to call in sick today, I thought as I began to work. It was 10:30 at this stage; I had to start working at some point in the day.

Later, Ray sent me an email. Not the most amazing thing to do in an office, I admit, but this was a joke one. Again, not amazing, but the thing is he never sent me jokes. I was never on his mailing list. He'd added me to his list! This might well be the start of something truly wonderful!

Ruth agreed that this was indeed a very welcome development. She nodded from her desk and said we'd talk about it later.

In that one day Ray sent me five jokes on email, and I was beginning to wonder if this was what Ray did all day. Was he in fact one of those people who look like they're working when they're not? If so, how the hell did he do it? Whenever I took a few minutes off to surf the net or send a joke I looked so guilty you'd actually think I was looking at porn or something.

Sometime around midday Ray stood up and sidled over to my desk. He leaned over the fax I was looking at. His tie swung gently, wafting some nice aftershave at me.

"What are your plans for lunch, darling?" he asked.

"We're going to the café around the corner."

"Who's we?"

19

"Ruth, Jack and me. Would you like to come?"

"Very much so," he smiled.

I ignored his double entendre. "Great, we go at one. All right with you?"

"That's great," he said as he straightened up and went back to his desk.

I could see Ruth staring over; her face was a picture. I smiled sweetly at her, but when I started to type again my hands were shaking.

A few minutes before one o'clock Ruth and I exchanged small nods. This meant we were both ready to go. Jack stood up right on cue and we all gathered around Ray's desk. He looked at us as we approached and held his finger up in the air, while finishing a phone call. We stood silently looking at each other, ignoring Ray as though he was some type of embarrassment. We waited patiently until the call was over and Ray hung up. He grabbed his coat and we left the office. Office etiquette is an odd thing. A lot of gestures and nodding that only seem to be acceptable in the office environment. If I was on the phone at home and someone decided to talk to me, my sticking one finger in the air would only leave me open to all kinds of smart comments and possibly a dead arm. Meanwhile, in the office this is perfectly acceptable and no one takes any notice; we all just shut up and wait till the finger resumes its natural position.

We got to the café and after a lot of ordering we all sat down with our food. Again I was doing battle with a plain chicken sandwich on wholewheat and coveting Jack's Pringles with all my heart. Ray and Jack sat together eating all around them while Ruth and I sat opposite them, silently praying that one or other boy would choke on their Pringles.

Neither one did choke, and lunch seemed to be passing off without any conversation at all. Then Ray turned his attention on me.

"So, Amelia sweetie, what's your game plan?"

I looked at Ruth; she was as nonplussed as I was.

"What do you mean?" I asked.

"What's the plan? Retire from this job at sixty-five or what?"

"Oh," I smiled. I'd played this game before. "Marry a rich doctor and retire to Foxrock."

Ruth and Jack nodded.

"That's a plan all right," Ruth agreed. "I, on the other hand, don't care what my husband does for a living as long as he's really good-looking."

"It doesn't matter what the doctor looks like – let's face it. I'd never see him. He'd be in work all hours," I said.

Ray looked at Jack. "I think they've played this game before, Jacko," he laughed.

Jack agreed.

"I actually would rather marry a surgeon than a doctor, preferably a plastic surgeon. He could practise his liposuction on me," I announced.

"Sorry, Amelia, a doctor can't work on a family member. I'd say that covers surgeons too," Jack advised me.

"What? Why not?" I was aghast; this had been a back-up plan of mine for some time.

"It's against ethics, the ethical code of practice or

21

something like that," Jack explained.

I was irritated. What made Jack the authority on doctors and all things medical all of a sudden?

"That doesn't matter. I'm sure he'll have a surgeon friend who won't mind sorting out my figure for me." I smiled at Jack, sure that would shut him up.

"He may not – especially if he works all day – he'll probably have no friends," Jack pointed out.

"He'll have friends in the hospital. Other doctors will be his friends," I pointed back.

Jack shrugged.

"Anyway, how do you know so much about it, Jack? Sidelining in medicine, eh?" I quipped.

"God, no. My brother's a doctor. I remember from when he was studying."

"Oh, I never knew that," I said, feeling a little put down.

Jack smiled but didn't say anything else.

Ruth leaned in and began to question him about his brother. "Well, Jack, tell us this. Is your brother married?"

"Yes."

Ruth and Ray both looked at me and smiled sympathetically. I began to feel slightly bad about ever saying anything about marrying a doctor. I wasn't quite sure why though. I think I felt I had just come off looking like a money-grubber.

"What? I'm not looking for a married doctor. I want one of my own!" I said.

"I should hope you don't want a married one," Ray said. "You don't quite fit the 'Other Woman' criteria, do you? A little too much sugar and spice about you, sweet-heart!"

He smiled but I got the impression there was a veiled insult in that remark. I looked at Jack but he wasn't looking at me at all. Maybe I was being a little sensitive about this.

Ruth continued, "Does your brother – what's his name?"

"Richard."

"Does Richard see much of his wife?"

"Well, they have three children, so I'm presuming they see enough of each other."

Again everyone looked at me. I felt like I should defend myself again, but I didn't know where to start.

Ray turned his attention on me again. "So, Amelia – pretty name, by the way."

"Thank you," I gushed.

"What would you be bringing to the union? I mean, he'll be bringing brains, money and status."

"I'd be bringing my stylish good looks, my charming personality, my own career such as it is, my car, my cat, three goldfish, my wardrobe and a bit of money. A woman's touch to his bachelor pad. I could go on."

"And those hips!" Ray laughed.

"*What?*" I was mortified.

Jack and Ruth stopped eating and watched my reaction.

"I was joking with you, sweetie," Ray smiled. "You're very sensitive. I must remember that for the future."

I smiled at him, blocking the hips remark from my

mind, focusing instead on his "future" comment. He will be remembering something about me "for the future". That showed promise.

Jack walked beside me as we made our way back to the office. He loped along for a few minutes in silence. I could see him from the corner of my eye. He was watching me for some reason.

"Jack, girls have peripheral vision too, you know."

"Not as good as men though," he smiled.

"Who says?"

"My brother, the doctor, remember?"

I flashed a condescending smile at him. "How could I forget?"

"Anyway, I was wondering."

"Were you now?" I said.

"Yes, are you really set on this plan?"

"The 'marrying a doctor' plan?"

"Yes."

"No, not really. It'd be a nice thing to marry money, but I've hit a small glitch in my plan."

"What's that?"

"I don't know any doctors. And it's unlikely anyone I know will suddenly change careers at thirty-odd."

"So does that leave the door open to suitors outside the medical profession then?"

"Yes, I suppose it does," I sighed.

"Well, that's nice," he said, in true Jack style.

The word bland came to mind very strongly.

"Jack, is your brother really happily married?" I joked.

"Yes, I think so."

"Crap! Well, keep me posted if he changes his mind," I laughed.

Jack smiled at me, but something in his eyes made me feel embarrassed all of a sudden. Should I explain again that I was joking? Was it not taken for granted? He looked at the cars passing on the road, then back at me.

"Maybe you should think about hanging out around the College of Surgeons. If you want a doctor that badly. I mean, if looks and personality don't matter. If it's just the status you're after."

"Jack, I was joking. I don't want to marry a doctor. Not to the exclusion of all other professions anyway. God, it was a joke!" I laughed in exasperation.

Jack didn't laugh. He just nodded and held the office door open for me. I walked in and went straight for the bathroom. Ruth followed me in.

"What the fuck was that remark about your hips, Amelia?" she fumed from her cubicle.

"That's nothing. You should have heard Jack having a go at me on the way back here!" I told the reflection of her cubicle door.

Ruth emerged and washed her hands while I reapplied my lipstick.

"Forget that," she said. "Ray was really out of order. That was very rude."

"Ah, I'm not too bothered by that. Jack took that whole game a bit seriously, didn't he?"

"I didn't think so." Ruth shrugged.

"I think he did," I complained, brushing my hair.

"I just can't believe you let that shit-head get away

25

with that comment about your hips!"

"He was only joking. He said so."

"I don't know. I didn't like it."

"I didn't love it myself, but he was joking," I soothed her as we left the toilets. "We're just not used to his humour, that's all,"

"I don't think it was a joke."

I realised that she could not be consoled, so I stopped trying.

"Look, it was nothing. Forget about it," I said as I sat down at my desk.

I glanced at Ray as I turned to my computer. He was sitting at his desk reading a fax. As if tipped off by some sixth sense, he looked up at just that moment. He winked at me. I smiled and could feel my cheeks flush a little.

He was gorgeous, so what if he had absolutely no tact? I'd just have to develop a thicker skin. That was no bad thing; I was always being told I was too sensitive. This would be a good thing.

5

The cable was down in Clontarf, so I was in my mother's watching TV and trying to enjoy my family circle.

It was very hard though. For starters, my younger brother Luke was asleep on the chair closest to the TV and his snoring was drowning out everything we tried to watch and secondly my sister Jenny and her boyfriend Mike were on the couch, making me very uncomfortable. They always sat very close together on the couch, touching and tickling one another and giggling at private jokes. The private jokes wouldn't have been so hard to take except that they spoke loud enough for you to catch some of it. Pet names like Mr Plod, and conversations about Mr Plod's truncheon should be kept to yourself. And worst of all, when Mike was around Jenny seemed to think it was necessary to speak in a baby voice. The girl was thirty-one years old and that was too old, too old! It made my skin crawl, it really did.

This brings us nicely to the small matter of Michael Elliott, Jenny's boyfriend at the time. They'd been dating for two years and I knew by now I should have made up my mind about him, but I hadn't. He still made me a little uncomfortable, and I had no idea why. There was nothing I could put my finger on about him, it was just him. I mean, he sounded perfect: he was polite and gainfully employed, he drove a BMW and owned a nice house in Malahide. He seemed very keen on Jenny and I should have welcomed him into our family a long time ago, but I hadn't and it was becoming a problem.

After about five glasses of wine sitting at the kitchen table the previous St Stephen's Day, I tried to tell my mother of my reservations about him. She listened as best she could, also having consumed a number of glasses of wine. She couldn't understand what I was complaining about.

"Mike is wonderful. We love him," she said, pouring the last of the wine into her glass, not offering me any I noticed.

"I don't think he's that wonderful. I don't love him," I told her.

"Well, Jennifer does and he's very taken with her, so keep your nose out of it."

"What would I ever say to her about him?" I defended myself.

"You know exactly what I'm taking about: you being non-committal about Mike and undermining Jenny. He's a lovely boy and she could do a lot worse."

"I'd never tell her how I felt about him. I have some

28

tact," I sniffed.

"Do you? We never witness your tact around here."

"I do have tact," I argued. Then in a deflated tone added, "She'd never bother asking me about it anyway. She doesn't care what I think now, not since Mike showed up."

"Ah, we're getting down to it now, aren't we?" Mum nodded sagely. "This is more the problem than Mike."

"What?" I honestly didn't realise what I'd just said.

"You, my girl, are just feeling sorry for yourself. You're jealous."

"I am no such thing!" I was stunned.

"Yes, you are," she answered, not unkindly. "Jenny has a boyfriend and you have to move over!"

"Jenny's had loads of boyfriends. I never cared about any of them!"

"This time it's different and you know it," Mum smiled. "It's a good thing. I'm glad Jenny's found some-one. I look forward to the day when all my children find their someone special. And when they do, I hope they're all as nice as Mike."

"I hope mine's better looking," I smirked.

"Look, I know it's tough. I was like you when your Aunt Jean met your Uncle Aidan. She was completely besotted with him and I was left to the side. Jean and I went everywhere together – we were always called the terrible twins. Then Aidan came along and it was Aidan this and Aidan that, and I thought she wasn't interested in me any more. But things worked out; she married Aidan and I met your father and we're all great pals still.

Do you see what I'm saying?"

"Yes, but I'm not jealous of Jenny. Mike is awful."

"Oh, for heaven's sake, I didn't have eyes for Aidan either!" Mum exclaimed. "I was annoyed that Jean had met someone and I hadn't! And that he had taken my place!"

I knew what Mum was saying, I just didn't want to admit she was right. Maybe it was jealousy on my part. Jenny and I are very close, in age and everything else. There's only eighteen months between us and, like Mum and Aunt Jean, we've always been treated sort of like twins. Jenny never got anything that I didn't. We wore the same clothes and had the same toys, her stuff was always red, and mine was always yellow. Now Jenny had Mike and they did everything together. They were treated like the twins now, one name was linked to the other and I was a name alone. Like: "Who's home?"

"Mike'n'Jenny are in the sitting-room and Amelia is in the kitchen."

Mike is not Jenny's first boyfriend, far from, it in fact. At last count I think we were up to about thirty-eight. (Not as much of an exaggeration as you might think.) She had lots of them, but they were short-term. A month or so, six months tops. She was always switching and was never the least bit bothered that the fling didn't last. She had no problem with being single. She had been headed for thirty, unattached and revelling in it. She was always telling me that "now" was the time to be single and "out there".

"Have as much fun as you can, Millie!" she'd laugh as

she came home, legs buckling under the weight of Brown Thomas shopping bags. "We're young, free and very well paid!" She'd open a bottle of wine as she tried on her new purchases and she'd always make me smile. She'd often point out that Mum was married with two children by the time she was thirty and that we were so much luckier than that.

If I was honest, Jenny pairing up with a boyfriend, a serious one, also made me face up to the fact that I was single, nowhere even close to becoming part of a blessed union and not getting any younger. In fact, I was almost thirty and felt I was in very great danger of being left on the shelf.

It had been a shock to my system when suddenly, and without asking my permission, Jenny went out one night and met Mike in some pub off Grafton Street. And he was still there two years later. She was all happy and set-tled; she didn't laugh about being young, free and single any more. She smiled dreamily and couldn't go to the cinema with me; she'd already seen everything that's showing. She'd been to see it with Mike.

And it appeared Mike was going nowhere. He was always in the house. When I called in a week before that, he wondered aloud why I'd ever bought an apartment at all – as I was always in my mum's anyway.

"It was the weirdest thing," I replied. "I woke up one morning and looked around me. Somehow or other I had amassed a whole load of furniture and I didn't know what to do with it. I couldn't fit it all in my bedroom so I bought an apartment to store it in."

31

"Very funny – that's a reason I haven't heard before," Mike smiled. "Who did you steal that line from?"

"I didn't steal it from anyone. I simply believe in giving stupid answers to stupid questions."

"It was an obvious question. You're always here. Don't you have a cat? Who feeds it?"

"I feed the cat. The cat is well fed and cared for. He likes his own company. He thinks a lot. Anyway, I visit my mother on a regular basis. Your smart comments won't stop me from doing that."

Mike opened his mouth to make some further smart comment but Jenny stepped in and asked if we were watching the TV or could she change channel. We both knew what she was doing and we glared at one another silently.

We watched the TV in silence. I was determined not to move from the sitting-room but I was fuming and wanted to complain about him. After about ten minutes of watching another rerun of *Friends*, the need to whine became too much so I headed to the kitchen.

"What is it about him you don't like?" my mother asked me after I had whined.

"Well, apart from the comments about me being here all the time, which is none of his stupid business by the way –"

"Exactly," Mum interrupted, not wanting to get involved in that particular aggro. The wonderful Mike had been out of line, for perhaps the first time ever, in my mother's eyes but she was not overly keen on bad-mouthing him just yet.

32

"Apart from that, since Jenny first brought him home, he's been on the couch and I'm on the chair and I can actually hear him breathing."

"He has hay fever." My mother tutted at me. "You're not exactly Florence Nightingale, are you?"

"Can he not take something? Is there any Claritin in the house?"

"No, there isn't. Don't be so nasty, Amelia!" My mother laughed at me. "You really are a piece of work, darling. Have you no compassion for anyone?"

"Of course I do. I just don't have any for him," I moaned, taking a can of Diet Coke from the fridge.

"Well, get to like him, missy. I think he'll be around for a while."

"What do you mean?" I asked.

"I think Jenny really likes him. Don't make things uncomfortable for her."

"Fine, I won't."

I left the kitchen and went back to the sitting-room. The lovebirds were kissing when I got there. I stood for a moment in the doorway waiting for them to stop but they didn't. They didn't appear to have heard me come in at all. I left the room again and returned to the kitchen.

"Jesus, you're like Banquo's ghost!" Mum commented. "Why are you back?"

My mother is a sweetheart.

"Because this is my ancestral home and I am allowed to walk around freely in it."

She rolled her eyes and returned to the cookbook she

33.

was reading at the table: *Nigella Bites*. It didn't seem right that a sixty-year-old woman would be reading a book with that title. She definitely should not be reading it in full view of her family. Last week I found her reading *The Naked Chef*. Cookery has really got a lot sexier since the days of Delia Smith.

"Don't start chatting again, darling. I'm reading," she said, not lifting her eyes from the book.

I stood at the fridge looking for something to eat. Things were quiet and I was just thinking, apart from me and Mike hating each other, what a pleasant picture we made. Whatever they say about it, we were the picture of suburban blissful living. The perfect nuclear family living in our home. My mother put down the book and turned to me.

"Will you close the fridge door! It's freezing and you'll defrost everything."

So much for family bliss.

"Can I have this yogurt?" I asked, ignoring the request to shut the fridge door.

"Have whatever you like, just shut the bloody door!" was the polite reply.

I shut the door and went to get a spoon. I turned up the radio slightly.

"Are you going back inside, Amelia?"

"No."

"Well, be quiet then. I'm trying to read."

"I am quiet!" I protested.

Mum tutted and I sat at the table reading the headlines in the paper.

34

"What is wrong with you?" Mum asked.

"Nothing."

"Will you go back to the sitting-room – I can't concentrate with you sitting there."

I was honestly stung by the remark. "No, I can't. I have to stay out here."

"No, you don't. Amelia, you're making a nuisance of yourself. Go back to the sitting-room."

"No."

"What is wrong with you?"

"Nothing. Can I not just stay out here with you?"

Mum was having none of it. "Why aren't you going back inside?"

"No reason," I shrugged.

"What's going on in there tonight?"

"Nothing, I just don't want to be in there."

"Why not?" Mum stood up. "What are they at in there? They can't make you feel uncomfortable in your own home. Now I won't have that!" And she made for the sitting-room.

I followed quickly, trying to stop her.

"What's going on in here?" she asked as she swung the door open.

It appears there was in fact nothing going on. They were sitting watching TV quietly.

"What?" Jennifer asked in innocence.

"You've upset Amelia," Mum replied, pointing at me for emphasis.

"I've upset her? I never opened my mouth to her," said Jennifer, annoyed. "Amelia, what did I do to you?"

35

"Nothing. It's fine," I smiled. "Mum misunderstood me."

"You said you didn't want to come back in here!" Mum announced.

"No, I didn't mean anything. I just … well, I felt I was intruding," I tried to explain but Jennifer was instantly furious.

"Why didn't you want to come back in? What did we do to offend you, Sister Amelia the Pure?"

"I didn't mean it to come out like that! Oh God!"

Mum looked at me. "Amelia, you told me in the kitchen that you weren't going back in because they made you feel awkward about being in the house."

"We never made you feel awkward! Mike made a comment that you were always here, and he's right!" Jennifer snarled. "I have no idea why you bought that apartment, you're always here!"

"That's it!" Mum stepped further into the sitting-room. "Amelia can call to this house whenever she wants! She will not be made to feel unwelcome! Jennifer, take that back or you and I will fall out very badly!"

This was blowing up out of all proportion; it was shaping into one of those family fights that can last for months.

Luke woke from his snoring. He sat up and watched the row unfold with a dazed expression. It was most likely the shock of a row erupting that he had nothing to do with.

"Why should I apologise?" said Jennifer. "It's true!"

"Madam, you take that back right this instant!" Mum's

face was reddening.

"Sorry, Amelia," Jennifer sniffed. "Aren't you a little old for telling tales?"

"I was not telling tales! You sat there and allowed your boyfriend to make fun of me and you did nothing about it. And if I have to sit here and listen to one more comment about Mr Plod and his bloody truncheon, I'll cut his truncheon off with a kitchen knife! End of fucking story!"

Jennifer went an odd mixture of white as the colour drained from her face and then crimson as the colour reappeared in her cheeks. Mike just went seriously pale, and crossed his legs.

"*Amelia!*" Mum and Jennifer shouted at once.

"That's quite enough of that talk," Mum said. "I will not listen to this kind of talk from you girls. Jennifer, be a little more sensitive to your younger sister."

Mum left and went back to the kitchen. I was left to fend off the dirty looks and smart remarks in the sitting-room.

"Amelia, do you mind if we sit beside each other on the couch, or would you rather we sat on separate chairs?" Jenny asked.

"Shut up," I replied.

"Hey, I'm going to put my arm here, over her shoulder. Is that OK with you?" Mike asked.

"Do what you like. Just keep it clean," I snapped.

"Amelia!" came a voice from the kitchen. "Enough!"

6

Ruth was celebrating her birthday. In true Ruth fashion she had emailed the entire office to confirm there would be drinking and general debauchery going on in the Mercantile Bar on Dame Street that Friday and that everyone was to be there. She also advised that gifts were an optional extra. I read the note with gut-clenching mortification and a hint of jealousy at the sheer gall of the girl. I would never have sent such a note. I would have asked Ruth, Jack and maybe Ray if I was feeling lucky. I would ask politely if they'd mind meeting for a drink after work. I'd have stressed that it was no problem and that no one was to feel they had to go. I'd have ended up having one drink and going home. Again it was all too apparent that I was a shrinking violet with a tendency to under-emphasise things that were important to me. How was I ever to get on in life? Anyway, it was not my birthday, it was Ruth's and Ruth is no shrinking violet. The note was sent and people were making plans around the fax machine by 11:30. Everyone seemed eager to let their hair down; we hadn't been out for ages so the blood was up and we were all dying for a few bevies.

Ruth, Jack and I had decided to go to the pub straight after work and get some food before the serious drinking began. At about four o'clock Ray wandered over to my desk.

"I hear the three musketeers are off for a bite to eat before the pub?" he said.

"Yes, we need a bit of food to soak up the alcohol."

"Well, I'll be out later. I have to get home for a while. See a man about a horse."

"I see," I replied, quivering slightly but trying to keep my voice steady.

"Yes, but would you do me a huge favour?" he asked sincerely.

"What?" I asked. He sounded unsure, maybe a little nervous. My heart went out to him suddenly. Maybe he wasn't so sure of himself after all.

"I hate coming into a pub late, playing catch up with the drinking games, you know?"

I nodded.

He continued, "Would you keep me a seat?"

"Of course, I will!" I grinned, thrilled to be of any help to him. Particularly *that* help.

He smiled, looking hugely relieved. "Thanks, I really appreciate it."

With that he walked back to his desk and I fell a little

bit further in love with him.

Five o'clock finally arrived and we ran from the office. As a birthday treat we were ignoring, and in most cases going completely against, our WeightWatchers regime. I was actually going to have any dish as long as there was white bread, mayonnaise, cheese and chips with it. We were having dessert too. A dessert each, none of this one-between-us crap. We were having it all. Jack looked at the menu and announced that I was going to have the cheeseburger and Ruth would be eating steak sandwich with all the trimmings. Freakily he was right.

We ate until we were actually ill. It was sheer bliss. Ruth announced that she was about to be sick and left the table. Jack looked at me as if I should go with her to hold her hand.

"As if," I said.

"Go on. I can't go with her."

"Do you honestly think I'm going to hold her hand while she pukes?" I asked him.

"Well, shouldn't you do something? Just check if she needs a hand?"

I hated to admit he was right. I stood up and followed her.

"Ruth, are you all right?" I asked as I got into the toilets.

"Yes, I just needed air. I'm fine," came a voice from the last cubicle.

"Are you sick?"

"No, I just ate too much."

"Do you need me to stay here with you?"

40

"No. I'm fine."

"All right. Are you sure?"

"Positive."

I returned to the table and found Jack adding up the bill.

"No hand-holding necessary," I smiled.

"Great. It would have been a pity to lose a soldier before the battle even began."

I looked at him and smiled. Of all the things he was, Jack was not funny.

We had paid for the meal, observing the birthday-girl-goes-free rule, and were sitting over the last of our drinks. I vaguely wondered what was keeping Ruth in the loo. She had seemed fine when I was in there.

Suddenly there was a very loud buzzing sound. It sounded like feedback. Jack squinted slightly at the noise and looked over his shoulder.

Again it buzzed loudly.

"Jesus, what's that?" I said.

"Someone killing an amplifier by the sounds of it."

Again the buzz and this time a girl apologised. We listened, but thanks to the fact that we were sitting in an alcove we couldn't see anything. We decided to move seats to get a look at what was happening.

"Come on – I'll keep an eye out for Ruth," I said.

"Don't bother. I see her," Jack laughed.

I looked at the stage and there she was, a karaoke machine beside her and a man loading it up. She was telling him which song she was going to sing.

She began and to be fair to her she sounded great.

Maybe we were a little bit drunk, but to my ear she was carrying that tune very well. She was singing "Stop in the Name of Love".

When she finished she got rapturous applause from a large group sitting on the other side of the bar.

She decided another song was called for and this time chose *"Look at me, I'm Sandra Dee"* from *Grease*. Then one of the guys from Ruth's fan club got up and sang *"I Want To Hold Your Hand"*.

Ruth came and sat back down. Jack put a drink in front of her and she drank it quickly.

"Come on Amelia. Let's sing another song!" she insisted.

"No, I can't sing," I protested.

"Come on, please. Sing with me. It's my birthday!"

Jack encouraged us both. "Go on, the pair of you! Amelia, it is her birthday after all."

"Don't be so smug, Jack. You're next," Ruth told him as she pulled me by the arm.

"I can't sing – please, Ruth, don't make me!" I begged but it was too late – a microphone was pushed into my hand and Ruth asked me if I knew all the words to *"Stand by Your Man"*.

I knew them, so we sang it. Then we sang *"Waterloo"*.

A little while later Jack got up and sang *"Tie a Yellow Ribbon Round the Old Oak Tree"*.

It was getting late and the crowd from the office had all come in. Ray was still nowhere to be seen. I was keeping a look out for him when Ruth and Jack converged on me.

"We need you to help us be Abba," Ruth said in complete seriousness.

"I'm not singing again. I sang twice!" I told her.

"Come on, we need you. It'll be a laugh!"

"There were two fellas in Abba, Who else is singing?"

"Robbie said he would," said Jack. "Come on, Amelia. It's great fun."

"We're singing *"Does Your Mother Know?"*. You only have to sing the chorus. Come on!" Ruth was getting a bit worked up about it.

"Do I have to? Can't you get someone else?"

"No, I don't want someone else! I want you!" Ruth whined.

She was really very drunk.

"All right, but after this I'm finished," I told her.

"Hooray!" Ruth hugged me and ran up to the stage again.

Jack beckoned Robbie over and we took to the stage. To say we had a laugh was an understatement. We had a ball. We were fantastic! Even if I do say so myself.

We got off the stage and sat back down.

A little while later I noticed Ray had arrived. He was standing at the bar and ordering a drink when I saw him from where I was sitting. I jumped up and went up to the bar. Positioning myself close to him but pretending I hadn't seen him, I ordered a drink. He came up behind me and put his arm around my waist.

"Hi there, you!" he smiled.

"Oh, Ray, hi!" I turned around to face him. He was really cute.

"Have you been here all day?" he asked.

"Yeah, we had dinner and then started drinking," I grinned.

"And singing?"

"Yeah, actually, we did!" I slurred happily.

"Were you by any chance part of an Abbaesque thing going on earlier?" he said, smiling indulgently.

"I may have been," I grinned, feeling distinctly proud of my onstage swaggering.

"Part of the same Abba crowd that sang in different keys and out of time with one another perhaps?"

"That I'm not so sure about," I smiled, feeling a bit embarrassed now.

"You look very familiar to me. And I think it was you I saw dancing and howling on stage earlier on your own," he said, laughing.

"Oh, well … I was doing a bit of karaoke all right. Nothing to write home about," I backtracked, feeling less confident in myself.

"Well, never mind. You can't sing but I still love you." He smiled down at me.

I didn't feel so bad after that. I grinned up at him, trying to look sexy. Due to the level of alcohol in my blood, my take-me-to-bed-or-lose-me-forever look was decidedly the worse for wear. I leered at him, and to give him his due he was polite, but sidestepped me none the less.

I became aware of a girl hovering in the vicinity. She was close to his shoulder and was watching me intently. I smiled at her in a territorial way, then threw her a look full of pride with a little pity thrown in. I let her know I was once a lowly onlooker like her, but now I was shining, I was in Ray's sights and I was glowing in the limelight.

The girl wouldn't go away. She was feisty, I had to give her that. I stared at her, my smile becoming icier as she stared back. Did she need an announcement to be made over the PA system? Ray was spoken for: I was speaking for him.

She remained rooted to the spot, eyeballing me. She lifted two drinks she was holding to eye level. I thought she was offering me a drink. I glanced enquiringly at the pint glass, ready with my polite refusal just as Ray glanced around at her. Then lo and behold he smiled at her.

"Ah, there you are!" he said. "Amelia, this is Sarah, my long-suffering girlfriend."

He took the pint from her and kissed her on the cheek.

It was my turn to stand rooted to the spot. She smiled sanctimoniously at me.

Isn't it amazing how suddenly your mood can change?

7

It turned out that Jack had seen Ray walk in and had seen the girl on his arm before I had. We were waiting for the kettle to boil in the kitchen in work about a week after Ruth's birthday.

He told me, and I quote, that he was "amused to see Ray walk in with his girlfriend".

"Why were you amused to see it?" I asked.

He looked at me for a moment and smiled. "I didn't think he was still seeing her, that's all."

"Do you know her?"

"No, not really. We drink in the same pub some weekends. I see him from time to time."

"Oh," I replied noncommittally, secretly wondering how easy it would be to get the name of the pub without coming out and asking for it.

"I would have told you before. I just wasn't sure whether you fancied him or not."

"I don't fancy him – what made you think I do?" I lied.

"I don't know. I just thought you might."

"Well, I don't."

"Anything you say," Jack smiled and walked back to his desk.

So now he knew for sure.

And to my shame so did Ray.

To tell the truth, anyone who cared to hear about it now knew I fancied Ray. I had disgraced myself on Friday night. After he introduced me to Sarah I did the worst possible thing. I drank too much and got narky with Ray.

Every time he spoke to me I'd tell him he shouldn't be talking to me, his girlfriend might get jealous. Whenever he was anyway polite or chatty to me, I'd advise him I was not his girlfriend and maybe we should stop talking in case she got upset.

At one point he asked me what time it was, and I told him to ask his girlfriend. He said that he already had asked her, but that she was not wearing a watch. So he asked me again.

"What time is it?"

"I don't know," I told him.

"Let me see your watch there, Amelia," he said taking my wrist in his hand.

"Watch it! You don't want to upset Sarah. She might think there's something going on between us."

"No, she won't – I just want the time, Amelia."

"She might think I fancy you. I don't, by the way."

"I know you don't." He smiled, but his eyes told me he knew only too well that I did.

"I don't, you know. I think you're really nice, but I don't fancy you."

"Five past ten, thanks," he said and stood up. Then he turned back to me. "Oh, by the way, Amelia," he said, leaning in close to me, *"The lady doth protest too much methinks."*

With that he walked away, and I was left feeling seriously embarrassed. Ruth put a drink in front of me and smiled. It was a fizzy orange. I stared in disbelief.

She sat in beside me and told me to drink up and shut up. I tried to look wounded but I knew she was right.

I drank the orange and got to work on sobering up. Ray and Sarah left at about midnight. I watched them go and wished for better judgment when it came to men.

8

About three weeks after the Karaoke Friday I still couldn't bring myself to be alone with Ray. Whenever he came into the room I'd make an excuse and leave. I really didn't want to be around him. The memory of that night was still too fresh in my mind.

One evening I was in the office kitchen alone, waiting for the kettle to boil and reading a trashy magazine I'd found on the counter, when Ray walked in behind me.

"Amelia?"

"Yes," I replied, not looking up from the page and not realising it was him.

"I think we should talk."

My heart lurched as I recognised the voice.

"There's really no need, is there?" I smiled.

He looked serious. "Well, there might be."

Crap, I thought, but smiled innocently at him.

"Look, I know you were seriously drunk the other

49

night. It seemed you were offended when Sarah came in with me."

"Of course I wasn't. She has every right to be out with you on a Friday night. She is your girlfriend."

Thank God she was there, I thought. I would have hated to have really thrown myself at him only to find out about her later.

"Well, she isn't any more, but she was," he said with a sorry smile.

"Oh, I'm sorry about that," I said, and truly I was sorry for him. "Are you very unhappy?"

I suddenly got a weird déjà vu feeling, and realized we sounded like we'd just stepped out of a *Friends* episode. I made a mental note never to sound like that again.

"No, I'm fine." He grinned, rallying slightly. "Look, Amelia, I just wanted to say sorry and clear the air. I flirted with you a lot over the last few weeks and I knew I was still seeing Sarah. I shouldn't have done it."

"That's all right; I was a bit flirty too," I laughed.

"So does that mean you actually fancied me then?"

"Of course not. I was just indulging in some practice flirting."

"Practice flirting?" He laughed. "I've never heard of it and I've heard of most things."

"Well, then, you take flirting far too seriously. You should get in some practice. It's fun."

"Maybe I will," he said as he took my cup of tea and returned to his desk.

I watched him leave and sort of enjoyed waiting for the kettle to boil again and making the second cup.

The air was much clearer from then on. Ray and I chatted and emailed as before. Everything was bliss in the office again.

It was time to sort out the weight problem. I needed to lose about a stone to be a healthy weight, about three stone to look like Jennifer Aniston. So Ruth and I rededicated ourselves to the WeightWatchers regime and as it was coming into the summer we went walking in the evenings.

Life was good. In my first official week back in WeightWatchers, after a few false starts, I lost four pounds. That's huge progress, and Ruth confirmed it.

"Wow, Amelia, you look great!" She nodded approvingly. "You can see it all gone from your face."

"Thanks," I beamed, choked with emotion.

I had to restrain myself from kissing her.

The following week I lost another three pounds and when the girl in WeightWatchers stuck the little seven-pound sticker to my booklet I actually shed a quiet tear of joy.

I was getting somewhere, and my excess weight was not coming with me!

9

My experience might not have been vast, having dated about twelve men in the previous sixteen years.

But I did know this: as soon as one part of my life seemed to be headed in the right direction and gaining some momentum, another part just fell flat on its face and the whole thing crashed on top of itself.

A bit of an overstatement? I didn't think so.

Ray and I were getting along like a house on fire, I was doing well in WeightWatchers, having lost twelve pounds in the last month, and I was on a roll in the office. Everyone I put forward for interview got the job and I was cleaning up on commission. It was like a fairytale. Was I getting the happy ending that as a child I'd been duped into believing was out there?

It would appear not. I was enjoying the false sense of security we're all warned about. I was about to have the rug pulled from under me in a most undignified fashion.

One Friday afternoon I got a call from Jennifer. I was to come to Mum's house straight from work that night. There was something she wanted to talk to me about.

I got home about 6:15 that evening to find the house in a bit of a fuss. Mum was rushing about, dusting anything that stood still long enough. Luke's college notes were hidden under the stairs, along with the exercise bike. This was serious – that bike had been taking pride of place in the sitting-room since January 1st.

"Quick, don't just stand there. Help tidy," Mum said, handing me a duster.

"The place looks fine, Mum," I said, taking my coat off.

I went to put it on the coat-stand in the hall, but I found it handed back to me quick as a flash.

"Stop it. Put that upstairs. I need the stand for Mike's parents' coats." Mum ushered me up the stairs.

"All right," I said as I went up. "What are Mike's parents coming over here for?"

I glanced back. Mum was looking up at me with a giddy grin and it suddenly clicked with me.

"No way!" I shouted as I rushed on up the stairs.

"Yes! Isn't it great?" said Mum, her voice muffled – she was under the stairs.

I stood at the top and shouted, "So Jennifer is preggers, is she?"

I could hear the stifled screech from under the stairs.

Mum reappeared. "Amelia! What a dreadful thing to say about your sister!"

"Is that not why they're coming over?" I asked, feigning innocence.

"Don't be such a little cow, you! You know full well why they're coming over. Now help get this place in order."

I came downstairs and finished tidying the sitting-room while Mum started to make the dinner. I was glad to see that Luke had been dragged into the preparation and was outside doing battle with the front lawn. Dad's car could be heard screeching up the road and reversing at speed into the driveway.

He appeared at the door looking a little flustered. He pulled me into the sitting-room and showed me a bag of red and white wine, and four bottles of Moet champagne.

"Is this stuff all right, love?" he asked.

"It's fine. You have loads there," I nodded.

"But the Moet – is that nice stuff?" he asked, concern in his voice.

"It's grand. Everyone drinks it."

"It's not the best, but it was all they had. It'll be fine, won't it?"

"It'll be grand, Dad. Don't worry about it." I gave him an encouraging hug.

"It's great news, isn't it?"

"Did you know about it?"

"Yes, Mike asked me about a month ago."

"Really?"

Dad nodded.

"Talk about exciting, Dad!"

"It is a bit," he agreed.

Jennifer, Mike, his parents and his younger brother arrived for dinner at about 7:30. They all came in and we stood awkwardly in the sitting-room for a few moments. Then Jennifer shot her hand in the air and shouted triumphantly, "Who wants to see my ring?"

Luke snorted with laughter, Michael gave an amused sigh and poor Jennifer looked stricken for a moment. Mum completely ignored the situation and pulled Jennifer's hand over until they were both standing under a lamp. Mum looked at the ring from every angle and then nodded approval.

"Very pretty. Well may you wear, sweetheart!"

We all crowded in to see the ring and then it was passed from finger to finger and we all made wishes on it. At first it was passed just among us women, but then Luke took it from me.

"No, it's just the girls who wish on the ring," Jennifer said.

"Why?" Luke enquired, trying to push it down on his finger. "Are you the only ones who can make wishes?"

"No, but it's just the tradition." Jennifer looked slightly confused.

"Ah, let me make a wish!" he said, laughing.

"All right, but it might not come true," she told him.

I think she may have been seriously warning him – as if any of our wishes were likely to come true!

"I'll put on a girl's voice when I make the wish and the ring will think I'm a girl."

"Don't wish for a woman or money – that won't work,"

Mum advised him, nodding indulgently at him.

He winked at her in an over-exaggerated gesture and made his wish.

Dad, who had been watching from a distance, came over and took the ring from Luke. It was passed among the men. Mum was not impressed.

"This is ridiculous – you're making a mockery of the whole tradition now," she scolded him.

"Never mind, the ring won't mind," he said, smiling.

In hindsight it was not the best-planned dinner party I'd ever been at. We maybe shouldn't have drunk all the Moet before dinner, or perhaps we should have left dinner for a little while. As it was, we were all giddy and the hunger had gone off us just as dinner was being served. Nobody ate much and we drank a bit too much.

Mum insisted that the bubbles had gone to her head a bit.

"Yeah, Mum, the bubbles, not the alcohol!" Luke laughed.

Mum smiled at him but her eyes advised him to put a lid on it. Which he did.

Jennifer cleared her throat, clinking the side of her glass with her knife just before dessert came out. Dad looked slightly concerned as he watched the glass. It was Waterford Crystal brought out especially for tonight. Everyone looked at her.

"Mike and I just wanted to say a few things while we have you all here."

I looked at Mum, and she glanced back, a slightly uncomfortable expression in her eyes.

56

"Yeah," Mike took over. "We just wanted to thank you all for coming over tonight, and thanks a million to Maggie and Joe for the drinks and dinner tonight."

Mum and Dad nodded and smiled at everyone.

"We just wanted to ask everyone to keep Saturday the 4th of September free," Mike grinned. "And if you could all be at Corpus Christi Church in Drumcondra at about 1:30 that'd be great."

There was silence for a moment.

"September this year?" Mum asked.

"Yes," Jennifer replied.

"You're getting married in four months?"

"Yes," Jennifer giggled.

"What's the hurry?" Mum glanced at me, the concern barely concealed this time.

I was a bit concerned too.

"No hurry, we just chose that date," Jennifer laughed. "The church, the hotel and band are all booked. Everything else is easy. I just need to get going on a dress. I've seen a few. Amelia, will you help me look some weekend soon?"

I nodded. Mum didn't look convinced.

10

That night Mum had wanted me to stay over, but I didn't want to.

"I had a really busy week in work, Mum, and tomorrow I really need to get a few things done. I want to be up and out early," I replied.

"You can stay here. I'll wake you up as early as you want."

"No, I'll go. I'd prefer to."

I called a taxi. She nodded, standing at the gate waving me off. We both knew why I wanted to go home and it had nothing to do with a busy week or an early start in the morning.

I paid the taxi driver and let myself into my apartment. I went straight to the bathroom and washed my face and teeth. I could feel the tightness in my chest and the sting in my eyes. Tears of frustration rolled down my cheeks as I brushed my teeth. I hated myself. Why couldn't I be happy for her? She was my sister and she was getting married to the man she loved. What kind of a person was I, standing here crying tonight? Was I that horrible? That selfish? Perhaps I was.

Maybe I wasn't that nice a person after all. I mean, had I not just flirted my socks off with a guy who turned out to have a girlfriend? And I did brush Jack off whenever Ray appeared, I knew I did it. I just couldn't seem to help myself. Jack was boring, Ray was not. But in truth that was no excuse for my behaviour of late. I should have been happy for Jenny and nicer to Jack, I was a bad person and I was getting worse. This selfish attitude had to change. I looked at myself in the bathroom mirror as I took off the last of my make-up.

"Enough, Amelia, enough of feeling sorry for yourself and enough of this crap! You go into that office on Monday morning and get Ray Donnelly to notice you. If he doesn't take the bait then it's time to move on!"

With that I went to bed, feeling dishevelled but defiant.

The mood changed again the following morning when Jenny rang at 9:30.

"Millie, good morning!" she boomed

"Hi," I replied, still trying to wake up.

"Mum said you were busy today, but I don't actually believe her. Are you busy?"

"Well, I have bits and pieces to do, but not too much. Why?"

I don't know why I bothered. I knew the reply.

59

"I was thinking we might go looking at dresses. What do you think?"

To be honest, I would have preferred to have my teeth pulled out without anaesthetic, but what kind of a person would I be if I admitted that?

"I'd love to," I lied. "Have you any ideas about designs?"

I really did try to sound light and interested, but Jenny heard the falter in my voice and picked up on it.

"If you'd prefer to do something else just let me know," she said, not unkindly.

I felt really bad now. "Of course I want to, I can't wait! I'm just not really awake yet. What time were you thinking about?"

"As soon as you're dressed!"

I could hear the excitement in her voice and made a concerted effort to sound very excited indeed. "Well, that's fine then. I'll be dressed in half an hour. Will you pick me up?"

"Will do, see you then!" Jenny was about to ring off when she thought of something I hadn't thought about. "Millie, make sure you have nice underwear on – we might see a nice bridesmaid's dress for you!"

"Groovy!" I smiled, but the fear in my eyes could only be believed if you'd seen it, like I did in the mirror. My chest hurt with the sudden pulling of my heart as it leapt crossways over my body.

I'd known I'd be a likely candidate for bridesmaid; as her only sister it was an honour I was expecting most of my life. But now that we were actually here, announcing

60

engagements yesterday, looking at dresses today, I was finding it hard to get my head around the speed of it all. It wasn't that I wasn't happy for her; it wasn't as cut and dried as that. I was happy for her – she was my sister and I loved her, of course I was happy for her. One half of me was anyway, the other half was bitter with resentment and fear. I was being left alone; I was going to be the spinster aunt. Me. The thing I feared most of all and it was happening.

I know that a lot of what I was feeling was self-pity, but it was real. I felt it acutely. It was all I could do to stop myself from actually crying as I showered.

The doorbell rang, and there stood Jennifer, grinning like the Cheshire Cat.

We got into her car.

"I have a list of shops," she said. "Don't laugh now. I've made a list of where we can go first to make the most of the time we have before town gets too crowded."

"You made a list, like a timetable?" I asked, not quite believing it.

"Don't look at me like that! It makes sense. I have a list of all the north-side shops and all the south-side ones. We'll start on the north side at Alexander's and work our way through."

I realised suddenly that Jenny was in great danger of becoming somewhat "Stepford-like". I would have to keep a very close eye on her and drop some hints if things didn't improve.

She parked the car and led the way to the first shop.

The assistant fussed and pulled dresses from racks.

61

Jennifer stood in the middle of the shop holding bodices up to herself and trying on tiaras, turning back to me for approval for ones she liked herself. I smiled on cue and shrugged at ones I didn't like.

"Millie, you look around for bridesmaid stuff. I have no idea for colours – just pick some out and I'll choose my favourite!"

The assistant turned her attention to me.

"Are you the maid of honour?" she asked. "We have lots of colours, but I think a rich colour would really look lovely on you."

She disappeared into a room at the back, leaving Jenny and me looking at each other.

"Should you follow her?" Jenny asked.

I shrugged, taking the opportunity to go and pull at a dress in the window that had caught my eye. I lifted the mannequin's skirt and revealed its underskirt. Jenny came over, telling me to leave the dress alone. She ushered me away from the window, but I noticed she took the opportunity to look at the mannequin's underwear as she did so. It wasn't wearing any.

The assistant arrived back into the room, carrying an armful of vividly coloured dresses. We gasped at the pretty colours.

"Yes, they always look really stunning after all the whites," she agreed, before turning to me and continuing, "Try some of these for a start."

She unloaded the armful of heavy, boned dresses on me. I almost buckled under the weight. She pointed me towards the changing-rooms and gave me a slight push.

I headed off. Alone in the dressing-room I looked at the heap of dresses on the chair in front of me.

The nightmare had begun.

11

Ruth had no sympathy for me at all; in fact she believed I was being a "moany cow".

We were in the kitchen at work and I was telling her about the various dresses Jenny and I had tried on and then discarded the previous weekend. The dress hunt was becoming manic; we'd been out every Saturday for the last three weeks. Jenny had tried on every dress she laid her hands on. At last count she'd been fully fitted out – shoes, dress, tiara and veil – twenty-three times. In one shop they even gave her a few lilies to hold. She had looked fabulous, so much so that I was genuinely surprised that she was the same Jennifer I'd lived with all my life. I had honestly never noticed she was so pretty. It would appear that I am not the most observant person alive.

Mum had come with us last weekend and cried in every one of the five shops we'd been in. Jennifer had narrowed down the list and we were now looking at five dresses with a serious view to a purchase.

We had chosen a dress for me in about an hour that first day. I was wearing a chocolate-brown straight-cut skirt, with a boned corset-like top. It sounds sexier than it really is; in fact, there's a lot more dress than I've just described and it's very pretty.

Jenny had opted for a full skirt and tight bodice with a long trailing veil. She appeared to be favouring a very classic look. It was a look Mum really loved and she was getting into the preparation in a big way.

"Ah, some day, Amelia," Ruth sighed dreamily, "that'll be me. I'll be wearing white and people will all be looking at me."

"Of course it will, it'll happen to us all sooner or later. Well, maybe not to Jack," I giggled.

"Do you still not like Jack?" Ruth asked, sounding a little surprised.

"Oh, he's fine," I conceded. "He's a nice guy." I was joking.

"Just a nice guy? Do you not think he's good-looking?"

"No, not really."

"God, I think he's lovely." She smiled to herself.

"Really? He's not an ugly person, far from it – but lovely? I think that may be pushing the boat out."

Ruth looked at me in surprise. "I have to say I think he's really good-looking," she announced. "I'm surprised you can't see it."

"Sorry, I don't," I said, watching her reaction. "He's very nice, but not gorgeous."

65

"I think he is."

"Do you fancy him?" I asked, realising that I'd never noticed this before. Could it have passed me by?

"No, I don't fancy him, not Jack!" she giggled.

"Why not?"

"He is lovely, but no," she said, shaking her head, dismissing whatever thought she'd just had. "No, there's no point."

"Of course, there's a point, if you like him and he likes you."

"No, I don't like him like that. No way would I fancy him." She shook her head, this time with vigour.

"Mmm," I replied, eyebrow raised. "He's still awfully quiet, don't you think?"

"No, he's quite the opposite if you ask me. I think he's very chatty."

"Well, then, it must be me. He never opens his mouth to me – which I find very boring," I sniffed, not the least bit bothered in truth.

There was silence for a moment while I studied a very unflattering photo of Pamela Anderson in the magazine we were sharing. It's always nice to see cellulite on a celebrity.

"Ruth, phone!" said Jack.

We jumped in a very guilty fashion. He was standing in the doorway. I think Ruth and I had the same thought: how *long* had he been standing there?

We left the kitchen and returned to our desks feeling more than a little bit jittery. Jack watched us from the safety of his desk for a little while before starting to work again. Later Ruth worried that the conversation had been overheard. I said that there was no way he'd have heard anything, but secretly I did wonder.

It was only slight at first, but his behaviour did change over the next few weeks. He didn't come to lunch with us the following day, then a few days later he was meeting someone and again a few days after that he went to lunch early, claiming he was starving. He didn't call Ruth when he went outside for a cigarette. Ruth would call him and he'd either be gone or just coming back from a break. He was perfectly polite about it but there was something in his manner that had changed. I could see it and so could Ruth. She was miserable.

"He heard us talking about him," she moaned over lunch one day, not for the first time.

"He couldn't have. We weren't talking loudly," I assured her, not overly convinced myself.

"He heard us, now he's avoiding us."

"Well, we weren't saying anything awful about him. He shouldn't have been listening. Eavesdroppers hear no good of themselves. Serves him right!"

"Amelia, he heard you saying he was boring and that he never opens his mouth!"

My smile froze, as it did every time I remembered what I had actually said. That wasn't the nicest thing I could have said about him. Especially if he was going to have to hear it.

"Worse still," Ruth continued, "he heard me saying he's great. He'll think we fancy him!"

I couldn't follow her logic there. "We? He won't think

I do. Nor you either, come to think of it. Don't you remember? You said no way would you ever fancy him."

"He'll never come near us again!" she wailed.

"Ruth, I don't think he's avoiding us. He's meeting his friend for lunch, that's all. He was chatting to you and Ray earlier on today, was he not?"

"Yes, but he seemed different. He never comes for a smoke break any more – you heard him on Tuesday."

"Yes, but him giving up smoking has nothing to do with us."

"He was looking straight at me when he said he was giving them up." Ruth looked at the ground, then back at me. "And why he was giving up."

I shuddered at the memory. "He had no right to look at you, or anyone, while making a statement like that."

"He was doing it to prove a point."

"What point was he proving?" I asked, recalling the snippet of conversation as I spoke and again shuddering with disgust.

Jack had announced quite loudly that he was "trying to give up the cancer-sticks". He said that he'd read a report linking smoking to low sperm count and how he wanted to give his "Jack Juniors" the best possible start.

I had been sitting at my desk, passing the time watching Ray work and I'd overheard him. Now, I had become fonder of Jack in recent months, but I could happily have lived out the rest of my days without hearing those particular words from him.

I had looked over, ready with my disapproving stare, but he never noticed me. He was standing with Steve and

68

some guy from Accounts, all three of them grinning like a group of bold schoolboys. I watched for a moment, still ready with my stare, but he never even glanced my way.

As I watched a thought struck me. For perhaps the first time I realised that men are simply little boys who have grown taller. They may be respectful and polite to you most of the time but, underneath it, they are all made of the same thing: slugs and snails and puppy-dogs' tails. Now, I'm no man-basher, in fact I'm quite a fan of men in general, but I do have to thank heaven for little girls. For starters, could you imagine if we were all made of slugs and snails?

Could you imagine if women spoke about themselves in the same way as men do? Discussing their inner workings at the top of their voices or naming their boobs like some men do their parts? Yuck indeed.

I looked at the three boys again but they were still laughing and gesturing wildly about something to each other. I had a fairly good idea what they were alluding to and all I can say is it was vile.

I had looked over at Ruth, ready to roll my eyes, but she wasn't looking at me. Her eyes were burning a hole in Jack.

"Ruth!"

"Did you hear that? He's really annoyed with me!"

"With you? You don't think that was all aimed at you?" I asked in bewilderment. "Why on earth would it be?"

"He heard us discussing him and saying he wasn't exactly the best catch on the planet. He was making a point that he was a good catch."

"What, because of his sperm count?" I asked, honestly wondering how on earth his mind was working. Or Ruth's for that matter. "Haven't they all got one?"

"Not just that! Can you get by his sperm count? That's not the point!"

"Excuse me? Get by his sperm count? With pleasure, it's disgusting!" I complained. "He really shouldn't be discussing it in public, not while there are ladies present."

"Are you calling yourself a lady?" Ruth sniggered.

"I most certainly am," I replied stony-faced. "Are you trying to make something of it?"

"No, and that's not the issue either. Look, he was saying he was already thinking about children. Most men these days seem to be all about work and drinking and being a lad. They claim they don't want babies at all – you practically have to beat them into admitting that they'd consider having a baby by the time they're forty. He was making the point that he is already man enough to admit in company he'd like some children!"

I could feel my eyes popping out of their sockets. God, she'd really lost it! That was crazy! "I think you're taking this all a bit seriously, Ruth. I think he was just being gross with the boys."

"I don't, and I think he was saying it to prove a point to me."

"Why you? I was talking about him too!"

"I don't know exactly, I just think it was aimed at me. I can't explain it."

"Fine, you drama queen!"

It was hours later that a much more convincing

explanation of Jack's weird behaviour occurred to me. Was he demonstrating that he was *not* boring and that he *could* open his mouth?

In which case, it was aimed at *me*.

12

Luke was sitting his final exams in college and the house was deathly still while he studied. He is someone who needs complete silence to think. I always need some music in the background, but I insist on a tidy work area. Luke is the opposite; he needs complete silence and as much of a mess as possible – papers, books and notes strewn around the floor like dead bodies in an old war movie.

As a result Mum and Jenny were taking refuge in my apartment. I had opened the door to find them both standing there holding a bottle of wine and a packet of HobNobs.

"We're refugees!" Mum announced very loudly. "We've made the journey all the way from Griffith Avenue and we need to stay here for the night."

Jennifer giggled a little but then gave Mum a disapproving nudge and told her not to be shouting about being refugees. "Millie, we need to get away from Luke. He's wrecking our heads. Can we watch TV with you?" she asked as they walked straight by me into the sitting-room.

"Sure," I said, taking the wine bottle from Mum. She had been trying to open the HobNobs with one hand and it was looking like everything was about to land on the floor.

Jenny went into the kitchen, where she threw open the press and reappeared with three glasses and a corkscrew. We sat around my tiny table and ate the HobNobs. Jenny picked her bag up off the floor and out of a small bag came a huge number of rolled-up magazines. All bridal, all dog-eared from reading.

"Well, now that we're all together, have a look at some of these ideas I had!" She beamed at us.

Mum sat forward, eyes glowing with excitement. I topped up our glasses, gave myself a drop extra, slapped a grin on my face and leaned forward.

The dress had been chosen, the florist was booked and the invites had been sent the previous weekend. Things were moving fast and, I had to hand it to her, Jenny was well and truly in control of all situations. If it was to be within three miles of Drumcondra the day of her wedding, Jenny knew its name and its date of birth.

Now we were discussing wedding favours, table centre-pieces and table plans. In other words the boring stuff that takes on a life or death significance on the big day. Mum told stories of seating arrangements that had gone horribly wrong in the past. Old enemies, feuding for generations, sitting at tables together with only the local clergy sitting between them. Personally I'd have enjoyed an hour at that table. I bet they wouldn't have noticed if the centre-piece got up and served them the starters. Of course I couldn't admit this, and spent an hour looking at flower arrangements and candelabras of varying size and design.

"I would always err on the side of caution with these things, Jenny," I ventured when we had looked carefully at a particularly large centre-piece for the fourth time. "Less is more. The guests should be able to see one another."

Mum agreed, thankfully. If I'd been seen to steer Jenny wrong in anything, I'd have been excommunicated without a word of warning.

"She's right – you don't want anything gaudy-looking. They should be tasteful, people shouldn't even notice them but they should enhance the room."

"Well, if they're not meant to be noticed, then why have them?" Jennifer asked crankily, still eyeing the huge centre-piece.

"They should be understated" Mum soothed. "We must have them, but anything too big would be vulgar-looking."

"I want people to notice them though. I want people to see them and say they're pretty."

Jenny was coming undone slightly. She was getting very upset about a bunch of flowers. We all needed to take a step back before she produced a gun and took Mum and me hostage or something. Mum smiled sympathetically at her. Then I said something really stupid, but in my defence I thought I was helping.

"Jenny, what kind of losers sit at a table discussing the centre-piece – it's not that big a deal."

Well, all hell broke loose at that point. I am presuming it was an accident; all I know is that one of my wine-glasses collided with the wall close to my head and Jenny never fully apologised for it. She was very upset and shouted abuse for some time. After what felt like an hour, she calmed down. The sobbing had subsided and now she was tired and pale from the exertion.

"I'll get you a new glass, Millie," she sighed.

"It's all right. They're not that special," I conceded.

Jenny sniffed loudly and wiped her nose in a half-hearted gesture. She sighed heavily and shuddered a little before opening a new magazine and calmly announcing that we would leave the centre-pieces until we all felt a little steadier.

I looked at Mum and she shook her head at me.

"That's fine. We've done good work tonight," she soothed.

"Right, let's discuss favours," said Jenny. "I was think-ing about little candles I've seen. What do you think? They'll put our names and the date on them."

Mum looked slightly aghast for the briefest moment, but rallied. Pulling the magazine closer to her side of the table, she studied the photos. "Those look really pretty, sweetheart."

I agreed. They were lovely. They were small fat can-dles, wrapped in white netting with ribbons on the top. The ribbon would be a chocolate brown, like my dress.

They would have Michael and Jennifer and the date printed on them.

"God, they *are* lovely," I announced.

I realise now that I put the emphasis on the 'are' and not the 'lovely' as I should have done. The sentence came out wrong and again Jenny lost the plot.

She launched herself over the table and grabbed me by the ponytail.

Thank God for Mum, I really do think she may well have saved my life that night.

"Enough, stop it, the pair of you!" she shouted. "We've done enough tonight! Jenny, we'll go home now."

Jenny stopped and straightened up, looking embarrassed to have been caught threatening my life. Rightly so. It was just a bloody candle and I had been agreeing with her: they *were* lovely.

13

Jack had gradually thawed towards us. Ruth and I helped the thawing process by staying on our best behaviour. Any fool could see we were sorry, we looked so miserable and guilty every time he so much as looked at us. So he forgave us.

It was the end of July and I had only six weeks left before Jenny's wedding. I really did not want to go alone. I toyed with the idea of asking Ray, and if all else failed maybe Jack.

I spoke to Ruth about it over a coffee.

"I was thinking about asking Ray to Jenny's wedding. Is it a plan?"

"I think not!" Ruth laughed.

"Why not? I need a date."

Ruth shrugged but the look on her face was clear: asking him would be social suicide.

"Well, if I can't ask Ray, what about Jack?"

Her features darkened. "Jack? What on earth would you ask him for? You don't even like him."

"I do like him," I laughed.

"But you can't," Ruth's voice faltered.

"Why not? It's just a date."

"Yeah, but . . ." Ruth flushed.

"But what?"

"But it's *Jack*."

"What does that mean?" I asked.

"Please, all I'm saying is, don't ask Jack." Ruth's eyes pleaded with me and I felt sorry for her. I was never really going to ask Jack, definitely not if she fancied him that much. I just wished she'd admit it.

"Don't worry. Your Jack is safe. I would never ask him."

"Why wouldn't you? What's wrong with him?" Ruth looked wounded.

"Nothing, he's fine, but you like him," I smiled at her.

Ruth said nothing. She just blushed crimson.

"Look, I'd never have the nerve to ask Ray out, but I might just turn on the charm with him."

"Really?" Ruth looked surprised.

"Why not? Is his girlfriend back on the scene?"

"No, I think he's still single." Ruth nodded, then on reflection she smiled and said, "Yeah, go ahead, I give you my blessing. Just don't let him say anything nasty to you."

I laughed but I knew what she meant. I wouldn't let him upset me, not this time.

The following morning I got up early and dressed in bright, sunshine colours. I walked into the office, all of my charms set to flirt. It worked extremely well: it worked on the postman, the corporation workers who were all busy looking down a hole on Dame Street, it worked on the young boy who was at the station and then sat opposite me on the DART. It worked wonders on Jack and Stephen in the office – they sat on my desk and offered me coffee all day. It would have worked wonders on Ray, if he'd been in.

I walked in to find his desk empty. I waited patiently until 10:15 before I asked innocently if he was running late.

"He's off for the rest of the week," was the reply from Louise, the manager's secretary.

"Oh." I could barely keep the despair out of my voice. "Will he be back Monday?"

"I think so."

"Is he sick?" I asked, wondering about sending a get-well card.

"No, I think it's holidays." Louise eyed me with good-tempered suspicion. "He's taken a long weekend. He'll be back Monday."

"Fine, I'll ask him about that file he wanted then," I said, pretending to think aloud, rushing back to my desk to cringe in private.

The following Monday, again the glad rags got an airing. This time Ray was sitting at his desk and looked up approvingly as I passed him.

I flashed him a friendly smile and went to my desk, pleased with the result.

Boys are so easy sometimes! I was sitting reading a new

CV that had come in, when Ray appeared like a vision in front of me, his aftershave wafting towards me in just the right quantity. I watched him lean against the desk, smiling down at me.

"Hello there," he beamed.

"Hi!"

"Did you miss me?" He leaned forwards and flicked through a magazine that was sitting on the desk.

"Very much so," I grinned, feeling Ruth's eyes burrowing holes in the side of my head.

"Who did you practise flirting with while I was away?" he asked, replacing the magazine and turning his attention back to me.

"There was a young boy on the DART last week, also the corpo men are always up for a quick flirt. Other than that I was good as gold." I smiled, congratulating myself on how well this was going.

"Good as gold? We'll have to remedy that. A girl like you should be decidedly bold whenever the opportunity arises."

"I tried, but the boy was only about fifteen and the men were a bit unshaven. The pickings have been slim."

"Well, I'm back now. I'll save you from the minors and the beer-bellies."

"Thank you so much, kind sir," I gushed.

"What are you doing for lunch?" he enquired.

"Nothing at the moment."

"Well, we'll do nothing together," he said, smiling.

He returned to his desk and I looked at Ruth. She was stunned; she told me later that she never expected a

result the very first day. We had a result though and it was
a good one, in fact make that a fantastic one. This was no
practice. This was the real thing. The flirting had begun
and I was doing very well.

Ray came to lunch with us all week and openly flirted
with me. Never missing an opportunity to touch my hair
or my leg. His hand rested on the back of my chair as I
ate my lunch and he walked to Trinity College with me
in the evenings, before heading down Nassau Street for
the 46A bus. Ruth looked on in amusement and nodded
approvingly from behind his back when appropriate.

All in all this was working a dream.

Time was running by, though. It was now the 12th of
August and I had only three weeks left. Ruth pointed this
out to me one afternoon in the toilets.

"I know. I know," I told her reflection as I brushed my
hair.

"You need to take charge of things. Sorry, but you
might have to think about asking him out straight."

"God, that's embarrassing. What if he said no?"

"I really don't think he will. He has been seriously flirting. I think he actually likes you."

"Thanks, don't make it sound so surprising!" I laughed.

"Well, you know what Ray's like. I wasn't sure at first.
But now I think he likes you."

"Umm . . ." I studied my reflection. "I don't know
about asking him though. I don't actually think I could."

"See how things pan out on Friday," said Ruth.

On Friday we were going for drinks after work. It was
being paid for by the boss because some bigwig in

accounts was leaving. We didn't know who it was and we didn't care. There were going to be free drinks and cocktail sausages. We were there!

Friday morning came round after a very long week. I had carefully chosen an outfit that could easily be transformed from day to evening wear by simply adding a fancy belt and higher heels. Ray appeared at my desk at 9:30. I knew by the look on his face that there was a problem.

"Are you guys all going for drinks after work?" he asked

"Yes," I nodded.

"I don't think I can make it."

My disappointment must have been palpable.

"Sorry, Amelia, I can't get out of a thing I have to do. Look, I'll try to get in later. Give me your mobile number and I'll give you a call and let you know."

"OK." I brightened a little as I rhymed off the number.

He wrote it down and winked at me, then went back to his desk.

14

We all sat in the cordoned-off area in the pub around the corner from the office. The boss was at the bar asking everyone what their drink of choice was.

The platters arrived soon after with cocktail sausages and chicken wings. We fell upon them and ate them in about three minutes flat.

The boss left sometime after seven and the real drinking began. I don't know why we always get so excited about a drinks session that the boss is paying for. You can't ask the boss to order you a tequila slammer or a vodka and Red Bull. You can't be seen to order your own drinks, or drink faster than the boss. He always drinks slower than anyone else, talking and laughing, drinking a pint of Guinness in about fifty minutes, the rest of the group watching thirstily as he downs the last mouthful and sits chatting for another twenty minutes before making any move towards the bar. Then there's the long wait while he takes all the orders again and waits at the bar to be served. All in all, these nights out are a bit of a let-down. Still we all go, and we all look forward to them. We are creatures of habit. Wave alcohol in front of most office workers on a Friday night and they'll do pretty well anything.

We did a fair bit that night.

Jack and I were sitting together talking about, among other things, rugby. Ruth was sick of the conversation, not liking rugby, and she was dancing in the corner with Louise and John. She was complaining bitterly that there was no karaoke that night. Jack and I were sympathetic to a point; there really is only so much you can say about karaoke.

We carried on discussing the finer points about the last Six Nations. He was amazed that I knew so much about the sport, and I was amazed that he ever played it. He's not a big guy, but he informed me he was fast. He was a winger for St Mary's all through his secondary school years. Then he was in the college team in DCU.

I told him that I'd been in the girl's rugby team in college myself.

He hardly concealed his suspicion. "Liar!" he laughed.

"Yes, I was."

"What position did you play?"

"Well, we never sorted that out," I admitted.

"How can you not sort that out?"

"We didn't play any actual matches. We formed a club, then no one got round to organising a match as such."

"Did you train?"

"Em . . . no, not really."

84

"Did you have a shirt? What number was on the back? I could tell your position from the number."

"I don't think I ever saw our rugby shirts – the boys' ones were blue and white though."

He began to smile, a broad grin that was infectious.

"What do you find so amusing, Jack?"

"You were never in a rugby club – you were in a fan club. You big fool!" He playfully pushed my shoulder.

"Yes, I was! I joined the club thinking we'd play rugby. It wasn't my fault no one thought of organising a game."

"Have you ever played a game of rugby?"

"No," I admitted.

Jack smiled smugly and pointed at my glass. "Want another?"

"Yes, thanks."

"Back in a minute, groupie!"

He got up and went to the bar. I was left grinning to myself. I had never thought of myself as a rugby groupie, but maybe I was. Someone came and stood in front of me.

"Hello there, you!"

I looked up and there was Ray, looking fabulous, smiling down at me. I jumped, kicking the table by accident.

"Hi!" I smiled.

He came around the table and sat down beside me, exactly where Jack had been sitting.

"How's the night going?" he asked.

"Fine, you made it in then?"

"It would appear so." Ray put his pint down on the table, pushing Jack's empty glass out of the way. Something about the action stung me a little. Ray then turned his whole attention on me, smiling and showing off a set of near-perfect teeth. His front teeth crossed over just a touch at the bottom, but to my eyes it made him cute. "I just had to meet a friend and sort out a thing before I got in. It's all done and dusted now, so I'm all yours for the evening."

"That's good to hear!" And it was! But I wanted to know what he had to sort out, but I wasn't sure how to ask.

Ray pushed my hair off my shoulder, and looked appreciatively at my neck. He was really very cute this close up. His eyes were a little unfocused – he looked like this was not his first pint of the night.

"So, were you out earlier on?" I asked

"I was in my local for a quick pint. Why?"

"No reason. Well, you look a little drunk. Are you?"

"No, I only had the one." He smiled before adding, "Well, one of everything at the bar actually. I may be a little foggy."

"I see," I nodded.

He leaned forward a little and seemed to make a gesture towards kissing me. I know it sounds ridiculous as I'd been openly flirting all week, but I got a bit of a fright. I moved just a fraction in the opposite direction, away from his face. He straightened up quickly, and took a mouthful of his pint. I was left sitting beside him, slightly unsure of myself. Ray turned to the girl sitting opposite us and flashed a winning smile at her. I excused myself and headed for the bathroom.

When I got back, a drink was sitting on the table

waiting for me. Always a happy find. I turned to Ray.

"Thanks," I smiled taking a sip from the glass.

Ray nodded, turning his attention back to me. The other girl looked a little deflated.

"Look, sorry about that earlier," he said. "I'm a bit giddy. I was pushing my luck. Forgiven?"

"Of course, it was nothing. I'm just a little too sober for … you know . . ."

He knew what I meant. Leaning in closer he whispered, "I'll keep an eye on you and kiss you later, agreed?"

"That could be arranged." I could feel a smug little grin on my face.

"Excellent, wait there and don't move. I'm just getting another drink." And he kissed me on the cheek.

I glowed happily, checking only briefly to see if the other girl was watching. She wasn't, but it didn't make the victory any less spectacular.

Ruth had seen at least some of it. She rushed from her corner, where she had been dancing happily.

"Well, look at the flirty smurf!" she laughed.

I smiled innocently, but I was giddy with excitement.

"When did he get here?" she asked.

"About twenty minutes ago. He came over and sat right down beside me. Did you see it?"

"Yes, I was watching you." She raised an eyebrow that told me she'd seen the failed kiss.

My cheeks flushed a little. "Did you see the other thing?"

"Yes, I did. You were dead right. He can't come in here and kiss you just like that! He needs to spend a little time

– small talk and the like!"

Ruth was laughing but she was serious and I agreed with her. Ray was really gorgeous but I was not to be bought, and even if I was, I was a bit more expensive than vodka and Coke. Ray came back, carrying drinks for both of us. He put the vodka in front of me and turned to Ruth.

"Sorry, babe, didn't see you there. Are you all right for a drink?" He kissed her on the cheek.

Ruth beamed at him, very merry indeed. "I'm fine. I have one here." She jerked a bottle of Miller towards him. "Next time though!"

"I promise." Ray swayed a little and turned back to me. "You, sweet thing that you are, should develop a taste for beers. That vodka was nearly a fiver."

"I don't care. I have expensive tastes. So sue me," I quipped, comfortable in the knowledge that he was mine for the night.

Ray sat down beside me, fishing a mixer bottle of Coke out of his shirt pocket.

He put it on the table in front of me, looking me in the eyes with a sort of intensity that gave me butterflies. Ruth made herself scarce, waving her goodbyes from over heads as she disappeared back into the crowd.

Ray continued to stare at me, but made no comment and no further moves towards me. The butterflies were receding; now I was feeling a little nervous.

"Am I freaking you out?" Ray laughed.

"Just a bit," I smiled, trying to sound lighter than I was feeling.

"I'm just wondering about something." He sounded

a bit serious.

"What's that?"

"Doesn't matter. It was nothing." He shook his head.

"What?" I asked again.

"Forget it. It was nothing. I shouldn't have stared at you like that. Sorry."

I didn't ask again, but I couldn't help wondering what was going on in his head. I flicked my hair, taking the opportunity to look away from him for a moment. He had made me a little uncomfortable with all the staring.

I noticed Ruth with Steve and Jack in the corner. Ruth was dancing beside them – well, make that twirling – she was holding Jack's hand and twirling happily in the corner. Jack was ignoring her for the most part, but was quick to steady her when the twirling got out of control. He was a solid, dependable person and I couldn't help smiling at the back of his head. Thinking it was a pity that Jack and Ruth didn't get together.

Ray stood up, telling me he was off to the toilet and that he'd be back. I nodded, still looking at Ruth and Jack. Jack looked over at me and waved. I nodded back, before it occurred to me that he had gone to buy me a drink just before Ray came in. It then dawned on me that it was Jack, not Ray, who had bought me the drink I'd found on the table when I came from the bathroom. And I suddenly recalled that Ray had sat in Jack's seat and that I'd ogled him for the last hour and ignored Jack. My heart lurched and I got up to make my way over to Jack.

I pushed my way through the crowd and arrived at his shoulder.

"Jack, sorry. You bought me a drink and I never thanked you."

"That's all right. I saw Ray was there so I left it on the table for you."

"I forgot completely about you."

Jack gave me the slightest glance, and I realised I had put that very badly.

"Never mind," he replied in a slightly stiffer tone.

"I didn't mean I forgot you," I tried to backtrack, blushing slightly. "I didn't forget you. I just forgot about the drink."

I blushed even more as Jack took in my obvious discomfort. He was not too ready to let me get away with it. He looked a little amused and made a point of looking at my neck, which I know was burning hot.

"Look, Amelia, it's all right. I know what you mean." He turned back to Steve.

"Do you want a drink? I owe you one?" I carried on, obviously not knowing when to shut up and walk away.

"No thanks, it's fine."

"Are you sure? I owe you one."

"I didn't buy you a drink just to get one back, Amelia, I don't work that way. You certainly don't owe me one." He smiled, but his eyes were focused and the implied message was not lost on me.

I stood for a second, looking at him, before turning to Ruth. She had finished twirling and was watching the exchange. She looked at Jack and raised an eyebrow at him. He shrugged off the look with a slight twitch of his lip.

Ruth looked back at me, smiling too broadly.

"Hello, there," Ray's voice came from behind me. He wrapped his arms around my waist and I turned to face him.

"Well, hello!" I gushed, putting a little kick in my voice for Jack's benefit although I was not sure why I was doing it. I just knew I had been given the brush-off. While I was aware that I had owed Jack an apology, the fact of the matter was I had apologised and he was not very gracious in his acceptance. You can be a bad winner, I thought to myself.

Ray smiled down at me. His eyes were so blue and they sparkled when he flirted.

He leaned close and whispered in my ear, while I shuddered a little from the heat of his breath on my neck. "Will we shoot off soon?" he asked.

I glanced at my watch, then back at Ray. His face was kind and his eyes were fixed on mine with an intensity that was breathtaking. It was 11:45 and all of a sudden the idea of leaving the stuffy atmosphere and heading off with him was very appealing.

I glanced at Ruth who was watching closely while talking to Steve.

"Come on. I'll get my coat," was all I said as I untangled myself from his grip and headed for my coat.

Ray followed behind me and we left the pub in seconds flat.

Once on the street we were faced with the important yet embarrassing question of where to go. I was a little nervous about bringing up the subject; luckily Ray had no such shame.

"I'm living with my parents at the moment, so back to yours?" he said hailing a taxi.

"All right."

That was it, sorted in one sentence. We got a taxi back to Clontarf and Ray allowed me to make him coffee. After his third cup he leaned forward on the couch and kissed me. This time I did not move in any direction and allowed him to kiss me.

He pulled away slightly, smiling dreamily at me. "Sorry about that. I thought you were going to offer me another coffee and three really is my limit." He moved towards me again, pushing my hair off my shoulder. The look was unmistakable. He stared at my neck and then back at my face, looking right into my eyes.

"I love the look of a woman's neck. It's got to be one of the sexiest things about a girl," he whispered as his lips brushed the edge of my ear and he kissed my neck lightly.

He nuzzled my neck, between my ear and shoulder, his breath hot and his aftershave filling the air around me. He sighed, moving back a little to look at my face.

"I love your hair. It's really soft. Girls' hair always smells so nice. What shampoo do you use?"

I was a little surprised by the question. "Pantene usually," I smiled, allowing myself a little giggle.

Ray looked at me and smiled. "Sorry, I always ask that. Men's hair never smells as good as girls'. I don't know why that is. Have you never noticed?"

"No, I can't say I have."

"Well, it's true. Smell my hair."

I swear to God, this is true, he actually bowed his head for me to smell. Worse fool me, I leaned forward and smelt the back of his head. "It smells like gel. That's what all boys' hair smells like."

"Yours smells nicer," he said, pulling a small handful to his nose and smiling at me.

"Well, it's no big secret. Pantene, smooth and silky. The blue bottle."

"Thank you. That's good to know." He laughed before leaning back on the couch and announcing that he hadn't had the grand tour of the flat yet.

"I like to refer to it as an apartment," I joked, but I realised that in fact I do.

"The 'apartment' then. I still want to see around it. How many bedrooms?"

"Just one."

"One? Where are you going to sleep then?"

"In my bed," I replied.

His eyes lit up.

"Alone," I said, raising an eyebrow at him.

"That's what you think!" he laughed.

I showed him around the apartment, my stomach a little knotted after the last remark. I knew he was here in my apartment, and I knew I was almost thirty, but I wasn't sure I wanted him to stay the night and I definitely hadn't decided if he was staying in my bed.

The decision was taken out of my hands as soon as we got to the bedroom. He shut the door behind us and gently pushed me back on to the bed. He didn't force himself on me, not at all. He just had an end result in mind and he got it. Once that night and then again the following morning.

I was a disgrace. I had no self-respect and no discipline.

The following morning Ray got up and made us coffee and toast.

He sat up against the pillows, his hair tossed and a cheeky grin on his face.

"I'm seriously liking your apartment. Living with the parents is great for the creature comforts, but a place of your own! I'm very impressed."

"Is there any reason you never moved out?" I asked. After all, he was thirty-one and still living at home.

"I was living in Donnybrook for about two years, but the rent was ridiculous and I wasn't loving my room-mate any more."

"Girl or boy?" I asked, hoping he'd say boy.

"Alan, boy. He was all right, we met in college and it was handy to get a flat together. Sorry, apartment. But he was a bit of a slob and we didn't get on too well living together."

"I see." I toyed with the idea of telling him about the wedding. I mean he'd invited himself to stay over and was showing no signs of leaving. I didn't think it'd sound too clingy.

It didn't matter much. Ray asked me about it in the end.

"I hear you have a wedding next month," he said while he chomped his toast.

"Yes, my sister."

"Are you one of the bridesmaids?"

"Yeah, the only one as it happens."

"I love a good family wedding. Need a date?"

I had known he was self-confident, but inviting himself to Jenny's wedding was a bit of a bold move. I was too embarrassed to refuse him.

"All right, if you'd like to come."

"Do you want me to?"

"Yes, that'd be great."

"Well then, girlfriend, I'm there." He laughed, planting a kiss on my cheek. "Now get up before I have to do something rude to you. From behind this time."

That comment appalled me and it appears again I wore my emotions on my sleeve. I must have looked as shocked as I felt because he backtracked very fast.

"I'm only joking! Don't look so upset. I'd never dream of it!" he laughed.

"All boys dream of it, but you'll just have to keep dreaming," I told him, but got up very quickly anyway.

He followed me into the kitchen and left his cup in the sink. "Is that clock right?" he asked pointing at the cooker clock.

I nodded and he raised his eyebrows. "Can I hop in your shower before I grab a taxi?"

"Sure you can. Are you late for something?"

"Well, it's almost midday. My mother will be looking for me."

It seemed like a reasonable thing to say, so I gave him a towel and he disappeared into the bathroom.

The buzzer went. Jenny and Michael arrived at the door just as Ray was emerging from the bathroom.

Jenny looked at him with some interest as I made the introductions. Michael winked at me and in a moment of uncharacteristic affection for him I grinned back.

Ray got his coat and headed for the door. In the hall he kissed me before he left.

"I'll talk to you on Monday. Thanks again for the use of your couch." He said it loudly, smiling at me.

When I got back to the sitting-room Jenny was pointedly staring at the obviously unslept-on couch.

"Will Ray be coming to the wedding then?" she asked.

"Yeah, do you mind?"

"Not at all. He can sit with Luke."

Michael coughed and Jenny suddenly sprang into action. "Oh Millie, we're here for a reason really. I wanted to ask you something."

"What?"

"Would you mind doing a reading on the day?"

"Oh…" I really didn't want to read in front of every one. "That's great. I'd love to."

She handed me a novel – honestly, it was two pages long.

"Is this it?" I smiled, hoping I'd be told it wasn't.

"Yes, it's a lovely one. I really like it." Jenny saw the look on my face and laughed. "It is a bit long, but it really doesn't take long to read."

"That's all right," I smiled, my heart lurching as I spoke.

"Hey, you can get Jenny to do both readings and sing the homily when it's your turn," Michael laughed.

"I might just do that," I nodded.

15

The countdown was on. We were down to two weeks. Jenny was skinny as a rake and neurotic about everything. She had asked our cousin Sandra if her twins would be flower-girl and pageboy. Sandra was only thrilled to have her smalls included in the day. The problem was they were very young, just gone three years old. Sandra had been in the house every weekend for the last four weeks, discussing what should be done with Rebecca's hair. I had rarely seen a child with less hair than this girl. The child had about fifteen strands of white-blonde hair, so did it really matter?

The week before Sandra told my mother that Richard was very jealous of Rebecca's basket of flowers.

"He doesn't understand that she's the flower-girl. He wants the flowers," she said over a cup of tea.

"Poor little lamb," said Mum. "We should give him something to hold on the day. I wonder what we could give him?"

"Don't worry about him – he'll get over it by the time he has to walk up the aisle."

I wasn't so sure, and sat quietly fretting as I listened. I was now going to have to walk up the aisle, shepherding two tiny time-bombs.

Most of the preparation was over and the replies were coming in thick and fast. So far no one had declined the invite. We were looking at a total attendance of 150 for the meal with hundreds more for the 'afters'.

Dad was getting his speech ready and becoming very secretive about the whole thing. Jenny asked me to find out from him if he was planning something huge. He said he wasn't but that he was keeping it a secret until the day. I begged him to be nice about Jenny and keep the "funny little stories" to an absolute minimum. He promised he was going to be the soul of discretion and not to worry my head about it. I pointed out that I was not worried about it, Jennifer was.

He gave a little chuckle and patted my shoulder. Now I was as worried as Jennifer was, but I had to tell her it was all under control.

Jennifer had decided to go for small flowers and large candelabras for centre-pieces. They looked very pretty, as did the tiny candles she was giving as wedding favours. She had decided to give everyone the house wine during the dinner, and was happy with the decision until some-one in work with her pointed out that you could bring your own and have it corked for about a euro less per bottle.

At first I thought it was a lot of fuss for very little saving, but as the amount of wine 150 people might consume was totted up, I began to take an interest in cheaper options.

We had bought in various wines and were going through them on a nightly basis. We were drinking them each night with dinner. Suddenly Mum was cooking for the masses every night. I was home for dinner each night, Jenny and Mike lived in the kitchen, hovering around the wine rack, and Justin's PlayStation gathered dust in the corner. We sat around the table clinking glasses and making toasts for hours.

We decided on bottles of Wolf Blass – good price and everyone seemed to like the taste.

To be honest we didn't really care about the wine: top table was getting champagne throughout the meal. We all laughed and made smart remarks about the commoner garden guests having to make do with wine when we would be bathing in champagne. We all thought this was really funny until Luke realised he was one of the guests.

"Hey, I'm not on the top table. Will I get no champers?" he asked

We should have been nicer about it, but we weren't.

"No, you won't," Jenny giggled.

"That's great. The bride's brother and I don't get a glass of champagne!"

"You'll get plenty of drink in the run-up to the event," Mum said.

"Yeah, but that's not the same thing," Luke whined.

"Yes, it is. You'll be fine!" Jenny smiled at him.

"No, it's not. Why can't I have champagne?" Luke was taking this a bit too seriously.

"You don't deserve champagne. Stop complaining!" Jenny laughed, the wine making her cheeks all flushed and her eyes glassy.

"Why not?"

"Oh, Luke, shut up whining about it. You'll drink the wine and be glad of it," Mum told him.

This was amazing. It may well have been the first time I have ever seen my mother brush Luke off. Ever. Luke looked wounded. Jenny, who'd been trying to keep a straight face for a few minutes, snorted with laughter.

"Well, that's fine. Now I know how you all feel about it. You couldn't care less about me!" Luke sniffed, storming out in true teenage-girl style.

We should have been nicer; someone should have gone after him to see was he all right. We should have, but we didn't. Jenny collapsed onto the table in front of her, sniggering. The rest of us were left torn between watching Jenny unravel and going after Luke to coax him back down to the table.

We watched Jenny. She rarely gets this drunk any more and she was always an amusing drunk.

16

Things were odd in the office the first Monday after Ray stayed with me. It seemed to have got around very quickly. I most certainly didn't tell anyone, but everyone seemed to know. I'd have wondered if Ray had told them, but I was in the office before he got in, so he couldn't have.

I went out to the smoking shelter with Ruth that morning and she confirmed that everyone did know.

"We all know you left with him. No one knows anything else," she said, lighting her cigarette before adding, "We all know Ray though. People are putting two and two together. Are they getting five?"

I wondered about lying, but decided against it. "No, not really." I couldn't help but smile.

"You slut!!" Ruth grinned. "Tell me more!"

"He stayed."

"On the couch?"

101

"No . . ." I tried to keep a straight face while Ruth dissolved into very childish giggles.

"Well, was he as good as he thinks he is?" she grinned.

"What? How do you know he thinks he's great?"

"Ah, the lads give him stick. I think he told them about a few conquests years ago and they've never let him forget it." Ruth shrugged.

"If he says anything about me, I'll break his neck!"

"He won't. Come on. It's nearly eleven. We've to get back. Hurry up and tell me!" Ruth waved her cigarette at me.

"He lives with his parents, so he came back to my apartment. One thing led to another and he stayed."

Ruth continued looking at me, waiting for more information. "Is that it?" She looked as disappointed as she sounded.

"Yes, I'm not telling you all the gory details."

"I don't want them all – just a few would be nice. Has he a big one and does he know what to do with it?" Ruth sniggered.

"You're gross and yes to both."

"Oh, lucky you!" Ruth laughed as she put out the end of her cigarette.

We got back to my desk and Ruth leaned over, reading the same magazine Ray had looked at a few weeks before. I thought I should really throw it away soon. It was over three months old. Ruth was pretending to look at my computer as she skimmed the pictures. Ray walked over to my desk and sat on a pile of faxes I had just been handed.

"Hi there, you!" he said, smiling.

"Hello!" I grinned at him.

Ray looked at Ruth with the slightest hint of a good-bye. Ruth scarpered.

"How was your weekend?" he asked.

"Grand. I have to do a reading at the wedding. That was why my sister came over."

He looked as though he was trying to work out what I was talking about. "The girl who called in on Saturday? The blonde with the ugly bloke?"

I nodded.

"Oh right. Listen, lunch today, my treat. Just you and me."

"All right," I grinned.

I turned back to my computer, happy again. I glanced at Ruth, but noticed that Jack and Steve were watching me. Steve was openly laughing, so I stared at him until he realised he was being watched. He stopped abruptly, sliding off Jack's desk and skulking back to his own. Jack carried on working, not even pausing to look over.

That afternoon Ray brought me to the Mercantile for lunch and we had ice creams on our way back to the office. Let them all laugh; I was in love.

From day one Ray was sweetness and light personified. We would go out to lunch, all four of us. Ruth and Jack looked on as Ray carried my tray and helped with my jacket. Ruth had to admit that Ray seemed to be smitten and there was no doubting that I was.

Still there seemed to be an atmosphere in the office.

Jack was still not smoking, so was not eager to go outside with us and without him we had no inside track as to what was going on with the boys in the office.

There seemed to be something going on though. I could feel the eyes on me as I walked around the place. It wasn't the girls – they didn't seem to care about Ray and me. In fact, only that Ruth had confirmed it, I would never have realised they even knew. They did know; they just didn't care. It was the boys who cared. I could feel eyes on me while I worked or when I was faxing or photocopying. I would look up and there'd be some head diving behind a computer screen, or three guys standing at the water cooler looking at me. They were very interested in me all of a sudden and I had a funny feeling it was not because I had morphed into the most glamorous girl in the room. It was something else. I got the feeling it was just because I was seeing Ray. Louise, the manager's PA, was seeing some guy in Accounts and nothing was ever said about that. This was different. I couldn't put my finger on it and it bothered me that I couldn't. Were they jealous of Ray or did they pity him? And either way, why?

Ruth dismissed it completely. She said that she noticed no new atmosphere. There was always a bad atmosphere in the office. She thought it was a problem of too many boys in the one room.

"Testosterone," she confirmed. "Too many willies in too small a space – they get antsy."

"Why does everything in your life revolve around boys' willies?"

"Because most things do!"

"This doesn't. Why are they all behaving so weird?"

"They're not."

"They are."

"I don't think so. They're just the same as they always are. Mad as hatters."

"Um, well, I think there's something up."

"Well, I don't." Ruth stubbed out her cigarette and started to get ready to go back into the office.

On our way back up to the third floor in the lift Ruth told me she was missing Jack's company at smoke breaks and hoped he'd start smoking again really soon.

"Well, of course you miss him. You fancy the arse off him!" I announced, pointing triumphantly at her.

"Don't start that again. I miss his company that's all."

I was going to get to the bottom of this. I had a very good idea about how to get them together. I just had to get to Jack at the right moment. I would though and, when I did, this was going to be sorted out once and for all.

17

It was now the 27th of August and the house was on the highest possible alert. Mum was honestly about to combust, both with pride and nerves. She was enjoying her Mother-of-the-Bride status and was using it to full effect.

She had had the house painted inside and out. She was wearing a new outfit every day and making almost daily trips to the hairdresser. She was looking very well and she knew it. Luke was videotaping everything – all the families' get-togethers, every neighbour knocking on the door to hand in a present or wish Jennifer well. Mum was not telling him to put the camera away either. She was smiling and preening for all to see. On occasion she would forget herself and move Jenny out of the way as she smiled for the camera which was always being poked in our faces.

Luke would appear at the door of whatever room we were in and announce that I was to smile and say

106

something to Jenny about the wedding. I would tell Jenny she was mad, and that the cost of this wedding would have us all out on the streets by October. Without fail Mum would hear me, and the shout would go out from wherever she was in the house.

"Amelia, stop that! It's not funny. Rewind it and tape over it."

She would then appear into the room, smiling for the camera, her eyes burning into me with fury. She would wait, still smiling, as Luke rewound the tape and she would "supervise" as I gave my proper message. I would be encouraged to wish them a happy, baby-filled life together.

Mum would then smile for the camera herself, wishing Jenny well, telling her she was the favourite child and that she was best thing that ever happened to the world, never mind this family. The atmosphere was always a little icier while Luke and I looked at one another over her shoulder as she recorded her message. Mum never noticed anything, or if she did, she didn't care enough to say anything.

It was now seven days to the big day. The hen night had passed off without that much trouble. We had not hired a stripper. Jenny had warned us prior to the event that stripping of herself or anyone else would not be tolerated, nor would L-plates or condoms. On her way into the restaurant she announced that no one was allowed to flirt with the waiters as it was "common". To everyone's surprise my Aunt Jean tutted loudly and told Jenny to get over herself.

"It's not common – it's good sense in a restaurant like this. If you're quiet in here you'll never be served." She poked my cousin Louise in the ribs. "Catch that waiter's eye, would you, love?"

Louise was well up for the job, being only just eighteen, with the face of an angel and the body of a hooker. She batted her eyes at the shy waiter who was stationed at our table. He took her order for beers and ran like the wind. A few minutes later an Italian-stallion type appeared from the kitchen with our order. He danced attention on us and was tipped wonderfully for his endeavours. The shy lad was later seen serving tables on the other side of the restaurant, as far from us as was possible

The night went downhill from there. Everything that Jenny had said she hated, she then looked for. We had brought an L-plate for her and an old communion veil which she loved herself in. She posed around town, being kissed by men and having phone numbers stuffed into her pockets. She loved it. Louise produced a handful of disco-boppers from her bag, insisting we all wear them. She stuck a pair on Mum and Auntie Jean and they jiggled their heads making the boppers bounce. Jenny had a white pair and the rest of us had red ones. We all wore them until Mum inspected Jenny's and noticed they were little willies.

"Dear God, she has penises on her head!" she announced very loudly in a late-night bar.

"I know," Jenny sniggered. "So do you!"

"That's disgusting!" Mum removed them from her head. "Why would you young girls think that's the least bit funny?"

She was unimpressed; the rest of us were highly entertained.

The night ended up in a bar on Leeson Street. We drank too much alcohol, spent too much money and danced too much, and we all had blisters and hangovers the next day. Well, everyone except Louise: she was still dancing at six and was up by ten 10:30 the following morning.

There was a family meal on the Sunday night; cousins, aunts and uncles from all over the country and beyond were coming over. I took the opportunity to bring Ray and have him introduced to my parents. They should at least be able to recognise him when he showed up at the wedding the following week.

Ray looked amazing when he arrived at the door. He was charming and well turned out, a combination that thrilled my mother.

It has long been acknowledged that my cousin Keelan has bagged a great husband; his name is Matt, he's English, and extremely good-looking. Mike couldn't compete even though, my feelings aside for the moment, he was well liked. Ray was the real thing though and Mum knew it. She welcomed him in with smiles and gushing pleasantries. Ray accepted them, smiling, offering wine and chocolates. I was very proud, really I was.

The dinner went off without a problem. Ray and Luke

got on very well. Keelan's Matt faded into the background when Ray was talking. Although, Matt is really gorgeous-looking, and that voice yummy!

Ray found me after the dinner and cornered me on the landing.

"Are you staying here tonight?" he asked

"I don't know, depends on how much I drink."

"All right, listen, I might shoot off soon," he said, looking over my shoulder at someone coming up the stairs.

Dad passed us by and went into Luke's room, reappearing a moment later with the video camera.

"Come on, you pair! We're making a bit of a film of the night." He ran back down the stairs.

"Could I interest you in a night together?" Ray whispered.

"Perhaps, but I can't go yet. I have to stay and say nice things to Jenny before we head off. Is that all right?"

Ray pouted a little but then smiled. "Sure, whenever you're ready. I'll have another drink and talk to that Mike guy – he was nice."

We joined the family in the sitting-room and listened to all the stories about Jennifer, from her early arrival into the world at the Coombe Hospital. She was a week early and Dad was away. We heard all about her first nappy change and it appeared every nappy change until she was potty-trained at age two.

Then we got on to her schooldays and the stories went on and on from there. They ended up with stories about their first impressions of Mike and how we were delighted to have such a wonderful member of society joining our family. The world was certainly a better place now that Mike and Jenny had got together and it was only going to get better as time went on.

I know it sounds twee and silly but I was enjoying it, feeling a little sentimental about family ties and getting caught up in the stories of babies and happy family times to come.

I was smiling at Mum while she told yet another baby story about Jenny when I noticed Ray in the corner of the room.

He was looking decidedly bored. I felt sorry for him and got up to join him. He smiled as I approached but his eyes were pleading.

"Do you want to get going?" I asked.

He nodded, smiling. "Sorry, is that a huge pain?"

"No, not at all. I'll get my coat."

I got my coat and we said our goodbyes. Everyone was very sorry to see us go, and to be honest I was a little sad to be leaving too.

111

18

It was definitely odd to be getting up and getting ready for work with Ray in the apartment. I usually get up and dash around, tearing out for the train station with dripping wet hair, leaving behind a huge mess in the bedroom. With him there I felt I should at least try to keep things tidy and make some effort at trying to dry my hair. As a result we missed the train and we got to the office just after nine. Everyone else was on time and they all watched us walk in together. I felt as if it was printed on my forehead: *Slapper*.

Ray felt no such shame and strutted around the office making us both a cup of tea and sitting on my desk for a while before getting started on his own work.

Jack had come in the Monday before last and without warning had started smoking again. He never said anything about it, and no one knew why. He just appeared out in the smoking shelter again. Ruth was overjoyed she had Jack back. There was no explaining to her that Jack's smoking was a bad thing. She understood that this was indeed very bad for his health and that he was making a huge mistake starting to smoke again after five weeks off them. I still went with her for the break, as the boss hadn't a clue whether I smoked or not. He didn't and he never came near the shelter, so I was safe there. I have to say, since starting back on the cigarettes Jack was like a cat with PMT. Of course Ruth couldn't see it and thought I was the one being cranky. He complained bitterly about the weather and the amount of work he had to get through. We tried to lighten his mood but he wouldn't accept help from anyone and refused to see the bright side of anything. In short he was being a complete pain in the ass.

"So is Ray going to the whole wedding?" Jack asked. He and Ruth had been invited too.

"Yeah, he's meeting me at the church – there's no point in him coming to the house."

"Right. So he'll be at the church when we get there," Jack confirmed. "That should be fun."

"Why would that be so much fun?" I asked, irritated.

"Ray is such a party animal, isn't he?"

"He's good fun, and he's my boyfriend," I replied.

"Are you sure about that? Have you got it in writing?" Jack asked, stubbing out his cigarette.

"I don't need it in writing. I get all the proof I need, on a nightly basis." I smiled smugly, but the comment didn't sit well with me. It wasn't like me to be so coarse.

Jack looked at me disapprovingly. "Right, that's good

113

to know," he sniffed.

"Get lost with your 'holier that thou' crap," I complained.

"I never said a word. It was you who gave us an insight into your bedroom. No one asked for it," Jack replied stiffly.

"You know, Jack, you might want to stop smoking again, or at least change brands. You're very narky these days," I told him.

I could see Ruth cringe slightly, but I didn't care. Jack was awful lately.

"Am I really?" Jack answered.

You could tell from his tone that he was just itching for a row. I was more than willing to oblige.

"Yes, you are. What is your problem?"

"There's absolutely nothing wrong with me," Jack sneered. "I haven't changed at all."

"What does that mean? I've changed?"

"You? God, never!" Jack practically spat the words.

"I have not!"

"Oh yes, you have, sweetheart! Why tell us what goes on between you and Ray behind closed doors? Who asked for that? Certainly not me, and you would never have spoken about it before he came along. You're a different person and I for one preferred the old you! You know he's making a fool of you! Allowing you to chase after him like you are."

"What are you talking about? I'm not chasing Ray. He likes me and I like him. We're young and we're having a bit of fun."

114

"He likes you? You think that makes you special? He fancies anything that stands upright. He's not the great catch you think he is," Jack sneered.

This row was losing the run of itself.

"I never said he was a great catch, but he's a better catch than some." I looked Jack up and down

"You think he's a better catch than me, for instance?"

"I never said anything about you. But could that be the truth coming out?"

"The truth?" Jack laughed. "Don't make me laugh! What do you know about the truth?"

"What are you talking about?" I asked.

"I am talking about the truth and the fact that your boyfriend wouldn't know how to be honest if he was given private tutorials."

"What are you going on about? No one understands you, Jack," I said, covering my unease with a belligerent stare.

"Let me put it this way for you then: your boyfriend is a liar!" Jack replied, getting up and stalking back into the office.

Ruth and I sat looking at one another.

"What was that about?" Ruth said, looking at the door he had just stamped in through.

"What did he mean about Ray being a liar?" I said, leaning back, shaken by the row. I hadn't expected things to explode the way they did.

"I have no idea. I didn't expect him to get so worked up." Ruth was still looking after him.

"Nor did I."

Ruth looked at me. She sighed, looking down at her

shoes as she began to speak. "Look, forget about what Jack just said about Ray. He's just being bad-tempered at the moment. I think he's just lashing out more than anything. I don't think it was true."

"Well, you can't forget about something like that. If Ray is a liar what's he supposed to be lying about?"

"I don't think Ray is a liar. He's vain, but I don't think he's a liar. I think Jack was being mean, just lashing out."

"He shouldn't have been lashing out at me!" I said, feeling very put upon.

"You attacked him too." Ruth smiled, her eyes confirming that I was in the wrong too.

"I was defending myself."

"You were, in your eye."

"Should I apologise?" I asked, hoping she'd say no.

"No. He will most likely, but just accept the apology and leave it at that, OK?"

"Fine," I smiled.

I didn't actually want to be fighting with Jack.

Jack was glaring at his computer screen when we got back to the office. Ruth walked by him, patting his shoulder in a kind gesture and he smiled briefly at her. He looked back at his computer, glaring again.

I sat at my desk waiting for the apology, but none came. I looked up to check if he was waiting for some encouragement. No, he was looking at faxes and heading for the photocopier. I looked at Ruth – her head was down and she was working. Maybe he wasn't going to apologise. I was bit annoyed but decided to let it go. As I said, I didn't really want to be rowing with Jack.

19

The morning of the wedding had finally dawned.

I was awoken at seven by Jennifer racing into my room, leaping onto the bed and actually screeching, *"It's my wedding day!!"* into my face.

It was quite scary actually. We had both had to sleep with our hair in rollers and Jennifer's were falling over slightly. They gave her a wild air; this was not helped by the already manic look about her anyway. I suppose it is scary, getting married.

Anyhow, she leapt off my bed again and opened the blinds. The sun was shining and the birds were singing. Thank God, I thought to myself. It hadn't actually occurred to me what might happen if the day was wet – after all the preparation Jenny might have actually stabbed one of us.

The house was buzzing; we were all up and showered by eight. Dad was making everyone a fried breakfast. He wasn't running the risk of anyone fainting in the church.

Mum reminded him that heart attacks were a bit more of a problem than fainting, so he should grill and not fry the breakfast.

After breakfast we drove up to the hairdresser's. It took ages. We were there for almost two hours and there were only three of us. How long does it take for wedding parties that have three or four bridesmaids? I shudder to think. Five hours?

Mum and I were easy enough to sort out, Mum had a wash and blow-dry and my hair was pulled up high on top of my head with flowers stuck to it for effect. Having my hair piled high like that gave me a good two inches extra in height. Being only five foot two that extra height was very welcome. It also made my neck look long. I may try to perfect this look, I thought – tone it down a little and leave out the flowers. Yes, this hairstyle might well be used to excess in the months ahead.

Jennifer's on the other hand was a delicate and intensive operation. The girl took the curlers out of her hair with the same amount of care that a doctor would remove bandages from a burns victim. A second girl stood close by taking the old curlers and wiping the first girl's brow from time to time. Then the real work began, as they pulled, pushed, swept and pinned hair around Jennifer's head. They stood back, viewed the work from a different angle and set to work again. A third girl appeared at a door and gasped. She raced over and announced that there was a slight bump at the back when you viewed the hair from an angle of 37 degrees south and that this

118

would cause untold misery for Jenny in the years ahead. Three heads then tried to fix up one head, while Mum and I stared at the floor and the other punters.

Finally Jennifer's hair was finished and tiara and veil attached and pinned. There was a reverent silence as they twirled Jenny's chair around for us to look at her.

She was beautiful, truly she was. Her hair was really blonde and her sun-bed sessions had really paid off. She was bronzed and healthy looking, with a light sprinkling of freckles over her nose and cheeks. Her hair was piled high, with big fat curls falling down over the top of the veil, and the diamonds in her tiara sparkled under the spotlights. All in all, she was a complete success. She did also look slightly comical in her headdress and veil, not a scrap of make-up and a track suit. We didn't mention this to her though. We just smiled and clapped for her.

When we got home the make-up artist had just arrived. We all got our make-up done, then things really started to come together. Mum and I got dressed and then converged on Jenny. She needed help being zipped and clipped into her dress; this was a strategic operation if ever there was one. Mum and I came at her from a few angles before we worked out how to get the bodice over her head without disturbing the hairdo. We managed finally. A word to the wise: if you get a halter-neck, make sure it opens at the back of the neck. We didn't and there were some narrowly averted disasters in that bedroom.

As in the case of most things, the dressing did finally come to an end and the result was a resounding success. She looked like a movie star. White satin, blonde curls, cream petals and sparkling diamonds. And not so much as one petal too much. She was perfect. She looked stunning.

Dad and Luke came in to have a look at the finished product. Dad was smiling and shaking his head and Mum shed a tear as she straightened the back of Jenny's veil.

The doorbell rang and it was Sandra and the twins. She led Rebecca and Richard into the sitting-room and had a brief word with them before returning to the hall, smiling and telling us that they were very excited about the whole thing.

It turned out that they were so excited about the wedding that they didn't sleep the night before and they were "a little tired" and "a small bit cranky" on the day.

I remembered there was a doll and a toy gun (let's not get into the question of stereotypes) which had been bought for them, upstairs in my room. I thought they might do the trick. I ran upstairs and produced them.

Rebecca's face lit up like a Christmas tree, she was so delighted. Richard was quietly pleased with his gun and proceeded to shoot Luke. At first Luke threw himself on the ground, clutching his side and dying a long drawn-out death.

Richard screeched with laughter and shouted, "Again!"

Luke died again.

Richard shouted, "Again, again!"

Luke died a little faster, only to hear "Again!" before he'd even breathed his last.

After five deaths, we were all bored. Not least of all, Luke.

There was another knock on the door and this time it was the cars and that was it, no more time to think, just into the car and off to the church.

I travelled with the twins. Alone. It was scary. I would have no idea what to do if they decided to fight or go to sleep in the back of the car. Tempers were running high.

Back at the house, Rebecca had begun to covet Richard's gun. Her doll didn't make any noise, his gun sounded morbidly real when it was fired. She liked the noise and had wanted to see it for herself in the sitting-room. Richard had held tightly to the gun, whining loudly. Rebecca had shoved her doll into his face, as a trade-off I suppose. He was not the least bit interested in the doll and threw it on the ground. Sandra had leapt up and taken both toys from the sparring tots, turning them towards the TV.

"Barney is watching that behaviour!" she advised them.

Oddly enough, it worked and they stopped dead. They stood watching the TV. They looked a little zombified to me. This was not helped by the fact that Barney began to sing and they both sang and danced with him.

Mum gushed about how sweet they both were and Sandra practically exploded with pride. She was just stopped short of this explosion by the fact that Richard suddenly reached out and pushed Rebecca backwards. She landed on the floor with a surprisingly hard thump and began to scream. She was helped to her feet and promptly head-butted Richard in the stomach. Luke watched on from the door, laughing so hard that Mum

121

told him to make himself scarce.

"Sandra doesn't need you sniggering at her," Mum told him.

"I'm not sniggering at her – I'm laughing at her children!" Luke pointed out but he was banished to the kitchen.

The fight went on a little longer in the sitting-room, both children now crying and reaching out to pull the other's hair every now and again. They stopped when Sandra threatened to have their toys given to "the poor children".

I wondered who the poor children were, only to be then shocked by the reaction of the "rich children" in the sitting-room. The crying stopped short; both pairs of hands grabbed the toys in question and hugged them as though they were lifesaving medicine. There was silence in the house and harmony was restored.

I'm very sure I behaved just as badly when I was three, but I was bothered by their reaction and wondered what type of people the twins would grow up to be.

The atmosphere was volatile as we sat in the back of the car, me in the middle keeping a shaky peace between the two as we made our way to the church.

When the car pulled up outside the church there were hundreds of people standing outside waiting for our arrival.

People converged on the car, hugging me and gasping at how beautiful both I and the twins looked.

The twins stood beside me, looking shy and delicate, as cameras flashed and people patted their heads.

"Hello there, you!" The voice came from behind me. I looked around and there was Ray.

He looked stunning, in a dark brown pinstripe suit with a cream shirt open at the neck. Smart casual at its tasteful best. He looked like he'd stepped off the pages of a *River Island* magazine. I was dying for someone to take a photo of us, just to prove to my grandchildren that I too could pull a looker in my youth.

Luke arrived at the bottom of the steps of the church, shouted my name and took a photo. He got a charming photo of the back of Ray's head, and me with my mouth open replying to him. Only I was not smiling sweetly and saying "Yes". I had my mouth open, my eyes were half closed, and I was saying "What?"

The second car arrived through the gates and the driver beeped a few times as a signal for everyone to get inside the church. No one moved. I asked a few people to head for the seats.

"Jennifer's just arriving now, could you all go and take your seats, please?" I asked.

"I know she is. We want to see her," my aunt told me.

"She wants it to be a surprise," I lied. I just thought that at least some guests should be inside when she arrived.

"Get the boys to go inside; the women want to see her," my aunt insisted.

Thankfully word began to filter through and people began to head into the church. I was standing just inside the door looking up at the altar, making absolutely sure that Mike was indeed there, when I was slapped on the bum. I stifled a screech and looked around to find Jack and Ruth grinning at me.

Ruth and I hugged. Jack looked at his feet, and then smiled a little at me, stepping behind Ruth as he did.

"You look fabulous! My God, you're positively scrawny!" she beamed.

Ruth saw Ray as she stood at the back and headed for him quickly, leaving Jack behind.

We looked at one another, embarrassed.

"You look really great. Don't fall going up the aisle now," Jack advised, walking swiftly away.

I was left behind, feeling suddenly very aware of my feet. I was now convinced I was about to fall headfirst on the red carpet.

I heard my name being called and turned to see Jennifer getting out of the car. I raced into action. I held the bouquet, straightened her skirt, fluffed her veil and kept the twins at a safe distance from the dress. Their hands were always slightly sticky – though on this occasion no one had seen any food in their possession.

Photos were taken and people headed inside just before we settled into the procession to walk up the aisle.

At the last moment I produced the basket of flowers that Rebecca was to carry up the aisle. Richard took one look at them and held out his hand to get his basket. I told him they were only for Rebecca.

"You got the gun, remember?" I tried to console him.

He was having none of it. He pulled the flowers from Rebecca's hand and she howled.

The organ music began, and that was our cue.

Richard was holding tightly to the flowers and would not let go. Rebecca was crying and pulling her hair from its pretty fastenings. I had to think fast. I looked at Jenny. She was glaring at me from behind her veil. Even behind the heavy white net I could see the eyes burning into my head. Mum was gone, Sandra was inside too. Dad tried to console Rebecca, bribing her with a few coins. She took them from his hand and hurled them on the ground. Proof positive that the euro is a load of crap.

He then tried to wrestle the basket from Richard, who, by the way, is a very strong baby.

Finally we gave up. Richard walked up the aisle with the basket of flowers and Rebecca had to be carried, still crying, in my arms. She was a dead weight and my arms felt numb as we neared the altar.

The top of the aisle could not have come sooner. I dropped Rebecca down and my right arm got severe pins and needles. I prayed that I wouldn't drop Jenny's bouquet or anything else I was handed during the Mass.

The tingle subsided, though it took longer than I expected – but then again, I couldn't shake my arm, so I had to sit waiting for the blood to come back.

The rest of the Mass went off as planned. Except for the moment when, during the communion, Richard shouted to me that he needed to go to the bathroom. He was on the other side of the altar at the time, and didn't bother with the formality of coming over to me. He just called out to me from a distance of about ten feet. Jenny shot me a glance that would have turned me to salt if this was a biblical story. I went and took his hand with a fake smile and then luckily Sandra came to the rescue. She took both of them off into the sacristy. I was not getting caught up in the bathroom for hours with the pair of them.

20

The wedding was a huge success. The hotel did itself proud, the food was gorgeous, the drink flowed and the room was very tasteful.

We were all prompted by Mum to tell Jenny that the centre-pieces, and anything else that sprang to mind, were very pretty.

I spent a good half hour telling her how pretty everything looked and how much I was enjoying myself. She politely told me to stop drinking. I wandered off, slightly miffed, and went to find Ray and the others. They were in the bar. I allowed them to tell me how wonderful I looked and how expertly I had dealt with the twins. Then I further allowed Ray to buy me a few drinks. I had no purse with me and I couldn't locate Dad to get money from him.

"I had no idea your sister was such a looker," Ray told me.

127

"Yeah, well, she's now spoken for," I advised him.

"Amelia, on the other hand, is not," Ruth put in.

"And that's how I like it," I said quickly, noticing the slight but instant change of atmosphere at the table.

"Then who am I to take that from you?" Ray smiled.

"Who indeed?" Jack said, with something of an undertone.

He wasn't starting with the crankiness again? I was going to kill him if he did, I looked at Ruth but she didn't seem to notice anything amiss. Maybe I was the one being cranky.

We were all called for the meal and people stampeded for the function room. People were excitedly pointing to their names on the table plan and looking around for the table number. They were picking their way through the sea of tables and stopping to greet other guests. Loud laughter and screeches were to be heard from every corner. And from my vantage point I could see Jack and Ruth sitting with Justin. I wondered where Ray was. Presuming he was in the toilets, I turned my attention to the waiter who was offering top-ups.

At the last second Ray reappeared and took his seat, his hair a little tossed. He glanced at the top table and seemed to search me out. I could see him but pretended not to notice. He didn't try to catch my eye – he just seemed to be checking my whereabouts. But then, I'd just been doing the same with him.

The meal passed off without incident. The speeches were funny in their way, but a little boring.

Dad did himself proud. Telling us all about the various

proud moments Jennifer had given him over the years. Not forgetting of course that Luke and I gave him a few reasons for pride also, and there was always Mum to fill him with pride when none of the children were on hand to do it themselves. All in all, he painted a picture of a happy, proud and indulgent father. No one disputed it with him. No one brought up all the times he had grounded us, sent us to our rooms, stopped pocket money or turned off the TV while we watching it to make us do our homework.

He told a few embarrassing stories about Jenny, like when she was five and had to be brought to the doctor for a check-up. He had given her a lollipop as he discussed the check-up with Mum. It was a green one and she had wanted a red one, so she took offence to the colour, and while he sat talking she got up, walked around the desk and bit his arm. Then she handed back the offending lollipop and said, "Red one!" Then we were told about the time Jenny had tried to sell me, pram and all, to a neighbour's child for 50p. There was also a wonderful story about Jenny's first boyfriend. Then a funny situation with her second, a comment or two about her third. An uneasy stir went through the guests: were we going to get a comment on each and every one of her ex-boyfriends? And what exactly would Mike say or do while the list was being read out? Luckily Dad stopped there with the ex list and finished his speech with some extremely complimentary remarks about Mike.

Later on, when the band had started and the first song was over people really let their hair down. The band was your typical wedding band, lots of Neil Diamond and Sinatra. The dancing was your typical wedding dancing, women in circles shuffling and singing the songs word for word. Jennifer never got off the floor; she danced and hugged various aunts and neighbours of my mother's. Mike shuffled beside her. I have noticed that for the most part, boys are split into two groups: those who can dance and love to dance and those who can't dance and won't dance. It would appear that Mike's natural habitat is the second group but that night he was forced to join the odd, in-between world of the "can't dance but have to dance" group. He had not got a clue; he shuffled and stooped awkwardly beside Jennifer.

Unkindly, Jack and I stood at the side of the dance floor watching him, making him feel more self-conscious I'm sure.

"Come on. Stop staring at him. It's not fair!" Jack laughed.

"Stay, it is fair. He made me do a reading," I told him and bobbed up and down a little, pretending to dance when Mum caught my eye so she wouldn't guess why we were laughing.

She still looked suspicious and came over.

"Where's Ray?" she asked, looking pointedly at Jack.

"In the loo, I think," I said. "Mum, this is Jack, from the office."

Mum changed her tack and smiled welcomingly at Jack. "Well, hello, Jack. Are you having a nice time?"

"Yes, lovely." Jack smiled. "It's a great day."

Mum smiled and agreed.

I looked around to see if Ray was anywhere around. He wasn't and I couldn't help wondering where he was myself.

Mum left and rejoined the ladies who dance, smiling and singing as Jenny and Mike bobbed in the centre of the group.

I watched, planning how I'd get out of that particular shame if I ever got married.

"Where's Ray?" I asked Jack absent-mindedly.

"I don't actually know. Ruth's at the bar there." He nodded towards the bar.

Ray was nowhere to be seen.

I was just realising that I hadn't seen him in about half an hour and I was getting a little concerned.

"I hope he's all right," I said and I caught the slightest smirk on Jack's face. I didn't say anything.

"I guarantee you, that guy's fine."

"What do you mean?"

"Nothing. There he is, over there." Jack pointed at the door just as Ray walked in.

He waved at me and I went to meet him. He'd been outside, there was a cold air coming from him.

"Were you outside?" I asked.

"Yeah, I had to take a call. The reception is very bad in here. It's freezing out there!"

"Who was it?" I asked.

"What are you drinking?" Ray asked, ignoring the question.

"I'm all right, but who was on the phone?"

"No one important, just a guy I know," Ray replied

131

over his shoulder as he headed for the bar. He shook his head in a dismissive manner, indicating that the conversation was over. He was taking a call, that was all there was to it.

I joined Ruth and Jack who were now sitting together watching the dancing.

"Where was he?" Jack asked as I sat down.

"Taking a call," I replied.

"Again?" Ruth said.

"What?" I asked, suddenly alert.

Ruth looked uneasy as Jack and I watched her.

"Nothing, forget it. I actually have no real reason to say that," she said

I knew backtracking when I heard it, and by the look on Jack's face he did too. The fact of the matter is that I didn't really want to know about it tonight. It was only 9:30 and this was shaping up to be a very long night. I didn't want a row or bad feelings between Ray and me tonight of all nights. Not in front of my family.

Ray returned to the table. Putting my drink down, he kissed the top of my head.

"Will you be dancing at all tonight, Miss Slater?" he asked.

"I think I might," I smiled.

So we all took to the floor. At least that way I was not thinking about where he was. He was right in front of me.

21

The day after the wedding we were all booked into a posh restaurant for brunch before the newly weds departed for a fortnight in the Algarve. I will admit, the weather was dull but dry and I would have sold my granny, if she was still alive, for a ticket to the Algarve that Sunday morning.

We sat in the bistro talking excitedly about all the small disasters that had happened and that now didn't matter at all. Jenny was laughing about the fact that Richard first looked and then reached down the front of his trousers and did God knows what in front of the entire congregation during the Gospel reading and then later he told the photographer that he was too hot and needed to lie down during the photos.

There was a jazz band playing in the corner. This was meant to add charm and atmosphere, but they were simply too loud. We found ourselves shouting over them, the other punters were shouting over us, the band in turn were trying to play the music over all of us. The noise level was reaching a glass-shattering climax when abruptly it stopped.

This made everyone look at the door, such was our expectation that a celebrity had joined us. No one had walked in and little by little it registered that the band had simply stopped playing. Calm was restored and we passed a very enjoyable two hours in the bistro. Drinking more wine and eating more sugar.

I was coming out of the toilets when I ran into Mike. We stopped sort of awkwardly in the small hall. I was blocking his way to the gents' and he was blocking my exit. We smiled and did that stupid little shuffle. Neither of us felt comfortable or indeed wanted to touch the other. We held our arms close to our sides and smiled a little, trying to avoid the other's glance. Then Mike laid a hand on my shoulder and said, "Stay there."

I did. He moved around me and pushed the gents' door open.

Just as I was about to make my escape he called me.

"Yeah?" I replied, turning around.

He let the gents' door close. I held the exit door open.

"You don't like me, do you?" he asked.

"Yes, I do," I lied, thinking with shame that I must be very transparent.

"Amelia, I know you don't like me. I just wonder why it is?"

"Look, Mike, I do like you. I don't know what makes you think I don't."

"I think I know what it is, but I just want to hear it from you."

"Mike, I do like you!" But I could feel the blush creeping from my neck upwards.

"I'm not stupid, Amelia. I can see it in you. Is it what I think it is?"

What did he think it was? I will admit openly, I had no idea why I didn't like him. I just didn't. If he had a theory I was all ears.

"Look," I tried again, not sure what else to say to him, "I don't really know you, but you seem nice."

"It's my job, isn't it?" Mike said.

That shocked the hell out of me. I had no idea what the guy did for a living. I remember asking, but I never really took in an answer. Maybe no one answered. The longer I knew Mike, the less interesting I found him. I never really bothered to ask again. I didn't actually know much about him at all. I only found out he had a sister at the wedding. What *did* he do for a living?

"Your job? I don't even know what you do!"

I let the exit door close, shutting us into the small corridor again.

"I'm a funeral director," he said.

"What?" I laughed.

"Yeah." He let himself smile a bit. "Everyone thinks it's a bit ghoulish, but it's actually a lot of paperwork and organisation. I don't really see the bodies much at all."

"What do you do?" I asked, for the first time truly intrigued by this man.

"I tend to think of it as being the 'best man' at a

funeral. I look after the ordering of the coffin, I pay for the grave and the opening costs and the cars and really anything that the family want me to do. I take care of the nitty-gritty things and let the family do what they need to do without the hassle of organising the funeral."

I nodded. It sounded like he did an invaluable job at a rotten time. As he put it, it did sound like he was simply taking a 'best man' type role in the proceedings. It didn't sound ghoulish at all.

"What made you want to be a funeral director?" I asked. I felt it was an obvious question.

"What made you want to do recruitment?" he countered.

"I didn't, I fell into it and I've been searching for the out-door ever since," I admitted.

He looked at me with a tiny glimmer of interest, but ignored whatever question had popped into his head. Instead he replied, "Well, I didn't really wake up one morning and think 'I'd love to organise funerals for the rest of my life'. But I answered an advertisement in the paper and ended up in the job. I like it though, and I'm good at it."

"And you'll never be out of a job," I replied.

"Death and taxes," Mike said as he kicked the gents' door. This time he kept his foot holding it open and that was as good as a goodbye for me.

I reached for the handle of the exit door and went back to my seat. It was the first real conversation I'd had with him and it was not that bad. He was maybe not such a bad catch for Jenny. As I said, he'd never be out of a job.

It was also reassuring to know that there was no way on earth I would ever fancy my brother-in-law, no matter what happened. He was maybe becoming a nicer person, but he was still as ugly as the day was long. Sorry, but he was.

22

After the wedding things had returned to a sort of normal around the house and by degrees we were readjusting to the rest of our lives. Mum was constantly looking for me to come home and spend the evening with her. Jenny had moved the last of her things out and Mum was terribly lonely. She didn't want to ask Jenny to come back so she was busy enticing me back to the house with bribes of all kinds, from my favourite dinners to shopping expeditions.

I was running out of excuses, but I had to be strong. She would simply have to get used to the house with just Dad and Luke in it.

I was also making myself available for Ray as often as possible. He had taken to calling in at unusual times, sometimes late at night when he'd arrive with an overnight bag. We'd leave whatever I was watching on TV and head straight for the bedroom. Sometimes he'd announce he was coming home with me just as we were leaving the office. He'd tell me he was coming over to my place for a little amusement. We'd go straight home, straight to the bedroom and then order some takeaway as we watched TV later.

I was fine with this most of the time. I mean, what else was I going to do alone in the apartment? Most evenings were spent watching TV or reading. A little male company was no bad thing, most of the time.

The thing is, sometimes I wanted to go home and faff about the apartment. I couldn't faff with Ray around. He had a one-track mind and if there was a dip in the conversation at all we found ourselves in the bedroom. Which is nice – I'm not a prude!

But, to be honest, sometimes you simply needed to tweeze, wax and condition. This was not a spectator sport, definitely not if the spectator was your drop-dead gorgeous and still quite recent boyfriend.

Ray himself was kind of hard to get used to. He had his own way of doing things and he was very independent. This was no bad thing – I'm a very independent person myself. People are always saying it about me. I was sure it was a good thing about us.

We weren't one of those couples who did everything together; we were completely together but very separate people. We had our own friends and our own interests. I prided myself on the fact that I was not a clingy girlfriend.

I did have some reservations about us – well, in fact I had just one, I knew we had jumped into bed on the first night and had pretty much stayed there ever since. When we were together we were either eating takeaway or in bed. Embarrassingly, I knew what he liked to do in bed, but I didn't know how he liked his tea. In my darker moments this bothered me a lot. I was not really that type of girl and sometimes it was hard to roll with it like I was doing.

I would reassure myself that I was an adult, having an adult relationship in the twenty-first century. This was the new millennium and things were different now. People didn't court any more, a man didn't buy you flowers or kiss your cheek as he walked you to your front door. Doris Day this was not, this was the real world and I was in it, up to my ears.

It wasn't all hardcore sex, though. After a night of passion, Ray would get up and make us both tea. He would bring in mugs of black tea, milk, sugar and toast and we'd have breakfast in bed. As we ate we'd chat about the office and our plans for the day.

Ray was always busy; he always had plans for his weekend. He'd be meeting a friend to service a car, or helping someone move into or out of a new apartment. That was fine by me. I had plans of my own, plans like going to my mother's to go shopping or watch a movie with her.

I'd sometimes have to clean the apartment, really get into the corners and tidy out presses. It was silly but I loved it. I was big into my housework. I liked to sit back in a fresh clean apartment knowing the laundry was done, the beds were changed and fridge was stocked with food for the week. I was a 1950's housewife, but I liked it and I was completely comfortable with it. Ray thought I was hilarious. He'd tell me I was neurotic, then kiss me on the cheek as he stepped into the shower. Once he was dressed, we'd quickly arrange to meet up that night or the following afternoon and we'd say goodbye. He'd leave and I'd get on with the rest of my day. It was a casual thing, no big deal, and that was how we both wanted it.

Then, one Saturday Ray said he'd be back at the apartment about seven or half past that night, so at eleven I had the whole day to myself. I tidied up and went over to my mother's. She was always delighted to see me these days; she was still missing Jenny and loved to see a girl in the house. We had a lovely day; we watched an old black and white movie and ate chocolates while it rained.

As usual, just when I was making shapes to go back to the apartment, Mum started making dinner and insisted on counting me in.

"I'm not staying, Mum," I told her.

"Just stay for your dinner, love."

"No, I can't. I'm meeting Ray."

"When are you meeting him? Will you be getting some dinner?"

"He's coming over about seven and we'll order something in," I told her as I pulled on my jacket.

"Ring him and ask him over. I'll make him some too."

"No, we might go out. I don't know what the plans are yet."

"You'll order in a Chinese and that's not a proper dinner. There's no goodness in it," Mum complained as she put a handful of potatoes back in the bag, at least five huge ones.

141

"You didn't think I was going to eat all those potatoes, did you?"

"You're a growing girl. You need your food," Mum said.

"I'm not growing any more! I'm as fully grown as I'll ever be!"

"Well, they're good for you – you don't eat enough of them!" Mum defended her potatoes, like an animal defending her young.

"I eat enough – anyway I can't stay tonight," I told her as I collected my keys and bag. "I'm off. See you later!"

She came out with me to the door to wave me off.

"You don't have to run off, you know," she told me as I stood at the door.

"I know but I want to go. I have to be ready to go out in an hour."

"Oh, good thing I remembered!" Mum announced.

She always remembered some big news just as I was at the door. It usually meant me coming back in and helping her to find something.

"Jenny and Mike are back on Friday morning and they're coming over on Friday night. We're watching the wedding video and getting the photos out. Jenny hasn't seen any of them. I'll make a bit of lasagne and we'll make a night of it. Bring Ray along."

"Oh right." That sounded like fun. "Great, what time do you want us over at?"

"Anytime you like. What about seven?"

"Great, I'll say it to Ray, but I'll be there."

Mum waved me off and I hoped that Ray could come on Friday night. There was no reason he wouldn't, just

142

the whole parents thing. I didn't want to force him into coming over for dinner in my parents', I knew it wasn't his thing. No more than dinner at his parents' was my thing. I'd say it to him anyway, play it by ear I told myself, but I hoped he would come.

I got back to the apartment and changed my clothes. Hungry since I had smelt dinner over at Mum's, I resisted the idea of making a quick sandwich. I watched TV and ignored the hunger pangs, opening a bottle of chilled wine to stave them off. I began to watch a made-for-TV movie about a woman who had just found out her baby was switched accidentally in the maternity hospital. There's always a happy ending to these movies, with the mothers always getting along like a house on fire. Even though the other family had never suspected a thing until you knocked on their door and asked to see their three-year-old. This entire family of tall, flaxen blonds with sky-blue eyes. Then their third child looks oriental, it's so dark, with brown eyes and tiny features. And they expect you to believe they never noticed this?

According to these movies it happens a lot, usually in hospitals in mid-west America, and if you can prove it you can basically write your own cheque. I wondered if it had happened to me. Jenny and Luke are both blond, I'm not. It hardly seemed relevant that I was the image of Mum or that Jenny and I looked like a blond and dark version of one another. I may still have been switched and, if so, jackpot!

I wondered about how easy it would be to get records of the Coombe Hospital going back to 1973. Just as I was starting to really think about this as a possibility, the movie ended and so did the bottle of wine. I had drunk the entire bottle? I was suddenly ashamed.

My shame came to a sudden halt when I realized it was nine o'clock and Ray wasn't here.

I rang his mobile but it went straight to voice mail. I left a message asking him to call me. I tried to sound casual but I was annoyed. I hated being stood up. For an otherwise casual person I was very particular about that.

I was hungry but the wine had made me take against anything that I had to cook, or heat. It was too much like hard work. I wanted something I could take from the packet and eat. Pringles, chocolate, chips from the chipper, that type of food. I opened the Pringles and went back to the sitting-room. Trying to watch TV was tough – my stomach was in knots for some reason. I wanted to know where Ray was. I knew he was helping someone called Simon move apartment but I didn't know who this Simon was or where the apartment was. I wanted an explanation as to why it was taking so long but I didn't want to scare him off with a *Fatal Attraction* type of outburst.

Finally the phone rang at 9:40 and it was Ray.

"Sorry, sorry, sorry!" he began.

"Where are you?" I asked, controlling my tone for the moment.

"Things took much longer than I thought to get sorted here. We've only just finished moving the boxes into the apartment and we're completely jacked!"

"Are you coming over?" I asked, hoping to hit the right tone even though I wasn't completely sure of what that tone should be.

"It's late and Simon's ordering an Indian. Would I be a really bad boyfriend if I stayed on here and let you do your own thing?"

I could hear someone in the background shouting "Stay right there, Indian!" and a chorus of laughter. Ray cracked up and began to explain the joke.

"Yes, I know. Simon was ordering the Indian to stay in the corner – old joke." I couldn't help but smile; it was an old joke but it was still sort of funny.

Ray heard the smile in my voice and took it to mean he was off the hook.

"Thanks, Amelia, you are a truly wonderful girlie!" Then to the assembled crowd in the room I could hear him shout, "My girlfriend is the absolute best little thing!"

He said goodbye and told me he'd be over at midday tomorrow to take me out.

"Be here no later than that, Ray! You're not completely forgiven for tonight."

"I know. I'll make it up to you, I really will. Anything you like, we'll do anything you like tomorrow – as long as it's lying in bed all day!"

I could hear the chorus of laughter again and realised he was playing for an audience so I left it. I could talk to him in the morning.

I hung up, feeling slightly better knowing where he was, but slightly worse knowing I was alone for the night.

The following morning Ray appeared at my door just before eleven. He had a box of Quality Street and a big grin on this face.

"Do you still love me?" he asked as he followed me into the sitting-room.

"Who told you I loved you?" I asked as I fed the fish.

"A little birdie told me you were seriously in awe of me!" Ray put his hands on my hips and turned me around.

There's something about men and their gentle strength that always does it for me. The firm grip of his hands on my hips as he pulled me closer and wound his arms around my waist. Holding me in place, just loose enough for comfort, just tight enough to feel him against me. He looked down at me, his eyes sparkling and his white teeth just visible as he smiled at me.

"Am I forgiven?"

"Perhaps." I melted a little.

He kissed me, his lips just a touch apart and warm.

"Any help?" he smiled.

"Maybe."

He kissed me again, just a little deeper, and moved his hand up my back, taking a little of my weight as I leaned back. He pulled away, leading me back to the bedroom. Once in there he took his time. We had all the time in the world and all he wanted to do was touch me and kiss me and make me feel like the most important girl in the world. We spent a long time in that room and I have to admit I thoroughly enjoyed every minute of it. I woke up after a short doze and looked at Ray. He was lying back in the bed, sheets tossed and quilt thrown on the floor, his tanned skin so dark against the white sheets. I was so proud of him, he was absolutely perfect and he was mine. I turned on the TV and watched a *Dawson's Creek* marathon that was on. An ad break woke Ray from his sleep, and he looked around, bleary-eyed and dazed.

"Where am I? Simon?" he muttered as he came round.

"No, you're with me." I smiled down at him. "Were you dreaming?"

"Yeah, I must have been." He rubbed his eyes and pulled himself up on his elbows. "What time is it?"

"It's half past two," I replied.

Ray got up. He pulled on his boxer shorts.

"Where are you off to? I thought we had all day," I said.

"We do. I'm just heading to the loo, and I have to make a call." He smiled as he left the room.

The following Friday we were going to Mum's to see Jenny and Mike and the wedding video. I was really excited, and not just about the video. I couldn't wait to see Jenny again. She'd been away from almost five weeks and I had really missed her. She had gone all the way to Budapest for the honeymoon and had visited every country between there and Ireland en route back. I was really eager to hear the news and see her tan. Ray was coming straight home with me and we were heading to Mum's for about seven. Mum wanted us there early because she wasn't too keen on a late night, and neither were Jenny or Mike as they'd only got in that morning.

Just before four o'clock Ray wandered over to my desk.

"What are you up to this weekend?" he asked.

"We're going over to Mum's tonight – the rest of the

weekend is free," I said, looking up at him just in time to catch the look on his face. "What's wrong?"

"We?"

"Yeah, for Jenny's wedding video, remember? I said it to you last Sunday."

"Jenny?" He looked nonplussed.

"My sister who got married," I whispered, not wanting the office to hear that Ray couldn't remember who my sister was.

"Oh, her! Yes, of course I remember." Ray smiled, the memory flooding into his face. "Do I have to go over too?"

"Yeah, you were invited," I said.

"Would it be a biggie if I didn't?"

"Well," I faltered, "no, I suppose not, but I'd like –"

"Great. You know me – I'm not really big into family get-togethers. I hate my own ones, so other people's are pure hell!"

"Well, I'll have to tell Mum – she has you counted in for dinner." I was hoping he'd change his mind if he heard there was dinner planned.

"Dinner too!" He laughed. "Wow! That was some narrow escape!"

"You had no problem last week – you said it would be great." I couldn't help getting defensive. I felt like my family were being belittled.

"Sorry, babe, I didn't mean to offend you. I hate any family gatherings, not just yours!"

"I just thought we could do something together tomorrow. You know, make a weekend of it. Together." I smiled at him, realising suddenly that I was putting myself on the line and hoping I wouldn't regret it.

"Sure, we can do something, no problem. We'll organise it tomorrow – give me a call when you get up." He winked at me and sidled back to his own desk.

I was really annoyed as I rang my mother to tell her Ray wasn't coming. She could hear it in my voice.

"Don't be getting upset about him not coming. There'll be plenty of nights he'll be able to get to."

"Yeah, I know," I said, fighting back tears of frustration for some reason.

"Where's he going tonight?" she asked.

I was about to say he was going nowhere, he just didn't want come over but I stopped. I felt sorry for Mum. I don't know why but I did. I knew her and I knew she'd be hurt to hear that he was "dissing" her family night for no good reason.

"He has to meet a friend and help him with something," I said, knowing it was probably not a complete lie. He was probably meeting someone to move something or fix something. He did that a lot.

"Well, it's good to see he hasn't dropped all his friends just because he met you. That's a good sign." Mum was determined to see the good side of people.

"Maybe so," I said.

Jenny looked like a movie star when she came over that night. Tanned and rested, her engagement ring shone and so did another really large diamond ring that had appeared on her finger. It turned out diamonds are really cheap in Singapore and she bought herself a few rings.

She didn't buy me one but I didn't complain – I was just happy to see her home. They had so much news about their trip and they were really excited to see the video. We ate dinner and then retired to the sitting-room to watch. We got a great kick out of watching the terrified faces and nervous smiles of the bride and groom. We rewound and watched the footage of our house and outside the church. Luke's girlfriend Susan was dressed to impress on the day and the video camera loved her. She was always on screen, smiling and watching the camera. She was mortified when she saw it. The video finished and all the photos were scrutinised. Jenny told us all the stories from the honeymoon and we told her all about the wedding from our point of view. We sat up until two (so much for Mum's early night) and drank every drop of wine and ate every crisp in the house. We decided the evening was probably drawing to a close when Mike, Susan and Luke all fell asleep on the sofa. I went off home, sorry in a way that Ray hadn't made it. He would have liked it despite himself – who wouldn't? It was good family fun and there was food, drink and pretty girls wearing party dresses dancing for us!

The following day I rang Ray around lunch-time.

"Hi, Amelia, what's up?" He sounded distracted.

"Nothing. Just wondered what you were up to."

"Right – I'm a bit busy here."

"What are you doing?" I asked.

"Helping Simon with his car."

"Simon again?" I said.

"What does that mean?" Ray seemed ready for a row.

"Nothing, just you've helped Simon a lot recently." I was sorry I'd said anything.

"He's a friend, Amelia – don't get all clingy on me now!" He laughed but the warning tone was there and I was aware of it.

"I'm not. Listen, I just wondered if you had any plans for today?"

"Yeah, I'm helping Simon and then we're getting a bit of pizza."

"Oh. I thought we were doing something today. Remember, I was to ring you?"

"Yeah, but you didn't ring. So I made plans of my own."

"But I'm ringing now."

"A bit late."

"Right." I was feeling very low. "Can we do something tomorrow?"

"Sure, what would you like to do?"

"I dunno, maybe go to the cinema or something?" I felt silly and self-conscious all of a sudden and I had no idea why.

"Well, I'll ring you tomorrow and let you know, but yeah, that should be fine."

He hung up and I was left at a loose end. It occurred to me that the main problem I had was that I was content to wait for Ray and not make arrangements without considering him. Meanwhile he seemed quite happy to do all kinds of everything without me. Maybe I should take a leaf out of his book, become less available.

I got up early on Sunday morning, showered and took my time over dressing. I blow-dried my hair and fixed my make-up so that you wouldn't think I was wearing any. All in all I was very pleased with the look. It was a fabulous October morning, the sun shone and even though it was quite cold the tree-lined street where I lived looked very inviting. The trees hadn't lost their leaves yet, but they had all turned red and orange and they lit up in the sun. I was looking out my window taking in the fresh air and sun when the buzzer went.

I opened the door and it was Ray.

"Watching out for me, were you?"

"What?" I asked.

"I saw you looking out the window. Were you keeping a watch for me?" He kissed my cheek as he passed me by. "Making sure I wasn't off helping anyone else?"

"I wasn't. I didn't even see you coming in," I defended myself.

"Yeah, you were!" he laughed.

"No, I wasn't, honestly! I'm not that bad. Give me some cred!"

"Hey, it was a joke." He smiled. "I know you're not that bad. I wouldn't be with you if you were."

I smiled, but I was uneasy. Was I that bad?

He went straight to the sitting-room and sat down. I sat beside him.

"Want a coffee?" I asked.

"No," he replied a glint in his eye, "I want something very different."

He pushed me back on the couch and kissed me. His

152

hands were all over my top and then under it in no time. I was a little surprised but didn't want to stop him. It wasn't that he was doing anything wrong – just very fast.

"Want to take this inside?" He nodded toward the bedroom door.

I nodded, a little embarrassed and not quite able to call a halt to the proceedings.

We disappeared into the bedroom and if last week he had all the time in the world this week he was on a stopwatch. Talk about your wham-bam–thank-you-ma'am!

I lay there watching him in the early afternoon sun and, although I was still blown away by the fact that he was mine, I couldn't help but feel a tinge of guilt. It may have been my convent education rising to the surface, but I didn't like it when our relationship seemed to be getting by on nothing but sex.

Ray woke up and we got dressed again. No matter how I tried I couldn't get my hair to sit right or my clothes to look quite as good as they had before. The back of my hair had a funny kink in it, maybe due to the fact that I slept on it for an hour.

We went for a walk but at the video shop Ray had "a better idea", so we got a DVD and went back home, closed all the blinds and watched *A Few Good Men*.

I was bored to distraction by the film. This was not the Sunday I'd envisaged for us. Ray protested, saying that he was thinking of me when he chose the film because Tom Cruise was in it.

"But I don't like Tom Cruise! He's a short little man!" I complained.

"What are you talking about? He's gorgeous! I thought everyone fancied him!" Ray said.

"Well, I don't. I'm starving. Do you want something?" I complained as I headed for the kitchen.

"Yeah, what are you making?" Ray asked.

"Cheese sandwich?"

"Can you toast mine?"

"Yeah," I replied, pulling the toaster out of the press. I was furious and I couldn't tell him why. It sounded too stupid. The problem was I was disappointed. I was disappointed with the day I was having and the sex I'd had earlier and the way the evening was shaping up. I was fed up.

Ray must have read my mind because he came into the kitchen.

"What's wrong?" he asked.

"Nothing," I smiled.

"Yes, there is. You're upset about something." He came over and put his arms around my waist. "Tell me."

"I don't know what it is. I just feel like shit."

"Run-of-the-mill shit or is it serious stuff?" he asked, his face sympathetic.

"Just run of the mill, I suppose." I shrugged.

"Get up the wrong side of the bed? Didn't ask to be born?"

"Yeah, I suppose so," I smiled and just smiling helped lift my spirits.

"That's better. I hate it when you're sad. It makes me sad too."

"Sorry," I said.

"Hey, it's all right. No one likes a moaner!" He laughed

and hugged me.

"I'm not a moaner," I said into his shirt.

We made the sandwiches and brought in Coke and Pringles with us. We watched the end of the movie and when it was over Ray left.

He said he had a family meal of some kind to attend and that he wouldn't bother putting me through it, but he had to leave.

So here I was; six o'clock in the evening, thirty years old, in a brand-new relationship, and sitting alone in my apartment at a complete loose end. It didn't get much more boring than this.

A few weeks later Ray and I were on the DART on the way home from work when I decided it would be nice to go for a walk along the seafront when we got home.

Ray was up for it and was warned off getting to the video shop and going straight in. I was going out walking tonight and he was coming with me.

An hour later I was in a tracksuit and runners and we were walking. It was a fabulous night – late October but the weather was still nice. We were in the middle of an Indian summer. I remembered them from my childhood, there'd been a few. Rain all summer and then a glorious September and October.

As I say we were having a glorious October. People were still swimming although very few of them, but they were there. Dog-walkers and joggers jostled for position on the paths along the seafront. Dogs down at the shore were barking at the sea, and people were soaking up the last of the heat from the sun.

Ray and I chatted as we walked. Light-hearted banter about the office and what we really thought of various people in it. We walked hand in hand, dodging the roller-bladers. We chatted about the different toys from our childhood. I remembered Cabbage Patch Kids but Ray couldn't remember them at all.

"You must – they had scrunched-up faces and people in America really adopted them."

"No, I don't. Did they walk and talk?"

"No, they were just dolls and they had nappies with this guy's signature on the arse. And you got adoption papers and the doll was already named and everything. Mine was called Tilly Viviane. And their hair was woolly and plaited, except if they were boys – then they had their hair in loops. Like curly short hair?" I knew I was giving him too much information.

He was lost.

"They were dolls?" he said. "And they had wool for hair and they cost thirty pounds back in the eighties?"

"Yeah."

"And people paid thirty quid for a doll back then?"

"Yeah, I suppose." I felt greedy and mean for wanting one so badly. Thirty pounds was a lot of money back then and both Jenny and I got one each for Christmas one year.

"They didn't talk or walk or anything? They just lay there?"

"Yeah, but that was the thing with dolls then. They didn't walk and talk much. We didn't need them to."

"No, I don't remember them." Ray shook his head. "I do remember Action Man with his eyes that moved and his fuzzy hair and we had a K'nex and we had Pac Man on our Commodore 64 when no one else did."

"I remember that – my cousin was really good at the K'nex – it was like grown-up Lego, wasn't it?"

"No, it was steel and you screwed them together."

"Yeah, but it was like you grew up and went from Lego to K'nex," I explained. "Like from Fisher Price dolls' houses to Sindy and Barbie."

"Whatever makes you happy, you little madser!" He knocked on the top of my head to indicate I was mad. "I remember K'nex, but I don't remember the Cabbage Patch fellas. Are you making them up?"

"No," I said, feeling a bit embarrassed again.

We moved onto the topic of Christmases when we were kids. My stories all involved getting up at four and eating all your chocolate before breakfast, opening every toy and setting up a huge game using the new toys. It would be laid out all over the sitting-room floor and would go on for days. We'd play for hours, get bored and leave it. A little later we'd eat more sugar and the game would start again in earnest. The sugar would leave our systems and we'd sleep on the floor among our toys. Dad would come along at some point and carry us up to bed. We'd wake up the next morning and the game would start again.

Looking back, I don't know how Mum and Dad paid for it all, but without fail Santa would come and we'd have all the selection boxes and toys we asked for and there'd be food and drink in the press. I was smiling at the memory. We'd had a good childhood – lots of shouting and running around. Sun in the summer and lots of cousins and chocolate at Christmas, real coal fires and new nighties on special occasions – life was simple but very enjoyable.

I finished up, aware that Ray was not smiling as much as I was. My stomach flipped. Was I boring him?

"Sounds great," he said looking out to sea.

We were sitting on a bench away from the joggers and roller-bladers.

"It was fun – but what about you?" I asked.

"Not as much fun as you, I'm afraid."

I looked at him, and waited for more.

"My childhood was not the same – polar opposite to be exact. You had lots of fun with very little money. We had lots of money but very little fun. Dad owned the pub, as you know."

I knew his father owned a pub in Dalkey. He'd told me the name but I'd forgotten and I thought it would look rude if I was to ask him again. He didn't look at me, just at the sea, and carried on talking.

"We were completely happy to the outside world. We had everything – central heating, double-glazed windows, and we were driven around when no one else could afford petrol. We had it all. We had toys coming out of our ears, anything we wanted. I was the only boy in my class who was given a bike for making my communion. I didn't have to buy it – it was my present. Then things changed."

"What happened? Did you lose the money?"

"God, no – my father? He'd never lose money, it's far too important to him. He was so eager to keep up with the Joneses he didn't think twice about us. After my communion I was sent to Clongowes College as a boarder. I hated it. I was homesick for months and I begged Mum to take me home but she wouldn't. She was sure they were doing the right thing. Then Paul my brother was sent there too and it just got worse. Mum and Dad would go away during the term and we'd be at school when a postcard came. It'd be them saying hi from the Algarve or Spain or wherever. It was bad enough knowing I was stuck in the school but knowing that Mum and Dad weren't even in the country was too much. Paul was so homesick the head advised Mum to take him home, but she wouldn't. Dad wouldn't hear of it. He was sending us to Clongowes to give us a better start in life, he said. He wanted the best for us so badly that he was determined to keep us there at all costs. Mum kept saying it'd get better."

"Did things get better?"

"A bit. I settled a bit better than Paul did, but that was more to do with me than Paul."

I didn't understand that statement but Ray was not stopping and I wasn't going to interrupt him.

"We studied and passed our exams but Dad was never completely satisfied with the result, not from me anyway. He wanted a doctor or a solicitor or something. I hadn't got it in me, I wasn't clever enough and anyway I hated chemistry and the sight of blood does funny things to me. I passed my Leaving and got out. I went and did an Arts degree in DCU and when I graduated Dad told me the game was up, that I had to get a real job and that the joke of a degree I got had better do some good."

"What about Paul?"

"He was more of a success story as it turned out. He was really clever. He got nine honours in his Leaving Cert and went on to become a solicitor. He's making a mint and he's just announced his engagement to the boss's daughter. They'll have a combined wealth of about three hundred grand a year. Paul is the golden boy, no doubt about it. Dad looks at me and sees a waste of money. He sees all the money he threw at me over the years: the education, the toys, the college. He even gave me a plane ticket for a trip around the world for my twenty-first birthday."

"Wow, I think I got a watch and party." I smiled. Ray didn't.

"I was sent away for a year. I didn't get a choice. 'Travel broadens the mind, son.' Like I needed my mind broadened. He should have gone himself," Ray spat bitterly.

Again I was aware I was missing something but I was loath to interrupt him.

"As if I could change who I was by seeing the Great Wall of China? As if it made one whit of difference to me? Would it make me cleverer? He complained about the type of person I was, but I was a product of my upbringing. He was the one who sent me away there, and then complained about the person it made me! He's the hypocrite! I'm his son, his flesh and blood. This is me and he should love me. Everyone else's parents love them, so

160

why does my dad look so fucking disappointed when he sees me walk in?"

"I'm sure he doesn't hate you," I said, putting my arm around him.

"Yes, he does, and you have no idea how that feels. I've seen you with your parents – they adore you."

"Well, 'adore' is pushing it – they like me!" I smiled but it was lost on him.

It was true; my parents lacked money but not love. It seems Ray's parents lacked love and his father had a major personality clash with Ray. I sat quietly while Ray looked out to sea. It was getting dark and it had become very cold.

"Will we go home?" I asked.

"Yeah." He stood up, wrapping his jacket around himself. "Could I stay with you tonight?"

"Sure," I smiled and we headed back home. "Would you like to get a DVD?"

"Might do. Will we order a Chinese?" Ray brightened a little.

"Maybe pick up a bottle of wine?" I replied.

"Now that's a deal!" Ray's face lit up. "My choice of DVD of course."

I felt that one conversation changed everything between us. We were no longer just passing time together, we were closer than that. Ray opened up to me and I was more relaxed with him. Now I knew something about his life and it answered a lot of questions about him and his behaviour. I now knew why he was always rushing out to help people and making plans. He didn't get on with his

161

father and wanted to be out of the house. This was why he called in to me at odd times and stayed over a lot. That was why he was so against family gatherings: his own were just proof to him that he wasn't doing as well as his baby brother. He put his friends first because to him they were his family; he had made them his family.

It all made sense and I was so much more relaxed that it lifted a burden off my shoulders. I could take a step back. Let him meet his friends if he liked, I wouldn't dream of whining about it. He was one of those people who needed to be needed. He only felt he was needed when he was in the thick of it, helping and sorting things out. He was as insecure as the rest of us; it was just in a different way.

It all made sense and I was so relieved that I didn't even notice he was picking *Naked Gun* in the video shop.

23

I'm not a complete saint and it did still bother me to be left sitting looking out the window in a restaurant, while he talked on his mobile outside. I bit my lip sometimes when he'd dash off to help a friend jump-start his car or help someone to retrieve a box of belongings from an ex-girlfriend's house. I would remind myself time and again that this was just who Ray was. He was eager to be needed. That it wasn't his fault, and to give him his due, he was just being nice after all. Some days it was easier to make myself believe it than others.

Without fail he'd reappear, back to the table in the restaurant or back to the apartment, smile that fabulous smile of his and I'd melt. At the end of the day this was him; he was just Ray, trying to be all things to all men. I still felt a thrill when I saw him, and he was mine. I wasn't doing too badly at all.

I wasn't so blind that I couldn't see though. I knew he

wasn't perfect, I knew it. He was putting me on the back boiler while he sorted out his friends. I could see it. What could I do though? Tell him to choose between his friends and me? Not likely. I knew the deal; I shared him or I lost him. It wasn't a perfect situation, but who was I to demand perfection? I fall pretty short of perfection myself.

I did put my foot down at times. I would arrange for us to go to the cinema, knowing that I'd at least have him to myself while we watched the movie. I would insist that he turn off his phone when we were sitting in some nights. He would agree with me and say he was very sorry about the phone calls. He always seemed contrite and would promise that he'd say "no" the next time he was asked to wade in to someone else's fight. He went so far as to commit to switching the phone off one night a week. So for about three weeks his friends would be alone to sort out the world on a Wednesday night. That didn't last long. I knew it wouldn't. Yet again the phone became planted to his ear every night. I would sit listening to half of a conversation, trying to follow it and work out if I should bother pouring him a new glass of wine or not. I was getting good at it too. I could tell by the "hello" if this was a friend in need or a chat. I could also tell if he was being asked to come to the rescue, and I could hear he was trying to get out of it sometimes. Finally he'd put the phone down and have to go out and help. He'd put on his 'Godfather' voice, "Whenever I get out they pull me back in, and now I have to go help Steve get his car started."

I would sometimes toy with the idea of trailing along,

but he never asked me and I never said anything about it. I'd just turn up the TV and watch it by myself, then I'd have to wait for the phone call that would sooner or later come, telling me he was either staying at his mother's that night or that he'd be back in ten minutes.

Some nights it took longer than he expected. Smiling and apologising for the delay he'd arrive in with box of chocolates or a bottle of wine. He'd apologise and promise he'd try to be a better boyfriend. He'd smile and play with my hair as he told me I was the perfect girlfriend and that he was the luckiest man in the world to have me.

Sometimes this was enough and sometimes it wasn't.

When it wasn't I would tell him all the things that were wrong in our relationship, all the things he should do to make things better and he would listen.

He'd agree and tell me he was trying to sort things out. He'd tell me how sorry he was and then he'd take my hand and lead me to the bedroom. I was aware he was using sex to fix us. I knew I was at fault too. I was allowing him to do it. I should stand up to him, but what could I do – suddenly withdraw services? You read about women like that, using sex as a commodity, as if it was mine to take away. It was his just as much as it was mine and after giving in to him so quickly who was I to suddenly become a prude?

And then there was the whole burden of knowledge thing. After what he told me about his family, him taking me into his confidence like that. If I ignored all that I knew about him and how it made him the person he was, what kind of person would that make me? He'd opened up to me and if I just left him there or expected too much from him after all of that, I was just as bad as his father. I saw the person Ray was and although he wasn't perfect, he was human. And sitting in a pub watching other girls look after him I realised he might not be completely perfect, but my God, he came close.

Closer than I ever would. I was lucky to have him.

In early December, management got a fit of conscience and asked everyone to donate blood for the Christmas period. They did a deal with the Blood Bank and we were told to give blood at a designated time, tell them who we were and we'd all get a voucher for a free lunch and one free drink courtesy of the company.

They even opened the office at 10:30 that morning to allow us the time to donate. It was something I'd always meant to do, so I took the opportunity. Ruth and I went off early in the morning. The blood donation went off without incident. No one fainted or screamed when they saw the needle. It was only afterwards that things went downhill.

I had been a bit nervous about the needle, but now that it was over I was feeling fine. The nurse thanked me and slapped a Band Aid over the needle-prick. She asked how I felt and I confirmed I was fine. I jumped up out of the chair and rushed away. The smell of the disinfectant was making me a little lightheaded. The smell of a hospital always does that to me.

Ruth was waiting outside, full of beans. It seemed the male nurse who took her blood was extremely good-looking. She was all a-gush about him. We walked down the street, Ruth checking her plaster to see how much blood was coming from the needle-prick. It would appear it wasn't enough as she squeezed her arm to encourage it.

"Hey, if it keeps bleeding I'll have to go back to that male nurse, won't I?"

"God, stop it! That's sick-looking!"

I watched her from the corner of my eye, intrigued but disgusted, tutting to indicate I was not impressed. She didn't care, peering even closer at the cut. I watched, sickened but unable to keep my eyes off her.

Then she caught the minute cut with her nail and scraped at it. A small trickle of blood rolled down her arm. She screeched and grabbed her arm.

That was enough to push me over the edge.

"Well, it's sore," she agreed, holding the side of her arm.

"Stop it. I'm serious. I feel sick."

Ruth didn't take me seriously. She just laughed and inspected the cut again before replacing the Band Aid.

Then she glanced at her watch. "Shit. It's a quarter past ten. We'd better get going. Come on!" She glanced over her shoulder at me, then stopped abruptly. "What's wrong with you? You're white as a sheet!"

"I feel sick. You made me ill with the blood."

"Seriously? Are you that squeamish?"

"Yes," I said, leaning against the wall and taking a deep breath of air.

"God, sorry. I had no idea. Are you OK to walk?"

"Yeah, in a minute I will be."

I leaned on the wall for another few minutes and tried to breathe deeply for a while. Ruth watched the time and I was aware we were getting later.

"Come on. We'd better get moving," I said, still feeling a little queasy.

Ruth was torn between concern for me and concern that we were now late for the office. We ran down Dame Street, dodging the Christmas shoppers. We rushed in the office door at 9:40.

"Amelia felt faint," Ruth announced as she got to her desk.

Everyone stood up and rushed to me. People fell over one another trying to get the kettle boiling for a sweet cup of tea. I was put sitting on a chair in the middle of the room, and my head was stuffed unceremoniously between my knees. Someone had taken my scarf off me and was pulling at the neck of my good turtle-neck sweater, supposedly giving me air. There were at least ten people standing around staring at me – how much air was I liable to get? The intentions were good and I was feeling a lot better after a minute with my head down. I tried to sit up and Ruth pushed my head back down.

"Stay there – you might get the rest of the day off," she whispered.

I threw my head forward and moaned for effect. It worked; the supervisor came over and inspected my arm.

"You gave blood this morning? Do you always faint after needles?"

"I don't often get needles, but I fainted after my rubella shot," I told her.

"Me too," she agreed and lightened up considerably. "So your parents won't sue us or anything?"

"Not because I fainted!" I laughed, realising why she was concerned.

"Well, sit out in the yard there – get a bit of fresh air. If you still feel faint let me know. We may have to do without your services today." She smiled, knowing full well that I was going home now whether I was sick or not.

Jack sat in the backyard with me. Ruth was called to the phone at just the wrong moment and was furious to see Jack escort me out. I knew she had wanted to do it.

The backyard is a tiny concrete square where we keep the bins. There are the dead ends of various flowers in pots that we have tried to grow and make the tiny area look a little nicer. The sun hits this space for about three minutes every day, at dawn. Nothing grows, and for the most part the whole place has a cold, abandoned feel to it.

There was just enough space for Jack and me to sit on the doorstep together. Jack smoked and I sat chatting with my head still between my knees in case someone saw us.

"Are you all right?" Jack asked.

"Yeah, I was feeling a bit queasy when Ruth scraped her cut."

"She what?" Jack had obviously been under the impression that there had been some kind of a plan for me to cry off work.

"She was squeezing her cut to get more blood. She squeezed the top off it, and it made me feel faint."

"Did you actually faint?"

169

"No, but look how pale I am." I lifted my head for him to inspect.

Jack appraised my pale face, taking my chin in his fingers and pushing my head to the right and left. Then taking the tip of my nose in his fingers and pulling it out a little.

"Ow, stop that!"

"I just wanted to see if it was growing."

"Is it?"

"It doesn't appear to be. Fair enough – you may be ill."

"I am."

"Well then, sit quietly. Don't stand up."

"I won't," I replied, head back between my knees.

It was cold and the step was freezing. We both shivered a little as the conversation dried up for a while. Jack leaned in close to me, putting his arm around me. He was warm and he smelt of freshly ironed clothes. I leaned in and allowed him to hug me close. We sat in companionable silence together.

"Jack?" I said.

"Yeah?"

"There's something I was wondering about. If the answer is no, that'll be fine. I'll say nothing more."

Jack's arm around my shoulder stiffened a little. He took a deep breath and let it out slowly. "What?"

"I'm just going to come right out and say it – I won't beat around the bush."

"Don't. Just say whatever it is."

"Do you like Ruth?"

Jack's arm relaxed and he laughed. I pulled away from

his chest and looked at his face. He was a little flushed, but he wasn't annoyed.

"Why?" he said.

"I just wondered," I said.

"I don't know," he replied, pulling me over to him again. With his free hand he scratched the side of his head.

"What do you mean?" I said.

"I just don't know. I mean, she's lovely, and really good-looking and I think she likes me, but . . ."

"So what's the problem?"

"We're friends. We've crossed that magic line, you know."

I did know, but I pretended not to.

"Oh come on. Why should that stop you?"

Jack looked down at me, judging me for a second. "Amelia, why would I wreck a great friendship for the sake of one night?"

"It wouldn't be one night, would it?"

"I don't know. It might go completely wrong and then we'd be weird about it."

"I think she really likes you."

He stopped breathing for a moment and looked at me; something was working behind his eyes. "Really?"

"Yes, I think so."

He looked at the ground for a while, then shook his head. "Oh, for God's sake, this is silly. No. Honestly no. I wouldn't want to."

"I think you're mad," I told him, and I did. Ruth was perfect for him.

"Thanks."

"Don't mention it."

We sat for a few minutes more before the door behind us opened and Ray came out.

"Maguire! Step away from the girlfriend!" he shouted.

Jack jumped a little and let go of my arm.

"Hi, Ray." Jack smiled, standing up and brushing the back of his trousers.

"You're released. I can take over from here," Ray said.

I sat on the step smiling up at Ray.

Jack looked down at me. "How are you feeling?"

"I'll be fine, but I'm still going home. And I think you're mad."

"Thank you, darling," Jack called back as he headed back inside.

Ray came over and stood on the ground in front of the step. "Are you feeling better?"

"A bit."

"Good." Then he hunkered down in front of me. "You complete wuss!"

"No, I'm not. I hate needles and I gave blood this morning. I just feel a bit queasy after it."

"Yeah, I know, you wuss!"

"Ah Ray, I am sick. Be nice!"

I was feeling distinctly uncared for since Ray showed up. He wasn't being the least bit sympathetic. I was sick, maybe not enough to be looking to go home, but I was queasy and when I'm sick I like a little bit of TLC. Ray should have had more sympathy, so I pointed this out to him.

"I was being civic-minded. I gave blood and now I feel faint."

"Civic-minded? You were looking for the free lunch!" He laughed. "Push over and let me sit down there."

He pushed me up along the step and lit a cigarette, laughing to himself and shaking his head in disbelief. He was bugging me.

"Anyway, it wasn't the giving blood sickened you – it was Ruth picking at her cut," he pointed out helpfully.

"I was a bit off balance after the blood drive and she just made it worse. Anyway who cares why I felt faint, I just did!"

"Keep quiet. They'll hear you and know you're looking for the day off," he said, glancing over his shoulder at the closed door.

I sighed loudly; he was really getting up my nose. Why couldn't Ruth have come out instead of Ray? Why couldn't anyone else have come out? "I am sick. Did you even bother to give blood?"

"Yes, I did, and I didn't cry off. Fainting and the like."

"Fine." I was feeling very defeated.

"How are you feeling now?"

"All right."

"Great, let's go back inside. It's freezing out here."

"What time is it?"

"10:55, on the 19th of December, and we're freezing our arses off out on this step. Come on, get up and back to work, you!"

He stood and pulled me up by the arm, so we were standing together in the yard. He looked at my face for a

173

moment and, smiling, pushed my hair behind my ear.

"I know you're feeling sick, but sitting out in the cold's not going to make you feel better," he said, rubbing my arms up and down to heat me up.

I felt a bit better. He was taking care of me, in as much as Ray was capable of taking care of anyone. He was fixing me in his own way. He hugged me for a moment and I relaxed.

"I said it before and I'll say it again: it's freezing out here. Are you coming in or what?" He smiled into my face as he stamped out his cigarette.

"Yes, come on."

"After you," he smiled, standing back from the door, but he never opened it.

I stepped forward and pulled the heavy door open. It swung back and before my eyes, or should I say nose, Ray walked straight in. Leaving me to hold the door for him and lock it up after us. He watched me from the corridor as I battled with the latch. Then we silently walked back into the office.

I went straight over to my desk and began collecting my things together. Ray stood watching, holding my coat for me. He walked to the door with me, smiling and fussing a little about my bag and coat. I was irritated by him and left the office quickly.

24

I went straight over to my parents' house. My mother was delighted to have me back. She was clucking around me and making me hot chicken soup. I basked in the warmth of the coal-effect gas fire and the lights of the Christmas tree. Luke's nose was a little out of joint when he came home and found me there, soaking up the limelight in the sitting-room. Mug of tea in one hand, remote control in the other.

"What are you doing here?" he queried.

"I'm recovering. I fainted in work." The story had become lost in the telling at this stage.

He looked appalled, but didn't question me any further. He just made me move my feet so that he could sit on the couch too. And unceremoniously took the remote control from my limp hand. My reflexes weren't what they used to be and the war had been lost before it began. The TV was Luke's and he was not watching *EastEnders*,

Christmas plotline or not.

Ray redeemed himself later that night. He rang to see was I all right, and was happy to hear I was safe and well, tucked up on the couch in my parents' house. He said he'd see me in the office in the morning, if I was feeling up to it. I confirmed that as like as not I'd be available for work the following morning.

Jennifer and Mike came over for Christmas Eve and Christmas Day. All was jolly and festive in the house. I did well on the Christmas-present front, Jenny didn't. She got a flannel dressing-gown and candlesticks from her new mother-in-law. What was the woman thinking? Talk about your odd combinations.

Jenny looked slightly distressed when she opened the present. Mike smiled at her and oohhed at how nice the candlesticks were. She smiled falsely as she watched my mother give Mike a pair of Levi jeans. She appeared to be biting back tears as she agreed with Mike that his mother's gift was just what she needed.

Luke and I were holding one another up in the kitchen as tears of laughter streamed down our faces, recalling again and again the look on Jenny's face.

The newly-weds hotfooted it off to Mike's parents' house for St Stephen's Day and later on I returned to my apartment.

The cat was hungry; he got down from his shelf and circled my feet, purring and bumping my legs for some time. I fed him; he ate like a pig and got back onto his shelf. I went over to rub him down and was bitten for my troubles. Happy Christmas to you, too, fur-ball!

Ray came over on the 27th with my Christmas gift. He appeared at the door laden down with bags of brightly wrapped presents. Wine, CD's, DVD's, perfume and a huge pink bunny rabbit with a small box around his neck. I was bowled over by the sheer volume of gifts arriving in the door. I opened the box around the rabbit's neck and inside there was a pair of diamond earrings with a necklace to match. I put them on immediately.

What a difference it can make to your day, wearing some expensive jewelry! Ray's gifts made my gift of a brand-new mobile phone pale into the palest of insignificances.

We lay on the couch for hours, loved up and deliriously happy. Me with my diamonds, him with his brand-new, tiny mobile phone pressed to his ear every waking moment. We were together in our own private utopias.

That was how we passed the next few days, lying on the couch eating and drinking far too much and talking drivel. We had the best time! We watched *Willy Wonka and the Chocolate Factory*, stuffing chocolate into our mouths until we felt ill. We even watched *My Fair Lady* and I was feeling so secure in my new-found love that I sang all the songs on the top of my voice, not caring when Ray told me I was hitting every bum note possible.

Then on New Year's Eve Ray's parents invited us over for dinner. I was to meet the parents!

I wasn't really looking forward to it. I expected it to be awkward and embarrassing. Poor Ray was a bag of nerves. He kept telling me to be nice to his parents, that they weren't the worst in the world. I gathered he was embarrassed about telling me the things he had about them. I tried to explain that it was fine and that I'd never breathe a word of what he told me.

When we got there I couldn't have been more surprised. Ray's parents were lovely. They were rich and well-groomed and looked exactly like I expected them to. His mother was very pretty, if a little too tanned and his father was small and well-dressed. They were very welcoming and hugged and kissed me when I came in.

His mother cooed about me and told me I was perfect. She kept telling people how happy she was that Ray had finally found a wonderful young girl to settle down with. She kept refilling my wineglass and asking if I was all right. I completely relaxed and enjoyed the evening.

Ray's brother Paul was there with his fiancée. They were nice but, wow, talk about your perfect couple. They looked like they'd just stepped out of a Hollywood blockbuster. He was tall and handsome, a thinner, more sophisticated version of Ray. She was small, about a size ten, with blonde hair and the whitest teeth I've ever seen.

They wore the best clothes and dripped money, but they were very nice and Paul was extremely chatty. And very funny in a bitchy kind of way. I could suddenly see where Ray got his sense of humour. I was beginning to put the picture of Ray and his life together and he was becoming less and less of an enigma.

Over dinner Paul told stories of their childhood, and his take on what had happened to them was very different to Ray's. He seemed completely comfortable with the boarding-school education and his life at home. I watched Ray as Paul spoke; he looked uneasy and his smiled was forced.

"Do you remember that time you told an old girlfriend that Mum and Dad beat you up when you were a child?" Paul laughed.

"You never did the like!" His mother's face was scarlet. "We never laid a finger on you at all!"

"I was about sixteen, and it was just to get her to stop grabbing at me!" Ray smiled, looking at Paul.

"Yeah, we all know how you hate a girl to grab at you!" Paul sniggered. "Anyway, Mum, he told her that he had begged you to take him out of school but you wouldn't and you and Dad beat him. And as a result he couldn't bear to be touched by anyone!"

"That's an awful lie!" His mother laughed, shocked but seeing a funny side I was not so sure of.

"I did ask you to let me come home," Ray said quietly.

"Oh my God! You asked us in the first term, then you completely settled in and you loved it. You make us sound like we were bad parents – we weren't!"

"No, you weren't, Mum, and we loved you!" Paul stood up and rounded the table to hug and kiss his mother. He held his wineglass high over his head as he leaned down towards her.

She slapped his leg and told him to get back to his chair and not spill any wine over her.

They seemed very close and not the least bit reserved. I glanced at Ray, but he didn't seem to be enjoying the floor show as much as everyone else.

After midnight Ray asked if we could go back to my apartment that night. He seemed tired and emotional. Perhaps it was the drink or perhaps it was because his childhood was a little tougher that Paul's. It often happened that the younger ones had an easier ride than the older ones. Paul was definitely the golden boy. Maybe it was unfair, but I could see how it had happened. I was convinced that his attention was the secret to my newfound confidence. For the first time in my life when someone told me I looked really well I thanked them instead of denying it and blushing madly.

It was around this time that I began to realise I was funny. People would laugh at my stories and tell me I was hilarious. Again and again I would hear people say, "God, Amelia, I always thought you were really quiet!" And I would fight back the urge to say, "I know. I thought I was too!"

I was popular, and it wasn't because I had the latest doll or bike, it was because I was good fun and people wanted my company. It was such a change from the person I'd always been. I loved the new me. I really did.

I had always been the sensible one. I was clever – no big deal, just a fact, I was. As a result my parents wanted the best from me, so I studied. I worked hard in school and got my Leaving Cert with honours. I went to college and studied there too. I got my degree, again with honours, and kissed very few boys in the process. I was in college for three years, from eighteen until I was twenty-one. I was surrounded by a heaving mass of hormones; everyone I knew was sleeping with someone else. The entire class was sleeping with each other, it was becoming almost incestuous. I slept with one boy while I was in college. He was in the year ahead of me and the following week he dropped out of college. How was I meant to feel after that? He dropped out rather than ever see me again. Charming.

That one event took a lot out of me. I felt humiliated and dumped in the most exposed way. There were lecturers who knew I was dumped and, thanks to the college timetable, some of them knew before I did.

Any pride I had built up was knocked after that. I retreated to books and studied my way through the next two years. Boys would chat me up at the bar and then realise I was the one who "scared Niall off". They'd laugh and back off, telling me that they really had to finish college and I was some kind of jinx. This was hilariously funny to them, but it was crushing for me. I couldn't see the funny side to that, most likely because there is no funny side to it. Niall had his own reasons for dropping out; ten years on I am quite sure I had nothing to do with it. But the rumours took on a life of their own and I was never asked out again. Not until after college anyway.

Now I was back to the person I should have been. I was a smart ass, and I loved it.

I was pass-remarkable and people were surprised. I could see it in their faces, especially my mother's. She would smile at the group, while she rubbed her neck, or straightened her top and then look at me just long enough so that I'd see the smile had not reached her eyes. I could tell she wasn't happy with whatever anecdote I was in the process of telling everyone. I would keep going though and to my shame get a silent thrill from the stares and false smiles. I'd always been such a good girl; I was just being a little bit bold. I had never staged a teenage rebellion, I was far too sensible for that. I was rebelling now; call it adult rebellion if you will. I called it funny.

So did Ray, he thought I was hilarious. He laughed at my stories and encouraged me to be scurrilous about someone's clothes or make-up.

One night he went as far as looking up a thesaurus for more words to describe a particularly awful make-over we witnessed on *Changing Rooms*. We, of course, thought this was pure comedy. The room was hideous, ugly, unsightly, repellent, revolting, ghastly and vile, to name but a few.

We said we were increasing our vocabulary, and that was a good thing. So in fact we were gaining from our discussions.

We would sit on the DART, watching the other commuters. Every now and then I'd catch his eye just as a fashion victim walked by. We would smile knowingly at one another and then take them apart as we walked the ten minutes home from the station. We weren't hurting anyone; it's not like we were saying it to their faces. That person had no idea they were the topic of our conversation. Anyway, chances are we'd never see them again in our lives.

We were just gossiping, no harm no foul.

In work we were no better. We'd all head out to lunch. Everyone would sit waiting for the next instalment in the life of Mike and Jenny. I would be more than happy to oblige. I would tell them all about the annoying things that Mike did. Jenny was always complaining about him; I suppose she was just getting used to married life. The first year of marriage is the toughest – even I knew that statistic.

Anyway, I would tell the entire table all about the rolling of eyes, tutting and bickering. All highly entertaining stuff, I think you'll agree. We would thank God that none of us had the misfortune to marry Mike and that we were still young free and sort of single. I would smile over at Ray from time to time, so proud of him and his sexy little grin. He was all mine!

25

Late in February things took a turn for the worst. Ray was back to his old ways, taking calls while we were out and rushing off to help friends. Nothing new, but this time he wasn't coming back. He was staying in his mother's, and he wasn't ringing to tell me where he was. He would just appear in work the next day, always contrite. Telling me that by the time he realised the time, it was far too late to ring me and that he was sorry things had got out of control. The car was harder to start, the friends' problems were deeper and not as easy to rectify. Whatever the reason, he was always sorry that he'd let me down. He never seemed to get the point of my argument, that whatever his reasons were and no matter how sorry he was the result was the same: he'd let me down. He was always promising he wouldn't and then he'd go out and that's exactly what he'd do.

I had to face facts. He wasn't ever going to change and

it was up to me now. How long was I willing to accept this behaviour? And what was I going to do about it? Was I in fact going to do anything about it? Was I so used to Ray disappearing that I accepted it? Was it worth rocking the boat for? Was no boyfriend at all worse than a bad boyfriend? The truth was I didn't know and until I could decide I didn't want to rock the boat.

Ruth could see what was happening. "I can't believe you let him walk all over you like that!" she would berate me.

"He's not walking on me. He lives with his parents; I have the apartment. It's obvious we'd be at mine."

"His parents are mega rich. I'm sure Daddy would give him a deposit if he bothered to ask."

"I don't think his dad would actually."

"If you want my honest opinion," Ruth began, "I think Rayo tends to tell his own version of events. Don't take everything he says as gospel."

"He's not that bad," I told her.

"He's not a bad guy. I think he may be a fantasist though." Ruth smiled at me. "Are you understanding me?"

"Yeah, but I don't think he is," I answered, defending Ray again.

Ruth was of the opinion, not that I was lucky to have Ray, but that Ray was lucky to have me. I always thought it was just female solidarity. I never imagined that she really thought that way.

One evening as work finished I assumed Ray was coming back to my apartment. When I went to look for him at five, I was told he'd already gone. I shouldn't have been so amazed – as I said it was just an assumption, nothing set in stone. He was well within his rights to shoot off and go home, but I couldn't help being bothered when he did. I had sort of wanted his company that evening. I thought we might get dinner in a pasta place on the seafront. I would have liked a nice pasta dish with a bottle of wine.

It didn't matter though; I just bought a bottle of wine on my way home and made some pasta for myself. It was just as good and a lot cheaper.

It was after eleven and I was in my pajamas watching TV. The buzzer went, and I got up to answer, a bit concerned about the late hour. It was Ray. He wanted to come and have a chat.

Immediately I imagined it was "The Chat", and I readied myself to hear that "it wasn't working out". I could feel my stomach knot up and the lump in my throat as I let him in. How wrong I was.

When he got in he was a little drunk and very amorous. He watched TV with me. I was so glad that he wasn't dumping me I accepted him with little or no question. The thing was, I never did actually find out where he was or who he was with. He kept laughing at me and telling me he was out seeing a man about a horse. This was something he said a lot when I was first seeing him. He used to go off and meet up with people every few days and tell me they were discussing horses. He'd laugh as if this was hilarious and I should really know what he meant. I didn't. And this particular night I got the distinct impression that he was laughing at me and most definitely not with me.

The following morning in work, it was playing on my mind. I wanted Ruth to tell me it was nothing to worry about. So we went to lunch alone and I told her all about it. She didn't make me feel any better; in fact she made me feel worse.

"I would have told him to go straight home again," she told me

"I couldn't – he lives so far away – it was very late," I was aware that I sounded like I was being taken advantage of.

"He went out, never told you where he was going or who he was going with. Then showed up, drunk and horny, and you let him into the flat?"

"Yes." My cheeks burned when it was put like that.

"You fool!" she hissed.

"OK, no need to be quite so nasty about it," I replied, stung by the anger in her voice.

"You were a fool, and he was a pig to expect you to play along."

"It wasn't as bad as that makes it sound."

"Really?"

"Yeah, honestly, he was just a little tipsy," I explained. "And he was really sweet – he brought a bottle of wine."

"Oh, that changes everything then," Ruth said, sarcasm dripping. "Why on earth didn't you say that before?"

"Don't be like that. I did nothing wrong."

"Yes, you did. You accepted that kind of behaviour.

You should have made him tell you where he was."

"I did ask him."

"What did he say?"

"He laughed and said he was seeing a man about a horse," I giggled.

"What's funny about that?"

"I don't know. I just think it is," I laughed.

Ruth was not impressed. I was aware she was scowling at me so I stopped laughing. I did think it was funny though and I couldn't help but smile when I thought back on the conversation we'd had when he came into the flat . . .

Ray had stood in the doorway, swaying gently, hair tossed, friendly expression on his face. He smiled down at me with his eyes slightly shut.

"What has you here at this time of night?" I asked.

"I was thinking about you," he replied smiling at me.

"Where were you?"

"I was out with a guy I know, and you know what I did?" He swayed a little and leaned against the wall.

"What?" I said smiling at him.

"I told him all about you."

"Really?" I was flattered but I didn't really believe him.

"Yes, I was telling him about your face and your lovely hair and this flat, I mean to say apartment." He stopped, laughing a little as he hugged me.

"Were you now?"

"Yeah, I told him I was going to have to come over here and see you right this night." He was slurring slightly. "I had to come over to see you and tell you how lovely you are."

"Thank you very much," I smiled. "But where were you?"

"In the pub."

"Who were you with?"

"With a guy I know. Dave is his name. He's just a friend. We were talking about a horse," Ray ambled towards the sitting-room door. "Oh yeah, I brought you this."

He handed me a bottle of wine. I took it from him and followed him into the sitting-room.

"What were you saying about this horse?"

"Bit of this, bit of that. It had a very long face and we wondered why. That sort of thing!" He began to laugh at his little joke.

"And that brought you on to the topic of me?" I asked, Ray's laughter was infectious and I found I was laughing too. Even though truthfully I didn't think it was particularly funny.

"No, not at all. I was just telling him I was happily settled now. I found a sweetheart of a girl. And I was happy."

"Oh, that's very sweet of you." I melted a little.

"Well, I am happy. I would be even happier if you opened that bottle of wine and poured me a glass," he slurred. "I'd love a nightcap,"

"Are you staying over?" I asked as I went to the kitchen.

"Yes, do you mind?"

"No. Not at all."

I opened the wine and poured two glasses. I came back in and we sat together watching a late movie.

It wasn't that I was bothered that he was out without me; I just wanted to know what exactly he'd been doing. I never did get a proper answer from him.

Ruth wasn't in the mood for helping me out. She was not mincing her words.

"Look, he's not being honest with you. What was he doing out last night?"

"I don't care that he was out. We're not joined at the hip!"

"I know, but where was he? What pub was he in and who was this Dave? Why did he have to come back to your flat anyway? Why couldn't he have gone home?"

"I don't know. He was a bit drunk; I couldn't get an answer from him."

"I don't know, Amelia. You should put your foot down on that one. Don't accept that behaviour, otherwise he'll walk all over you."

"Yeah, I'll find out what he was doing when I see him tonight," I nodded.

"Do," Ruth said, and picking up the dessert menu she began to read it.

I took that to mean the conversation was over.

So, understandably I was not feeling any better after the chat with Ruth. I was feeling distinctly worse in fact. I went back to the office and watched Ray from a distance; I listened to his phone calls, waiting for him to say something about last night. I waited to hear if he might

190

give himself away. He didn't. All his calls were work-related and he barely looked up when anyone walked by. He was busy and I was feeling guilty for having thought anything bad of him and very guilty for having said anything to Ruth.

That night we went out for a pizza and I tried to broach the subject of the night before.

Ray just laughed and waved his hand in front of his face.

"Jesus, I was twisted. Sorry for calling so late," he laughed.

"That's all right, but I never did find out where you were."

"We were in that pub, the one on the seafront." He shrugged.

"What one?"

"The one near the beach, I can't remember the name of it. Why are you so interested?"

"Because you're my boyfriend."

"So? That doesn't mean you own me. I've told you where I was. I was out with Dave."

"Which pub on the seafront? There's more than one," I said, trying to keep my voice light, but I needed the information.

"I think it was the Yacht. Why the twenty questions?" Ray was beginning to sound irritated.

I began to think I was on to something. Why was he annoyed? He must have something to hide. Why else would he be annoyed? My heart began to beat faster, not with nerves this time but with excitement. I was about to trip him up. He wasn't going to get away with treating me badly.

"But you live in Stillorgan. What brought you and Dave all the way from the deep-south to Clontarf? It's a bit of a camel ride for a pint, don't you think?"

"I know where I live, thanks. I didn't think I needed an excuse to be out in a pub with a mate. Dave has a new car and we were trying it out. We went for a spin. We were actually talking about you and I said there was a great pub near your apartment. All right? That innocent enough for you?"

Ray was furious, and I realised only at the last moment that I had been pushing him too hard.

"All right, then why didn't you say that in the first place?" I bickered, feeling embarrassed to have made such a big deal of things.

"I was drunk last night. I wasn't aware that you were such a Fatal Attraction," Ray hissed.

"I'm not. I was just wondering –"

"Where I was! I know. I was out with a mate in a pub. I thought that was enough information for you. But as it's not here goes – I'll try to remember what we talked about. Let's see now, I might not have these in order, but here goes –"

"No, it's fine. I didn't mean anything." I tried furiously to backtrack but it was too late.

"We discussed the traffic, house prices, the price of a pint and the price of his car. The specs of his car. I think we also discussed the LUAS works and the port tunnel. Is that enough information for you?" Ray's eyes flashed with anger and I was really sorry I'd begun this line of enquiry.

"Yes," I replied, realising I was well and truly in the wrong.

So he'd been in the pub with a friend. He had done nothing wrong. He was completely innocent. I had made it into an issue and now I looked like a complete freak.

26

After that night I was far more lenient with Ray. I didn't want him thinking I was insane, or clingy, so I rolled with it as best I could. For his part he was nice about it. The fact remained that I had behaved like a madwoman. He knew it and, worst of all, I knew it too. He was nice about it and he was gracious in his acceptance of my apology. But I was living with the shame of it. I was the one who couldn't get over it.

I realised soon after that night that things had soured to the point of no return. It was a combination of things. I looked at the person I was since Ray had appeared, and I didn't like myself. I was an odd combination of totally self-centred and then self-conscious around him. He made me question everything about myself. On the one hand I was behaving like a clingy, silly girl around him, like someone who had no willpower of my own. I was led and said by him, I questioned every thought, every move

I made. When I wasn't thinking about all I was doing wrong, I was watching him and wondering about his motives. I was not this person and I hated it.

As awful as that was, I couldn't get away from the realisation that I was a complete cow when the humour took me too. It was all well and good being smartass and funny, but I was being cruel and bitchy. That wasn't cool and I was feeling dreadfully guilty about it. Mike wasn't a bad guy; he was dull as ditch-water but he didn't deserve the hard time I'd been giving him. Jenny certainly didn't and as for the innocent commuters on the train, well, I was awful. I realised I had become one of those bitches that I went to school with and had always wanted to take by the ponytail and shake. I wanted to ask them why they were being such bad people. Now I realised why they were doing it – for just the same reason I was: they'd fallen in with a bad crowd. Ray was my bad crowd and I had to cut myself loose from him. I hated the person I was becoming and I knew I would just get worse and worse while Ray was around to agree with me and laugh at my bitchy remarks.

I came to a decision and once I'd made it I knew I had to be strong and not go back. I had to give Ray his walking papers. He was a really great guy in his own way, and quite a catch for someone like me but I was unhappy and he wasn't helping me. He was gorgeous and I still very much fancied him. Believe me, I did. But he just had to go.

The following Saturday morning we were sitting in the

kitchen having tea and toast and discussing the previous night. After a few false starts. At first Ray thought I was talking to the cat, then about a movie we'd rented the night before and finally he thought I was reading aloud from the paper. After all of this I got around to telling him what was really on my mind. He listened quietly but not too seriously to my reasons and feelings about the break-up.

"I'm sorry. I just want to be alone for a while," I told him relying heavily on the one-liners of my youth: it's not you, it's me – I love you, I'm just not in love with you. We've all heard them and some of us have been lucky enough to use them. I rarely used them and as a result they sounded off. Ray knew it and tried to undermine me.

"Why?" he asked.

I hated him for asking. I knew he would but I was holding out a glimmer of hope that he would be gentlemanly about it. I had actually hoped he would take his cup to the sink, rinse it out, leave it to drain, grab his coat and toothbrush and leave. He did none of the above, he just looked at me. I was not backing down though and he was just going to have to bear with me while I talked my way out of this relationship. It was not going to be pretty.

"I don't know," I told him, silently cringing – always a good start. "I just think it would be better for us if we weren't boyfriend and girlfriend any more. I still want to be friends – it doesn't change the fact that I really think you're great."

"What have I done?" he asked, stony-faced.

"Nothing, nothing at all, you're great," I smiled, overenthusing just a tad.

"Then why do you want to break up?"

"It's just that … well … you see, the thing about it is this …" I trailed off as I caught the look on this face. A little ashamed, I stopped. "I have no real reason. It's just not what I want at the moment. Does that sound selfish?"

"Of course, it does, but you're a girl. You're all selfish little things underneath it all. It's no biggie." He took a sip of his tea and watched me crumble.

"I'm not selfish. I'm just looking out for myself. It's not my fault, it's not anyone's fault. Please don't make this harder."

He began to feel sorry for me; either that or I was sickening him with my girly show of emotions. "Look, it's all right. I just wondered why. If you have no reason, you have no reason. It's not like you were the one and only. I'm sorry about it, I still like you, but if you don't like me I can assure you it's for the best."

I was surprised by his complete lack of caring. It was as if, like he said, he was just enquiring as to why I was dumping him, out of curiosity. He didn't seem to care at all. I, on the other hand, was the one who was close to tears after this confrontation. I watched him as he looked back at me. He blinked slowly, then shrugged.

"What?" he said.

"I thought you might be a little upset, or bothered maybe."

"I don't cry over spilt milk, never have," he said matter-of-factly.

"Am I spilt milk to you?" I asked, aghast.

"It's just a saying, but yes, I suppose you are."

That was nasty.

"Don't look so hurt. I'm sure there are worse things you've been called," he continued.

"Worse than milk?"

"Yes."

I thought for a moment. I think as insults go that was a pretty odd one. Odd and therefore disconcerting. Disconcerting and therefore hard to argue with. I had been mentally thrown off course. This was bad news. I was liable to say something silly, just to avoid the silence.

"I think this may be the first time in my life I've been likened to a dairy product."

"Don't take it so badly. It was just a comment."

"An odd one, I think you'll agree," I said.

"All I said was I wasn't going to cry over spilt milk."

"Yes, but you insinuated that I was milk," I pointed out.

"So what? In the context of the phrase, a well-known and much-used phrase, you are the milk that has spilt, and I will not be crying over you."

"But milk?"

Just for the record, I know I was labouring the point but I couldn't help it – I'm sorry.

"Yes. Milk," he replied, giving an exasperated sigh.

"Skinny or fat?"

The question was out of my mouth before I could stop it. I hated myself for asking, really I did.

"What size dress do you wear?" he smirked.

At that moment I hated him, with all my heart I hated

him. I wanted to hurt him. I wanted him dead. I decided to go in all guns blazing.

"You know something? I was very unhappy with you. In fact, I was miserable. And you were very disappointing in bed as well."

I had lied on two counts in that statement. I hadn't been miserable, I wasn't altogether chuffed throughout our relationship, but miserable was pushing it. Also, he wasn't that bad in bed. In fact he was good, decidedly good, but let's not go there.

He flinched slightly, almost imperceptibly to the naked eye, but I was tuned in to it and I saw it.

I smiled at him over my mug. His eyes narrowed momentarily, then there was nothing.

"Why were you miserable?" He looked interested, not hurt.

"You're choosing to ignore the bad-in-bed remark?" I smirked.

"I know what you're doing. I also happen to know I am quite good in bed."

How conceited is that, I ask you?

"Really? Who told you that lie?"

"Never mind, I just know," he sniffed, picking up the paper.

"Girls fake it, you know," I looked at him, sarcasm dripping, a single eyebrow raised practically to my hair-line, I imagined. "A lot."

"Thank you for the heads-up, but I knew that, honey."

Damn. He was good at this.

"I was lonely a lot of the time, you know," I

announced. I had decided to leave the bedroom discussion where it was. I wasn't winning that one.

"Lonely?" he enquired, again interested, not too bothered.

"Yes. And when I look back I was only truly, really happy about fifty per cent of the time.

He stared at me. I sat there brazenly glaring at him for about five seconds, then I had to cough. I didn't actually need to; I was just feeling a little self-conscious all of a sudden. I felt as though I'd opened my heart to him for no reason at all.

"Fifty per cent? Really?" He didn't sound upset for me – again, interested is the best spin I can put on it. I tried it again.

"At first I was happy, most of the time, but lately... I don't know."

He was still staring at me. It appeared that at last I had his full attention. How odd that now, just as I was telling him I was sick of him, he was attentive. Typical – if he'd behaved like this last week we'd not be having this conversation.

He watched me, taking in each gesture I made. I really had his complete attention this time. It was suddenly a little off-putting. I was very afraid I was about to say something stupid. I have a dreadful habit of sabotaging myself when I finally get the spotlight. I usually fall over, forget lines, get a frog in my throat or start to speak in a high-pitched voice, all the things that make you cringe and basically throw yourself from the top of a high building.

Then, like bloody clockwork, I sabotaged myself. I forgot my point. I knew I had one when I started. I also know that I believed it to be a good one. Now I couldn't remember the damn thing. Shit.

He was still watching me, now willing me to finish. He nodded his head and waved his hand just a touch, beckoning me to continue. I couldn't think of anything to say. Why oh why was this always happening to me?

When all else failed I resorted to repeating myself. This, I find, is always a great way to trip yourself up. "Ray, I'm not completely happy. As I say, I look at us and I have to say I'm only really happy about fifty per cent of the time."

He raised an eyebrow, taking in and calculating the fifty per cent for himself. Perhaps for the second time.

"Well, that's not too bad. Half the time you're really, truly – let's never forget the truly – happy. That's a passing grade you, know. Not a bad grade, if you ask me."

"I don't want a passing grade. I don't want to look back in years to come and realise my whole bloody life was a D minus. I want an honours grade – passing grades are not for me."

"Not everyone gets honours, honey – you should be happy to pass. A lot of people don't."

"Well, I'm not a lot of people. I'm me. I want better out of life." I sounded like someone who'd overdosed on *Oprah*.

"Better than me?" Ray looked taken aback.

I stopped and thought for a moment. It occurred to me that he was right. Yes, I did want better than Ray. I

201

wanted better treatment than the treatment I was getting from him. I really was looking for someone better than Ray. Could that be true? The Ray? Was I over Ray?

"You're very nice, but yes, I suppose I do want better than you. I want someone who will treat me better than you've been treating me."

There. I'd said it.

He was shocked. "I treated you well. When was I nasty to you?" Ray's back was up; he felt he was being picked on.

"What about that milk comment?"

"Shut up about the milk comment. It was a remark."

"It was nasty."

"It was not, but in any case, apart from the milk comment, when was I ever nasty to you?"

I thought for a moment. "You were never nasty to me; you were just never reliable. You never stayed around; you were always taking calls, running off to help. I was always left alone."

"Were you bothered by that?"

"Yes!"

"You really thought I was unreliable?" Of all things, it appeared Ray thought he was reliable.

"Yes, you were. You were completely unreliable. Don't forget I was here. I witnessed it."

Had he not noticed me or something?

"Wow, I never thought that. Of all the things I thought of myself, I never thought I was unreliable. I never thought that would be why you'd dump me." He shook his head in disbelief.

202

"What did you think it would be?"

"I dunno, just not that." He looked at his mug. "I actually thought you were annoyed about other things. You know?"

"No," I replied, a little lost now. "What other things were there?"

"Oh, I don't really know, just other things," he sounded dejected.

"Ray, you were never here, that's the major problem. There's nothing else – you were never here to annoy me about anything else."

"Fine, if you say so." He picked up two slices of bread and made for the toaster.

"Yes, I do say so. It's true."

"Fine, I just didn't think it bothered you."

"How could you not being here not have bothered me?" I asked, allowing a good dollop of sarcasm to filter through for his benefit.

"To be quite honest, I didn't think I was gone the whole time."

I watched him buttering his toast. Was he mad? Had he been in some parallel universe for the last six months? He didn't think he was gone all the time?

The fact that he didn't seem the least bit bothered was not lost on me either. In fact, he was taking this very well. It hadn't hurt his appetite, that was for sure. How many slices of toast was he on now? Five?

He seemed curious about why I wanted rid of him, but that was all. I was irritated; he really should have been more bothered. I wasn't asking for tears. I hate to see a man cry, but a forlorn expression wouldn't exactly go amiss.

"Don't you care at all?" I asked, voice quivering slightly.

I had been nervous about bringing this up. I was careful about how I approached the subject and when I did it. Not when we were out for dinner, not while either one of us was drunk, not when he was down, all kinds of little notes to self. I worried about how he would take it. He was taking it very well, too well. I was the one who was upset. I had the hurt pride. I had been likened to spilt milk, and full-fat spilt milk at that.

I was bowing out of his love life and he was shrugging and buttering more toast. My pride was very hurt.

"Do you really not care in the least, Ray?"

"Of course, I care. Not enough to cry about it though. I never cry about these things. One thing my mother did right was tell us this." He sat up properly and cleared his throat. "Never cry over someone who doesn't love you. They are wasted tears and they blind you from seeing the looker who has just walked in and is giving you the glad eye.'"

I stared at him for a moment. Was he joking? He wasn't laughing. Could it be that his mother really had told them that?

"She told you that?" I could see the logic, but it was heartless.

"Well, the first part, I put in the part about the looker and the glad eye." He smiled his very winning smile and I was very tempted to take the whole thing back.

"I wondered about the glad eye part. It's not something you hear very often, especially not from a woman."

"My mother isn't just any woman though, is she?"

I didn't know what to say. I'd only met her once but, yes, she seemed very much like any other woman I'd ever met. She looked like any one of the hundreds of women shopping in Marks & Spencer as we spoke. I know I wanted to hurt his feelings, but picking on someone's mother was way off the mark. Even at my lowest, I was not going to take a jab at his mother. So I held back on all the sly remarks that flooded my head and replied, "No."

He took a bite of his toast, smiling at me as he said, "Don't worry, I'll get over it."

"All right, but just so you know..."

"You still really like me and you want us to be friends, I know. It's always the same old story."

"Well, that's not exactly what I was going to say, but I do want to be friends. I've seen how you run to help them when they need you. I want to be sure that I'll get the same treatment should I ever need it." I smiled at my own cutting wit, although it was wasted on him. He didn't seem to care in the least. Again I was struck quite dumb by his absolute lack of caring.

"Don't worry," he said his mouth still full. "I'll be there for you if you need it. I would have been there to help you even if you weren't my girlfriend once."

I tutted inwardly. He was always getting the last word, damn him to hell. Hold on one minute here – 'his girl-friend once'? I was taken aback by how quickly he'd moved us to a past tense. I'll admit to being hurt by that, more than a little bit. Was he really over it already? That was very fast, even for someone as slick as Ray.

"You really are OK about this, aren't you?" I said inwardly fuming.

"Fine, why wouldn't I be?"

"It's just I thought you'd care a bit more."

"I do care, but if you thought I'd cry and beg you to reconsider, you've got the wrong man."

"Fine," I replied and took my mug to the sink.

He watched me, while draining the last of his tea. He stood up. Taking his mug to the sink, he kissed my cheek and walked away. I looked after him, not sure what was happening next. He headed for the bedroom and I honestly thought he was going to insist that we sleep together one last time. Personally I think that's how my cousin Keelan got pregnant, but we're not allowed to say that. Anyway, what if that happened to me? What if I ended up pregnant, appearing on *Ricky Lake* looking for child support and telling my story about single motherhood and having to leave work, living on welfare benefit and working in topless bars for the tips?

Ray came back out of the bedroom and spoke to me. It was only then I realised I was in a cold sweat.

"Would you be on for it or what?" he said.

I stared at him: was he honestly asking me to sleep with him?

"On for what exactly?" I asked him, taking the high moral ground in my tone.

The look on his face told me I'd misheard him even before he repeated the sentence.

"Are you going for it or not, the new office in Fairview? Are you going for the job?"

"Oh, no. I don't think I'll bother," I replied, mortified.

"You should – I would if I were you." He turned away, but then looked at me again. "What did you think I said?"

"It doesn't matter. It was nothing."

He looked at me for a moment but seemed to think better of further questioning. "Anyway, I think you should at least look into it. The commute time will be halved at least. That's worth going for in itself."

"But I like the office, I like the staff – the other office might be full of wankers."

"I'd take my chances. And all our office staff aren't great, I can assure you."

"Well, I like them all."

This was ridiculous – why were we suddenly talking about the office?

"Believe me, not everyone in that office is a sweetie."

"Well, fine, I just hadn't thought much about it."

"You should. The closing date is the end of the month. I would." He picked up his coat.

"Then why don't you?" I asked him, not caring about the reply. I headed for the kitchen.

"Too far away. I would if I was on the DART line though," He ignored my rudeness and followed me into the kitchen, still talking. "Why wouldn't you?"

I was shamed into being more polite. "I didn't really think much about it. I like the job I have."

"Lie," he smiled.

Wow, he was still really good-looking.

"Why the interest? Do you want me out of the office?"

"No, I couldn't care less. I thought it was a good move for you. I was going to say it to you before, but I never did."

"Well, I'll think about it."

"Do." He smiled and headed out towards the front door.

I walked him out and he hugged me goodbye. Very grown-up and civilised. I shut the door and walked back to the sitting-room. I looked around for something to do. I was lost; I had nothing much to do and all day to do it. My breath caught in my throat as I realised he was gone. I was alone, I didn't feel triumphant, but I was doing the right thing. I was sure of it. The wind had been knocked out of my sails a little, but I was still afloat.

I sighed; going over to look at the fish I stroked Gandhi under his chin.

He accepted it with a quiet purr. I stroked him again, smiling at him as I did. This time he bit me on the finger. His tail lashed twice and he stopped purring.

With that one bite it was confirmed that all was normal in the world. I sighed again, louder this time, and picked up the phone.

27

No matter how old you get, or grown up you might feel for that matter, older siblings always have a certain power over you. We've all been there: the kitchen table/sitting-on-the-floor-in-the-sitting-room, 2 a.m., someone battling with a new corkscrew and a bottle of wine. Maybe two or three siblings, usually sisters, telling one another things that they really should think about telling a psychiatrist. As the drink flows so do the secrets, and while everyone is enjoying the camaraderie, there is a fine line between sharing gossip and just unloading your issues on some poor soul. Never forget that the wine will run out, the hangover will be rough, and you too will have to sit at the dinner-table with people who now know all about your exploits, sexual and otherwise, with that ex-boyfriend. The up-side, speaking as a younger sibling, is that it breaks down the ivory tower that older siblings have been living in since the day you were born. You suddenly realise they don't have a book of directions on the path of life. They in fact sometimes got a worse time of it than you did. It's thanks to their tears and tantrums that you enjoyed going to The Grove or any other school disco and got to stay till the end. They were the ones who had to be home from their first disco at 9:30. It's they who fought tooth and nail to be allowed to wear lipstick and eyeliner at sixteen. It's the younger siblings who get to shout: "But (insert name) was allowed to wear heels/ lipstick/ eyeliner/ stay out till eleven at the weekends/ have a boyfriend when they were my age!"

I should honestly send Jennifer a thank-you card every now and then; she fought the good fight for years about such things as make-up, wearing black and having boyfriends. It is thanks to Jennifer, and of course my own feminine charm, that I was allowed to have Carl Buckley call to our front door and ask me to go to The Grove when I was fifteen. I remember so well the look on my mother's face as she called me to the door and told me that a boy was calling for me. She beamed at me, and fixed the collar of my school uniform as I passed her on the stairs. I went on down gripping the banister for fear that my knees would go from under me. I pulled the door a little wider and there he was, all five foot four of him. (He was fifteen; he had his growth spurt at seventeen as far as I remember. He's now a good six foot tall, bless him, and still a bit cute.) I smiled and we chatted for a few minutes about the Inter Cert and how great The Cure were, and he offered to tape me an album he had. I accepted and thanked him, flushing a little, knowing it meant he would have to call in again. Finally he wondered if I was going to The Grove that weekend. I shrugged, my heart literally in my mouth. I didn't speak for fear it might fall out and land on the doorstep. That would have been a conversation-stopper; it would have taken a one-liner of biblical proportions to save me from that humiliation, never mind the fact that I might have died if it did happen. He then asked if I was going out with anyone. I shook my head and tried for nonchalant. He nodded and gave the impression that he was far more interested in the small weeds that were growing out through our wall from the neighbour's garden.

"So I might see you there?" he said.

"Yeah, I'll see you there," I shrugged.

"Maybe I'll meet you before we go in. It can be crowded; I might miss you."

"Sure, that would be fine."

Again he was engrossed, pulling heads off little pink flowers that I don't actually think were weeds, but I wasn't about to stop him.

"I'll meet you at the gates at ten to eight?"

"Sure, great. See you then."

He nodded, looked sideways at me, hesitated for a moment before putting his hands in his pockets and leaving.

My mother was standing behind the kitchen door and swung it wide open to dart up the stairs after me.

She sat on my bed, asking about him and where he lived and what I was going to wear to the disco. She wondered would we now be doing a line. I tutted, but have to admit the same thought was racing through my mind.

Not in those particular words obviously.

Jennifer moaned about only being allowed to date boys when she was sixteen, and that I was clearly under age, being not long past my fifteenth birthday. In the end she was overruled; again she had broken the boundaries and I was reaping the rewards. She was quick to point this out.

I could see her point even then, but I kept my mouth shut and smiled smugly as Mum told her that a boy had called with the intention of asking me out, that was a very special moment and that she was ruining it for me.

After that it was all downhill for Jennifer and onwards and upwards for me. I was allowed do what Jenny was doing, apart from make-up. Jennifer was furious and I can't really blame her. I'd have been furious myself. Then one night, when I was about eighteen and Jennifer was nineteen we happened upon one another in the kitchen late one night or perhaps ridiculously early one morning. I can't remember the exact timescale here. We had been out with our respective friends and came home the worse for wear, tottering about and giggling in the kitchen. We were both after the one thing, toasted cheese sambos and crisps. We sat together after cooking our feast and chatted about the ways of the world. Boys we fancied, boys who fancied us. Gossip about one another's friends and amazingly we chatted candidly about ourselves. I told her what I wanted most of all out of life – I think it was a pair of leather trousers and to be a D-cup – and she told me how to go about getting it. I shone light on the problems in her life too. It was bliss and sisterly love reigned about the house.

The following morning we awoke with dreadful hang-overs and fought like two alley cats for about a week. But, that aside, I found out that night that Jennifer was not half as cocky or sure of herself as she made out, and that she was also a very good listener. She listened and thought before she gave advice. I mean, she could have told me to get a credit card, buy the trousers and check into the Blackrock Clinic for implants; instead she told me to see about getting a Saturday job, save my money and buy the trousers and a Wonderbra. She told me a heavy chest is not always a blessing. After buying a Wonderbra a few years ago, I can now agree whole-heartedly.

The point to this is Jennifer is a great person to have around at a time of crisis. I know I was not exactly in a crisis at this precise moment, but I was down and I needed a pick-me-up. I rang Jennifer, hoping she would be in.

She answered after three rings, sounding breathless.

"Hi, Jen," I smiled down the phone.

"Hi, there. What's going on?" She sounded pleased to hear from me.

"Nothing, I was just wondering if you felt like a chat?"

"Always, I am my mother's daughter!"

I could hear her pull a chair from somewhere and sit down. I could hear the difference in her voice.

"What's up?" she asked.

"Oh, I just broke up with Ray and I was thinking I'd like to grab a bite to eat maybe and a bit of a chat."

"Oh, sorry about that, Millie. He was nice. How are you?"

"Good. Well, all right." I was getting a little down as I spoke.

"Who dumped who?"

"I dumped him, but I still feel a bit sad."

"Oh, I know. It's tough sometimes. Will we grab a coffee?"

"Yeah, that'd be nice. When suits you?"

"Now, anytime at all. I was just hanging clothes on the line."

"Are you sure I'm not interrupting?"

"Well, the laundry is all I'm doing, so feel free to interrupt."

"Where's Mike?"

"Playing golf. Would you like to come over or will we meet up somewhere?"

"Let's get a bit of lunch," I smiled, always eager to eat out.

"Fine. I'll pick you up and we'll talk then."

Jenny hung up and I felt better. She was one of life's positive people; she'd puff my ego and tell me I was doing the right thing. My ego needed some serious puffing: my thirtieth birthday was less than five months away and I was alone in the world. I felt I would be abandoned by civilised society and would die a spinster in my expensive little apartment on the north side of this expensive little city.

I shouldn't have worried – well, I shouldn't have worried about it right then. Jenny had just arrived and was all smiles, hugs and good advice. Without a trace of married smugness in her voice.

We sat down in a small café on the seafront and ordered from the lunch menu.

Jenny smiled and flirted with the waiter and got a free glass of wine for her troubles. He made me pay for mine. I tried to flirt, I smiled and flicked my hair at him but he was looking at the people at the next table who were gesturing for their bill. The story of my bloody life. A series of near misses, missed opportunities, glances ignored and flirting wasted on people who couldn't really care less.

I wondered sometimes, could it be that God thought I died a few years ago? When I was knocked down on my way home from school when I was seven? I broke my arm and got concussion, the doctor said I was lucky to be alive. I banged my head off the bumper of the car. Could God have thought I died that day and now he thought I was just a silly spirit who kept praying for a life I didn't have any more? Was that why my prayers, no matter how trivial, were never answered?

"So tell me what happened?" Jenny said as soon as the waiter was out of earshot.

Why do we all do that? As if the waiter cares about what's going on in our lives? Do they not have enough going on in their own lives?

"Oh, it was nothing really – he was just a bit annoying."

"What was annoying about him?" She sounded surprised.

"He was nice and everything, but he was just a bit unreliable."

"He was gorgeous," Jennifer said, more to herself.

"I know he was. Wow!" I agreed. "But the thing is, he was always running off."

"Running off?" She stopped drinking.

"Yes, he was always getting these phone calls and racing off to help people."

Jennifer had stopped eating and was staring at me. "What people?"

"His friends – they'd ring if they were locked out, their car broke down, they were fighting with girlfriends, all kinds of things. And he'd rush off to sort it out."

"Rush off from where? Out of bed? Away from dinner?" She was smiling but she was annoyed. I recognised the furrow on her forehead.

"Dinner, night in with a movie. Usually he switched off his phone at night. But while it was on, it was basically a free-for-all. Whoever called was sorted out."

"And you accepted this?"

"Not accepted it, I was annoyed. He knew full well how annoyed I was, but it was complicated."

"How?"

I didn't want to get into it with her about his family life. I still felt I owed him some confidentiality. "He had a tough time as a child. I don't want to go into it, but he wasn't given any affection. I think he needed to be in the thick of it, helping his friends to feel good about himself. So I let him do it."

"Sounds like a cliché to me. How tough a time had he?"

"He wasn't beaten or anything – just, not really

loved. You know?"

"Sounds a bit like crap to me. Are you sure that he was telling the truth?"

"I don't think he'd lie about that."

"Don't you?" she sneered. "Men don't think the same way we do."

"Yeah, but that's a bit much. Telling me his parents neglected him, just to get out with his friends? No, I think he was telling the truth on that one."

"Did you meet his family?"

"Yes, twice."

"And?"

"They were nice. They were very nice in fact. His mother was very chatty."

"Did you think they were the type who'd beat their child?" Jenny asked, her voice stony. She hated cruelty. She gave money to all the charities for animals and children.

"They didn't beat him. They weren't cruel to him."

"What did they do?"

"They just didn't hug him and stuff." I still didn't want to talk about it. I felt it was just a step too close to gossiping.

"He wasn't hugged? And he says he was neglected?" Jenny sounded more irritated by the second. "Millie, start from the beginning because this sounds like a crock to me."

So I did, under some protest at first. But after a while I was spilling the beans like a pro. I told her what he told me. No hugs, just money and holidays, but no love. She nodded and listened. She looked like she was mellowing to him. Then I told her about the phone calls and him leaving to run out and help. Me, sitting in restaurants while food went cold, waiting for him to get off the phone and come back. His hurried apologies and quick exists.

Her mood changed. She wasn't impressed. To be honest, neither was I. Hindsight is twenty-twenty vision and I could see perfectly well that I had been used. While his story was sad, it was not really Barnardo's or St Vincent de Paul kind of stuff. I tried to put a pleasant spin on it and changed the subject completely.

"He was really gorgeous, wasn't he?" I smiled.

Jennifer didn't. She just pursed her lips and frowned at me. "Yeah, but that's not all that counts, you know." Again she sounded irritable.

The nasty side of me wondered if that was just sour grapes. Mike's no looker. I fought very hard to keep this thought from my mind, but it was hard.

"Well, that's the story. I dumped him anyway," I announced with a resigned tone.

"Should I sympathise or tell you about the sea and all those fish in it?"

"I like the fish story – tell me that one!" I laughed.

So she did. She also topped up my wineglass, so at 2:30 in the afternoon I was very giddy and when I went off to the toilet I was disappointed to see I had the telltale rosy cheeks of a novice drinker.

28

After Ray and I split, things became strained in the office. Again I got the distinct impression I was being watched, and I know it sounds conceited but I got the impression I was being talked about. Conversations would stop when I walked in or people would smile a little too politely when I said good morning to them. There was nothing I could really put my finger on, but this had happened before. When Ray and I got together I had noticed it and said it to Ruth. At the time Ruth had said I was being paranoid; this time she listened which made me realize I was right. She denied it,, of course, and told me I was mad. But I was sure of it. I caught Steve looking at me while I photocopied some CV's so I stared at him and he looked away. I went back to my desk and caught him watching me again. I looked over and asked him if he wanted me.

He shook his head, smirking. I looked at him with my

best attempt at disdain but it's hard to look disdainfully when in fact you're feeling completely self-conscious. Try it some time – you'll soon realise it's very hard to do.

Then the following week Ruth let the cat out of the bag. She confirmed that people were indeed talking about me. She didn't mean to. It just slipped out.

We were in the kitchen area making tea, watching the kettle and hoping to God it would never boil and we'd get to stay there till home-time. I was breaking with tradition and having a coffee. I was sitting on the countertop stirring my milk and instant ground.

"Louise said you were right to dump him by the way," Ruth told me.

"What's it to her?" I looked up at her.

"She never liked him. She was surprised that it lasted as long as it did." Ruth was still watching the kettle.

"Is that a veiled insult to me or to him?" I asked.

"I think it's an unveiled insult to him," Ruth smiled. "Anyway the buzz is you were far too good for him anyway."

"What buzz?" I asked, truly shocked by this.

"From the others. Public opinion is with you on this one."

"Am I the topic of conversation in the loos?" I asked, anger rising in my heart.

"No." Ruth blushed and I knew she was lying.

"Am I?" I raised an eyebrow.

"Sort of." Ruth was looking mortified.

"What are they saying?"

"Just that you were right to dump him, that sort of

thing." Ruth was now crimson.

"Why is it such a big deal? Are we the first office romance in here?"

"I don't know why, but at least they're all with you. It'd be worse if they were all crowding around Ray and telling him you were ugly." Ruth reached for the kettle that had just boiled. "Will I pour for you?"

"Yes, thanks."

"Come on. Let's get back." Ruth picked up her mug and headed to the door.

I felt really bad after this exchange.

Then, as if that wasn't enough, there was the problem of Ruth and Jack. I know. I'm never satisfied. I know!

I had openly encouraged Jack to pursue Ruth before Christmas, but that was when I had Ray. The world is a different place when you're part of a couple and I was all for Ruth and Jack getting together. They weren't taking the bait back then. Now, in line with "Murphy's Law" they were flirting away happily and I was single again. Openly grinning and touching one another in a most inappropriate fashion. I was increasingly feeling like a gooseberry in their company.

One afternoon Ruth got a glob of mayo on her cheek after biting into her sandwich. I was happy enough to let her sit there for the obligatory ten minutes before I mentioned it to her, but Jack saw it and told her. Not only did he tell her, but he leaned over and wiped it off with his napkin. She blushed and looked all doe-eyed at him as he wiped her face. He smiled down at her and rubbed her cheek with his finger when he was finished. I watched, feeling all green and hairy. I know I'd told Jack to ask Ruth out, but then there were four of us and it wouldn't have been a big deal if we happened to be two couples. Now we were looking increasingly like becoming one couple and me. Yes, the winds of change were blowing and I was becoming surplus to requirement.

Then one fatal day Jack and Ruth were giggling over some private joke when I sat down with my tray. Ruth's collar was stuck inside her jacket and she was doing battle with it. Jack leaned over and fixed it for her. He lingered around her neck for some time and for her part she held her hair up for a very long time. He took advantage of the view and ran his fingers over her skin just a little too long for my liking.

"Can you stop that? I'm here too," I sniffed.

"Sorry." Ruth flushed a little.

"What are you whining about?" Jack laughed.

"I'd rather you kept your grabby hands off each other in front of me," I told him. "They invented private homes for that type of groping."

"Look at you pretending to be all shocked and horrified by me and Ruth," Jack said, still laughing.

"I am shocked and horrified," I said, biting into my sandwich.

"By what? I was helping her with her coat."

"You know that's not all you were doing, young man," I pointed out.

"Yeah, right, and who appointed you guardian of Ruth's chastity?" Jack laughed, picking up his sandwich.

"No one. I just felt that someone should be looking out

for her virtue. You appear to be intent on taking it from her."

"Yeah, just 'cos Ray helped himself to yours!" jeered Jack.

"Ah, you're wrong there, Jack. My virtue was well gone before Ray got his hands on me!" I laughed.

"I'm glad to hear it, as Ray appears to have taken the virtue of every man, woman and beast in Dublin city."

"Man and beast?" I laughed. "Not quite man and beast, Jack – give the guy credit where it's due. He's a maniac but he's completely straight!"

There was a moment's silence.

"Ray? Straight?" Jack smiled, then looked over at Ruth.

"What? Why are you laughing at that?" I asked, looking from Jack to Ruth.

"You are joking about the straight remark, aren't you?" Jack looked at me, a smile playing on his lips.

"What are you talking about?" I asked.

I looked at Ruth and realised there was something going on here that I wasn't in on. I was the only one out of the loop and it appeared "the loop" was about me and Ray.

"Nothing. It was a stupid remark. Nothing," Jack picked up his sandwich and started to eat.

I looked at Ruth. Her eyes were wide as she stared at Jack, her face ashen.

"What is going on here, Ruth?" I asked.

Ruth looked at me and back at Jack. "I think you should talk to Ray, Amelia," she said, still looking at Jack.

"I'm speaking to you, Ruth!"

"Please, Amelia, just talk to Ray."

"No, tell me what's going on here. I can see by the look on your face that there's something."

"Sorry, it's my fault. I should never have said any-thing," Jack said. "It was none of my business."

"Was Ray two-timing me?" I asked, suddenly ready to hear he was. It would have explained all the rushing off.

"No, not that I know of," Jack said.

"He wasn't," Ruth agreed.

"Then tell me what's going on?"

There was silence for a moment as Ruth and Jack looked at one another. Then Ruth gave the slightest nod of her head before turning to me.

"I would never do anything to hurt you or embarrass you," she began.

This was the worst opening statement you could possi-bly hear in this situation. I was about to be embarrassed. I tried to brace myself.

"But I don't think Ray was completely honest with you."

"About what?" I asked.

"About himself," said Ruth. "What did he tell you about his private life?"

"Home life? About his parents and school and stuff?" I breathed a sigh of relief – I knew all about this.

"No, not exactly. More his love life?" Ruth was sugar-coating this for me and it was excruciating. I just wanted her to say it.

"What are you talking about? Just spit it out."

224

"Did he tell you about Alan?" Jack asked.

"Who? No." I remembered the name being mentioned, but nothing more.

"He lived with a guy called Alan for a while. Did he never mention him to you?"

"He said they shared a flat for a while, but then he moved back home."

"He never said why?" Jack leaned over the table.

"I never asked." My heart was thumping in my throat now. I had a feeling where this was going. I just didn't want to believe it.

"They weren't just flatmates. Are you following me?" Jack said.

"I think so," I replied, but it was too awful to contemplate.

"Either you are or you're not," Jack said.

"Tell me then."

"Look, Amelia, Ray should have told you this. It shouldn't be coming from Ruth and me."

"Just tell me!"

"Ray swings both ways," he told me, his face sympathetic.

"He does what?" I'd heard him but it seemed odd to my ear.

"Swings both ways – you do know the saying?" Jack said, his blank face staring at me.

"Amelia, Ray likes boys too," Ruth cut in with a mercy killing.

"How much does he like boys?" It was a stupid question. What did it matter how much he liked them?

He liked them!

"Just as much as he likes girls," Ruth told me.

I stared at the table. My sandwich suddenly looked like a brick.

"I don't believe it," I said.

"That's up to you," Jack sighed. "It really doesn't matter if you believe it or not, but it's true."

"He likes boys?" I repeated in disbelief. "How much?" I was fixated on this 'How much?' point.

"Enough, believe me. Enough." Jack looked at Ruth for back-up.

"Do we really need to spell this out, Amelia?" Ruth asked.

I stared at her. She and Jack were in focus but nothing else was. I tried to speak but nothing came out. I nodded to verify I understood what they were saying. Ruth thought I needed it spelt out. So she did.

"Amelia, sweetie, Ray sleeps with men *and* women. He's bisexual." She reached out to hold my hand.

I sat staring at her. Other things were beginning to come into focus. It was sinking in. I was completely aghast. "Are you telling me my ex-boyfriend was sleeping with men and never bothered to tell me?"

"No, I'm sure he was faithful to you," Jack assured me. "I don't think he was seeing anyone else at the time."

I fumed inwardly. "What possessed him not to tell me?"

"We don't know," Ruth said.

"How long did you know?" I asked her.

"Jack told me on Monday."

"You've known for two days and never told me?" I was

focusing my misplaced anger on Ruth. Jack was quick to wade in to defend her.

"Hey, it wasn't Ruth's fault. Ray should have told you. He should never have left it to us," he correctly pointed out.

"I know," I said, frustrated by the amount of anger inside me and having no one to shout at.

"Amelia," said Ruth, "as soon as I found out I wanted to tell you but, the question was, was it better to let sleeping dogs lie? I wanted to spare you the hurt."

"Well, thanks," I muttered, still furious.

I began to think back. Why hadn't I seen the signs? Were there signs? Was I just incredibly thick?

"Did you know all along?" I asked Jack.

He nodded with a sad smile.

"Did anyone else know?"

Jack looked at his half-eaten sandwich. Ruth stared out the window. Everyone else knew.

So how come I was the last to know? Was I so close to the situation that I couldn't see the full picture? Couldn't see the wood for the trees?

I took it all in for a moment and to my shame I realised I was biting back tears.

"That bastard, he never bothered to tell me," I said, my voice cracking slightly.

Ruth swapped seats and came around the table. She hugged me around the shoulder. "He's a prick. He should have told you! Of course, he should!"

"He should. It was stupid of him. It's not as if you'd never find out or anything," Jack pointed out.

"And everyone else knows?"

"Well, the guys all know," said Jack. "We've known all along. I dunno about the girls. I'm sure some of them do."

"That's why Steve was watching me," I said, more to myself than anyone else.

"As time went on we thought you knew about it. We just thought you were really open-minded," Jack said.

"Did you honestly think I wouldn't care about that?" I asked him.

"I was a bit surprised, but who was I to comment? It's all live and let live these days." Jack shrugged.

"Oh God, not only did you all know my boyfriend was eyeing up my brother, but you thought I was a slapper who didn't give a damn about it. Great!"

"No, no!" Ruth hugged me closer.

"No!" Jack agreed. "He didn't fancy your brother!"

This was Jack's attempt at a joke. I just glared at him.

"I am going to kill him," I said. "Stone dead, I'll kill him,"

"That's my girl. You do that," Ruth smiled, still holding my hand.

29

I left the café and walked back to the office. Jack and
Ruth were rushing to keep up with me. I was on a mission
and no one was slowing me down. I barged up the road
through the office workers and punters on the street. I got
to the office door at two. I stood for a moment to collect
my thoughts. Ruth rushed up behind me.

"Thank God you stopped. Are you all right?"

"No, of course I'm not all right," I hissed.

"Don't go in there and shout your head off. You still
have to work there," she urged.

I could see her point but it made no difference to me
right there and then.

"I told you I was going to kill him and that's just what
I'm going to do," I told her calmly, my tone belying my
true feelings.

"Please, Amelia, don't throw a wobbly in there," Ruth
pleaded.

It was too late: I saw Ray through the window. He was laughing and smiling with one of the new receptionists, the one with the blonde hair. He was batting his eyes and smiling at her, flirting. I knew the stance. I could read the signs. I was furious. I opened the door and stood there for a moment. I knew Ruth and Jack walked in behind me, but to be honest I don't know where they went after that. I was watching Ray; he was still talking to the blonde. I thought her name was Mairead; it didn't suit her at all.

After what seemed like an age but was in fact about twenty seconds, Ray looked over and saw me, did the quickest double-take and smiled at me. His eyes never left me as the smile froze on his face. We stood for a few seconds staring at one another.

"Hi there," he smiled falsely at me.

I looked at him for a moment, hating him with all my heart. Then I remembered he didn't know why I was so angry. I would enlighten him.

"You, come out back – I want to talk to you," I said, walking by him and gesturing to the back door.

His smile flickered for the briefest moment. He beamed at Mairead and said something witty about being right back. Then he followed me out the door.

He was nervous; he fidgeted and cleared his throat as he walked behind me. I walked out to the yard and waited for him to come outside. I nodded to him to close the door behind him. He did and we stood looking at one another for another minute. He had stopped smiling and was gone very pale indeed. It was like a scene from a cheap western: we stood face to face, about three feet between us, not moving. Me flushed with anger, him pale with worry.

"What is it? I'm worried," he said.

"Are you now? Well, fear for you, you arrogant pig!" I whisper-shouted.

"What are you talking about? What's this all about?" he asked, fear catching in his throat.

"I hate you, Ray Donnelly!" I hissed.

"What? Why?" he asked, half a smile on his face.

"You are a fucking lying sack of shit!" I shouted, fury burning and making me ignore that fact that we were in fact still in work.

"What's wrong with you? Why are you 'effing and blinding at me today of all days?"

"You lied to me and you made a complete eejit of me in front of the entire office!"

I looked at him with contempt.

"What did I do that made a fool of you?" he asked, and again the uncertain smile played on his lips.

"Don't look at me with that smile on your face," I told him.

His smile faded and was gone. "This is all highly entertaining stuff, Amelia, but why are we out here?"

"Because I want to know something, and I don't want everyone else hearing me," I told him, in a tone I would usually reserve for talking to a small child.

"Then perhaps you should stop shouting at me?" he replied, using the same tone.

"You're an asshole," I said, making sure to keep my voice controlled.

"Perhaps I am. Was that it?"

"No."

He looked at me, an eyebrow cocked in a self-assured manner. I hated him.

"When were you going to tell me that you sleep with men?" I asked and watched his face freeze.

When he replied his voice came out thin and high-pitched. "Who told you?"

"I was told. The real issue is why the information didn't come from you!" I hissed.

"I didn't think about it," he replied, his voice small.

"What do you mean you didn't think about it? For six months you never gave the fact that you fancy men a second thought?"

"I'm sorry. It never really came up. And then it was too late, and I didn't know whether to say it or not." He stepped towards me, his hands out in a begging gesture.

"No, stop that. Don't start that." I backed away a step as he moved forward.

"Look, I'm just trying to explain."

"Well, do it from over there if you don't mind."

I pointed to a spot on the ground and he stepped back towards it. It was almost comic. He looked at his feet and lined them up with my finger. I nodded and folded my arms. He stood at the appointed spot and tried to explain from a distance.

"Look, Amelia, the thing is this," he began, but he looked fussed. He started again. "I really don't feel comfortable having this conversation here, in work. Can we meet up after work?"

"And save you the shame of being embarrassed in work?" I asked in my best sarcastic tone.

"Save us both. They'll hear us inside. This won't be a quick conversation, will it?"

"Oh, for God's sake!" I hated him but I could see his point. "All right," I replied grudgingly. "But just tell me this. When were you planning to tell me?"

"Honestly?"

I nodded.

"I don't know. I was putting it to the back of my mind to be honest." He looked at his shoes, and then back at me.

"The back of your mind?" I asked, fury burning in my chest again. I was flushed. I could feel it. "I can hardly believe my ears, Ray!"

"I wasn't being bad – it's just complicated." He smiled a sort of surrender. "It's not as easy as you seem to think. It's not what I want to be."

I looked at him, standing with his hands in his pockets, head bent, eyes pleading. The fury subsided a little, just a little though. Enough for me to agree to a chat in the pub later on.

We went back inside and Ray sat back at his desk, looking sheepish and unhappy.

For my part I wasn't exactly jumping for joy on my side of the room. I tried to keep busy but my eyes stung and my mind wandered. I couldn't concentrate. I kept thinking about all the times Ray went out at night, "To see a man about a dog." I tried not thinking about it.

I looked down at my diary to see what was next on my

"to do" list. As I did my vision blurred, and a tear ran down my cheek. I was crying! In the office! I was furious. How dare he make me cry at my desk! I looked over at his desk, fury burning in my throat. He was typing, head down and busy at work. I watched him for a moment and saw that in fact he was working. His head just bobbed up and down every now and then. He was concentrating hard. Mairead wandered by his desk smiling at him from time to time but he never looked up. She seemed a little crestfallen as she returned to the reception for the third time, carrying her third glass of water. I felt a little sorry for her, then again I was actually saving her from the social suicide I had just committed. Here I was, sitting at my desk crying over a man who had been lying to me from Day One and everyone else in the office knew about it before me.

I glanced at Ruth and she jumped from her seat and gestured towards the smoking shelter. I followed her.

"What the hell happened? Are you crying?"

"I'm all right. We're meeting later to discuss it."

"What did you say? Ray looks faint up there – what happened?"

"Nothing much. I called him outside and I told him I knew."

She leaned forward nodding.

"He nearly died," I said, "and asked that we meet up to talk about it later."

"Well, I suppose he has a point, no need to shout the odds in the office."

"I know," I said.

We sat in silence for a moment. Tears stung my eyes again; Ruth saw it and held my hand. It was all right; we were alone in the smoking area. I sniffed and wiped my eyes.

"I hate him. How dare he make me cry, in work – that's the last straw," I sniffed.

"I know. He's a prick," Ruth agreed as she breathed out a cloud of smoke.

We sat there, saying nothing. I blotted my eyes on the corner of my sleeve. It left a black mascara-stain on my cuff. I hated him for that too. Another misdemeanour for my list.

30

Ray and I met after work. We found seats in the quietest corner we could. Ray gestured to the lounge boy and we ordered two drinks.

"Do you want to see a menu?" He asked.

"No," I replied folding my arms.

"Fine."

Ray shook his head at the lounge boy, who promptly left. We were alone. Ray shifted in his seat and took off his jacket. He loosened his tie as the lounge boy reappeared with our drinks.

"Right. What was going on in your head that you thought this was never going to come to my attention?" I turned to face him as I spoke.

"Before we get started on this, I just want to say I'm really sorry. I never thought you'd hear it as office gossip."

"I didn't. I was told. Very specifically."

"Who told you?"

"Guess."

"Jack!" he spat.

"Don't blame him – he was doing me a favour," I hissed.

"Yeah, he wasn't looking out for himself at all!" he sneered.

"What are you talking about?" I queried before I realized it was yet another diversionary tactic. "No way, pal, keep to the subject. You're the baddie here,"

"I am not the baddie. I'm bisexual. That doesn't make me a bad person,"

"No, just an indecisive and greedy one."

"That's a load of shit! My sexual orientation is no more my choice than yours is."

"Whatever," I replied in my most dismissive tone. I was furious, but I wasn't that narrow-minded. I knew it wasn't his choice.

"Don't you 'whatever' me!" he berated me.

"OK, it's not your fault or anything. I know that. That's not the issue. I don't mind or even care that you're 'bi'."

"You don't mind? How very gracious of you!" He stared at me, rage fuming behind his eyes.

"Look," I said, looking away from him, trying to regain some control of the conversation, "you know what I'm saying. I don't want you to explain your preferences, but I do want you to explain why you never told me. Especially when you told everyone else."

"For starters, I never told everyone else. I told no one in work. They found out and asked me. Which I think

237

was very rude of them, by the way. I never denied it. I never would. I'm not ashamed of it. I just don't advertise it."

"How did they find out?" I asked, my nosiness getting the better of me.

"I was seen in a pub with someone. It was years ago. It hardly matters."

"Who saw you?" I asked.

"Why does it matter?"

"Well, how did they see you? Were they in the pub and, if so, what were they doing in a gay pub themselves?" I asked, leaning forward, eager to make my point.

"It wasn't a gay pub. I was in Howl at the Moon with Alan. We were having a row; things were fizzling out between us at that stage. Anyway, we were arguing about something just outside the toilets and Steve walked out, almost on top of us. He heard us, put two and two together and asked me the following Monday."

"That was a bit presumptuous of him."

"Not really, we were bickering like a couple of old marrieds and everything about the situation told him we were more than friends," Ray shrugged. "So that was it. I was outed and everyone in work knew about it."

"Did Steve tell everyone?" I asked, feeling a little sorry for Ray.

Why do I always end up feeling sorry for them?

"No, not really. I told him, other people heard and before I knew it the office knew about it. As I said, I'm not ashamed of it. I wasn't hitting on anyone in the office." He paused, smiling at me. "Not at that stage

238

anyway, and definitely none of the boys. So, it made no odds to me who knew."

"Why did you not tell me any of this?"

"I actually thought you knew. Were you not around when it all came out?"

"I dunno, when was this?"

"Well, Alan and I broke up before he went to Canada, so it was about four years ago." Ray looked heavenward for inspiration, his eyelashes fanning. He was fabulous, no doubt about it.

"I'm only working there three years," I confirmed.

"Ah, then you wouldn't have heard," he nodded. He was very relaxed and matter of fact about it.

I sat back. Was I satisfied with this explanation? No, quite frankly, I wasn't. None of this explained why he never told me. 'He thought I knew' was just not good enough.

"Hang on, why didn't you tell when we started dating? All the things you told me about your childhood . . ," I paused for a moment. "Oh my God, that's why your parents are annoyed with you! That's why your father and you are at loggerheads. They never beat you – he's annoyed about your sex life!"

"Yes," he said, sitting forward and resting his elbows on his knees. He rubbed his eyes and stifled a yawn.

"Why would you tell lies about your family? And why didn't you tell me the truth when you had the chance? I gave you the perfect opener! You just chose not to tell me!"

"I didn't choose not to tell you."

"Then what?"

"I just didn't know whether to say it or not."

"Did you think I'd never find out? That we'd go our separate ways and never meet up again?"

He looked off into the distance, thinking for a while. "If I had told you all about it, would you have been interested in me?"

"Maybe. I mean it would have been my choice to make," I replied.

"Would you? It doesn't matter now, so you may as well be honest. Just tell me."

"I don't know."

"Yes, you do. What's your gut instinct? If I met you and I told you I was bi, would you want to know me?"

"Yes, I'd have no problem," I said, deliberately misunderstanding his question.

"You know what I'm saying. Would you have slept with me, if you knew?"

I looked at him and to my shame I had to admit, gorgeous and all as he is, I wouldn't have slept with him. I shook my head. I had just confirmed what he already knew: nice girls don't sleep with the likes of him.

"See?" he said. "Do you think men are any different? A lot of them don't want me when I tell them I like women. It's a vicious circle."

"It may well be, but you still should have told me. I would have told you if I was HIV positive." I blanched as a thought hit me. "You are careful, aren't you?"

"What? Yes! Of course I am!" He looked appalled. "Amelia, I'm not that kind of a person! I don't sleep

240

around with just anyone!"

"When was the last time you got to grips with a boy?" I asked – perhaps a personal question.

"Excuse me?" Ray thought it was.

"Come on, I want to know. Who was your last boyfriend?"

Ray sighed and thought for a moment. "It was a guy called James, about a year ago, and we went out for about three months. Since then I was with Sarah for about a month and then you."

"Were you completely careful?"

"Yes."

"Ray, this is serious: did you take any chances, any at all?"

"No, just like with you I used a condom every time – I always do," he said, looking me in the eye, and for once I believed he was being honest.

"You understand why I have to ask?"

"I understand the question, but I'm offended that you think I'm that stupid."

"You slept with me for the last six months and never mentioned this, and now you're offended by the fact that I ask you if you're careful?"

Ray looked away, annoyed. "Amelia, I'm not as bad as you think I am. I have some social conscience."

"Have you really?"

"Yes. It's not that I was deliberately keeping this from you. I wanted to tell you but things moved very fast and there was never an opportunity."

"Yes, there was!" I fumed. "We practically lived in each

other's pockets – you had plenty of time and opportunity to bring it up!"

"I'm sorry. I should have told you."

"Yes. You absolutely should."

"I wasn't thinking straight. I'm sorry." He smiled. "I really am sorry. I never would have done this on purpose. It's not my style."

I looked at him for a moment, then suddenly it hit me. Simon. Who was this bloke Simon and how bloody close were they?

"Jesus, Ray, were you seeing Simon behind my back?"

"Well, this is just off the scale now, Amelia. You've lost it!" he said, but he smiled as he said it.

"For once in your fucking life just be honest, Ray!"

"What? I am being honest … what's wrong with you?" he said, but again there was a stifled laugh in there.

"Amelia, you're really clutching at straws now."

"I'm right. Oh my God I'm right!" I said, my heart pounding. I was seeing the situation very clearly now, and I couldn't believe my own stupidity. How had I not seen it before? "That's where you kept racing off to! No friends, no broken-down cars or fights to sort out – just that Simon! Ringing you, while you sat with me! While I was sitting there waiting for you to come back! You were out with him. You would come back and sleep with me, in my bed, after spending the evening with him! You prick!"

Without thinking of the consequences I lashed out and punched him in the face. He reeled from the punch, covering his eye with his hand. I stood up and looked over my shoulder, but no one else in the pub had noticed anything amiss in our little alcove. This wasn't a scene, yet. I looked at the table, then at Ray – he was feeling his cheek and eye for damage. I picked up his pint and tipped it over his head.

"Drop dead, you prick!" I smiled as I turned, picked up my bag and walked out.

The walk to the door was surreal. I felt like I was walking on legs that didn't belong to me. I kept expecting Ray or someone to shout after me, tell me I was barred or something, but no one did. It was the perfect crime. I had just been involved in a pub fight! For the first time ever I had thrown a punch and it had connected with the other person's eye! I was a bad ass!

I'd think about facing Ray and his black eye in the morning.

31

I called to see Jennifer and Mike on the way home from work a few days later. It was an unplanned visit and Jenny was thrilled to see me. We sat in the kitchen over cups of coffee and later we ordered from the local Chinese.

Jenny sent Mike to the off-licence to get plenty of wine while he was picking up the Chinese.

After dinner Mike went to the gym and left Jenny and me to chat.

We sat for a while rubbing our full tummies and complimenting the takeaway. I was a little tired and found that I was staring into space as I listened to the radio in the background.

"Wait until I tell you the latest instalment of my love life," I said, still staring into space.

"Go on, I love to live vicariously through you. It's so much fun!"

"Fun? Well, there's not –"

"I really do think you have the most fascinating life, Millie," Jenny butted in. "Don't rush into marriage. Have lots of fun." She smiled and took my hand in hers.

"Promise me you'll have lots of fun before you marry anyone?"

"I'll try," I laughed.

"No, do it. You must. Don't settle Millie, never settle." She looked off into space. "Don't sell yourself short."

"I won't," I said and not for the first time I wondered about how happy she really was.

I thought about asking her, but I didn't know if I really wanted the truth. "Well, listen to this for fun!" I started, trying to change the mood that had become a little melancholy. "Ray is bi."

"He's what?" Jenny jerked awake.

"Bisexual."

"Why, how, I mean, what do you mean?" She sat up straight and looked at me.

"It turns out he was all along and he never bothered to tell me about it. He said he didn't think it was a big deal."

"Right, start from the beginning and tell me everything."

So I did. From the start, all about Alan, about everyone in work knowing all about it, and finally about being told by Ruth and Jack and having it out with Ray in the yard at work. With each new revelation Jenny's face lit up in equal measures of disgust and delight. When I told her about the punch she cheered, spilling her wine all over her top.

"I can't believe it! You actually punched him? In the

face? Did it hurt your hand?"

"Yes it did, but not until much later. I was feeding the fish and I noticed that hand was stiff, but it's fine now," I confirmed, examining the back of my hand for bruising.

"Did he have a black eye?"

"No, it was all bloodshot and his cheek was red for a few days, but no shiner. Sadly enough," I smiled.

"How do these things happen to you?" she asked, laughing. "What do you do, Millie?"

"I have no bloody idea," I laughed. "I think that I'm gullible is the problem."

"Well, at least you can always tell your grandchildren you lived," she said.

"What grandchildren? I have to have children first, and going by my luck I'll never have any of those."

"Yes, you will. You're only just gone thirty. What's the rush?"

"I'm thirty is the rush!" I complained. "I'll be thirty-one in ten months and I have no boyfriend and no prospects of one either!"

"I'm thirty-two. I was thirty-one before we even discussed getting married. You'll meet someone and settle down very quickly. Wait and see."

"I'll have to," I moaned.

"Anyway, I'm thirty-two and I have no wish to have babies yet."

"Don't you want any?" I asked, surprised.

"Someday, but not now."

"Oh," I replied, filling both of our glasses up. "What about Mike, does he want them?"

"Yeah, but not yet," she said taking a mouthful of wine.

"Well, that's a lie. He wants them now, but he understands."

"Understands what?" I asked.

"I'm not ready."

"I see. What does he say about it?"

"Nothing much. He's all right about it."

"That's good."

"Yeah, he's a dote, but he's really old-fashioned sometimes."

"Old-fashioned?"

"Yeah, he wanted me to take his name, change all my ID's, that kind of thing."

"Have you?"

"No, I like my name. I'm used to it. Anyway, it's not the name that bothers me."

"What bothers you?" I asked.

"Mike thinks I should be pregnant already."

"I thought you just said he understands!" I said, sitting up a little.

"He does, most of the time. But sometimes he gets a little grumpy about it."

"Grumpy?" I said

"Yes, grumpy. He'd like a baby and I wouldn't. It leads to discussions."

"What kind of discussions?"

"Nothing bad, just the usual. It's fine."

"It's not fine if you're rowing over it," I pointed out.

"It's just a little thing. Anyway, he understands. He does." She stopped. "Don't look at me like that, Millie!"

"Does he really understand?" I asked.

"Yes, he does. He has to, and let's face it, I should have the final say in this. I should be allowed to have some say in it anyway." She looked at me and her eyes glistened with tears. "I should, shouldn't I?"

"Yes, of course you should. Absolutely."

"I'm not a bad person; I just don't want any kids yet. I thought I did, but now I'm not so sure."

"What do you mean, you thought you did? Are you pregnant?" I asked, my heart thumping and I didn't know why.

"God, no!" She sniffed a little and shook her head. "Oh God, why are we talking about this?"

"Because you brought it up," I said, not unkindly. I was worried and I wanted to know if there was something going wrong in Jenny's marriage.

She shuddered a little. "Mike wanted a baby as soon as we got married. I was all on for it at first."

"Then what happened?"

"I don't know. I just went off the idea. I'm only thirty-two. I don't want dirty nappies and sleepless nights. Is that bad of me?"

"No, absolutely not. I understand that completely," I agreed.

"Anyway, Mike says it's all right but I know he's upset." She sighed. "He's upset and I feel to blame. I feel like it's entirely my fault."

"Well, it's not," I told her. "You don't need to be having babies if you don't want to. There's loads of time for babies – statistically women are having babies later and

248

later. I saw a thing in the *Irish Times* the other day about the average age of mothers being about thirty-five or something. Anyway, look at that Bridget Jones woman, she was thirty-three when she had Colin Firth and Hugh Grant fist-fighting over her! You're a lot prettier than her – they'd be attacking one another with machetes to get at you."

Jenny laughed and the stress washed off her face. She laughed for a long time, and when she finished she dried her eyes.

"Thanks for listening. Please don't think things are going bad with Mike and me. They're not. It's fine."

"I know, it's just really hard. The first year of marriage is meant to be the hardest of all," I told her.

"I don't know about that, but deciding to have a baby is a real tough one. That's what I mean when I say have fun before you marry. Once you marry, sooner or later someone's going to want a baby. And it's us who have to carry it, put our lives on hold and get the stretch marks when it arrives."

"But having a baby would be nice. It's not the baby you disapprove of, is it?"

"No, of course not, the baby would be great. I just want to live a little more before it arrives. I'm not being bad. Please, don't think I'm awful!"

"I don't. I just wondered."

"It's not just the baby thing," Jenny said, looking at her wineglass.

"What is it?" I asked, looking at her face.

She looked at the wall for a moment, biting her

lip."Oh, I don't know. It's just a bit messy."

"What's messy?" I asked.

Jenny looked at me. She took in my face for a moment and then smiled. "Life, Amelia. Life is messy. Don't believe anyone who tells you different."

I sat looking at her, waiting for her to expand on the last sentence, but she didn't. I wanted to know what was wrong with her and why she was so disillusioned with life. A car pulled into the driveway and I heard the familiar rattle of keys in the door.

Mike walked into the sitting-room.

"Are you guys still here?" he laughed.

"Where else would we be?" Jenny asked him.

"Walking off the food," he took in the glasses and the empty bottle, "and the drink?"

"We can't. We're too tipsy!" Jenny grinned up at him from her seat on the floor.

All conversation was dropped and Mike turned on the TV.

I left just after nine. Mike gave me a life home. Before I left, Jenny asked me not to say anything about what she told me. I agreed but asked if we could talk more about it some time. She smiled ruefully and told me that we would, to be sure.

32

Ray and I had not spoken a word since he came to work with his bad eye. Everyone asked what had happened to him, but he never mentioned my name. I think it was more to keep his dignity intact than to help me keep my job. We sat across the room from each other, glaring at each other and not speaking for about a month before it became too much for the rest of the office.

My supervisor sat us both down with someone from Personnel and asked us to tell her what the problem was. We sat in silence for a minute or so, looking at the personnel girl. Then Ray announced that I had punched him during a row.

"She took me unawares and punched me in the face," he said.

"What? Amelia, you did that to his eye?" The supervisor started to laugh, but stopped. "Ray had a bit of black eye last month," she told the personnel girl, who then looked at me with a new awe.

"It was completely out of character for me, and I had been provoked. He two-timed me and then laughed in my face when I confronted him about it . . . and other things." I looked at Ray.

"We broke up and she took it very badly. What can I say? We argued about it and she punched me. I will not be talking to her again, why should I?"

"Ray was sleeping with another guy while he was dating me. I confronted him and I punched him," I announced. Two can play that game. I was not being branded the bully here.

The personnel girl began to choke; she was out of her depth on this one.

"Could we maybe stick to the issue of work?" said the supervisor. "What goes on after hours is not any concern of ours."

"Fine by me," Ray sniffed.

"Fine, I have nothing to hide. I was completely honest. It's he who has a problem with honesty." I glared at the side of his head.

"Bite me," he replied under his breath.

"I might get rabies," I replied.

"All right, we're not going to get anywhere here, are we?" The supervisor could see this escalating out of control. "Could you both agree to keep things civil in the office? I don't care what you do in your personal lives, but in the office I want peace and harmony. All right?"

"Fine, we will," we replied in unison.

We didn't mean a word of it.

We went back out to the office and back to our desks. For about twenty minutes things were quiet, then it began.

"Amelia, have you got the file for ICS?" Ray called out..

"Yes, it's here on my desk," I replied.

"Well, office procedure is, when you're finished with it, put it back in the filing cabinet. Could you put it back, please?"

"If you want it, come and take it," I told him.

"I really need you to put it back in the cabinet, Amelia. It is the correct procedure after all," he called, still looking at his screen.

I stood up, walked over to his desk and handed him the folder.

"Just take the bloody thing," I told him.

And so it began. I got emails, yellow stickies on my computer, but most often I got shouted at. It was as if Ray had read and memorised the employee handbook suddenly and was not letting me get away with any little indiscretion. When a person gets a job we should not only update the computer but locate their hardcopy CV and move it to another cabinet. Nobody actually does it and every six months or so someone takes about a week to update all the paper files. It's been this way forever; it is actually faster and easier than everyone pulling files and moving pieces of paper each day. But Ray was being a stickler with me, and he would leave me little notes asking if I'd updated the paper file or if I knew why this CV had not been moved. Then he moved on to my job

253

descriptions and my wording. He said he felt I was not being PC, or that I was deliberately putting the emphasis on female or male candidates.

Finally I confronted him as he was making coffee in the kitchen.

"Ray, what are you playing at?"

"What's wrong with you?"

"I cannot believe you are being so fucking childish! Stop checking all my work, it's not your job and I do not need you or anyone else looking over my shoulder!"

"Oh, I think you do. You appear to be lacking in some of the more basic skills for the job – your job descriptions are very basic and you have actually specified gender in that ad you did for Emma the other day. That's a complete no-no. Everybody knows that."

"The ad was for a midwife in the bloody Coombe! And they specifically looked for a woman. You cannot keep this up, Ray. I'll complain about you."

"Well, do what you like – but if you complain about me, I'll just go to Larry and let him know my reservations about your ability to do this job."

I stood and looked at him: he wasn't joking. He was actually going to complain about me to the boss.

"You know, Ray, I'm just sorry I didn't hit you harder that time. If I had one more shot at you, you'd wake up next year some time."

I walked back out of the room and back to my desk. Ray emerged from the kitchen area a few seconds later and looked straight at me. Something in his eye made me feel a bit nervous. Maybe I shouldn't have actually threatened to hit him again – had I gone too far that time?

I comforted myself in the knowledge that if it all did blow up in my face and Personnel were called in again, I would have had grounds for the threat. He was harassing me too. I may have punched him but he was wrecking my head and no one could put up with that type of crap without losing it after a while.

I decided to ignore him and go back to work – I was not going to have him pull me up on my work load as well as everything else. I went to my emails, hoping Ruth had sent me a joke or a note of some kind.

Nothing from Ruth. But there was a note from Larry, the manager. I opened it, my heart thumping in my chest. He only ever emails you to tell you you're fired. To my absolute horror he was requesting that I come to see him in his office at 4:30 that afternoon. I was sickened to my stomach. Was I fired? Had Ray already gone to him about me? Had he heard me threatening to punch Ray? The more I thought about it, the more I realised I was fired. As surely as I was being harassed by Arse Face. I looked over at Ruth but she wasn't there. I checked Jack's desk and he was gone too. I guessed they were out smoking together and really she had enough on her own plate without me adding to it. Anyway, if I was in big trouble I wanted as few people as possible to know about it.

The hours ticked by until 4:30, when I stood up and walked to the manager's office. His secretary, Louise, looked up at me.

"I have an appointment with Larry," I told her.

"Do you?" she asked and looked at his diary. "Oh yeah,

I'll just tell him you're here."

She disappeared into his office and came back out smiling at me. "Go on in."

"Thanks," I said walking into the office, my heart in my mouth.

"Amelia, come in and sit down," Larry leaned over his desk and offered me a seat. I took it. "I bet you're wondering what this is all about?"

I nodded, still feeling very uneasy. Our boss is not the most hands-on man I've ever met and chats in his office are never about the weather.

"Well, a few things have come to my notice lately." He looked at me as though I should understand what he was talking about.

I guessed it was about me and Ray, but why was Ray not invited to tell his side of the story too? Had Ray been here already? Had he got his side of the story out and blamed the whole fiasco on me? I braced myself for the attack.

"I do see what's going on out there and I am aware of the history between yourself and Ray Donnelly."

I looked at him. Was I in trouble for inter-office dating? "Ray and I are well and truly over, Larry. It was never a serious thing anyway," I began to explain.

"Please, it's none of my business what you do in your private life and I wouldn't have mentioned it except for the fact that things appear strained as a result."

"We're fine. There was a little tension between us at first, but we're fine. I think Ray's just messing, with all the comments about CV's and job descriptions and that. I had a word with him just this morning and I think it's all sorted now. Just to let you know it is in no way getting in the way of our work." I stopped, wondering why I was fighting to keep this job when in fact I hated it so much.

"Amelia, it's all right. There's no problem. I can see that the work level is still strong – I have no problem with that. I just wanted to have a chat with you."

I looked at him, waiting for him to continue, nervous about what I was about to hear.

"I am aware that you have been out of sorts lately," he said quite kindly. "Amelia, I have daughters about your age. I see how Ray gets to you, and I will be having a word with him about it, believe me. I can see it's upsetting you and I do not blame you in the least." I felt myself begin to blush; I knew I looked like some silly girl who was finding it hard to come to terms with a break-up.

"I'm fine. This will all blow over and everything will go back to normal around here, Larry," I assured him, even if I was feeling very unsure myself.

"It's all right. You're not on trial here!" he said, holding up his hand in a gesture to calm me. "As I said, I have daughters of my own – I'm not worried about a few harsh words. That's not why you're here."

That sort of stopped my train of thought. "No?"

"Not at all. I have a proposition for you. I wondered if you might be interested in moving out to the Fairview office when it opens up. What do you think?"

"Well," I began, but I really didn't know what to say, "is this to get rid of me, without firing me?"

"Not at all – the opposite, in fact. I have seen for some

time that you're a great worker. You're a self-starter and that's exactly the type of person we need in Fairview. We need someone with experience of how we like things done around here, and someone I know we can trust completely. You fit the bill. Also, there would be a promotion involved and a significant pay rise." He looked at me, then added, "I thought it might be a bit easier on you, all things considered."

"Thank you. When would I have to give you an answer?"

"As soon as possible, but don't rush into it. Think about it." He stood up and leaned over the table to shake my hand.

"Larry, did you offer this arrangement to Ray?"

"No, I didn't, but that has nothing to do with my personal opinion of either one of you. I thought long and hard about it. You were the one who looked like the best candidate, and that's why I asked you, no other reason."

"Thanks, I'll let you know as soon as I can."

I left his office and went straight to the bathroom. I was still shaking and looked flushed. I stayed in there for a few minutes to get my head together then I returned to my desk. I'd got an email from Ruth while I was away. Jack and she were going out on a date the following night; they were going to see a movie.

33

I wondered about the pros and cons of the job-change all the way home on the DART and then as I made dinner, ate dinner, watched TV and as I tried to sleep that night. The fact of the matter was, I really hadn't got enough information to make a considered decision. I must admit though, the proposition was looking somewhat more interesting as the night went on. I sat up in bed making a list of questions I needed to ask about the job, the salary, the responsibility and who else would be in the office with me.

I went in to work the following day and put my questions to the boss. He confirmed that there would be a pay rise, although he was not completely "give-ish" with the actual amount of this pay rise. I was still no nearer a decision and so I went to see my father and asked his advice, "If all else fails ask Daddy" being a motto I lived by. He advised that I should go for the new position, a change being as good as a rest, and it would give me all the perks of starting a new job without the hassle of working from the bottom up again in some other office. So I took the job, a little blindly I know, but it was a fresh start and it was a pay rise. Also, it was away from Ray.

The new office wouldn't be open until early the following autumn so it wouldn't exactly be a quick getaway. I was bound to the city office for at least another four months.

I had to break the news to Ruth. She would be furious that I was leaving her here alone – but, after all, now that she had Jack she wouldn't be alone. Maybe this was all meant to be – things falling into place without our knowledge, fate perhaps?

"Leaving?" Ruth screeched.

Everyone in the smoking shelter turned and stared at us, took in my blushing face long enough for me to blush even more and then carried on smoking.

"Not for ages yet," I told her, and the guy in the corner who was still staring at us. I looked at him and he looked away with a wounded expression on his face.

"But you're going," said Ruth and then dropped her voice to say, "Is it all because of Ray?"

"No, not really. I was asked by Larry and I went home and thought about it. It seems like a good idea,"

"When are you going?"

"Not until September or October,"

"Why did he ask you?"

"He thought I was a good candidate," I shrugged. I was not about to go into the mortifying exchange about me being upset in the office.

"Well, he always liked you," Ruth said, smiling but looking a little sad. "Good luck. I'll miss you but a promotion is a promotion."

"Hey, enough about me, what about this date tonight!" I laughed.

Ruth threw her head into her hands and groaned. "I'm sick. What am I doing?"

"The right thing," I confirmed for her. "What are you going to see anyway?"

"The latest Hugh Grant movie, I can't remember its name. Something safe,"

"No love scenes?"

"Hopefully not!" she laughed. "Imagine if we accidentally went to see *9 1/2 Weeks!*"

"*Last Tango in Paris!*"

"God stop, I'd never be able to look at him again!"

"Oh, it's 10:50. We'd better get moving."

Going up in the lift I told Ruth not to tell anyone in the office about my move. She promised. I knew she wouldn't – she had too much on her mind anyway. She was really very nervous about the date. I told her I thought it was really sweet that both she and Jack were nervous about the date. I was slapped on the arm, very roughly if you ask me, and told not to be so condescending.

That night I left work just as Jack and Ruth were both getting up to leave. I waved to Ruth. It turned out they were heading for a bite to eat and a movie later on.

I ran to the station and squeezed onto the DART. Over my dinner I wondered how their date was going. Ruth had promised to ring me when she got home.

My mobile rang at half past seven. I glanced at the clock. If this was Ruth, it was a very bad sign. It wasn't Ruth. It was Jenny.

"Hi, Millie!" She sounded very happy.

"Hiya!" I replied.

"Where are you?" she asked.

"At home, where are you?" It sounded like she was in a nightclub, as loud music pounded down the phone; it was very early on a Wednesday night though.

"I'm out with the work crowd – I wondered if you were out and about."

"Oh, no, I'm at home."

"Maybe I'll call in to you on the way home!"

"Yes, why not?" I replied, wondering how drunk she'd be by the time she got here. "What time were you planning on leaving town?"

"We're not in town. We're in Booters…"

Just then someone interrupted her loudly and I didn't hear the rest of the sentence. Then she giggled and said that she'd call to me the following night instead. She shouted goodbye down the phone and hung up.

I took it she was in Booterstown, although what she was doing all the way out there was beyond me. I also took it that she was having a good night. I turned on the TV and sat down, and just as I did Gandhi got up on my knee and in a gesture that was completely out of character he began to purr and settle down. Things around here may be changing, I thought to myself.

I flicked stations until late. Gandhi remained on my

knee, staring me down whenever I had to breathe or move a finger. My leg was dead and there were hundreds of pulled threads in my trousers from him marking time on my thigh. At about 10:30 the phone rang again. This time I knew it would be Ruth. I jumped to grab it. To my surprise it was Jenny again.

"Amelia, could you do me a huge favour?" she asked, her earlier good humour well subdued.

"Yeah," I replied, thinking she probably wanted something taped on TV.

"Can you come and collect me, please?"

"Where are you?"

"I'm in ... I'm on Kenilworth Square, in Harold's Cross." She sounded lost.

"What are you doing, a tour of the south side?"

"No, not really. Can you please come and collect me?"

"Fine – is there a landmark close by that I could meet you at? I don't know Harold's Cross that well."

"Neither do I. I'm completely lost – no, wait, there's a cinema across the road – The Screen – I'll be outside it." She sounded like she was about to cry.

"All right, stay at the cinema and I'll find you. Harold's Cross can't be that hard to find."

I cursed her as I locked the door and made my way to the carpark. I turned towards town and headed for Christchurch. Town was busier than I expected it to be but, as I passed the Olympia I realised there was a show just coming to an end. That explained the crowds and the idiots who thought standing in the middle of the road waving at every car was the best way to hail a taxi. I always hated driving through town late at night, and that night was no exception. I headed south at Christchurch and watched for signs It took a while but I finally found her, standing outside the cinema, hugging herself against the night air. She looked the worse for wear and I was surprised by her appearance. She usually looked so tidy, but tonight she was well and truly dishevelled. I pulled up and she got in.

"Thanks," she said quietly. The smell of smoke and drink from her was overwhelming.

"What happened to you?"

"Nothing – we just had a few too many on a work night."

"You look a little shaky. Is something wrong?" I asked, looking at her profile as she hunched in the front seat.

"No, I'm fine." She turned to me and smiled. "I'm absolutely fine. I just drank too much."

"All right." I decided to say nothing else, but she was definitely not fine.

We drove home in silence, though every now and then Jenny would cough or sigh. She had stopped hunching and was now looking out at the city as we drove along Dame Street.

"Do you want to go straight home?" I asked.

"I'd better. Mike will be looking for me."

"Jenny, who were you out with tonight?"

"The gang from work. We just drank too much. We decided to go back to one of the guy's houses. It wasn't the best of plans – as soon as I got there I wanted to come home."

The Trouble with Boys

"Why didn't you call a taxi?" I asked, trying not to sound like I was complaining about collecting her.

"I didn't know a number. Look, I'm sorry about calling you, Amelia, but I didn't know what else to do."

"Why didn't you call Mike?"

"I did. He wasn't there. He might have been in the shower or down at the gym."

"Well, you're home now. Do you still want to come around tomorrow night?"

"Yes, I'd love it – we could get a takeaway and have a gossip." She smiled.

"Great, see you tomorrow." I hugged her goodbye.

She smelt like aftershave. As she jumped out of the car she looked back at me. It must have registered on my face because she put her hand to her neck in a guilty gesture and rushed up the driveway.

When I got home it was just after midnight. There was a message from Ruth. She sounded disappointed that I was not there. She said they'd had a great time but that Jack hadn't tried to kiss her, so there was nothing to say on that score. She also said they were going to meet up on Saturday night for a quick drink. That sounded very promising. I turned off the lights in the sitting-room and unplugged the TV. I rubbed Gandhi as I passed his shelf and he hit out with his claws at me. Horrible, horrible cat.

Ruth talked non-stop about her date. It seems things had gone exceptionally well the previous night. I was happy for her and I listened to all the details, such as they were.

They'd gone to see a movie, Jack had paid for her dinner and the tickets into the cinema. I nodded, agreeing that he was very generous. He'd wanted to pay for the popcorn but she'd refused and paid for it. I listened to all the details, but I was thinking about Jenny. I wondered what had gone on last night. She was definitely not happy when I picked her up and she was hiding something. I wondered about telling Ruth but she was so happy with her date and, anyway, I didn't want anyone thinking that Jenny was doing anything she shouldn't have been. After all, she'd just gone out for a few drinks with the work crowd and, as she said, things may have got a little rowdy for a Wednesday night. It can happen – it's happened to me on a Monday night.

Jenny rang me in work that afternoon.

"Sorry about last night – I was very drunk."

"That's fine – how are you feeling today?"

"All right." There was a pause. "Actually, not great, that's why I'm calling you. I can't make it tonight. I really need an early night. Is that all right?"

"That's no problem."

"Maybe next week I'll get over to you?"

"Yeah, any time."

She said goodbye and I hung up. She wasn't coming over and now I was at a bit of a loose end. I stared off into space for a moment before focusing in on Ray and Mairead flirting at his desk. She was sitting on his desk swinging her hair in front of him. I watched them for a few minutes. Oh, just ask him out already, I thought to myself. I could feel myself getting irrationally irritated by them so I stopped watching. I turned to take my mobile out of my bag and as I turned I noticed my boss standing at his door watching. He was watching Ray. Then he looked at me, his eyes full of pity.

Oh crap, now he thinks I'm still pining for Ray.

I took my mobile out of my bag and read a text message – anything to look like I wasn't watching Ray.

The boss came over to my desk. "Amelia, you're doing the right thing in moving to the new office," he said conspiratorially. "Just think of the travel-time from Clontarf to Fairview – you won't know yourself."

He walked away. I knew he was clapping himself on the back for averting me from a bout of tears at my desk.

34

The following week Jenny did call over. She arrived one night unannounced just after seven.

"Hi," she smiled as she walked into the sitting-room. She was carrying a bottle of wine and a box of Cadbury's Roses. *"Thank you very much for picking me up the other night!"* she sang, in the vein of the old advert.

I smiled, taking the Roses from her and heading to the kitchen for glasses and a bottle-opener. She was watching the TV when I came back in.

"Sorry for calling in like this. I would usually ring before I came over, but Mike was going over to his mother's and I just decided at the last second to get a lift from him. It was all very last second. I should have rung you – sorry."

"Will you stop apologising. It's lovely to see you and the chocs are an added bonus!" I grinned, pouring the wine into two glasses.

We sat in silence for a while, watching the TV, and for some reason feeling a little uncomfortable about things. We watched *Coronation Street* together but there was something hanging in the air between us. I wasn't sure what to say about it or how to approach it.

It was Jenny who finally spoke: "I want to tell you about last week. The truth. Please just listen."

I muted the TV and turned to face her. She was looking at the TV screen but her face was serious; she looked almost scared.

"It's no shock to anyone to hear Mike and I are not completely thrilled with married life. Well, Mike is; I'm not." She glanced at me, then back at the TV. She looked like she might cry and I felt a horrible wrench in my chest. I didn't want to hear she was unhappy. She was my sister and I loved her.

"Mike wants the happy families and I'm not ready for it all. I don't want a baby, or to give up work or change my name! He wants Doris fucking Day, and I can't, I won't be that person. Why should I? Who says I should have to give up all of me just because he put a ring on my finger? So what if we're married six months and no baby? So bloody what?" She began to cry, tears of frustration spilling onto her cheeks.

"So the baby's becoming a huge problem?"

"Sort of," she sniffed and took a mouthful of wine.

"There's other stuff too, but it's going to make me sound like a complete weapon. I can't help it though!"

"What stuff?"

"Please don't think I'm a bitch when I tell you this. I

269

know I'm in the wrong, but I can't help myself."

We both drank a mouthful of wine, fortifying ourselves for what lay ahead.

"Mike is a nice guy and I love him, I really do, but he's not exciting. He's your average good guy – good job, nice suit, nice car, you know?"

I nodded.

"There's a guy in work. His name is Frank. He's really gorgeous." She glanced at me. I tried to keep my face neutral, but she could tell I was appalled. "Please, Millie, don't look at me like that!"

"Are you having an affair?" How alien that statement felt, how was it that I was asking that question? It didn't quite fit with my quiet suburban life style.

"No, I'm not!" she replied, shaking her head emphatically. "But I did a really stupid thing. We've been flirting in the office, but nothing too much, just the usual. Smiling and eye-catching, tipping each other as we pass – you know the kind of thing I mean?"

I nodded, sick to my stomach.

"The other night when we were out, the flirting went up a notch. We were sitting together in the pub and I thought we were only messing but things got out of hand. Frank asked me back to his place and, Christ, this is so embarrassing, I said yes." She began to cry again. "I was really thick, I should never have done it, but before I knew it we were in a taxi headed even further out into the south side. We got to his house and we went in. He made us a drink and then things moved on. I only kissed him, I swear to God, but it was awful. I felt so guilty that

270

he wasn't Mike and I got upset. I said I didn't want anything more and wanted to go home. He was furious. He told me I was a prick-tease and was shouting at me about coming all the way home and him thinking he was on to a winner and all that. He wouldn't call me a taxi and told me to get out and walk home. He threw me out of the house and flung my coat after me. I was in the middle of a housing estate, so I walked up to the main road, but there were just houses there too. There was nothing – no landmark and no taxis passing. I walked for a while but I was getting a bit lost and I didn't want to wander into any dodgy areas so I rang you. Then, of course, I saw that cinema and I stood there."

"You did the right thing." I was unsure of what to say next, but at least I knew she'd done the right thing in leaving his house and not wandering blindly around the city.

Jenny sat silently crying for a few minutes.

"Does Mike know any of this?"

She shook her head. "But I think he knows I fancy someone in work. He said it to me one night. It was when we were first talking about me giving up work to have a baby. He asked if there was someone in work I didn't want to leave."

"What did you say?"

"I said there wasn't, that I just didn't want to give up work." She sighed and refilled our glasses.

"How have things been with this Frank asshole?"

"Not good. We don't really speak any more, but I'm mortified. People in the office know I went back to his house and they, of course, think the obvious."

"Would you tell a friend what really happened?"

"I did. She just said it was none of her business. So I have to grin and bear it. It's entirely my own fault anyway. I was in the wrong."

"He was the one who flirted with a married woman and kicked you out! He's more guilty than you are!"

"He's not married and he was flirting with someone who fancied him. What did he do wrong?"

"What? He flirted with a married woman, took her back to his house and then kicked her out on the street when she refused to go any further than a kiss!"

"Thanks for your support but I'm the bad guy here. I am, after all, the married one. And I was the one who agreed to go back to his house. Anyway, we can debate who the villain of the piece was till the cows come home, but the fact remains I was flirting when I shouldn't have been and I was willing to go back to this guy's house. Knowing that Mike was sitting alone watching TV and waiting for me to come home."

I watched her for a while, as she drank a little of her wine and ate a chocolate.

"So the flirtation is over, is it?"

"Yes, it's completely over. In a funny way it actually proved to me that I love Mike completely and utterly. Odd, isn't it?" She gave a watery smile.

"I don't think it's that strange," I shrugged. "I mean, you just needed to prove it to yourself and now you have. You do love Mike –" I fought the urge to say: dull and all as he is.

"It's not perfect. We still have the whole baby thing to resolve and even more than that, the whole Doris Day thing. He wants me to be someone I'm not and never will be!"

"Tell him," I said. "Tell him you're not ready to be a 1950's housewife and that you need to keep your job and your own name. It's not the end of the world if you do, is it?"

"I don't know. We row a lot and it's always about the housewife stuff. Ironing and cleaning and stuff. You know I was never much use at housework, but Mike thinks I should be well able to do it all."

"Sounds like a communication problem and you'll need to sit down and talk it through. Don't be pushed into anything you're not happy with – make sure he listens to you."

"I will. I'm just not sure of what I want. I always thought I wanted the baby and the house and family car, but now that the pressure is on I'm not so sure."

We sat in silence staring into space. I sensed that the last comment needed no reply. I couldn't make her mind up for her and she really didn't need me telling her she was lucky to be able to give up work. I was no help on this one, so I just sat there and listened, refilling our glasses from time to time.

It took longer than you'd think for the whole story to come out and for the aftermath to be properly dealt with. It was nearly eleven when Jenny called a taxi and headed home.

I watched her leave and waved from the door. When I

got back to the sitting-room I looked around me. Only then did it register with me: Jenny's marriage was in serious trouble if they didn't take it in hand. And it seemed neither of them knew exactly how to take control. Was there any control in this situation? They were both grown adults and they wanted different things. Someone would have to give way, or at least compromise and I had no idea which of them would be willing to do that.

I tidied up and watched TV for a while, but nothing I watched was making any sense to me. I turned off the TV and went to bed.

The following morning Ruth grabbed me and led me into the bathroom as soon as I walked into the office.

"Well, just so you know, Jack and I finished last night," she said.

"*What?* What happened?"

"A disaster and I don't want to talk about it." She was looking around to see if there was anyone in the cubicles.

"It was weird!"

"What was weird?"

"We just didn't click for some reason. Everything we did was out of sync and we couldn't get a conversation going to save our lives. We sat in complete silence most of the time." She shook her head at the memory.

"Did you kiss?" I asked.

"Yes, and that was the worst part."

"How?"

"It just felt weird."

I looked at her, waiting for more information.

"It was – he's a good kisser all right – there was nothing wrong with him as such. There was something missing though. It felt like I was kissing my cousin or my brother. There was no spark."

"That's awful!" I said, feeling very sorry for her. I knew she really liked him.

"Tell me about it!" Ruth laughed in spite of herself. "Anyway, we didn't have to say anything. He just dropped me home and I got out of the car and ran to the door."

"So you just left it like that?" I asked.

"Yeah, but we were under no illusion. It was a stupid thing to do and now it's over. Maybe it's for the best." She looked at herself in the mirror again, and shuddered at a private thought. "We should never have tried it – we were stupid."

"No, you liked him and he liked you. There was nothing wrong with meeting for a drink. Sorry it didn't work out," I smiled sympathetically.

"Thanks. We'd better get back," She shrugged as she turned from the sink and grabbed the toilet door. "Please don't mention it to Jack, just let it go. Best forgotten."

Ruth may have wanted it to be forgotten and perhaps she was right that it would have been best forgotten, but it wasn't. We still went to lunch together and ate the same food from the same little café as before, but that was the only thing that remained the same. Ruth and Jack were awkward around each other and in trying to be polite and relaxed with one another they were in fact stilted and brusque. They did talk but it was nothing more than comments about the weather and the price of melons, absolutely nothing of any consequence. I would sit there like a prize duck in the middle, talking crap for an hour. It was excruciating. I would regularly come back to the office after a break in their company and feel like sleeping for an hour, I was that exhausted by the whole thing. Ruth and Jack were enjoying it even less than I was, but what was the alternative? Sitting in silence?

I was aware I was being snappy in the office. Ray wasn't helping matters there, still calling out my mistakes to me as he checked all my work. And lately he'd taken to announcing that I was being very cranky.

"I note Amelia is her usual sweet-tempered self today!" he'd call from his desk.

"Shut up," I'd reply.

"Ah yes, dulcet tones," he'd smirk as he worked.

Sometimes this was a good tension-breaker for me. I could snap at Ray without fear of repercussion. We'd spar for a few minutes, back and forth a bit. But after about a fortnight of this, I was getting sick of it. It was just another show I had to perform in. Keep them smiling in the cheap seats, Amelia.

I felt as though I was constantly working to keep things ticking over. I was getting nowhere. Ray was taking a lot of energy from me and, as for Jenny and Mike – well, I didn't want to think about that one. Jenny was still unhappy, that was for sure. I could see it in her when we met. She was quiet and drawn. I hoped she hadn't done something stupid like telling Mike about the night in Harold's Cross. If nothing happened he didn't need to know – that's if really nothing happened. I didn't want to know too much detail on that one.

I could see the signs. Things were becoming complicated and I needed a break.

I went home and ran a bath, raiding all the goody-bags I'd got for Christmas that year and pouring all kinds of everything into the water. I poured too much in and turned the bubbles blue, and the entire apartment smelt of lavender. I put on the radio and sank into the bath. It was wonderful. Hot water and plenty of bubbles really do help you to see the world in a fresh light.

I lay in the bath singing along with the love songs and I could have done this until midnight but the water got cold, so I had to get out. I smothered myself in strawberry-smelling lotion and got into fresh pajamas. I was feeling better in my body but not so much in my mind it has to be said. I had been so busy singing along with the love songs that I had not got around to thinking about the problems in the relationships around me. To my chagrin, my head was not rested by this time out. It was in fact buzzing with details from various conversations I'd had over the last fortnight.

I sat on the couch and turned the TV on. I sat there watching but I couldn't concentrate. I was thinking about Jenny and what was going on in her life. I hoped she was working things out and that Frank guy was gone for good. The more I thought about it, the more I wound myself up in knots, but there was nothing I could do. It was her marriage and I had to watch from the sidelines like everyone else. I hated it.

There was very little I could think about that didn't upset me. My new job for instance; that should have been really good news but had I bitten off more than I could chew? A self-starter, the boss had said. But was I really a self-starter and a go-getter? I sometimes gave that impression, but underneath it all I felt I was in fact just a well-organised pen-pusher. I was good at paperwork and keeping my desk and files tidy, but did that translate into good management skills? I could manage myself, but an office of new staff all looking to me for inspiration?

And I'd have to leave the familiarity of the Dame Street office. I liked the status quo, but things around me right now were anything but status quo. Boats were being rocked and situations were changing all around me.

I looked around the apartment: it could do with a face lift. The walls could be painted and the furniture could be updated. Then my eye fell on the fish. Their water was filthy – I had meant to change it three days before but I didn't get around to it. I picked them up off the shelf and took them to the bathroom. I filled the sink with water and released the three musketeers into the sink. I washed out their bowl and their pebbles. Then I scrubbed their little plastic castle and their fake seaweed. It was while I was scrubbing the castle that I realised I was crying. I had no idea why, but the tears were flowing down my cheeks and there was nothing I could do to stop them. I filled the fish bowl with water and replaced the fish. They swam around in the new water and I watched them for a few minutes. The tears kept coming; they blurred my vision.

Then I did perhaps the worst thing I could have done

under the circumstances. I put the fish back on the shelf and went to the fridge, opened a bottle of wine and poured myself a big glass. In my defence, I thought I was doing the right thing. It was only as I was halfway through my second glass and feeling suicidal that I recalled that alcohol is actually a depressant. I flicked stations and ended up watching *Prime Time*. It was about the aftermath of Chernobyl, not the most uplifting thing for a girl in my condition to be watching. I sat there alone, drinking and crying. I was a sorry sight. .

The buzzer in the flat went at ten o'clock. I stopped dead. If I sat still they wouldn't know I was here – forget the little formality of my blinds being open and my lights being on. I sat quietly on the couch. The buzzer went again, this time with more gusto, a longer and louder buzz. I got up and pressed the button.

"Yes?"

"Amelia?" a male voice replied.

"Luke?" I replied, even though it didn't sound like him.

"No, it's Jack. Can I come in?"

"Jack?" I was shocked. What was he doing at my buzzer?

"Yeah, I was passing and I thought I'd call in. Are you busy?"

I suddenly realized I was being rude, so I made amends.

"God, not at all. Sorry, come in. I'm in my PJs." I don't know why I put that in – he'd see for himself in about a minute – I just wanted to have it out there.

"Fine, as long as they're not see-through." Jack laughed and I heard the main door shut behind him.

I opened the hall door and waited. Jack arrived around the corner, looking at door numbers before he saw me. He grinned when he saw me.

"Hiya, I was really bored at home and I went for a bit of drive. I was around the seafront and I remembered you lived around here." He smiled as he passed me into the hall. "Through here, I take it?"

"Yeah, go on in. Would you like a glass of wine?" I headed to the kitchen to get a wineglass.

"Why not, just the one if you're having one –" His eyes fell on the half-empty bottle and my glass as he spoke.

I was embarrassed. "I don't usually drink alone in here or dress for bed at dinner-time – you just caught me on an off night." I cleared the table a little and pushed the cushions around until the room looked a little tidier.

Jack was sitting down, pouring what was left of the bottle into the two glasses and opening one of the packets of crisps I had put on the table. He leaned back on the couch and sighed, "Wow, this is really comfy! It's a big apartment, isn't it? How many bedrooms?"

"One, why?" I smirked.

"No reason at all, I was just asking!" Jack blushed.

"I'm only joking. It's just that that was exactly what Ray said the first time he came over here." Now it was my turn to blush.

"And I think that might just tell us a little more than we needed to know!" Jack grinned as he looked around the room. He stopped and looked back at me. Then he did the quickest double-take and took a sip of his wine. He looked at me again. "Are you all right, Amelia?"

"Yes, I'm fine."

"Sorry for saying so, but you don't look too fine. Have you been crying?"

"No," I laughed, but it sounded off. "I was watching a documentary about sick babies and I had a bit of a cry. I'm fine though."

"Sick babies?" Jack looked surprised.

"Yeah, it was about Chernobyl – it always makes me cry."

"I see," he said, half smiling at me.

"Well, I shouldn't watch these things but I do, and I had a bit of a cry. It was nothing."

"I don't believe you."

"Well, that's up to you," I smiled, but I could feel my chest tighten as I spoke. My voice sounded high-pitched. I looked at him and confirmed that he had heard it too.

"Amelia, I don't mean to pry. I'm just concerned. I call in and find you crying into a bottle of wine. What kind of a person would I be if I turned a blind eye and never said a word?"

"Honestly, I'm fine. I'm just being silly," I replied with a sigh but the sigh was ragged and caught in my throat.

"You are not fine. What's wrong?" Jack sat forward, his face concerned.

"It's just silly things, no one thing just a load of little ones. You know how it is . . ." I smiled, but I could feel my eyes sting and the look of genuine sympathy on Jack's face was just too much for me. "It's Ray."

Jack looked surprised but said nothing.

"I'm completely over him, but I'm just disappointed to

be back here, alone on a Tuesday night. I'm right back where I started. I'm lonely I suppose and I'm annoyed with myself about how things with Ray worked out. I feel hard done by – does that make sense to you?"

Jack nodded. "We all know how it feels to be lonely, and disappointed. You're not alone there."

"I don't know what's wrong with me. I mean, I don't have the least bit of interest in him any more, but does he have to flirt with Mairead and make fun of me in the office?"

"He doesn't make fun of you. What gives you that impression?"

"He sends me emails and sticks notes on my computer about anything and everything I do. He seems to have memorised the rule book and if I don't do things to the letter he comes over and tells me where I'm going wrong!"

"That's harassment. Everybody cuts corners. We all do it. Have you tried turning the tables on him, watching what he does all day?"

"Yeah, he's playing it to the letter these days," I sighed.

"Amelia, what can I say? The guy's an asshole. He always was. He has great cheekbones and a shitty personality." Jack smiled at me, his eyes sympathetic. "He doesn't seem to realise that his looks will only take him so far – he needs to be a nice person to hold on to a relationship. That's the trouble with little boys though, isn't it?"

"You're a boy. You're not like that," I said. I realised there was a tear hanging off my eyelash and wiped it away.

"Ah, a common mistake. I am, in fact, a man – there is a difference!" Jack laughed, digging in his pocket and handing me a tissue.

"Thank you," I smiled, taking the tissue from him. Then, dabbing my eye, I stopped. "This is clean, isn't it?"

"Yes, you ingrate! I wouldn't be passing around used tissues!"

I laughed for a few minutes at the good of the joke.

"So is that all that's bothering you – Ray?"

"No, not just that." I had an audience. Jack seemed to be a good listener and so I was going to use him while he was there. "With you and Ruth not getting along, lunch is really hard work at the moment. I worry that we'll stop meeting for lunch and then we'll all drift and I like us hanging around together. And then there's my sister. She's so unhappy. I think her marriage is a sham." I looked up and found Jack staring at me. "Am I unloading on you?"

"No, that's fine. I don't mind at all," he said. "Don't be worrying about Ruth and myself. We went out twice and it didn't work out. It happens all the time."

"But you're not talking to each other and I feel like piggy in the middle."

"Well, you're not piggy in the middle or anything like it. You take too much on yourself. What's happening between Ruth and me is between Ruth and me. We'll get back on an even keel in a while, so until then stop worrying about it."

"I just feel like everything in my life is out of my control and I hate it."

"Yes, other people are out of your control. I certainly

am, so don't give yourself grey hairs trying to control how I behave. I'm my own person."

"Wow, your own person!" I laughed through my tears. "You're quite the hard man when you get going!"

Jack rolled his eyes. Luckily, he took the jibe in the good humour it was meant. "Shut up, I was trying to help!"

"And you did. Thank you," I smiled at him, picking up my glass and draining it.

"That other problem – Jennifer," he said. "Do you want to talk about it or will I leave that one?"

I put down my empty glass and looked around for the bottle: it was empty. I did want to talk about Jennifer, if only to get it off my chest. I wanted to hear I was being silly and that she was as happily married as Paul Newman. So I told him about my fears.

"She doesn't want a baby and her husband does – he wants the perfect housewife and she's not interested in being housewife and mother. To be honest, he's a complete bore and I couldn't understand why she married him in the first place, but she admitted to me a few nights ago that she kissed a guy in her office and now there's no hiding from the fact that she's unhappy and things are not working out between them. I hate to see how different she is now. It's like she's aged about ten years since she married him. I hate it!" I could feel my chest tighten again; just saying it aloud made it real and frightening. What could I do for her?

Jack listened, his mouth shut, eyes watching mine with an intensity that made me feel like I was the only person in the world and that nothing I was saying would ever pass his lips again. When I finished he put his hand on my knee and squeezed a little. It was a sympathetic gesture but one I was not ready to deal with. I jumped a little and he removed his hand very quickly.

"Sorry, I'm just not great with sympathy," I apologised.

"No problem, sorry!" Jack held his hand in the air.

"Look, I'm sorry about calling in like this. And I never would have pushed you to talk about your worries if I'd known what was happening. No wonder you're upset."

"No! It's actually nice to say it all out loud. Get it all off my chest. I can't talk to anyone at home, especially about Jenny."

"That's understandable," Jack nodded. "Listen, I know it may be a completely different situation but I remember when Richard, my brother, first got married. I was sure he was having a tough time. He'd just got his practice up and running and his wife got pregnant very quickly. I know that wasn't the plan. Things were very tough on both of them for about a year but they got over it. The practice took off and Lily is four now – she's a complete sweetheart and they wouldn't be without her."

"That's very sweet, but I don't think they have quite the same problem," I said as politely as I could.

"I know. But the thing is I thought Richard was unhappy, but he wasn't. He was actually really happy about Lily, and he knew the practice would just take a while to get off the ground. Looking in from the outside I saw only the downside and his wife being all hormonal and crying the whole time. But in fact they were happier than we thought. They were happier than they thought they were."

"Yeah, I can see your point, but I don't think this one will be fixed with a baby. I think the problem is deeper than that."

"Well, if it is then they have to deal with it head on. Them and only them." Jack looked me straight in the eyes. "You have to let them deal with it alone, and give them space to deal with it."

I nodded. He was right. I could see his point but it didn't stop me from worrying about it all. I sat forward and rubbed my face, exhausted all of a sudden.

"May I make a suggestion?" he said.

"If you must!" I replied through my hands.

"I think I must, just briefly. Now, this is just a suggestion, and don't jump down my throat before you hear me out . . . I could see you eyeing that empty bottle . . ."

I looked at him, knowing what was about to be said.

"Don't open another bottle of wine. Have a cup of tea. In fact, I'll make it for you."

I began to protest, but it was only Tuesday and I was quite drunk. I nodded as Jack headed for the kitchen and located the kettle. I followed him in and sat at the table giving brief nods and pointing towards presses where cups and tea bags and spoons were kept.

Jack made two cups of tea and we sat in the kitchen at the tiny table. Jack looked around this room with more disdain than he had the sitting-room. The kitchen is tiny in these apartments. While the bedroom and the sitting-room are really big and airy, the kitchen and the bathroom leave a lot to be desired. But I was happy there and the tiny kitchen had served me well. I had no complaints.

"This room is very small," he said looking at the ceiling.

"Don't be dissing my kitchen," I told him.

"I'm not. I'm just stating the obvious. It's small."

"Compact is how I like to describe it."

"Quite," Jack looked at me and grinned.

I looked away, laughing but pretending to be offended.

"Go away. There's nothing wrong with this apartment!"

"I'm joking with you. It's a lovely spot and you're most likely sitting on a small fortune. How much did you pay for it?"

"Oh please, let's not get into house prices. If I hear one more time that I was mad not to pay the extra thirty grand and go for a two-bed, I'll scream!"

"I see." Jack put the mug of tea down. "Have you had this conversation before – perhaps with your mother?"

"How did you guess?"

"Been there, bought a number of tee-shirts and now wear them on a regular basis."

"Have you a house?"

"No, I looked into buying one years ago and didn't bother – now all I hear is about how I missed the boat and all that jazz."

"Marry a girl who's minted and move into hers – that's what I plan to do when this one bed gets too small," I told him.

"You plan to marry a girl?" he laughed.

"If she's minted I won't be picky," I smirked.

"Ah yes, your marry-money scheme, still going strong on that one?"

"Yes, but no one I know is loaded – other than Ray, that is. And I'm not marrying him! What's your situation?" I eyed him.

"I have a minus figure in my bank account at the moment. An overdraft that's like a mortgage and a credit card that I can only use once a month on pay-day. Sound inviting?"

"Sounds like a mirror image of me. How do we get into these financial holes? I'm only twenty-nine – I should be in this much debt only when it comes to sending my children to medical school!"

"We are the see-it, want-it, buy-it generation. We all buy on credit and never actually repay it," Jack replied, swirling the tea at the bottom of his mug. "I'm not actually as badly off as I make out. A small overdraft and a huge credit card, that's my problem."

"I know. Me too. Credit limit bigger than my belly – they keep upping it and I keep letting them."

"Will we ever learn?" Jack raised his arms in a dramatic beseeching gesture.

"No, I don't think so. At least not while we're watching *Sex and the City* and *Will and Grace*. They have too much and we want to emulate them, so we just buy, buy, buy!"

"How very articulate of you. Amelia Slater, the voice of a new generation!"

"Thank you, I read a lot," I replied and we both

laughed for a while, until Jack glanced at the clock on the cooker.

"Is that the right time? And more to the point, are you so anal that the clock on your cooker is correct?"

"Yes," I nodded triumphantly, "and yes again," I nodded with a little less umph.

"Does your stereo have the correct time on it too?" he asked as he stood up from the table and made his way to the sitting-room.

"Yes, but there's a good reason!" I called as I followed him in.

"And that reason is?" he said as he looked disbelievingly at the stereo complete with precise time display.

"That stereo is never unplugged and the zeroes flashing in the corner of the room were distracting when I watched TV in here," I lied.

I am anal and I had set the times on all my electrical equipment. What's worse, I used to go around before bed and change them all when the clocks go forward and back. 'Spring forward; Fall back' was my motto.

"The real decider is: do you know how to set the timer on your video?" Jack asked.

"What has that got to do with anything?" I complained.

"Just answer the question!"

"I don't know."

"You don't know if you know how to do it or you don't know full stop?"

"I can't remember," I sidestepped, trying to avert the question.

"Just be honest!"

"Yes, I know how to use it, but I have a very simple video!" I protested.

"I bet you can change a plug and take spiders out of the bath with toilet paper!"

"No, I flush them down the drain like every other girl in the world. And I leave the water flowing for about twenty minutes so I'm sure he's really gone."

"All right, under that façade there may well beat the heart of a girl."

"Of course, there is! I don't know the off-side rule and I hate spiders and mice! I can assure you I am as girlie-girlie as the next girlie girl . . ." I trailed off at the end as I sounded stupid.

Judging by the look on his face Jack was highly entertained by the outburst. "As much as I am enjoying your tantrum I really do have to get home. By your precise clock on the stereo there it's almost 11:30 and I should be home before midnight."

"Will you turn into a pumpkin if you don't?" I asked.

"I left that one open for you as a test. You took the bait, I notice." He smiled at me from where he was standing, very close to Gandhi, whose tail was just starting to twitch. "And the answer is no, but my car will and I will be turned back into the lowly servant I am. Didn't you pay attention to the actual story of Cinderella?"

"No, I'm a girl and I was too interested in getting to the end of the book and seeing the dress."

"I see. Well, I'd better get out of your way and let you get to bed." Gandhi's tail was now lashing. As Jack turned to leave he caught sight of him and his face lit up. "Has this cat been here all the time?"

"Yes, but I wouldn't touch him," I said.

"Why not … *Oouch!*" Jack's hand shot up in the air and he gripped his thumb tight.

"He's not very friendly," I couldn't help but snigger.

"Jesus, no shit!" He laughed but his face betrayed he was hurt and most probably bleeding from a thin deep claw wound. I was used to them at this stage, but Jack was not.

"Sorry, let's see it. Did he cut you?" I went over.

"No, I'm fine." Jack presented a thumb with blood running down the side.

"Run it under the tap in the kitchen and I'll get a Band Aid," I told him.

He ran the tap for a while and when I came back the bleeding was almost stopped. I put the plaster on his thumb and fought the impulse to call him a big baby. He wasn't used to cats and I shouldn't forget that they can be vicious little buggers at the best of times.

Jack left and I locked up. I turned off the TV and put the glasses and bottle out into the kitchen. I cleared up the mugs and biscuits we'd used and wiped down the counter. I went to the bathroom and washed my teeth. It was only when I was doing this that I looked at myself. I was grinning from ear to ear. I'd had a really good night and I'd laughed a lot.

Maybe Ruth was right, maybe Jack was a bit of a riot.

35

I woke up the following morning in great form. The alarm went off and instead of pressing snooze and then lying for ten minutes feeling around for any sniffle or pain, I turned the alarm off and got up. I jumped in the shower, dressed and fed the cat with a very definite pep in my step. I felt good about myself and was in time for the early train, getting to the office in time for a croissant and a cup of coffee before I turned on my computer and started to answer emails from the day before.

Ruth walked in just before nine and Jack arrived just after her. He went straight over to her desk and chatted for a while as he took off his coat, and then took hers with him to hang up while he was at it. I watched from the corner of my eye, aware of their movements even before I was aware I was watching them. Jack returned to his own desk and gave me a slight wave as he settled down. I was a little disturbed to realise that I was smiling my best smile, reserved for potential squeezes, as I waved back at him. This, I reasoned with myself was just me being silly, an involuntary reaction to the opposite sex. Nothing at all to be thinking about. In fact I had given it far too much thought already, so I stopped.

I returned to the job at hand and opened some post I'd been given earlier on. It was as usual a bundle of CV's, only three of which had cover letters, all unimaginative – my name is this, my age is that, I have been working as a secretary for the last six months and now I want to be a dentist/a doctor/a rocket scientist, but I would like to work only nine to five and only three days a week. I looked through the bundle to see if anyone had a realistic view of their own talents, but sadly no, they had all sent in their CVs and letters to a recruitment agency but none of them seemed to want to work. I set to work, putting the post in bundles for callback. I began with the ones most likely to get some work and most likely to take it up.

Two hours later, after leaving countless messages on mobiles with varying types of message-minders, I gave up. I was very unsure about what was going to come of the message I'd left with someone called Eileen who claimed she had "just stepped out to buy a sheep and would be back within the hour". I presumed it was a joke and told her I'd got her CV and we would arrange a quick interview just to get her on the books officially, but to be honest and judging by her CV I really didn't know.

I was sitting at my desk thinking about a coffee break – it was 11:30 and my stomach was beginning to growl a little. I glanced at my emails and found that I had one from Ruth, but before I got a chance to open it she rang me.

"Diet Coke break?" she asked.

"Lovely," I replied with a smile.

We stood up and headed for the smoking shelter, stopping at the Coke machine to grab two cans as we passed.

"Did you get my email?" Ruth asked.

"I saw it. I didn't have a chance to read it. What?"

"I need a bit of advice. Jack asked me to meet for a drink tonight," she opened her can with a loud smacking noise that thankfully concealed the sound of me squawking in reply.

I regained some composure. "He asked you out again? Why?"

"I don't know – he was saying that he was sorry about the way things worked out. And he wondered if I wanted to have a drink and clear the air."

"How do you feel about it?" I asked.

"I don't know. Maybe I should." She took a slug from her can and shrugged at the same time, not the cleverest thing to do as she dripped Coke down her blouse. She busied herself in wiping it off before she looked up at me.

"What are his motives? Does he simply want to clear the air or is it a case of wanting to start things up again?" I asked, my heart thumping loudly in my ears for reasons of its own.

"He says to clear the air, but I'm not so sure. I think there may be other reasons!" Ruth grinned, confirming she was hoping for other reasons.

"Well then, go," I replied, a fake grin pasted on my face, and to be honest I was not really sure why it was fake. I mean, what did it mean to me that Ruth and Jack were going out for a drink? Why was I bothered?

"Oh, I may as well go and hear him out," Ruth was saying. "I mean, what have I got to lose?"

"Nothing," I told her.

So it was decided: Ruth and Jack were heading out that night and I was feeling left out.

Jack sent me an email later that afternoon, asking if I was feeling OK today and saying sorry he'd stayed so late. He went on to say that, as I probably already knew, he and Ruth were having a drink that night. He said he wanted to clear the air with her, that after talking to me last night he realised things were not great between them and that they should sort it out. He finished by telling me that I had a gorgeous flat. I sent him a quick note thanking him most kindly and telling him that the term used in Clontarf was in fact "apartment". He replied with a LOL (Laugh Out Loud) and that made me wonder what he does in his spare time.

At five I headed for the door, waving at Ruth as I passed. I gave her the thumbs-up and raced out, wanting to get home as quickly as I could. I realised, just as I was about to cross the road at Trinity, that I had no change for my ticket – I'd only had enough money for a one-way ticket that morning. I'd have been shot if I'd appeared at the cash desk with a fifty-euro note, and while I'm at it why is there no smaller change given out by bank machines? What's happened to all the fives, tens and

twenties? Anyway, I digress; the point is I went back to
the Centra to buy a magazine and a packet of crisps to get
change. Which put me back almost a fiver!

I came out of the shop only to be confronted by the
sight of Jack and Ruth heading into the Mercantile. He
was holding the door open and ushering her into the pub.
I felt an odd lurch in my chest for some reason. I scolded
myself for being so silly about it. What was I doing standing here watching them like this? What if they saw me?

And finally I had to wonder, why was I feeling so
incredibly left out?

I turned away and headed for the train station, resolv-
ing to get a life of my own.

36

A most unusual thing happened when I got home. Luke rang. He never uses the phone and he most certainly never rings me. He said he was coming over and that I was to be ready for a surprise and hung up.

I rang back and Mum answered. I asked what was going on with Luke but she didn't know. She said that he'd got his exams and passed with flying colours last week. I had known that. I was there and we'd been out to dinner to celebrate. She had no idea what he was so excited about but told me to be nice to him when he came over. I have no idea why she'd have to prompt me to be nice to my only brother but I agreed to be nice to him and hung up.

I waited for the knock on the door. It came, and in walked Luke who used to have dark brown hair and was now sporting bleached-blond, very short spikes. I screeched when I opened the door. I thought he was a stranger stepping in on top of me.

"Your hair!" I gasped.

"Yeah, and Mum likes it so don't go complaining to her about it."

"Let's see it," I said, beckoning him to lean forward and step into the light while I examined his head. "Will it cost a fortune keeping the roots from showing?"

"It looks good with some root showing. It's all the fashion now," he replied, walking over to the cat and pulling its tail with a quick tug and then dodging the slap with reflexes that have to be praised.

"Mum didn't lose the rag when she saw it then?"

"She was in shock for a while but then she realised it looked good,"

I raised a sceptical eyebrow.

"Anyway, it isn't my hair I'm over to show you," he went on as he fiddled with the waistband of his jeans.

"If you got pierced, keep it to yourself," I told him, very seriously.

"No, look out the window." He walked to the window and pushed the blind out of his way.

I took it from him and jerked it up to where it should have been. There outside in the carpark was a brand new Ford Focus.

"Is that yours?" I pointed to the car, hardly able to believe it.

"Yeah," he said, pride in his eyes. "Mum and Dad gave me the deposit for it when I got my exams."

"Wow, I got a bloody pair of jeans!" I moaned.

"Yeah, well, you're not the beloved son in the family.

Do you want to come out for spin?"

"Absolutely!" I headed for the door.

We rushed down the stairs and out into the carpark. I made straight for the Focus and went round it to the passenger side. Next thing, the car beside it beeped and I jumped. It was a small black Peugeot 106 and Luke was in the driving-seat. My mouth dropped open.

Luke leaned over, opened the passenger door and I got it. I *oohhed* and *aahhed* at the dashboard, and the quiet engine, and the fact that there was only 40,000 miles on a seven-year-old car. I had no idea if this was good, bad or indifferent, but Luke was pleased with his purchase and I was really pleased for him. His face shone with pride as he drove out of the carpark and headed along the coast road. The car was a good little mover and judging by the whiplash I was suffering every time we took off from a green light there was nothing wrong with the accelerator.

"So how much did it cost?" I asked.

"Three thousand. Mum and Dad gave me the six hundred deposit and I had another four hundred in my bank account. So I got a loan for two grand."

"Well done, you! How will you pay it back?"

"They're keeping me on at the office for another three years and I'll have it paid off by then," Luke grinned and again I could hardly believe that this messer beside me was actually an accountant now.

"Well, good for you," I smiled, "but I'll just say one thing." Luke looked at me. "Please do not get stupid-looking alloys – and no fear stickers – and please don't get a sound system that's bigger than the car!"

"I won't get a radio, but I am getting alloys."

"Fine, just remember, less is more!"

We drove up to Howth and had dinner in a pub on the seafront. This was most unlike us; we never do anything like this and certainly never together. We had a good laugh though and when Luke dropped me home just after eight I was sorry to see him go.

I had just changed into a tracksuit to sit and watch TV when the phone rang. I debated for a moment as to whether I'd pick it up and while I was sitting there the machine clicked into action. It was Jack. My stomach flipped. I was very aware of the sensation and it was not welcome.

I picked up the phone.

"Hi, Jack, how are you?"

"Oh hi, screening calls eh?"

"No, I was in the kitchen and the machine picked it up before I got in," I lied.

"No matter, just wanted to know if you were around?"

"Yeah, why?" I asked, guarded.

"I just dropped Ruth home and I wondered if I might have a quick chat?"

"Yeah, how did it go?"

"Not great, that's why I wanted a chat."

"Fine, come on over," I said, looking around the sitting room – it could do with a quick tidy.

"Thanks. I should be there in about ten minutes."

He hung up and I tidied, and got myself cleaned up too. I brushed my hair and wiped off a splodge of cream I'd applied with a heavy hand to a spot I had on my left cheek. I was about to reapply some make-up but stopped myself – that was stupid behaviour. Instead I settled for a dab of concealer. I looked at myself in the mirror and have to admit I was embarrassed by the way I was preening. After all, Ruth liked him and I was certainly never going to step on her toes. My head had been turned because he'd ridden in on his white horse last night, complete with hankies and a shoulder to cry on.

I closed the bedroom door and came back to the sitting-room. I was just the victim of a misplaced crush. We all know that women are famous for falling in love with their gynaecologists – now there is a misplaced crush if ever there was one. I was just one of those unfortunate people who get crushes on the wrong person, but now that I knew what it was I could fight it and I would.

Jack arrived a few minutes later and my stomach flipped again. I ignored it and offered him a cup of tea. He went into the sitting-room while I boiled the kettle. Everything was going fine until he came in behind me and spoke to me.

"Need any help?" he asked.

"Oh!" I jumped. "Sorry, no, I'm fine. It's not that difficult!"

"I brought a bottle of wine to replace the one I finished on you last night."

"Thanks, there was no need at all! Will we open it now?"

"No, not for me. I won't have a drink tonight." He came over and opened the press, took out two mugs and put them on the counter.

"Will you open that press over there and grab the HobNobs?" I asked.

He obliged and put them out on a plate for me just as the kettle boiled. He stood right next to me as I poured the water, waiting with the milk in his hand. His close proximity made me nervous for some reason and my hands shook a little as I poured. He noticed.

"You have a shake in your hand. I noticed it last night too," he announced.

"Yeah, I always have had," I lied. I had never had a shake. My hands were usually completely steady. I stopped pouring and put the kettle down. "So tell me, how did things go?"

Jack poured a little milk into his tea and took a HobNob. "It was all right, not great though."

"Really?" I picked up the HobNobs and headed to the sitting-room. "Now tell me what exactly was it you were trying to do over this drink?"

"What do you mean?" Jack asked as he followed me.

"Well, was it a last-ditch date or was it just to put that whole thing to rest?"

"Oh, put it to rest, definitely."

We sat down and I muted the TV.

"We had been dodging each other and things were left very up in the air. I just wanted to make sure we were fine. After what you said last night I wanted to sort it out."

"And did you sort it out?"

"Sort of. We're friends again and I'm delighted about that. But we're not going to go out again – we definitely put the last nail in that particular coffin."

"Are you bothered by that?"

"A little. I would have liked it to work out. I wouldn't have asked her out otherwise. But it could have gone a lot worse."

"Never mind, at least it's all done and dusted now. And at least you're not fighting the way Ray and I are."

"You and Ray are not fighting. You just have issues that you both bring to the office!" Jack laughed.

"Well, I hate the atmosphere in there. That's why I'm moving to the Fairview office."

"Are you sure about that move? I mean, if it's just to get away from Ray, is it clever?"

"It's not just to get away from him. I could do with the change and the commute-time alone is reason enough."

"I'll miss you and so will Ruth – she was just saying it tonight."

"Believe me, I'm not making a mistake. I want to leave the office and go to the new one."

"Well, good luck to you! When are you off?"

"It'll be open in three months but I think I'll be gone about a fortnight before that just to get things set up."

"Well, that'll be a night out to beat all nights out!" Jack raised his mug and clinked it with mine.

"Yes, it will," I agreed. I needed more info on the Ruth situation. "So you're glad you had the talk with Ruth?"

"Yes, very much so. It needed to be done and now we can all get back to our ordinary lives again."

"You're right – when at all possible it's best to just clean the slate and get back to normal. You tried it out, went on a date or two and it didn't work out. There's no use it trashing a great friendship just because you kissed," I replied.

"I know. It's just that cleaning the slate can be very embarrassing!" Jack laughed.

"True, but it was worth it. We can all start eating lunch again for starters."

"And how are you feeling, Amelia?"

"What?" I was surprised by the sudden change in topic.

"After last night. You were really upset."

"Oh that! I'm a lot better thanks. I just needed a good old sob and a shoulder to cry on, and your shoulder was more than adequate for the task."

"That's good to hear," Jack smiled. "So we've both sorted our lives out – it's amazing what a good cry and a chat can do for you."

"It certainly is."

Jack was looking at the dregs of his mug of tea before putting it down and looking at the muted TV in the corner. His eye was attracted by the cat's tail; he looked at it and instantly looked at his finger, still bandaged. His mouth flickered in a sort of smirk and he stood up. He headed straight over to the cat and flicked its tail, pulling his hands behind his back quickly as he did so.

"He'll scrape your face if he can't catch a finger," I told him. I'd seen this played out by dozens of visitors who thought they were faster and cleverer than the cat – a common mistake, but a mistake none the less – only Luke actually was.

Jack continued to tip the tail, and after a few successful

tips he got a little more courage and tipped the cat's back.
The cat spun his head backwards in a move that was reminiscent of *The Exorcist* and bit him hard on the back of
the hand.

"*Yeeowww!*" Jack squealed.

"I have no pity for you at all," I told him as I put my
mug of tea down, getting ready for the show-and-tell that
was about to commence: 'Look what your cat did to me.
Your cat just bit my hand' etc. These people were always
so surprised by the fact that the cat bit them.

"Dear God, that cat is the Antichrist – he just bit me.
I didn't think cats bit like that, just like a dog!" Jack presented his hand, shoving it under my nose.

"I know what it looks like," I laughed as I took in the
familiar sight of four tiny fang-dents surrounded by red
skin. "You got off lightly – sometimes there's a little cat
spit for good measure!"

Jack looked horrified. Then realising he was not getting anything like the sympathy he got the night before,
he took back his hand and followed me into the kitchen.

"Give me your hand, you big eejit!" I smiled. "Run it
under the tap there for a few minutes – is it bleeding?"

He inspected his hand. "No."

I pulled out my first-aid box and dabbed some antiseptic cream on his hand.

"Now will you leave the cat alone? He's very angry; he
has issues."

"I will. Me and that cat are finished. I don't like him."

I rinsed out my mug and put the kettle on again, Jack,
who had carried his mug out, also rinsed his. He went to

the press and pulled out the tea bags. This time, instead of taking a seat at the tiny table in the corner, we both stood at the counter pretending to watch the kettle boil. Well, I don't know about Jack but I was pretending: I was enjoying the fact that I was standing so close to him. He was tall and always smelt of freshly ironed clothes. I glanced up at him as we waited and caught his eye. My stomach flipped as I realised I wanted him to kiss me. I wanted Jack, beige Jack, to kiss me. I glanced at him again, but he was staring at the mugs in front of him, and without looking at me he asked if I had any crisps in the house.

"Crisps?"

"Yeah, I feel like a packet of Cheese and Onion," He smiled at me. There was no unspoken lust in his eyes, no Mills and Boon moment just waiting to be played out, just a childish grin and the munchies.

"Yes, I should have Pringles in the press over there, but Luke was here today and I don't know if he took them with him. He always tends to leave with a fistful of good-ies he didn't arrive with."

Jack went straight to the press and took a packet of Pringles out. He shook them and satisfied himself that there was enough in the packet to relieve his hunger. Coming back just as the kettle boiled, he leaned over me and took the kettle. He made the tea and I followed him back into the sitting-room. We sat down.

Jack announced he was going to have to go after this cup. I wasn't really listening to him; my mind was still back in the kitchen with that glance and my somersaulting stomach. I needed to be alone to arrange my thoughts on that one. This was silly. I was sure it was the guy-on-the-white-horse syndrome: he came and held my hand as I cried and I got the obligatory crush on him. But with me a crush was usually well and truly crushed if the object of the crush ever tried to kiss me. I always enjoyed the romance of being infatuated with someone, but I didn't usually enjoy the nitty-gritty of it. Him being in the house all the time, drinking tea and using the bathroom before he left. But I liked it with Jack. I liked him being here and although I did need a little space to think about what had just happened in the kitchen, I still wanted him to call again tomorrow, and the next day and the day after that.

This was going to get messy, very messy indeed.

37

The following morning I was at my desk when Ruth got in. She came straight over.

"Did Jack call in to you last night?" she asked, moving some post and leaning up against the desk.

"Yeah, how did you know?" I knew I was blushing. I hoped my make-up would cover it for me.

"He said he might give you a shout as he was passing. After he dropped me home." There was not a hint of annoyance in her voice and no death stare in her eyes.

"Did he tell you about last night?"

"He said that things were finished between you in that way."

"Yeah," she sighed heavily.

I gave her a hug and a smile.

"It'll be okay, Ruth. If it wasn't to be maybe it's best that it didn't drag on for months."

"I know. At least now we all know where we

stand," Ruth agreed.

Jack came in at that point. We both watched as he walked to his desk. I know my heart skipped a beat or two as he took off his jacket and fixed his tie.

"I shouldn't be so annoyed, but I am," said Ruth, lowering her voice to a murmur. "I mean, we hadn't been flirting any more and he wasn't exactly dancing attendance on me. Not like he used to."

"Well, look at it this way: he still really likes you as a friend. That's good, isn't it?"

"Oh yeah, thrilling. That's exactly what I was looking for, being pals with the guy I fancy."

"Things could always be worse – he might be openly flirting with someone else in the office and making your life hell," I told her, masking my bitterness with a grin.

"Oh, Amelia, I'm sorry!" Her hands shot up to her face. "I forgot about Ray and that whole situation."

"Oh, don't worry," I said, "but be thankful things aren't that bad between you and Jack."

Ruth shrugged and walked back to her desk.

Ray was no longer sending me ten emails a day – it was down to about five or six, still pulling me up on every move I made. A part of me wanted to do everything by the book and give him nothing to complain about, but a bigger part of me wanted to show him that I didn't care, even though I did. A lot. Another charming development was that Ray and Mairead had stepped up the flirting a notch and were now openly touching one another and flicking hair to beat the band. I was not as bothered by this as I had just let on, but it was a bit of a nuisance that when I did have to speak to Ray I was now looking at him over the top of Mairead's stupid head as she sat on his desk and ducked down out of the way, instead of getting up and going back to her own seat when it became apparent that other people were actually working in the office while they flirted.

I felt for Ruth. I really did. I resolved at that moment not to allow my feelings for Jack to get any stronger and to do absolutely nothing about them. Ruth was my friend, first and foremost.

I opened my emails and there were seven new ones, including one from Larry, the boss. It was about the new office. I'd have to go out and meet the new manager and some new staff next week. I should go out on Tuesday morning, he'd come too (joy of joys) and we'd get lunch out in Fairview. He was wondering if I knew anywhere that would be nice.

As I was wondering where to advise for lunch, Mairead came over with a bundle of post and handed me a few envelopes. She grinned at me, a little too widely to be honest. I smiled back at her, so fast it hadn't got time to reach my eyes before I turned away from her.

I looked at the post I was handed – CV's and letters of reference. I put my head down and began to work. My father told me once that if all else failed you should throw yourself into your job, and that it had saved many a man's sanity. In the last few weeks I was realising the wisdom of those words.

Tuesday rolled around and we met the new staff for the Fairview branch. They seemed nice and they all seemed

310

---

quite impressed with the fact that I had worked in the business for almost four years. Larry gave me a glowing reference, and on one occasion actually referred to me as "one of the company's star players". As you can imagine this was news to me and certainly an exaggeration of the truth. I just smiled, accepting all praise, and he led the Fairview branch to believe the office in Dame Street might actually go to the wall after I was gone.

We went for lunch in Trotters opposite Fairview Park and I was back at my desk just after three o'clock. All in all, a good day's work. The new staff were impressed and I was feeling all puffed up from the praise.

It was only when I got a note from Larry the following morning and realised that the new office was opening on the 13th of October that I began to panic. It was now the 3rd of September; there was very little time for sitting around gloating about the lies Larry had told. The fact was, I was moving to a new office in six weeks, I had a huge workload to tie up and I was not as great as Larry thought I was. I had to put my head down and work, so I did.

38

The weeks were going by in a blur since I said I'd take the new position. When I said yes and we were talking about the office opening in October, it seemed like years away. Now we were almost there. The autumn was not only coming, it was here. Soon winter would be closing in on us.

And then some really annoying people began to brag about having started their Christmas shopping already. Like Mum.

I was over in her house one evening, telling her for perhaps the twentieth time since I was a child that I didn't like dark chocolate and not to buy me a box of Black Magic as a Christmas-stocking filler this year.

"You always liked dark chocolate – when did you change your mind about it?" Mum questioned, her face a mixture of interest and disdain. She'd obviously already decided I was getting dark chocolate and I was probably disrupting her shopping list. She hates that.

"I have always hated dark chocolate, and don't look at me like that. It's not the end of the world!"

"When you were a child you always ate the dark chocolates out of the box. I remember it so well. I used to buy you Bourneville bars."

"You never did, Mum," I told her.

"Well, who did I buy them for then?"

"Me. I like them," Jennifer said.

Mum and I both looked at her. She'd said so little during the conversation that I had forgotten she was there.

"You?" said Mum. "Are you sure?"

"Yes, very sure. Although I can't eat them at the moment." And her cheeks flushed a little.

I noticed it but didn't really take it in. "Now, Mum, I told you I never liked it!" I said.

But Mum was still looking at Jennifer. "Why can't you eat it?"

Mum must have already bought the chocolates and was now looking for someone to unload them on.

"They make me a little ill at the moment, but I should be better soon."

"What are you talking about?" Mum asked, obviously extremely bothered about those chocolates.

We had all stopped what we were doing and were now watching Jennifer intently.

"Dark chocolate is turning my stomach just at the moment because I'm pregnant and it's not unusual to go off something you like while you're pregnant!" This time she blushed crimson and looked at me.

I stopped breathing for a moment: Jenny was pregnant. So she'd lost the battle of wills with Mike.

Mum threw her hands in the air and rushed around the table to hug her. I quashed the butterflies in my stomach and queued to hug her too.

"So what's that? Almost three months?" Mum asked.

"It's ten weeks," Jennifer replied, smiling a little but not particularly animatedly.

"So when are you due? Who else knows about it? What's been happening?" Mum was flushed with excitement and grinning like the Cheshire Cat.

"I'm due on the fourth of March, and I have no news really. No one else knows. I have to go to the hospital in three weeks for a scan and that's it."

"So what hospital are you going to? Have you seen the doctor yet?" I asked, already working out my holidays for next year.

"I'm going to Holles Street, but I really don't want to talk about it. I don't want to jinx it."

"Ah, you won't jinx anything by telling us when you're due, don't be silly!" Mum laughed. "So are you going private or what are you doing?"

"Private. I didn't care – I thought the price was very high but Mike insisted."

I was aware that Jennifer was not the glowing mum-to-be that I'd hoped she'd be. I watched her, hoping I was wrong.

"He was quite right. It is expensive but it's worth it. I heard Mary Singleton saying that Sinead paid a huge amount for her stay, but that it was great to have the room to herself and the attention when she was in the delivery room."

"Ah Mum, we all get the same attention in the delivery room, I'm sure," Jennifer said.

"Well, I think Mike was right – you should pay the extra if you have it and get the full service!" I put in.

"Anyway, you'll do this maybe twice or three times in your life, why not do it in comfort?" Mum said.

"Twice or three times? Once, Mum!" Jennifer said, not smiling.

"Ah you say that now, but wait till you see that baby – you'll want hundreds!"

"No, I won't."

"Have you been sick at all?" I asked, uneasy about the expression on Jennifer's face.

"Yes, a little bit – nothing like what they lead you to believe though. I'm not throwing up – I'm just nauseous most of the time."

"That'll pass and you'll feel a lot better!" Mum said.

Jennifer smiled. "Maybe, but I really don't think I'll be having any more. I'm not the mum type, not like you."

Mum cupped Jenny's face in her hands. "This is so wonderful. Wait till your dad hears about it. Where's Mike?"

"He's in work, but he'll be over later to pick me up. I'm not allowed to get the bus or walk anywhere on my own."

"Well, that's only right – you wouldn't be walking from here to Malahide, now would you?" I told her.

"No, but I'd like to be allowed to walk to the shop!"

"He's just taking care of you – that's lovely. Anyway, nine months is a long time. He'll get used to it and you'll be allowed to walk anywhere you like."

"I'd better be. He's driving me mad!"

"Tell me everything, darling! I want to know from the beginning!" Mum was sitting with a mug of tea in her hand, ready for the full story.

"We talked about it and Mike wanted a baby, so we decided to go ahead and have one. So here we are," Jenny shrugged.

I watched Jenny's face – was there any trace of pride or excitement in her eyes?

"And just like that, a baby. You're blessed. That's truly wonderful," Mum said, tears gleaming in her eyes. My heart went out to Mum – she was so excited and she was right. It doesn't happen just like that for everyone. Jennifer should try to smile.

She must have read my mind because she smiled at Mum as she replied, "Yeah, just like that."

Dad came home from work and appeared in the kitchen. He took one look at Mum wiping tears from her cheeks and immediately thought there was something seriously wrong, and that Luke was at the bottom of it.

"What's he done now?" he asked, looking from one face to the next at the table.

"Nothing! Jenny has some news!" Mum grinned, still crying.

Dad looked at Jenny and then at me. I was grinning too so Dad began to relax and smiled around the room.

"What? What's the news?"

"I'm pregnant," Jenny said, again no visible smile on her face.

Dad threw his arms around her and rocked her for a moment. "That's the best news I've had for ages, love!"

She pulled away, nodding and flicking her hair a little. She was very dismissive of him and of us all.

"Smile, Jennifer. It's good news!" I told her as I could hold it in no longer.

Jennifer shot me a dagger look. "I am thrilled but I've had ten weeks to get used to it, so I'm not grinning about it any more."

Part of me believed her, but the bigger part of me still wanted to kick her in the shins and tell her to grow up.

39

The boredom that is our office progressed quietly enough over the next few weeks. I was encouraged by the fact that I would soon be leaving, encouraged that is, until I saw the stack of paperwork on my desk each morning. Some of this I knew I could leave behind but there were loose ends, such as people who had been on our books for a year or more. They would be sent for interviews, would get the job, then ring a fortnight later to say they had left and were back on the market. In most cases they would claim the boss was rude or the office too constricting, that a nine o'clock start was too early for any self-respecting artist – oh yeah, they were all looking to work while they chased bigger and better rainbows. The number of people in their late twenties, walking around Dublin still believing they will be the next Bono or Colin Farrell if only they can find the right café to sit in until they get discovered! This, despite the fact they haven't a note in their heads, written a word of a song, nor ever even heard of the Gaiety Stage School. Anyway, there are plenty of them out there and I was lumbered with coaxing them into attending interviews, taking the job and staying there long enough to get trained and make a few friends. There was also the cascade of new CV's and letters received each day. These in turn had to checked and each person interviewed to get them on to our books, before we in turn tried to get them on to someone else's books, in the shape of a permanent job.

I remember when I started that job, thinking how rewarding the whole process would be. I thought people would remain in the job you so kindly found for them. I thought they might even thank you for the work you put in, in finding them an interview and setting it up for them. But sadly no. What's more there was never even a backward glance as they walked out of the office, except the girls who practically gave themselves whiplash when they noticed Ray. I was trying to tidy things up as much as possible for Emily who was taking over my position – she was currently working around the office, filing, typing and faxing for other people. So I really wanted to leave things so that she could slip into my role and carry on working. That meant I was working like a slave to try to get lots of people interviewed and on the books, then farm them out to other interviews and get as many of them jobs as I could before I left. It entailed a lot of late nights. Leaving the office with the cleaners every day for a week was not helping my self-esteem, especially when they talked to each other about the office staff and how filthy the office was, in front of me as if I was not there. I began to feel very guilty about throwing away any rubbish and would get down on my knees and pick up crumbs from under my desk at the end of the day. The cleaners would arrive about 5:30, so every night just before they were due I would disappear under my desk and begin to clean. I'm sure the others in the office thought I was losing the plot, so I became sneaky. I would wait anxiously until they had all gone home and then get to my knees under the desk to clean up for the cleaners.

As I knelt there one Tuesday night a thought struck me. Was this in fact a mind-game played by cleaners on the rest of the world? The stories of people cleaning the house before the cleaner arrives are legendary. The cleaners knew they had the upper hand, that people were terrified of being seen as unclean, so would clean the house or office before they arrived, thus halving and perhaps eliminating the work altogether. Office-workers have all gone home by the time the cleaners arrive in the office, and I presume most people would be out when the cleaner visits their home. So the cleaner may well be sitting watching *Oprah* and drinking our mineral water and we have no one to blame but ourselves: we have after all been shamed into cleaning up ourselves and then paying someone else to come in and take the praise.

I stopped what I was doing and looked at the pathetic few crumbs and pieces of fluff in the palm of my hand. I could feel the prickle of heat on my cheeks. This was either from the exertion of picking up the crumbs or the embarrassment of finally realising what a fool I was. I don't actually know. I sat back up at my desk, still cupping the crumbs in my hand. I pondered throwing them back on the ground as an act of rebellion, but who was I kidding? I threw them in the bin, straightened the papers on my desk, fixed my hair and washed my hands.

I was so busy that the time flew by, and before I knew it or was ready for it the time was up and the new office was opening. I was to leave on the tenth of October and it was now the ninth. All my work was finished. I had interviewed and registered a grand total of twenty-three people in the last fortnight, the paperwork was up to date and various people on our books were to be found around the city adjusting their ties or the hair-clips as they readied themselves for interviews.

I was sitting at my desk at about 10:30 when a few things struck me. The first was that I had no work. I had worked so hard over the last few weeks that there really was nothing left, not a "t" to be crossed and not an "i" to be dotted. As the thought struck me I sighed and realized that every muscle in my body was tense. I had to relax. I couldn't be this tense starting a new job. I'd go in wound up like a spring and most likely snap at all around me for a fortnight, and by the time I'd relax the new staff would hate me. I'd have made my bed and would be forced to lie in it until my sixty-fifth birthday, and then noone would show up at my retirement party and I'd be sitting in a room all by myself holding my gold watch and smiling at my family, telling them that the guys at office must be working late. We would be sitting there until the catering staff began to pack up around us and the balloons we'd put up were beginning to deflate. That is how much they would hate me in the new office. Dear God, sometimes I can go off on a complete tangent and stress myself out until I can't actually breathe. This was one of those times. So much for relaxing myself.

My second thought was not much better. I realised that I liked working in here, I mean really liked it. Ruth, Jack, Emily and to an extent even Ray – I liked them and they liked me. I was comfortable and I enjoyed the chat. What if all the staff at the new office were boring? What if they hated me? This might be the worst mistake I ever made. What if it was and I wanted to come back? Would I be allowed? I wished I'd asked Larry that before I accepted the job. Damn me and damn the lure of a fatter pay cheque. Damn it to hell!

I had to push these thoughts from my mind; it was just my subconscious as usual trying to trip me up when I was taking a chance, putting myself in the path of a new opportunity. Without fail I would undermine myself with thoughts of what could go wrong. This time I was on to myself and I would not be swayed.

Just as my resolve was steadying itself Ruth came over to my desk holding a little gift-wrapped box.

"This is for you. It's just from me. To say goodbye and I'll miss you," Ruth handed me the box.

"Ruth, what's this? You shouldn't have," I smiled as I opened the box to reveal a small bottle of Ghost perfume, my favourite. "Ruth, this is really expensive!"

"What of it!" Ruth waved it away but her voice was cracking and even as I was hugging her I knew I was probably squeezing a few tears from her and she wouldn't thank me for it. I looked at her and right enough she was wiping her eye with her sleeve. "Stop it, don't make me cry. I'll take it back if you do!"

"Out of my cold dead hands!" I told her, putting the bottle of perfume back in its box and into my bag.

"Well, I just wanted to give it to you myself, before the big presentation and all that."

"What big presentation?" I asked, my heart thumping in my chest. I knew there'd be a farewell clap on the back, but a presentation?

"We couldn't let you go without a slide show of all your best bits now, could we?" Ruth laughed.

"Ha-ha, very funny. You are joking, aren't you?" There is a projector and every now and again they do make promotional videos in the office, not to mention the video camera that's produced every Christmas at the office party and played for us, as a treat, the day we break up for Christmas. I have been in one or two in my time, and my blood was running cold as I thought of it.

"I might be, but then again, I might not!" Ruth hurried back to her desk before I could catch her.

I looked around. Was there anyone I could trust to tell the truth? I looked at Jack's desk – he wasn't there. I looked for Ray – he was gone too. Something was going on. Jack came out of an interview room and headed to his desk. He looked at Ruth and then over at me, the tiniest grin playing on his face. Ray came out of the same room

323

about three minutes later. He looked directly at me and winked. Behind him Mairead came out. Mairead too? She looked a little flustered, her hair tossed at the back, but she was grinning. I was now wondering what the hell all three of them were at in the interview room. I was also sorry I hadn't noticed them all going in – you can see into those rooms from the bathroom door. And I would have had a good nose as to what they were doing.

As things stood, the mind boggled.

I shouldn't have bothered. As it turned out, the next day all was revealed.

I arrived into work on my final day in the Dame Street office. It was a mild day for October, grey sky with the sun breaking through. The trees rustled in the wind and I was happy my life was turning a corner. For starters, Jack would not be sitting just in my line of vision and I would hopefully forget about him, no doubt helped by the fact that I would fall hopelessly in love with some other guy who was equally off limits. I might try my hand at falling for a married man this time. I mean bisexual men, men already taken by my friends were all so old hat for me – a married one might be just the thing. Lord knows I would never pick an eligible bachelor if there was an ineligible one in the vicinity.

I walked into the office and stopped dead in my tracks. My desk was covered, and I do mean covered, in cans of Diet Coke and balloons. I walked over and picked up a can – at least I tried to pick one up. It wouldn't budge. I tried another, then another. It appeared that someone had managed to stick about thirty empty Coke cans permanently to my desk. Then they had stuck balloons all over my computer and chair. I stood looking at the desk for a few minutes before Jack came in and walked over to survey the damage.

"Who did this?" I asked, lost in amazement.

"Ruth, Emily, Louise and me."

"How long did it take?" I asked, trying again to pick up a can. "And where did all the cans come from?"

"It took about an hour and the cans came from the recycle bin," he grinned. "OK, we'd better get them off before the boss comes in."

"They won't come off."

"Sure they will!" He leaned over and pulled a can. It didn't move. He tugged it again, still nothing. He looked at me, his eyes wide. "Shit! We'll have to pay for a new desk!"

I started to laugh at the situation.

"Stop laughing! Help get them off – get some water maybe!" Jack's tone was urgent. We were still the only ones in the office but the others would be in soon.

"I don't think water will help. What did you stick them with? And also, *why* exactly?"

"They kept falling over when anyone walked by, and it seemed like a good idea."

"To whom?"

"What?" Jack was still pulling for all he was worth.

"Who thought it was a good idea?" I pulled at another can.

"Steve said it first, but we thought it was a plan. We

got Evo-Stick."

"Well, it certainly stuck!" I laughed.

We pulled for all we were worth and finally one of the cans came away, but the veneer on the desk did too. We stared at each other in silence, wide-eyed like two rabbits in headlights.

"Jesus!" Jack said and put the can back down.

"What the hell are we gonna do?" I asked, not laughing any more.

"Where's the nearest hardware shop?" Jack asked.

"Capel Street?"

"Go out quick and tell them what we've done – they might be able to recommend something. Get a few of those scrapers – you know, the ones they use for scraping wallpaper!"

"Right. You used Evo-Stick?"

"Yeah, from a tube!" Jack shouted after me.

The man behind the counter in Caple Street laughed so hard I thought he was going to have a heart attack. He told the young guy stacking the shelves and they both laughed.

"Yeah, well, it wasn't me," I said.

"Then why are you here buying the paraphernalia to take it off?" he asked, still grinning.

Good question. I wasn't too sure about that one.

"It was my desk," I replied curtly.

This made them cry with laughter. I realised before they pointed it out that I was a fool to be running around town looking for and paying for something to remove Evo-Stick I hadn't put there.

Finally the man behind the counter stopped laughing long enough to dry his eyes and point me towards some bottles in the corner.

"Try that, love. It's meant to remove tar off the streets. It might just work!"

"Thanks," I said walking over and picking up the bottle. It was one of those bottles of potion you see advertised on TV. You know the type: this tiny bottle will remove all the tar from the M1, from Dublin to Belfast. And as if that wasn't reason enough to buy it, if you order now they'll throw in a second bottle and special cloth that'll make taking the tar off the road even easier. All for the amazingly low price of fifteen euro.

I bought it and ran back to the office, praying that it would live up to its own hype.

When I got there Jack was waiting.

"Thank God!" he said as he took the bag and took out the bottle, doing a double-take as the size of it became apparent.

"It's concentrated; there's enough there to last a year," I told him, quoting from the placard that was above the display.

"Let's just pray it works."

We got to work on the desk. Ruth, Louise and Steve helped. Thankfully the stuff worked. We got the cans off the desk and no more veneer went missing. This stuff could actually take the tar off the road by the looks of things. I was impressed. There was also a good half bottle left when we finished.

The rest of the day was a subdued affair. Maybe it was

due to the can disaster or maybe because they were saving the best till last. About 3:30 I got a phone call asking me to please come into Interview Room 3 to meet with Personnel and have an exit interview. I was a little taken aback by this. I'd been led to believe this wasn't going to happen because I was transferring to another office not out of the company. These exit interviews were renowned for being awful. A false smile or word and they took back every nice word they'd ever said about you in their reference. This is why I asked if I was having one and when they said no, I didn't prepare.

So here I was looking blindly around me, panic-stricken, hoping someone would help me get a sentence in order. There was no one around; they were all gone off somewhere in my hour of need. How typical.

I stood up on shaky legs and made my way to the Interview Room. When I got there the room was packed, but not a soul from Personnel was to be seen. Just everyone from the office, crammed into this one small room. Seriously, there were serious health and safety issues here. The room was designed for four people to sit around a desk. There were about fifteen of us, a desk, a television and video all crammed in at the moment. I stood at the door, wide-eyed. My mouth opened and shut but nothing came out. I must have looked for all the world like a fish with camera fright.

Larry stepped forward and welcomed me into the room.

"Amelia, come in. Shut the door. We've been waiting for you!" He grinned at me. Putting his arm around my shoulder, he walked me further into the room and shut the door.

He produced a chair, again covered in balloons, and told me to sit down and relax. I sat down, looking at the balloons and ensuring I didn't burst any. That, I believe, would have been social suicide, even at this late stage. I looked over my shoulder at the coloured balloons and wondered how many there were. It was a small chair and it was absolutely covered in the things. It suddenly occurred to me what Ray, Mairead and Jack were up to in the office yesterday, blowing balloons up and here was me thinking the worst of all three of them.

Then came the real showstopper: Larry made a quick speech. He chronicled my life in the office from my beginning as office junior three years ago to my leaving today, covered in glory. He wished me success in my new job, thanked me for taking it on and told everyone that I would be an asset to the Fairview branch and very much missed in the Dame Street one. I swear to God if I had come into the room late, I'd never have imagined he was talking about me.

Finally came the pièce de résistance: they had edited every office video I'd ever had the pleasure of appearing in and there was a twenty-minute montage of me. There was me doing mock interviews for camera in a training video, me at my desk working hard in a promotional video and about fifteen shots of me at various stages of intoxication at Christmas parties. Plenty of make-up, beautiful hair, no tolerance for alcohol, bless me!

I cringed silently. In some of the footage I looked very

well, very young and skinny, but as the tape rolled on I was getting fatter and older, but my clothes and hair were getting nicer, so that was a plus.

The piece ended with me and Ruth dancing a jig of sorts in the office accompanied by our own rendition of Riverdance. We were humming the music for ourselves and adding in *dum, dum, dums* here and there as drums were needed. I had no recollection of the night in question, but there it was in full colour for all to see.

When it ended the office clapped and I blushed profusely. Larry again made a small good-luck type speech and they presented me with an Arnotts voucher for one hundred euro. While I was thanking everyone and kissing various cheeks around the office they opened the customary warm white wine and we drank it from plastic cups. All in all it was a great goodbye and I felt I would miss this office and the people. Even Ray. After all, as Larry pointed out, on average we spend more quality time with our office colleagues than with our families. Scary thought, it certainly made everyone in the tiny interview room look at those around them in new light.

The work day over; we walked the hundred or so feet to the Mercantile Bar. A corner had been cordoned off for us and we were quick to occupy the space. The drink was flowing and the mood was jovial. So many people came over and wished me well. I had no idea some of them knew who I was. People were hugging me and as the night progressed the good wishes were more poetic and heartfelt – that was before the person would forget my name at the all-important moment or lean over and ask me who it was who was leaving again?

Jack came over just before eleven.

"Hello there," he smiled down at me.

"Oh, Jack, hi!" I grinned up from my seat, my head spinning a little from the drink.

I pulled his trouser leg to indicate he was to sit down. He hunkered in front of me and pushed my fringe from my eyes. That was a really good idea. I had thought the bar was very dimly lit; it now appeared I had hair in front of my eyes all the time.

"There you are. I can see you now!" I giggled.

"Yeah, listen, I have to get going."

"No!" I threw my arms around him. "You can't! It's only early!"

"It's almost eleven," Jack pointed out. "I want to grab the last bus. We've been drinking since four o'clock and I have to mind Lily tomorrow,"

"Who?"

"My niece Lily, and I'd better not go hungover. She's four and you really need your wits about you."

"Did I tell you Jenny is pregnant?" I slurred.

"Yeah you did. That's fantastic news," Jack tried to stand up.

"Oh, Jack, please stay!" I pulled his arm to keep him where he was.

"No, honestly, I have to go but I was going to say that I'd call in one night next week maybe?"

"Oh, OK." I felt better; I still didn't want him to go though.

"Will I ring you?" he asked, finally standing up.

"Yeah, that'd be great," I grinned up.

Jack put his arms out for a hug. I obliged and hugged him. He smelt like smoke but under that was the familiar smell of freshly ironed clothes. He pulled away and smiled at me for a moment before he left. He grabbed his coat, waved at Ruth and was out the door in a flash. I stood watching him leave. God, he was lovely. The type of guy who creeps up on you – you think he's nice and polite and then you wake up one day head over heels in love with him. And he's done nothing different. He hasn't been extra nice to you or given you a lingering glance over the water cooler. He's just been himself: polite, good-mannered and unassuming. And you've fallen for him hook, line and sinker. And now he was walking out the door and out of my life. The door swung behind him and he was gone.

I looked at Ruth, expecting her to be watching the door as well. She wasn't, she was talking to Mairead and draining the last of her bottle of Miller into a glass. She glanced at the bar as her bottle emptied and carried on talking. I turned back to my table and looked at my half empty glass. I had been drinking since four; maybe I should get a Coke this time. Ray came over and tipped me on the shoulder.

"Can I buy you a drink, for old times' sake?" he said, his baby-blue eyes dancing.

As much as I hated him, he was still irresistible.

"Go on then, just the one," I replied, smiling to let him know bygones were bygones.

"Bacardi and Coke?" He pointed at my glass and I

nodded, all thoughts of the Coke on its own disappearing.

He reappeared with my drink and scooted me up the couch so he could sit beside me.

"I'm sorry we left it on such a bad note," he said.

"Yeah," I agreed.

"I shouldn't have lied to you about my history. I knew what I was doing and that was nasty." He was looking at me from beneath his eyelashes. "I think there's something wrong with me."

"What?" I wasn't sure what was happening here.

"I think I may be a compulsive liar. I lie to everyone; it's not just you. Does that make you feel better?"

"No, not really." I sat up a little straighter, looking at him more closely.

"No?"

"Absolutely not. Not content with concealing the fact you're gay, now you tell me you also concealed the fact you're a compulsive liar?"

"I'm not gay, I'm bisexual. Big difference," he corrected me.

"You're greedy, that's what you are," I dismissed him.

"Anyway, what makes you think you're a compulsive liar now?"

He began to laugh and announced. "I don't think I'm a compulsive liar – I was joking! I said it just to get a rise out of you! Jesus, you are so wound up! You're going to die of a heart attack before you're forty!"

"You really do defy belief, Ray," I told him, turning my back on him.

"Oh, get a life, Amelia. I was joking. So we dated and

it didn't work out. Get over it. I did!"

"I am over it. If you'd been honest with me from the word go we'd have gone our separate ways and no one would have cared. You lied all along, not just about being bi – all that stuff about your parents leaving you in boarding-school. They weren't being nasty to you. You settled in just fine. So did Paul. There was no huge drama in your schooling. Your parents are really nice people. You should be ashamed of yourself telling that pack of lies about them. What kind of a freak tells lies about their own mother?"

"A compulsive liar," Ray smiled. He was not taking this seriously and I wondered about how drunk he was.

"Go away, Ray. You wreck my head," I said and stood up to go.

"Ah, you're no fun!" Ray complained as he stood up to let me out. As I walked away he called after me, "So no chance of a nightcap back at yours?" and then dissolved into laughter.

I wondered about a cutting remark, but what was the point? I'd spent the last six months throwing insults at him across the office, and the only one who'd been upset by it was me. As much as I pretended to like a good row, the truth was I hated them. I always took to heart what the other person said, and people say dreadful things when their backs are against the wall. Ray was awful and a clean break would help me. As he said, I was too wound up and Ray was the one who wound me up.

Ruth came over; she'd seen me walking through the crowd.

"What's up?" she asked.

"Nothing," I smiled, but I was tired.

"It's not nothing – what was Ray saying to you?"

"He bought me a drink and I thought he wanted to clear the air, but he didn't."

Ruth steered me toward the bathroom. "What did he want?"

"Just to tell me another pack of lies and laugh at me."

I could feel myself begin to cry. I hated this. Lately when I got too drunk I became emotional and cried over everything and anything. I blinked the tears away. I was not about to exit my leaving bash in tears. Not without good reason anyway, and Ray was not a good reason.

"What did he tell you?" Ruth took my arm and led me to an alcove.

"He said at first that he wanted to buy me a drink for old times' sake, and then he said he was sorry that he was a compulsive liar."

"He was lying about buying you a drink?"

"No, he bought the drink," I waved the glass in front of me. "Then he said he was joking, that he's not in fact a compulsive liar. He was saying it to get a laugh out of me. I just didn't understand him."

"You didn't understand him? I don't think anyone understands him!"

"Well, anyway, he said I was too wound up and that I'd have a heart attack if I didn't loosen up. Then he shouted after me he supposed that a nightcap back at mine was out the question."

"Is he on drugs?" Ruth asked and it occurred to me that

this was a plausible answer.

"I have no idea, but I'm just sick of being the butt of all his bloody jokes. He takes it out of me – every time we're in contact he leaves me feeling shattered."

"Look, he's gone now – after tonight he's out of your life. And I was talking to Mairead just now. It turns out she's been seeing him outside of work for the last three weeks and she knows all about his 'switching sides'. She doesn't care. She says she's just having a bit of fun and that he's no great shakes in bed. I think he'll get his comeuppance soon enough there."

I half shrugged, half nodded. I was not the least bit interested in Mairead. "Do you like Mairead?" I asked Ruth.

"She a child. She's only nineteen. I had no idea people had full-time jobs at that age. I certainly didn't."

"No, those of us who went to college weren't in work at nineteen," I sniffed.

"Oh, *miaow!*" Ruth laughed. "Saucer of milk coming up!"

"I know," I laughed. I had heard myself and I knew I was being mean. "Sorry, I just don't like her. She wears ridiculous clothes in work and she'd always packing more and more make-up on her cheeks."

"We all know what she's like. Don't take it personally," Ruth advised. "The younger generation seems to be wearing belly-tops in December as a matter of course!"

"And they spend all their time combing their blonde hair and looking in their compact mirrors!"

"Have you noticed they all seem to be blonde?" Ruth laughed.

"Yes, where has this generation of Irish blondes come from? Are we not all meant to have brown hair and fair skin with freckles?" I laughed.

"Yeah! No more Roisin Dubh's walking down Grafton Street these days!"

"Absolutely!" I giggled.

"So I saw you looking after Jack tonight when he left," Ruth said as we walked up the stairs back to the bar.

"Who, me?" My heart lurched. I knew I had been. I just didn't think Ruth had seen me.

"Yes, you. What's the situation there?"

"Nothing. He was just apologising because he had to leave early."

"Oh my God, your tongue was hanging out for him!" Ruth laughed.

"No, it wasn't."

"Oh, come on. I was looking at you."

"You were not. You were talking to Mairead," I told her, instantly realising I was admitting I was watching out for her reaction.

Ruth copped it straight away. "Oh, was I now!" She grinned. "And how would you know if you weren't watching for my reaction?"

"I was just curious!" I laughed, tipping my empty glass at her, gesturing at the bar and turning to leave her.

"Nice try, I'm coming with you." She followed me through the crowd.

I ordered my drink as she carried on her interrogation.

337

"So carry on. Let's see how much more of your foot you can stuff in your mouth," she said, smiling at me over her bottle.

"I have not put my foot in my mouth," I insisted.

"OK, let's get one thing out in the open: you fancy Jack," she announced.

My mouth opened and shut several times before I could get anything out. The truth was, I wasn't sure whether to agree or try to argue.

"He is lovely," I conceded. "But I know you like him, so there's no way anything is going to happen."

"I used to like him," Ruth smiled. "Past tense."

"You're only saying that! Don't worry. I won't touch him. I don't know how or why I suddenly got to like him, but I won't do anything about it. I swear!" My hand was actually resting on my heart as I spoke.

"Please don't make promises you have no hope of keeping." Ruth turned and walked back to the table.

I ran after her. "No, Ruth, I do intend to keep it. I'll never see Jack again. I would never stand in your way!"

"What are you talking about? Jack and I are history. I have no further interest in him. Anyway, he's fancied you for years. As soon as he realises you fancy him, he'll be in like Flynn."

"He fancies me?" My face lit up. I know it did as my cheeks instantly ached from grinning.

"Are you really that unobservant?" Ruth laughed.

"I must be. I thought he fancied you."

"Briefly, while you were with that Ray thing."

"I thought you really liked him!"

"I did. He was lovely. You know that yourself. He really is the best. But he's not my type."

"So what is your type?"

"No one type, just not Jack." She smiled. "He is lovely – he's just not lovely enough for me."

I looked after her as she headed into the crowd, glancing over her shoulder at me. She was laughing. I followed her again. This time I caught up with her at the table back where the work crowd was thinning out.

"What do you mean 'not lovely enough'?" I asked.

"Look, I'm not sure how far it's going to go, so I wasn't going to say anything yet, but I have a new squeeze."

"Oh my God! What's his name?"

"His name is Chris and he's gorgeous!"

"How long? Where did you meet and how did it happen?" I asked, shoving a load of coats out of the way as I made room for both of us to sit down.

Ray came over, put his drink on the table and ran his fingers across my shoulder to get my attention. I looked around at him, annoyed at the interruption.

"What?" I asked.

"Hi there, you!" He smiled into my face.

"Hi, Ray, I'm busy." I turned away and back to Ruth.

"Go on, tell all!"

"You really are a great-looking girl," Ray continued.

"Did I ever tell you that?"

I looked around again, and confirmed it was in fact me he was talking to.

"Ray, I'm talking to Ruth about something. Can you leave us alone?"

"Sure, what are we discussing?" He leaned over us.

"It's private. Can you go away?" I said, trying to be polite, not wanting to antagonise him too much

"Look, there's Mairead. Go over to her," Ruth put in.

"No, I don't want to. I want to talk to Amelia." Ray smiled at me and ran his hand over my hair.

"Stop that!" I turned back to him. "Ray, please. This is private."

"What, Ruth, what are you admitting to? Let me guess. You're actually a man?" Ray began to laugh.

"Get lost, Ray!" Ruth replied.

"No, seriously, let me guess. You're pregnant and it's Jack's? No, that couldn't be it – old Jackie wouldn't have it in him." Ray pondered for a moment. "You're leaving the office to pursue a career on the stage?"

Without even looking at one another, both Ruth and I replied as one: "Fuck off, Ray!"

He stopped laughing and looked at us. "What?"

"You heard us. Sling your hook," Ruth told him.

"Well, fine. If that's how you feel about it!" And he was gone.

That would be the last time I spoke to Ray Donnelly. He was a bad egg and I wouldn't be sorry.

I turned back to Ruth. "Tell me!"

"Well, it's really early days. I'm not calling him my boyfriend or anything, but he's really nice. I met him at a thirtieth birthday party I was at. Remember my friend Gillian's birthday?"

"Yeah, that was in August." I counted the months.

"Two months ago? You're seeing a *buachaill* for two

340

months and you never said anything?"

"No, not two months and we're really only getting together now. I kissed him the night of the party and he said he'd ring, but, of course, he didn't. He called about a fortnight later and I was really stand-offish with him. But he explained that his father had had a heart attack and they were all in St Vincent's for the last ten days and, of course, nothing else mattered to him at the time."

"Oh shit, you really couldn't say anything to that, could you?" I agreed.

"No, but thankfully I hadn't said too much. So anyway, his dad is fine, out of hospital and all that. So he was really sorry about the delay, but would I like to meet for a drink?"

"When was that?"

"About four weeks ago, so it's really early days. We still arrange another date before we part. There's no such thing as 'see you tomorrow'!"

"That is fantastic news!" I laughed, hugging her.

"I know, I am thrilled and he is gorgeous. Quite literally tall, dark and handsome."

"Wow, we must meet up to give me a look at him."

"In time, my friend, in time!" Ruth grinned. She flicked her hair and took a mouthful of beer. "Anyway, the main thing is Jack is all yours, I have no interest in him. I bagged a real looker!"

"I think you're being nice," I laughed. "I think you are, but I'm not sure!!"

"I'm being nice!" Ruth laughed. "I'm being nasty to poor old Jack, but nice to you!"

"Well, thanks! I can have Jack then?"

"With my blessing!" Ruth held her drink up to mine and we clinked them in agreement.

"Thanks, but I wish I'd known that about two hours ago!"

"Never mind. I'll drop a few well-timed hints next week," Ruth nodded sagely. "You leave it all to me."

"Please, don't make me look like a loser!"

"Trust me, I'm good at this!"

Just then the bar lights flashed and we were told to drink up and get out.

Twenty minutes later we were being asked about where our homes were located, a further ten later we were standing outside the bar, cold and sobering up far too quickly as taxi after taxi sailed by with empty back seats or one person smiling smugly from the back window.

I stood closing my flimsy coat over myself. What was I thinking, buying such a light little raincoat, in Dublin in October? So what if it was a fabulous pale blue with those pretty flowers on the lining? It simply didn't cut it as a real raincoat, or as any kind of shield from the cold weather. As for the scarf I was wearing, well, just don't get me started. It was crocheted with lots of balls and knots in it. These balls and knots were attached to one another by string. Again, not the smartest item to be wearing on a cold October night. I was freezing cold, my coat was just that bit too tight across my chest and the buttons gapped. I was again reminded of the sad fact that I am not now, and never really was, a thin girl. I cursed myself for letting my guard down with my food intake. I had allowed

342

myself to become a "plump" girl again.

I had heard it with my own ears just last week but I had chosen to ignore it. Now, my coat not fitting and my heart heavy, I had to admit my Aunt Jean had a point.

She had been in the house last weekend and I'd overheard my mother and her talking about all of us cousins.

They were sitting in the kitchen looking at photos and discussing each of us in turn. There was a photo of me and Jenny sitting beside one another. Mum was cooing over how pretty we both were. Jean was tight-lipped; she usually is when someone else's child is being praised.

"Look how dark Amelia's hair is – I never noticed how dark she is," Mum was saying. "Of course Daddy was very dark all his life, wasn't he?"

"Yes, he was. Everyone is always saying Keelan is just like him. Both colouring and looks." Jean looked at the photo again.

"Yeah, Keelan is the image of him – she definitely has his features, his nose in particular."

"Are you saying Keelan has a big nose?"

"Not at all, she has Daddy's nose, that's all," Mum smiled.

Mum and Jean are old hands at giving a compliment with one hand and taking it back with the other.

"A big nose," Jean replied.

"I never said she had a big nose. You obviously think she does, but I never did," Mum said. "Like I said, she has Daddy's nose."

"Keelan is very pretty, you said so yourself." Jean was feeling wounded, and rightly so.

"Of course she is. I never said she wasn't. You said she looked like the Kilbrides and I agreed with you. For that matter I think Amelia is getting more like them as she gets older – the eyes and facial expressions."

"The Kilbrides were never heavy people, Maggie," Jean said, putting the photos down on the table.

"Heavy? Who's heavy now, Jean?" Mum's back was rising as she spoke.

"Amelia was never a slim child and she's a plump girl now."

"She's maybe a little plump, but she's not heavy. Anyway, she's lost a lot of weight doing that WeightWatchers. She's very slim now."

"Oh look, it was just a comment. I love Amelia, she's a ticket she really is, but I did notice she was heavy at that party," Jean was backing down a little.

They always knew when it was time to take a tactical step back. It's a time-honoured tradition and a good battle, fairly fought, is actually a thing of great beauty. Like a mating dance of birds with beautiful plumage.

"She was plump, but she's not any more," Mum said, more under her breath than to Jean.

I had heard the full exchange and the only part that stood out in my mind was that Mum had agreed I was plump. Which actually meant I was heavy. Mum would never have allowed the word 'heavy' to escape her lips. Not about one of her own children anyway – one of Jean's kids was fair game. I had been plump but I wasn't any more. That was not the compliment it seemed.

As usual I had gone back to my apartment and done

what I always do. I ate like a pig and wallowed in my self-pity. I opened a bottle of wine, ate a packet of crisps and then went in search of anything else I could possibly eat. I found a Mars Bar – I have no idea where it came from, they are not a favourite of mine and I never buy them. But it was in the press waving at me, sending out flares and making a flag out of its wrapper to be sure I saw it. So I rescued it, fed it some fluids and took it with me back to the sitting-room. Once there I betrayed its trust and ate it.

I drank two glasses of wine, big ones that meant half the bottle was gone. I looked around me; my stomach was round and full, the bottle was half empty. Yes, half empty; this was not a glass-half-full situation. The table was strewn with empty wrappers, a corkscrew and a broken cork. There were crumbs on the table and the floor around my feet and I was ashamed. I hated myself for doing it but here I was again, gorging and then 'guilting' about it. I never allowed myself to become so guilty I threw it back up; instead I would just sit and whine to myself about the amount of weight I had just gained.

Then the sugar would wear off and I'd be hungry again. Then I'd go to the press again with the thought "might as well be hanged for a sheep as a lamb". This was foot-shooting mentality at its best, but it allowed me to eat one last bar of chocolate before I gave it all up again and ate only green vegetables for the rest of my life.

Now here I was, three weeks later, weight gained, and coat not closing. I was cold, a little sick from alcohol and now it appeared fat too. I pulled the scarf to try to lengthen it, I heard a rip but upon inspection there was no hole forming, no new one anyway. I sighed, hugging myself for warmth and also to keep others from seeing my ill-fitting coat. I always hated this part of the evening, but then again, this is not part of the evening. It's part of the following morning – this and the hangover.

40

The new office opened its doors on Monday morning at
nine. I got there at 8:30 and was met by three other staff
members as I walked in the door.

I nodded greetings at them and headed to my desk. All
our desks had our names stuck to the front of them, a bit
like starting school again. I wondered about drawing
flowers on my plaque.

A guy in a dark grey suit and pale pink shirt sidled over
to me. "Hi there, you're Amelia?"

"Yes, pleased to meet you," I smiled. "What's your
name?"

"Jeff Ryan. Sorry, but I have to say, you look really
familiar."

Dear God, is it not early days to be flirting in the
office? Not to mention early in the morning?

"I do? Wow!" I said, trying to sound noncommittal. I
really didn't want to get caught up in any office flirtation
this early in the game.

"Yeah, and this is not a pick-up line. I think we have met before. Do you live in Drumcondra?" Jeff was standing back, away from me with his hands in his pockets, no flirtation in his body language at all. I sat forward a little.

"Drumcondra? Yeah, I used to." I was now wondering who he was and why I didn't recognise him.

"Have you a sister called Jennifer, with blonde hair?"

"Yes, how do you know Jenny?"

"I don't know her, but I knew you for a while."

"Really? How?" I asked, blushing slightly the way you always do when someone knows you and you have no recollection of them at all.

"I was a friend of Gary Redmond."

"Oh my God, Gary!" I laughed. I had gone out with Gary for three weeks around the time of my Inter Cert and for some reason we were linked for years afterwards. People would meet me and say "Oh, you're the one who went out with Gary!" We never saw one another after we split up, and it was hardly a heart-wrenching break-up. I got a friend to call into his house and dump him for me while I waited around the corner. He sent word back that it was fine; he was going to dump me later that night anyway. We didn't trade insults; we just agreed that it was best for everyone in that case and went back to our respective lives. For some reason our names were linked though and here it was again. Almost sixteen years later I was being remembered as the girl who once dated Gary Redmond.

"How is Gary?" I asked.

"I have no idea. We lost touch after school. He got married last year but other than that I haven't a clue."

348

"Wow, he got married?" Even as I was saying it I knew it sounded ridiculous. We were both thirty at this stage – why was it so amazing that one of us was married? "Are you married?" I asked Jeff.

"No, not yet." He smiled. "You?"

"No," I smiled in return and that was it. The conversation was over and we were left, me sitting and him standing in an awkward silence. Smiling at one another and nodding slightly.

I looked up at him, wishing that he'd just move off. Just go away now, I thought to myself but he stayed where he was.

"I saw your name and I was waiting to see if it was you. You look the same."

"Really? God, is that good news?" I laughed, not expecting an answer. At least not the one I got.

"Ah, it's not the worst news. You were run-of-the-mill back then, and you still are. You've plumped up a bit though. Only to be expected – what are you, thirty-odd now?" He turned on his heel, not waiting for a reply.

I looked after him in disbelief. How do I manage to get put down like this, no matter what the circumstances?

I watched his retreating back. Prick, I thought to myself and put his name in my mental notebook. I was second-in-command around here and I would not forget that one.

He walked up to a desk on the other side of the room and chatted to some girl sitting there, making her squirm a little in her seat. I watched the exchange. She was blushing madly and I wondered what on earth he was saying to her. I thought about calling him over to tell him what I'd seen and demand to know what was happening. I did not want any harassment issues so early on either.

He walked away from her desk and went to another one where he spoke to some poor guy who was reading the paper. The guy closed the paper and shifted uneasily on his chair. I watched this with a growing unease of my own. Was I going to have to talk to the boss about this so early on? He couldn't go around the office making others uncomfortable every morning. I looked around for his desk. I saw no Jeff Ryan name-tag anywhere. I watched as he left the guy's desk and walked around reading the posters on the wall and checking the plants. He was looking the whole place over as if he owned the office. Then it hit me. I looked at the door of the manager's office. And there it was: my heart sank. I was second-in-command. He was first. I took in the 'P' in *Mr Jeffrey P Ryan*. His name. Stuffy prick, I thought to myself.

I looked at the clock. It was 8:50 and the room was filling up fast. People were coming in, finding their name and smiling sheepishly at one another as they set up home at their desks.

One girl even brought in a small Busy Lizzie. I hadn't seen one of them since Granny died three years ago. I was never around old people now and young people don't seem to go in for Busy Lizzies the way the elderly do.

I waited until nine and then went into Jeff's office.

"Hi, Jeff, I just wondered if you had a plan for how you'd welcome the staff to the office? Are you going to have a speech or a few croissants or anything?"

"All in good time. I have it all under control." He

smiled. "You go back to your desk and make sure they're all working,"

"But they don't have any work at the moment," I pointed out. We had no clients on our books and no CV's just yet. The Dame Street office had sent out a newsletter telling employers that a new office was opening up, but there would be a quiet period before word got around and CV's began to drop on our mat.

"Well, just make sure they're not out there reading the paper and chatting."

I really didn't relish the thoughts of being the one to go out and ask people to stop talking to one another.

I left the office and headed to my desk. Just as I was about to sit back down, I decided to do my own little meet and greet.

I went from desk to desk telling people who I was and that I hoped they'd all settle in and enjoy working in the office. I felt a bit like the queen. The staff sat up straight when they realised who I was. God forgive me, the tiny bit of power was wonderful and I completely enjoyed it.

And joy of joys they all seemed nice and they all seemed to like me!

Just before ten o'clock Jeff's secretary announced that we should all make our way to the meeting room at the back of the building. We all stood up and followed one another down the small corridor and looked dumbfounded when we opened the meeting-room door to find an empty room. We made our way in and sat down around a large table. We sat there for about five minutes before anything else happened. We were making small talk about the office and the smell of fresh paint and varnish. The door opened and Jeff walked in – no coffee, not a croissant or a scone in evidence. Part of me was happy to see him make such a cock-up on his first day, another part of me withered thinking about the months and years to come, dealing with such a fool and wondering how on earth he landed the job as manager. My question was answered about two minutes into the first meeting.

Jeff told us all that he was a Trinity graduate.

I remembered a joke that was doing the rounds a few months before. Question: *How do you know if someone has been to Trinity?* Answer: *They'll tell you.*

How apt, I thought to myself as he went on to tell us that he'd worked in New York and London before coming back to Ireland when he heard through the grapevine that there was something called a Celtic Tiger and we were making plenty of money back in the old sod. I could see the demeanour of the group around the table change; each face was registering the same disdain. Jeff had just confirmed he was back in Ireland to make as much money as possible, nothing else. Then he introduced me, telling the group that he and I were old friends who danced at the same disco back in the late eighties. I looked at him in dismay: the late eighties? I know it was technically the truth, but did he have to say it like that? The staff wouldn't hear the "late" part; all they would remember was the eighties part. I looked around the table: most of these people were *born* in the eighties! I was fifteen when I danced at that particular school disco and to be honest there wasn't much dancing; we were all too busy posing and checking each other out. He hoped I would be happy in the office and then asked if I had anything I'd like to add.

I quickly confirmed exactly how old I was back in the late eighties and exactly what I was doing at that disco. I made it quite clear that Jeff and I had never danced together nor done anything else together. I welcomed the new staff, telling them I'd been with the company for three years, coming as I did from the Dame Street office and that I was very sure that we'd have just as close a staff and just as much fun here as in the office I'd just left. I knew this would help my status. Three years isn't long but it was longer than anyone in the room, other than Jeff, would have held down a full-time job. I looked at the faces around me and realised that three years ago these people were probably doing their Leaving Cert. God, I hated that thought. It made me feel old. I looked at Jeff and suddenly I felt decrepit. Decrepit and plump. Was that word going to follow me for a while? Would I never actually graduate to fat – always be thought of as a plump girl?

How can you meet someone and instantly take such a dislike to them, I wondered.

Jeff commented that noone had brought a notepad to the meeting and he said that he would be having a team meeting each Monday morning at 9.30 a.m. sharp. We would all be expected to bring a pad and a pen. I stopped myself just short of rolling my eyes as I caught a girl's eye across the table. She rolled hers, stopping abruptly midway through, realising who I was, I presume. I smiled to let her know the feeling was mutual but I couldn't roll with her just yet.

41

About a week after opening, the office had that lived-in feeling. People had spilt coffee on the carpet and we'd worked out a coffee and muffin run. We took it in turns to run to the café around the corner just before the Tec let the students out for breakfast and they clogged up the cafés and newsagents around the area for fifteen minutes. There was a certain amount of disdain between the students and the staff. The students were doing drama and the like; they would look at us in our suits and heels and feel sorry for us. We in turn would look at them in their jeans and jumpers and snigger behind our mochas while we worked out how many of them would be in with us before the year was out looking for jobs. The "them and us" mentality bubbled under the surface and was never outwardly admitted to. But I think we all enjoyed it, the students perhaps more than us. We did have jobs and we had to return to the office in ten minutes whereas they would sometimes be seen leaving the college at midday and not returning for days and in some cases weeks. We would sit at our desks looking out at them standing at the bus stop and wish for that kind of leeway. Also, the students drank much more than we did and seemed to enjoy it much more than we did too. They were far louder than us.

About a fortnight after we opened, the holiday was over. We had CV's waiting on the doormat each morning and companies asking for secretaries and temping staff all over north County Dublin. We had to get people in and interviewed and farmed back out very fast if we were going to look professional. It was great to see there seemed to be a good work ethic in the office. People worked as a team, perhaps because we were all new and trying to put our communal best foot forward, or maybe because we'd been lucky and had found a really great team. Whatever the reason, everyone was helping and there was no one who was slacking. People shared CV's, telling others that a great one had come in and it might just suit a place they were trying to fill. In the Dame Street office legend has it that Claire once ate a CV she'd received in, because she knew it fitted a position perfectly that Steve wanted to fill. Claire hated Steve – we never got to the bottom of why that was, but in any case, she ate the CV for fear he would find it and fill the position. In hindsight, perhaps we were not the "Brady Bunch" type of gathering I liked to tell people we were.

So we were very busy and work showed no sign of slowing. I was about three weeks into the new job when the phone rang.

"Hi, it's Ruth, can you talk?"

"Always," I replied.

"You will never guess what happened in here last week. I would have called you sooner only we haven't stopped talking about it long enough to dial the number!"

"What happened?" I asked, turning away from my computer for fear it would distract me.

"Ray and Mairead had the biggest bust-up in the pub on Thursday night. We were having some drinks after work and everyone was there, even Larry Boyd. They had some row about some misdemeanour last weekend, and she threw a pint over him."

"Another pint on the head! Was he furious?" I laughed.

"His head went so red I thought he'd burst a blood vessel. Anyway she ran away when she'd done it – I think she got a bit scared – she ran to the toilets shouting that his bits were tiny and that she faked it every time."

"Oh my God!" I was in complete shock.

"Yeah. Were his bits tiny?"

I thought back for a moment; it was almost eight months since I'd actually seen them. "No, in fairness to him, they were about average."

"Average meaning small?"

"No, average meaning neither huge nor tiny. I wasn't shocked by them one way or another."

"Anyway, the best is yet to come. She ran to the toilets and a bouncer went after her. So Claire and Louise went with him, trying to persuade him that she wasn't a lunatic, that she was just really annoyed with Ray. About five minutes later they all arrive back up and Mairead is shouting something about Ray and her doing it in the interview room by the toilets one night while we were all working late. The bouncer just picked her up and carried her out – still shouting about Ray. That was last Thursday and she hasn't been back since. We don't know what's happening. When we ask they just say she's on leave at the moment."

"You know what that means."

"Yeah, she's out sick until Personnel find the paragraph in the handbook that lets them fire her."

"Damn right," I agreed. "What about Ray?"

"He left really fast and then next morning he was called into Larry's office. I don't know what was said but he's been quiet as a mouse ever since."

"He got a warning, I bet. That's about his fifth," I shrugged.

"His fifth?"

"Yeah, he told me he got a few when he started over his time-keeping."

"I thought you only got three and then you got your P45?" Ruth sounded confused.

"They only sit on your file for six months or something. So he never had three on his file at the same time. That's what he told me anyway."

"Jammy bastard," Ruth tutted. "Anyway, that's the news."

"Well, that's news all right! So you say they did it in the interview room while we were all working. You can see into that room!" I was appalled – people were having sex in the office while I was working overtime? Talk about your no-fair situations!

"Yeah, seems so. It must have been in July – we were really busy, remember?"

"Yes, I do. Gross!" I laughed in spite of myself. "Has anyone asked Ray about it at all?"

"I don't know. The girls haven't asked him anyway. Some of the boys must have but no one is saying and now everyone is kind of ignoring it and trying to pretend it didn't happen. The smoking shelter is jammed all day with people discussing it behind his back though."

"Poor Ray, how embarrassing!"

"Poor Ray! Good enough for him! He's been a complete asshole for years."

"I know, but I still feel sorry for him."

"Well, don't. He deserves it," Ruth advised.

"Have you plans this week or could we meet for a drink?" I asked, thinking for the first time in three weeks of Jack. He'd never rung me after he left the pub that night and I wouldn't mind finding out where he was.

"Yeah, I'm going out on Saturday but what about Friday?" Ruth said.

"Great! I could meet you in town?" I said, thinking that I might just see Jack if I went anywhere near the office.

"No, no need. I'll go out to you and we'll go to that nice pub out there. I'll get a train out to Clontarf and meet you at the station."

"Fine, see you Friday," I said, a little disappointed at

not being able to see Jack.

Friday came and right enough there was Ruth waiting at the station just after 5:30.

We jumped in a taxi and headed straight to the pub. We ordered a bite to eat and two drinks.

"So tell me what the new office is like?" Ruth asked, taking a mouthful of her Miller.

"My new boss is a prick," I told her.

"Really, what's wrong with him?" Ruth rubbed her hands in glee.

"His name is Jeff and I used to know him back in the year dot when we were in secondary."

I began the story and by the time I'd finished Ruth was gobsmacked. She could hardly believe the pushing thirty and plump comments.

"What a prick!" she laughed but I knew she was horrified for me.

"And he's not any better with the others in the office. He makes everyone uncomfortable – even the guys squirm when he talks to them."

"Larry's beginning to look like a complete darling!"

"Believe me, Ruth, he is a darling!" I laughed. "But the rest of the office crowd are great. They're really nice. I think we may have a bit of a romance beginning to blossom between two of them, but I don't know."

"Really? Excellent."

"Yeah, and while I'm on the subject how is your romance?" I congratulated myself on how well I'd steered the conversation around to Ruth.

"We weren't on the subject, but my romance is fine. Chris is a dote and he's still absolutely gorgeous!"

"When am I allowed to meet him?" I grinned.

"Oh God, you will. I just don't want him thinking I'm showing him off to my friends. You know how that looks really pathetic and then the following week they dump you."

"All right, but don't go dumping him until I get a look at him!" I told her.

"Believe me I won't. I'll keep this one as long as I can. Did I tell you he's gorgeous?" She laughed as she called the lounge boy's attention and ordered more drinks.

"Maybe just the once, but you didn't harp on about it so I didn't think it was true."

"Oh it's true, it's very true!" She grinned from ear to ear. "Not as good looking as you think Jack is, of course."

"Well, I don't know. I've never seen this Chris guy, I only have your opinion on his looks. Maybe he's a minger. Anyway, leave Jack out of this. This is all about you and Chris!" I laughed but I could feel myself blush as I spoke.

"Oh now, leave my Jack out of it!" Ruth mocked.

"I never said my Jack!" I laughed, but I was now turning crimson.

"Go on with yourself! As if you're not dying to hear all about him. Look at you, you're scarlet!" Ruth laughed.

"Anyway, we shouldn't be laughing at him. Poor old Jack is very sick at the moment. He's been out sick for the last two weeks. He's got some kind of flu and he really cannot shake it. He's looking desperate."

"That's why he didn't call me!" I blurted out.

"What?" Ruth's eyes widened.

Now I was crimson. Wonderful. "He said he'd ring me and he never did. It must have been that he was sick."

"Were you waiting for the call that never came?" Ruth looked genuinely sorry for me. "Poor you! And I could have told you!"

"No, it was fine. I'm just thinking that must have been why."

"Poor old you! Poor old loser you, waiting by the phone!" She started to laugh.

"Like you never waited for a call that never came!" I threw back.

"I would never tell anyone I did. I would take it to my grave if someone promised to call me again and never did!" she laughed.

"Shut up!" I giggled. "Anyway, you were saying he's been ill for two weeks?"

"Yeah, he was really sick the week after you left. I was giving him stick about being lovesick when you left. He was denying it, of course, but then he got really sick and had to go home. He looked like death, and I felt a bit bad for slagging him. He hasn't been back since. The last we heard he should back in on Monday."

"Poor Jack," I said honestly.

"Yeah, poor guy all right. But, the real order of business tonight is this!" Ruth sat forward grinning from ear to ear. "By the way, you can thank me later!"

"What? Thank you for what?"

"He is single as single can be!"

"How did you find out?" My heart was beating faster – had she come out and told him I liked him? Nothing would surprise me about her.

"I asked a few well worded questions and he told me."

"What did you say? Tell me the exact question." Tact was something Ruth used very sparingly indeed.

"I leaned seductively over the photocopier as he was making some copies and said 'Hey, big boy, what's the story? Are you getting it on a regular basis?'"

My mouth dropped open, "Please say you're lying!"

"Of course I am," Ruth laughed. "You're so literal!"

"What did you really say?"

"OK, I admit it – I did ask him if he was getting any – I made out it was a joke, but I watched for his reaction."

I narrowed my eyes at her. "Congratulations, Ruth. You are officially the most tactless person in the world."

"Look, I got the information. He said, no, not at this precise moment."

"Not at this precise moment? So is there someone he has his sights on, I wonder?" I asked, trying to think of any girls he'd mentioned while we were in the apartment.

"Yeah, you. He's had more than his eye on you for ages," Ruth said looking around for the lounge boy again.

My heart skipped a happy beat as I allowed myself to believe what Ruth had just said. I had no idea if it was actually true, but it was nice to believe it for a while.

The lounge boy came towards us and from a distance of about thirty feet shouted, *"Same again, is it?"*

We nodded and waved a twenty at him, perhaps to entice him a little closer.

362

"Flavour?" he shouted again.

We looked at one another and then at the table. What was he talking about?

"Breezer? Orange again?" He shouted, walking backwards towards the bar as he spoke.

"Orange!" I shouted to him, then to Ruth, "Jesus, I had no idea what he was talking about, did you?"

"Not a bull's notion. I thought he said favour," Ruth confided.

He came back over and placed a Breezer and a Miller on the table between us. We gave over the money and an exorbitant tip to keep him sweet. We really needed him to keep bringing drinks for us as the bar was filling up steadily.

The next few days were lovely. I would remember Ruth's comment and think: Jack's had his eye on me for ages! And things wouldn't seem so dull or boring. I would allow my mind to drift to Jack, and suddenly I would have a new lease of life. In work during the following week, it lifted my spirits and helped during stressful moments. Like the one I was having at the moment with Jeff. Talk about your unforeseen nightmares! He was mine. I wondered how we'd never met on the day I spent out here with Larry before we opened the office. He wasn't there, at least not at the lunch anyway.

We were in his office, sorting out holiday rosters and a "POA" for the coming year. POA is Plan of Action; Jeff likes to talk in Armyspeak. He asks every morning if anyone is AWOL – we are only open six weeks so the answer is no. Most days he comes out of his office just as we're doing the coffee run. He stands beside the desk of whoever is gone on the "run" and asks if they are Missing in Action. When we tell him for the one hundredth time that they are gone on the coffee run, because he's too cheap to sign off on a coffee machine for the office, he laughs at his own little joke. He tells us "No need for a Court Martial then, I suppose?" and goes back to his office. Invariably someone gives him the one-finger salute as he shuts his door. Someone is going to get caught doing that one day and I only pray it isn't me. I could take many things in this life: Jeff firing me is not one of them.

As I say, we were in his office looking at the new year's schedule and trying to work it around people's holiday arrangements.

"You're not on the list here. Have you no plans for a holiday this year?" he asked me as he looked at the year planner.

"I never book holidays this early. I'll wait and see what's available in a few weeks and take a week where I can."

"I'd prefer to see everyone take a block of two weeks' holiday. It's been proven to do you the world of good to get out of the office for a block of fourteen days in a row. I'm taking the first two weeks in August off."

"Really?" I smiled, biting my lip in an effort not to tell him to fuck off with his fortnight's holiday. "Sorry, but I really would prefer to wait a few weeks and see how things are going and take a few days here and there this year."

"No holiday plans? Or is it just that you have no one to go with?"

"No plans. And my sister is having a baby in March and I really want to see how that goes. I may take a week around then to help her out."

"Really? Did Jennifer get married or is she one of the un-marrieds?"

"She's married, but what difference would it make if she wasn't?" I asked, my hackles rising, the voice in my head telling me to back off. Just for the record I ignored it.

"No difference, just every second girl pushing a pram these days has no ring on her finger. As a man, and a tax payer, it is a little irritating to see it." His smiled indulgently to himself.

"One thing, has it ever occurred to you that a woman's fingers swell during pregnancy and maybe her ring doesn't fit any more?" I had been reading Jennifer's pregnancy magazines a lot recently. "And second of all, the woman rarely manages to do this all by herself. There is usually a man somewhere close by when the blessed event takes place. He's just as much to blame and he's usually got a naked ring finger too!" I could feel my voice reaching a higher octave as I spoke and my hands shook a little, adrenaline and hatred rushing through my veins.

"Hey, take it easy. I just asked was she married." Jeff laughed it off but I was still furious.

"Why did you feel the need to ask that of all questions? Why couldn't you just say 'congratulations' or 'oh really' and carry on with what we were doing? Why has there always got to be some loaded comment about everything?"

"I just asked if she was married because I was surprised that she was," Jeff replied, looking back at the planner.

"Why were you surprised?" I asked, my voice calmer.

"I actually thought she was headed for the convent personally."

"The convent? As in, to become a nun?" I asked disbelievingly.

"Yes, I thought she had a vocation. She always seemed aloof."

"You hardly knew her; she was two years ahead of you. Of course, she was aloof with you. You were Inter Cert and she was Leaving Cert – she wouldn't have touched you with a bargepole. Apart from everything else, that would have been social suicide!"

"Well, whatever the reason I never thought she was exactly marriage material. But you say she is and I believe you," he sniffed. "Now can we get back to what we were doing or are you going to get hormonal again?"

"Jeff, I am not hormonal. And you really shouldn't speak to me or anyone else like that," I said, and to my surprise tears blurred in my eyes as I spoke. I blinked them away as fast as I could.

"Get off your high horse – I was just asking if you were going to get all up-tight again. You're wound up like a poodle. Did your mother know your uncle a little too well?"

"*What?* Seriously, Jeff, that's going too far. You shouldn't talk to me like that!" This time my voice cracked, making him look up from the cursed planner and see that I was crying.

"What is wrong with you? Can't you take a joke?" He laughed.

"I don't think you're being funny. I'm really offended by the things you said." I wasn't going to let this drop, not without an apology. Start as you mean to continue.

"What, that I was surprised your sister was married? Well, I am. I was joking about your mother and your uncle." He shrugged and set the year planner against the wall beside the door. "Take the planner out and stick it on the wall by the water cooler, if you don't feel that would be offensive to you. Tell the staff that the holidays in black have been approved." He opened the door and I walked out, talking the planner with me. "And Amelia, if it is offensive, just stick it wherever you like, won't you?" His face was innocent but the comment was loaded and we both knew it.

"Where exactly would that be, Jeff?" I asked, my eyes tingling with uncried tears. He was not going to get the better of me.

"I don't know – you girls are all into that Fung Shui – stick in some nice spot that won't offend the decoration gods."

"I can think of one place to stick it, but I'm not too sure it would fit." I smiled at him as I turned and walked away.

One thing was certain: this was far from over. In fact, it was just beginning.

42

Christmas came and went with very little incident, just the one little incident in fact. We had a family Christmas with Jenny and Mike over for Christmas Day. As usual Luke cleaned up on the gifts. For some reason he does really well every year. He has done since we were small children; the joy of buying for a boy was too much for my mother it seems. She has never really grown out of the excitement. Here we all are twenty-six years later and he still gets bigger and shinier gifts than Jenny and me put together.

My Aunt Jean and the family came over after Mass. They crowded the house and whooped it up big style as the gifts were given out. There are very few occasions during the year when it's permissible to open wine and spirits at midday. Christmas Day is one of those precious days. My cousin Keelan and I opened the vodka and danced in the sitting-room to the Christmas songs being played back to back on VH1. It was only 12:30 and we were pouring our second vodka each, when a child began to cry somewhere in the house. We stopped and looked at one another. Suddenly Keelan slapped her head with the base of her hand.

"Jesus, that's Adam! I forgot about him!" She raced from the room and came back a moment later with Adam, who was wiping his eyes and carrying a packet of crisps. She kissed his damp cheeks and hugged him. "You weren't lost, baby. You were in the kitchen. Grandma was there. You were fine!"

"You were gone!" he wailed.

"I was in here all the time – you were fine, baby!" She took the packet of crisps from him and opened them. She took a few before handing them back to him. Why do parents do that to their children all the time? Could she not have got her own bag of crisps?

"Adam, what did Santa bring you this year?" I asked him, suddenly very excited by the thought that next year we'd have our own small person like this to lavish attention on.

"A Scooby Doo," he told me in his perfect London accent, his solemn eyes devouring me.

"Wow, did you bring him with you? Can I see him?" I turned to Keelan. "That voice!"

Keelan nodded agreement.

"No, he's at home. I have a Boobhaa." He was perking up a little.

"He didn't want to get Scooby dirty so he didn't bring him," Keelan told me, still smiling at Adam. She called to her husband Matt to get something called a Boobhaa from the back of the car.

He reappeared with a yellow furry blob with brown eyes and gave it to Adam before returning to his conversation with Mike.

"He's Boobhaa," Adam told me and pushed the doll's head into his body.

"That's charming," I laughed as it sprang back out and Adam pushed it in again.

"Yes – thankfully it doesn't speak. The Teletubby last year had us all at breaking point by midday," Keelan said, laughing.

"What did it say?" I asked.

"He said 'Eh-Oh, time for tubby custard!'"

Adam's eyes lit up remembering the Teletubby. He rubbed his stomach and stamped around singing about tubby custard.

Keelan picked up her vodka and took a mouthful before coughing and spluttering it back up.

"No ice, no ice!" she whispered as she grabbed the ice bucket.

You had to feel for her – hot vodka is one of the worst things you can drink. That, and gin. I absolutely hate gin.

Jenny came into the room and ducked around the back of the couch when she saw Adam. I thought it was an odd thing to do and I also thought it was really bad-mannered. Thankfully Keelan missed it, still being waist deep in the ice bucket.

Adam, of course, zoned in on Jenny. He smiled and headed straight for her. He showed her the Boobhaa and pressed its head again. She nodded and pushed by him to the chair in front of the TV.

"What's this?" she asked picking up the remote.

"We were having a laugh listening to the Christmas Number Ones," I said.

"Crap," Jenny tutted and flicked through the stations.

I know she's meant to be hormonal but she was being a royal pain in the ass for the last few months. I looked at Keelan, now out of the ice bucket.

"Jenny, how are you feeling?" she asked.

"Like I badly need a drink," Jenny snapped.

"Oh, I remember that very well. I had him just before Christmas so on Christmas Day I could have a few glasses. You poor thing, dry all through Christmas!"

"Yeah, and people constantly saying it to me doesn't help either!" Jenny stormed out of the room.

"Sorry, I didn't mean to get at you!" Keelan called after her. "It's completely worth it in the end!"

"Don't mind her – she's like a bag of cats at the moment," I put in.

"Is she still feeling sick?" Keelan asked.

"I don't think so. Mike, has Jenny still got morning sickness?" I called.

"No, she's fine. She's just tired, I think," Mike replied.

Keelan and I shrugged at each other.

"Personally, I think she's being a crank about the whole thing," I confided.

Keelan smiled non-commitally.

I was sorry I'd said it, but it needed to be said.

Jenny had a little bump at this stage, she looked really

pretty, her hair and skin were perfect, she was gone past the morning sickness – according to Mike anyway – and she should have been glowing. But her mood was far was glowing. She was dreadful company at the moment and anytime we asked how she was feeling she would list her ailments. Fat, tired, bored, uncomfortable, to name but a few. Sometimes I wanted to kick her; she was ruining the excitement for the rest of us!

The cousins left after a few hours and the house looked like a bomb zone. Dinner was just about ready and the smells were fantastic. We were sitting in the living-room, watching *ET* and eating someone's open selection box – noone knew exactly where it had come from as we were all a bit old for selection boxes, but it was tasty. And we were all digging in.

There was only one bar left and Mike picked up the box and offered it to Jenny.

"Here, have the last bar. You can eat all the chocolate you want because you can't drink anything," he said, his plain face smiling at her.

"I can't eat all the chocolate I want," she snapped. "I have to watch what I eat and I don't want to be eating the wrong stuff and piling on weight. Everything I gain I have to take back off before I go back to work. I will not be some fat cow going back to the office. And I am going back to work after this baby is born!"

Luke and I sat rigid, our faces turned to the TV but our eyes wide and staring at each other.

"All right, Jenny, I was just being nice. I'm sorry you can't have another drink. It'll be worth it all though."

Mike tried to placate her.

"Leave me alone," she snarled at him.

He looked at us and we smiled, pretending this type of reaction was common in expectant mothers.

"Some women get mood swings all through the nine months. That's what the doctor says anyway," Mum said.

He shrugged, putting the selection box back on the floor and kicking it away with his shoe.

"Don't kick that box – the noise is really annoying," Jenny glared at him.

I looked at Mike and for the first time ever I felt sorry for him.

"Jenny, stop being such a bitch about everything!" I said.

She turned on me. "Don't even start on me, you!"

"What is the fucking problem with you?" I sat up in my seat – there was no way she was turning this on me.

"I'm sick of being pregnant! That's what's wrong with me. I hate the way I can't sit comfortably for more than five minutes and the heartburn and never being allowed to eat what I want, and the stretch marks, and having to lie on my side in bed and no one ever wanting to talk about me! Just about this damn baby!" She stood up and ran out of the room crying.

We all sat staring at one another.

"That was not my fault," I announced.

Luke nodded. "What the hell was that about?"

Mum ran in from the kitchen. "Was that Jennifer?"

"Yeah, she's upset," I said.

"I'll go after her," Mike said and went off to find her.

"What's wrong with her?" Mum sat down.

"I have no idea, but she's not a happy bunny," Luke said.

We were all in shock at the outburst.

"Mum, I think she's got major problems with the whole baby thing," I said.

I looked at Luke and he nodded. "I think she's right, Mum. That is not the behaviour of an excited mother-to-be."

"I'll talk to her later. Maybe she's just overwhelmed. Being pregnant is a very emotional time. You're not always full of the joys of spring, you know," Mum said, but her eyes were worried.

But this was not a moment of panic – Jenny was not happy about the baby at all. She was getting worse instead of better. I couldn't help thinking back to the conversation we had last summer. About Mike wanting a baby and her not. What would she be like when this baby was born?

I looked over at Luke, then back at Mum. She was looking towards the sitting-room door.

"I'll talk to her later," she said. "Let's just enjoy the night and say nothing more about it." She stood up and headed for the kitchen.

Before she reached the door Mike and Jenny came back in. Jenny's face was tear-stained and her eyes were bloodshot.

"Are you OK?" Mum asked.

Jenny nodded.

"She just gets a little frantic sometimes," Mike told us.

"You all right, Jenny?"

Again she nodded, then she glanced over at me and gave a watery smile.

"Sorry, it's not your fault," she said quietly. "Now can we stop talking about it, please?"

We all nodded.

We carried on watching *ET*, but the mood was subdued. I couldn't help but look at the caramel bar that lay on the floor in its box. I looked up and caught Luke's eye – he was watching it too.

Finally he leaned over to pick it up. "Want to share it, Mill?"

"Yeah," I replied, the lure of chocolate being too much to resist for long.

Christmas ended, the tree came down and the chocolates were eaten, all down to the Turkish delights anyway. They rattled around in the oversized box for weeks after the chocolates should have been finished. Noone would actually throw them away, and no one would eat them; the wrappers were tearing off them and they were getting dirty. Every now and then someone would go to the press, open the box and stare in. The box would then be closed, returned to the press and the person would walk away. At this rate we'd have that particular box with the seven Turkish delights rolling around the bottom until next Christmas. Finally Mum opened the box and took one. It took about ten seconds before she spat it back out, complaining about why they ever included the likes of it in a box of sweets.

"What is the least bit sweet about those buggers?" she complained. She headed straight to the bin and dumped the box in. "That's it! I'm never bothering with them again!"

And, with that, Christmas was over. The last of the goodies were gone and we were all back to work, and diets.

I was in the kitchen when the chocolates were thrown away that night. Mum came back to the table and sat down. She opened her newest cookbook and began to read about how low fat didn't have to mean low taste. I was thinking about Jenny; the outburst at Christmas had bothered me. I couldn't help but remember the night at Jenny's last year when she confided in me that she didn't want a baby. And the night I picked her up from the other side of the city after that "thing" with Frank from her office. She never spoke of it again and I never brought it up, but lately I just couldn't get it out of my mind.

"Mum, have you spoken to Jenny?" I asked.

"Not today," Mum said from behind her book.

"About Christmas?"

"Oh." Mum put the book down and took her glasses off. "Yes, we had a chat about that."

"What's wrong with her?" I asked.

"Nothing's wrong with her. She's just jittery about the whole thing."

"Mum, she doesn't seem the least bit pleased about this baby," I said. Now that it was out I was scared of what Mum would say. She didn't say anything though. She just ran her hand through her hair.

"Jenny is happy. She's never been one to go shouting and screaming about things. You're our drama queen, Jenny is more . . ." Mum searched for a word, "I don't know, maybe more subdued about things."

"Mum, come on, she was complaining about the cost of the hospital before Christmas and then saying that going private was a waste of time. Then she's been whining about not being allowed to drink. And then the scene here on Christmas Day was something to behold. You know she dodged Adam like he was contagious when he was here?"

"That's nothing! I'd dodge him if I could! He's three. He's a pain!" Mum laughed.

"Seriously, what about the nurturing we all hear about. She doesn't seem to have any maternal instincts. What if she hates the baby?"

"Amelia! She won't hate the baby!" Mum said, half laughing, half appalled. "Look, she's a bit overwhelmed, but there's nothing to be worrying about."

I looked unconvinced.

"Don't you go saying any of this to her," Mum scolded. "I will not have you putting more worries in her head."

"I'm not going to say anything to her, but I am concerned," I said.

"Well, don't be!" She picked up the book and began to read again.

I really wished I could be as sure as she was, but what could I do?

43

We were back in work three weeks when the contract came in. An Australian pharmaceutical company was opening a branch in Coolock and they were looking for an entire workforce. This was big; we needed everyone to pull together on this one. And we needed it to go perfectly. Jeff and I went into his office to talk about it.

An uncomfortable hour later we emerged. It was decided that we should contact the Dame Street branch and talk to them about the situation; we would take instruction without handing over the business. They were the business headquarters and they needed to be kept abreast of contracts of this size.

Also, we needed the jobs filled in three months and they had much larger database to pick potential workers from.

I rang the office and spoke to Larry. He was like a child with a new toy.

"Amelia, have you any idea what this could mean to us, if we filled the places and kept them as a contract?" He spluttered excitedly. "The staff turnover alone would keep us going for years!"

"I know, but we really need to get the places filled, and filled right. If we send them over a gang of wasters they'll give the contract to another agency. We wouldn't have nearly enough people on our books."

"Take ours. I'll have Ray and Emily go through the files today and forward all the CV's we think are suitable."

"Thanks, that'd be great!" I smiled at the thought of Ray trawling through the database for me. It is regarded as one of the most tedious jobs in the office and has to be done usually about once a year. Ray would be doing it for the next fortnight. I would email Ruth so she could laugh at him.

"I'll get them to you by this day week. Anything further, give a call."

I hung up happy. Before I did anything else I mailed Ruth. She'd enjoy that one, I thought, as I went to the water filter to get a drink.

Jeff called me back to his office as I was passing by with my bottle of water.

"Amelia, a word please."

I went into his office and he shut the door. I wondered what this was about.

"Would you be so good as to ring the *Irish Times* and have the placement advertised in the Health Supplement this week and then ring the *Independent* and have it run in Sunday's paper?"

"Fine. Will you be needing to look at the advert before I ring it in? Is there a cap on the amount of words you can use in the advert?"

"No, I trust you. Just make sure they get into the papers this week." He opened the door and tilted his head in a gesture to tell me the meeting was over. "And Amelia, as usual, it was a pleasure to have you in my office."

"I aim to please, Jeffery," I smiled as I passed him.

I went back to my desk and worked on the wording of the advert. It was harder than you might think. I had to check if the company wanted to be named in the advert. They did and they wanted their logo too. I spent the rest of the day on the phone and fax trying to get the logo to the paper and confirm how much they would charge us.

Just after five everyone headed for the door. I was hoping to get out myself in the next few minutes. I decided to close my computer – the work would have to wait until the morning. Just before I closed, up popped an email from Ruth. She was inviting me out for a drink on Saturday, with the gorgeous Chris! I emailed back to say that I'd love to.

We met in O'Neill's bar on Pearse Street on Saturday night. It was quiet and we could all sit and talk. Chris was gorgeous, just as Ruth had said. He was tall, with dark brown hair and brown eyes that you could just drown in. He was really nice too, not a bit full of himself. Ruth had told me he was loaded, and that coupled with the gorgeous description made me nervous about what he'd actually be like. I shouldn't have worried. He was really polite and a bit shy – he even blushed when Ruth introduced him as "this hunk". I'd have been mortified myself, but it was nice to see a man blush instead of puff out his chest and agree.

Chris got a round of drinks and headed for the toilet. He knew the drill: leave us to dissect him for a while early on, let us get it off our chests, and then we could all relax and enjoy the rest of the evening.

"Well?" Ruth asked, knowing the answer already. What else could it be?

"He is fantastic," I beamed at her. "You know that though!"

"I do, but it's lovely to hear it from someone else!" She grinned.

"Well, I'll say it again, He is fan-bloody-tastic. Where did you find him again?"

"Bit of bad news though," Ruth frowned. "He has to go home early. Some match he has tomorrow."

"What?" I couldn't believe it. Had we uncovered his down-side already?

"Yeah, he has a rugby match and he takes the whole thing very seriously." Ruth looked disappointed.

"Oh," I looked away, afraid she'd see me involuntarily roll my eyes. I liked the rugby as much as the next girl, and maybe it is a girl thing but I was not so into sport that I let it affect my Saturday night's entertainment. Certainly not a Sunday afternoon kick-about type thing down in the local park.

"He's really good and the team really rely on him. I'm going to watch on the sideline – it's in Marley Park at half-past eleven."

I wondered why I was getting so much information here. In fact, I'm lying; I knew why I was getting it. I just didn't really want it.

"Would you come?" Ruth smiled.

"Do I have to?" I pleaded, hoping she'd say no.

"Well, I don't want to go on my own!"

"Who says you have to go?" I asked, unfairly I know.

"No one, I just wanted to, but I don't want to go alone. Please, Amelia?"

"All right," I caved. "What time?"

"Oh great!!" She laughed. "Half eleven, I'll pick you up at about eleven."

"Fine, but don't go hanging out with him and going back to his house. I don't want to be third leg any longer than I have to!"

"I promise you. I will go straight back home after the match."

"I don't mean that. I just mean don't have me play gooseberry all day." I mellowed, suddenly afraid I was sounding like a complete cow.

Chris came back from the bathroom and sat down. He glanced at Ruth and she confirmed that we had been talking about him but now we were discussing gooseberries. He smiled at her and she ruffled the top of his head, tossing his hair. He looked over at me, rolling his eyes before he grabbed her arm and made her toss her own hair. I have to say I have never felt more like a gooseberry in my life. To give them their due they didn't touch or kiss inappropriately and they never alluded to

382

any personal jokes "just between them". It was the atmosphere; you could cut the sexual tension with a knife and I was drowning in it. The only problem was there was no tension heading in my direction. I was the eunuch in this particular Roman get-together and I was feeling dreadfully left out. Again it hit me square in the face: I was lonely. I wanted a boyfriend; I wanted to be on the receiving end of some of that attention. Nothing major league, no show-stopping sex antics – all I wanted was this: someone to buy me a drink, hold my hand, listen to my rambling tales and scratch my back when necessary. I missed human contact. I know that's ridiculous –it wasn't as if I'd been living a life devoid of hugs and smiles. But the hugs and smiles from a family member are not the same, no matter how much you love your family. I sat there watching the pair in front of me grin and flash eyes at one another and finished my drink. I went to the bar and ordered a round. As I stood waiting for Chris's pint of Guinness to settle I looked back at the pair, still chatting animatedly, as though no one else existed in the room. I'd give them another five minutes of this before I insisted they include me in all other conversation.

A large group walked in, bringing cold air and traffic sounds in with them as they let the door swing. They weren't very loud but the pub had been so quiet that they made a few of the punters look around. The group must have been equally caught off guard by the quiet pub. They looked around them and lowered their voices as they sat down. They began to order drinks from one another and grab stools from around the bar.

I watched them as I waited. The pint was ready, all money had exchanged hands, so I picked up the drinks and returned to the table.

Ruth and Chris sat forward in anticipation. I threw a few packets of cheese and onion crisps on the table, always a surefire hit with the taste buds and later a sure-fire passion buster. Cheese-and-onion breath is a killer. I smirked to myself as Ruth dived in.

"You pet! A few crisps, yum!" She opened the pack and we all ate them.

The night progressed as usual, the pub filled up and we got drunker. Then at about 10:30 Chris stood up to leave. Ruth was distraught, an overreaction caused by alcohol. She hugged him and kissed his cheeks.

"I'll see you in thirteen hours!" she called after him.

He did the quickest double-take at her before he left the pub.

I pulled her arm and sat her back down, advising that a little of that talk goes a very long way. Ruth giggled and asked if she was very drunk.

"Yeah, you are," I smiled. "Tell you what. We'll just get a Coke this time." She looked disappointed. "We both will," I consoled her.

"Yes, but just one."

We drank our Cokes and I'm glad to say the hour or so without alcohol sobered Ruth up a treat; I was worried about how I was going to get her home if she carried on drinking like she was.

Soon enough the conversation got around to Jack.

Ruth was completely sure that Jack was just dying for the word and he would come running to be with me.

"Seriously, he has fancied you forever. Since you started in the office."

"Not that long. Remember my wine suit?"

"Yes, everyone remembers your wine suit," Ruth laughed.

"No one could have fancied me when I was wearing that suit!" I giggled.

"That's very true. I'm not sure about the suit, but he has fancied you for quite some time."

"Anyway, I don't completely believe you about this one."

Ruth looked wounded. "That is a hurtful thing to say."

"About this one!" I said. "I believe you about everything else, but that Jack's fancied me since 2001 I do not believe!"

"Up to you, but it's true. And he is lovely. Seriously, he's a great guy."

"And you'd know!"

"I would. Jack is my friend, first and foremost. And he is a good kisser!" Ruth grinned to herself as if remembering something.

"Stop that!" I told her. "Do not have that look on your face!"

"I have no look. That's my face!" She laughed, but the grin confirmed she knew exactly what she was doing.

"Jack is really nice, but that's it. I think I missed the boat on that one."

"What are you talking about? Are you listening to

me at all?" Ruth looked amazed. "Have I not just said he fancies you?"

"Ruth, you're drunk. You could say Mass when you're drunk."

"That was one time, years ago and I said I was sorry at the time!" Ruth joked.

"Hilarious!" I laughed as we got another drink.

Just as I was pouring my Diet Coke into my Bacardi, I glanced up at a punter who was passing the table. He was talking to another man who was scanning the bar for a seat. They both saw some seats at the same moment and headed towards them. It was only when he was gone by that I realised I recognised the face. I looked after them. It was Jack.

I watched as they both sat down and carried on talking. I watched at regular intervals for about half an hour. Girls came and went, some chatted and others asked for seats. They didn't seem to be waiting for anyone. There was no girl presence in their group; in fact, it appeared to be just the two of them. I watched for a while and when Jack got up to go to the bar I was ready.

"Don't look around just yet," I told Ruth.

Ruth looked around.

"I said don't look around!"

"Come on, everyone looks around. What are we looking at?" Ruth waved her hand dismissively.

"Over at the bar, it's Jack!"

Ruth's eyes widened as she looked around. There he was. Her eyes rested on him for a moment. "Go up to him," she said decisively.

"No, what would I say?" I was getting ready to go up anyway.

"Anything you like. He'll be delighted to see you. Go on!" Ruth urged me up to the bar.

I went up; I couldn't feel my feet on the ground. I knew that if I thought about them I'd fall flat on my face. I had no control over them whatsoever, my heart pounded and my head was light. Either I was very drunk or Jack had quite an effect on my equilibrium.

"Jack?" I said as I reached his shoulder.

He looked around him, and as soon as he saw me his whole face broke out in a smile.

"Amelia! How the hell are you?" He hugged me, the smell of fresh ironing hanging around him as usual.

"Great, how are you? I heard you were ill," I smiled.

"Oh, much better. Who are you here with?"

"Ruth, she's sitting over there. I just saw you at the bar and I said I'd come over."

"Well, that's brilliant!" He smiled down at me, his eyes moving all around my face as we spoke. "Tell me, how are you finding the new office?"

"The office is great; the staff are lovely. All except the boss, that is."

"Ruth said he was an asshole. Don't worry about it. There's always one, in every office. Is he as bad as Ray?"

"He's as tactless," I laughed.

"If he gives you any stick, tell him I'll be in to have words. No one gives you a hard time while I'm around," Jack smiled, eyes locking with mine as he spoke.

"I certainly will. I'd better get back to Ruth, she's by

herself," I said, observing the "leave before the conversation dries up" rule.

"Well. I'll see you later," he smiled.

I walked away, happy that the conversation had gone very well. I glanced back just once to check was he looking after me. He was.

I got back to Ruth.

"How well did that go?" she asked.

"Quite well."

"But why didn't he come and join us? Or invite us over?"

"Oh, I suppose he's stuck with his mate!"

"But he didn't even come over to say hello to me!"

"Oh, I'm sure he'll be over in a while."

About an hour later we were still there and Jack still hadn't come over. He was still engrossed in conversation with his friend and seemed oblivious to us sitting gaping at him. If I had been sober, that would have bothered me but the drink was going directly to my head, not wasting time with the stomach at all. Ruth was just as bad. She was trying to look at her watch. She was holding it close to her eye and moving it back and forth, trying to focus on it. Then she pulled her sleeve up past her elbow and held it up towards the light. She finally gave up.

"What time is it by you?" She leaned to the side and asked a stranger.

"A quarter past twelve," The stranger replied.

She sat still for a few minutes, looking at her drink and then at the bar. "We should head soon," she said finally.

"I think I may have drunk enough tonight."

I really wanted to stay until Jack was ready to leave, but I said, "Right, I'll just run to the loo."

I jumped up, taking in with some disappointment the fact that Jack was not at his seat. I'd hoped to "accidentally" bump into him on my way to the toilets.

But just as I was passing his table on the way back from the toilet I heard him call my name.

"Amelia?" he called.

"Yes?" I spun around.

"Are you guys leaving now?

"Yeah, why?" I asked.

"If you want to wait a minute I'll get my coat and walk out with you," he said, tipping his almost empty pint glass at me.

"Sure," I smiled

"You pair have been drinking all night. I'll get you to a taxi," He stood up and grabbed his jacket.

"Where's your friend?" I asked.

"Behind you. Amelia, this is Liam – Liam, this is Amelia. Ready to go?"

Liam smiled and shook my hand.

"So you're Amelia!" he grinned.

We collected Ruth and left the pub. As usual there was a huge queue for the taxi rank so we decided to get some food. Ruth and Liam went in and ordered fish and chips. I made an excuse to wait outside and just as I had hoped Jack volunteered to wait with me.

I allowed the alcohol in my veins to run straight to my head. I needed all the Dutch courage I could summon for the task in hand.

I had never done this before and to be honest I had no idea how it was going to work out. I took a deep breath and began. "Jack . . . now that I have you alone . . . ."

Jack stopped kicking the wall outside the chip shop and looked at me.

"I'm just going to say this," I went on, "now that I have the chance."

"What?" Jack looked concerned.

"I know I wasn't that nice to you for a while, but I really like you," I smiled.

"I like you too." Jack seemed wary.

"Good. Sorry about being so horrible to you last year. I was being stupid. You're lovely."

"Thanks," Jack replied, looking after a small group that passed by, hailing taxis and cursing them as they sailed by empty.

"Jack, this is serious. I want to tell you something before the others come back."

"Well, tell me, but, Amelia –"

"No, listen to me. I've let enough things pass me by and not said a word. I am not such a shrinking bloody violet!"

"Yeah, but do you really need to say this tonight? You're very drunk."

"That's why I'm saying it. Listen to me!" I stamped my foot and almost overbalanced. Jack put his hand out to straighten me.

"I'm all right, but just ... listen ..." I stood up straighter. "Right, I like you."

"We covered that," Jack smiled.

"No, I *really* like you. I think you're great." I grinned at him.

"Amelia, please stop. You're really drunk."

"It doesn't matter if I'm drunk or sober, I'll still think you're gorgeous when I wake up in the morning," I told him.

"Oh Jesus!" he muttered. "Amelia, stop, there's no point."

"What do you mean? You like me, don't you? Ruth told me you liked me!"

"Amelia, it makes no difference at this stage."

"Jack, we really like each other. I'm single, you're single! I'd like to go out with you. What's the problem?" I said it far too loudly, waving my hands in a dramatic fashion.

"I'm not single," he said.

"What?" I said, stopping dead, sobering up very quickly.

"I have a girlfriend," Jack smiled.

"Why didn't you say something?"

"I tried, but you won't be stopped once you decide to get something off your chest!" he pointed out.

"I feel like a fool!" I wailed, my cheeks burning. "You could have told me to shut up!"

"I'm sorry, Amelia, I tried to stop you. But I wasn't sure what you were going to say anyway."

"Well, you had a fairly good idea!"

"I'm sorry, what can I say?" Jack tried to be diplomatic about it. "I'm really flattered."

"How long have you had her?" I asked, dejected and rejected.

"Not long, about a month."

"What's her name?"

"Her name is Brenda."

"Is she nice?" I asked, for no reason but to compound my own sorrow later tonight as I lay in bed cringing at the memory of this.

"I think so. She's very nice. But, Amelia, let's not talk about her."

"No, it's fine," I replied, sounding lighthearted. "So you really like her?"

"Yes, I do. She seems really nice." Jack smiled and my heart pounded.

He was lovely and I'd blown my chance with him. I could feel my chest cave with the first telltale sign of tears.

"That's good," I said and smiled as I looked at the cars passing by.

Jack touched my sleeve and I looked back at him.

"Ruth was right by the way – I did like you, a lot," he said simply as the others came out from the chip shop and passed around the bags of chips.

"Thank you," I said as he handed me a brown bag full of greasy chips soaked in vinegar.

He held my eyes for a moment and smiled. "Are we still pals?"

I nodded, my eyes locked on his.

He looked away as Liam and Ruth started to walk on.

We walked in silence. The chips I'd been starving for only moments before now felt like lead in my mouth. I ate about three and threw the rest in the nearest bin. Jack flung his in after me. We hailed a taxi and finally one pulled up. Jack and Liam gave it to us and said they'd hail another one. It made sense. I wanted to get as far away from Jack as possible; also, they were going south and we were headed north of the Liffey.

We got in; the taxi had barely left the kerb when Ruth turned to me.

"What's happened with you and Jack?"

"Can I talk to you in the morning?"

"All right, was it bad?" She put her arm around me.

"It was worse than bad," I said quietly. "It was awful."

We were silent, watching the city speed by outside the taxi window. The taxi dropped me off and I climbed into bed, make-up still adorning my cheeks, teeth unwashed, no glass of water, no headache tablets. I would pay for this in the morning but right now I just wanted to get to bed and cry.

44

The hangover was in full swing when I woke up. Head pounding, mouth as dry as Gandhi's flip flop and eyes stuck together with mascara. The alarm went off at ten o'clock and for a God-awful moment I thought it was Monday morning. I was delighted for about four seconds, then I remembered the night before. I pulled the covers over my head and moaned at the memory of last night.

I was just about to curl up and pray for death to come quickly when I remembered the rugby match. I pulled myself out of bed and crawled to the bathroom. I ran the shower and made myself stand under it until my body took over and I washed my hair and face.

I pulled jeans and a jumper out of the wardrobe and dressed while I was waiting for the Disprin to dissolve. I drank it down as Ruth got to the door.

"Ready?" She came in, sprightly and upbeat.

"How are you not sick as a pig this morning?"

"I drank a pint of water and took two Hedex before I went to bed last night," she replied, poking the cat on the side. He lashed at her.

"I feel really ill."

"Did you go straight to bed?"

"Yes. I was not happy."

"Maybe an hour standing in the brisk wind is exactly what you need," Ruth smiled, linking me as we walked towards the door. "And you can tell me about the Jack incident while we walk."

I told her all about it in the car as we travelled to Marley Park.

"He's not fucking single!" she complained. "Also, what possessed you to tell him you were interested in him?"

"You told me he was single and just dying to jump me," I covered my face, cringing from the memory.

"Oh dear God, I didn't know you were about to profess undying love for him!"

"I didn't!"

"You may as well have," Ruth laughed, shaking her head as she looked over at me.

"Stop looking at me. I am already ashamed!" I told her, covering my eyes again.

"Anyway, he told me – he said he wasn't getting any."

"He might not have been at the time. But he is now."

"Well, he's a fast mover if he's getting it now and wasn't when I asked him! And she must be a slapper! I mean what type of a girl gives it up on the first night?" Ruth looked at me for back-up.

I couldn't give any. I was that slapper. I had "given it

up" to Ray more than once that first night. Not my finest hour, but it left me in no position to throw stones at anyone else.

Ruth realised what she'd said and backtracked furiously. "You know I don't mean you. What happened with Ray is a very different scenario."

"No, it wasn't. I was weak and I fancied him. I am that slapper!"

"No, you're not. You're not a slapper. You're just … you're …" She trailed off, unable to decide what I was.

"I'm thick, that's what I am!"

"No!"

"Yes, very much so. I am thick. God help me but I'm awfully thick. Sleeping with Ray on the first night, telling Jack I fancied him when he'd given no indication he fancied me! I am the stupidest girl in Christendom!"

"Well…you just don't seem to think things through." Then she saw the funny side and began to laugh. "Sorry, I shouldn't laugh at you. It was awful what happened last night. It really was."

"All right, stop it now," I told her. "Anyway, when exactly did he tell you he was single?"

"I don't know – but quite recently, at the fax machine."

"What did he say exactly?"

"He said – I asked him if he was getting any," Ruth replied, concentrating very hard on such a lame statement.

"And he said?"

"Nothing, he just smiled," Ruth said and flushed a little as she realised her mistake.

"He *just smiled?* And you interpreted that as meaning 'No, I don't have a girlfriend'? What? Are you serious, Ruth? That meant he was getting some and was too polite to say anything!" I couldn't believe this discrepancy in the story. "Do you actually know Jack at all? Of course, he wasn't going to shout about it. This is Jack!"

"Why did I get the impression he wasn't seeing anyone?" Ruth muttered, more to herself than to me.

"Because you weren't listening to him!"

"But I was. I don't understand this at all." Ruth looked over at me. "Oh Amelia, I'm sorry. I really thought he wasn't seeing anyone. Otherwise, I wouldn't have said anything. You have to know that!"

I looked out the window for a moment, reliving the horror of the conversation.

"Yes, I know you wouldn't do it on purpose. I just wish I'd heard that part of the story before I opened my mouth to him."

We parked the car and went to get out.

"I never knew you were about to ask him out, Amelia. I would have advised against it."

"I know. Maybe that's why I never told you," I replied as we began to walk towards the playing fields.

"You know Chris has lots of rich, cute friends. Maybe I could put in a good word?"

"No thanks, there's been enough matchmaking I think."

"Are you sure? You're looking very pretty today. A hangover brings out the colour of your eyes a treat."

"Shut up!" I laughed.

45

It was hard to do but I tried my best to put Jack to the back of my mind. He was a lost cause. I was a lot of things, but I was not one of those girls who made a play for someone else's boyfriend. It had been done to me a few times in my life and it was the worst feeling on earth, especially when the boy walked off with the new girl on his arm. I would not be stooping that low.

I threw myself into work, leaving Jeff to his own devices as much as I could. Our working relationship had gone from bad to worse. He never missed the chance to have a sly dig and I made it my business not to let any remark go unnoticed. It was only a matter of time before one or other of us brought a gun to work, disgruntled postal-worker style. As of yet neither of us had managed to locate the means of getting our hands on a gun, so the office was safe. I was looking into poisoning the water cooler though and he kept moving the fan so that it was just about to fall off the shelf on to my head as I passed by.

Office politics at their very best.

You can then imagine my delight when I realised that he was going to be on holidays the week that the contract with the Pharmaceutical Company was being signed and handed over. I was going to have to deal with it. I was terrified, but I was not about to tell Jeff that. This was a big contract and whoever signed over and met with the Australian committee would be the first point of contact with them from then on. It was important and Jeff was going to be in Majorca! The joy!

He rang his girlfriend to see if they could cancel but the response was a resounding no. I sat back at my desk smiling broadly as I listened to one side of the phone call. His week in the sun was going to be costly for our Jeffrey. He came out of his office looking ruffled and called me in.

"As you know I am away early next month," he said.

"Yeah, I saw it on the year planner. You're taking a week. I thought you said we must all take two-week breaks?"

He ignored my sniping. "I didn't realise when I booked the break that it would coincide with the Australian contract."

Tough shit! I thought to myself, being careful not to say anything out loud.

"Will you be all right to look after things alone?" he asked.

"I should be fine – I have done this type of thing before," I assured him. This was true in one way but a complete lie in others. I had looked after things like this, but never alone.

"Perhaps we should give Larry a call and let him know you'll be dealing with this alone and you'll need back-up."

"If I need back-up, I'll call Larry. If not I'll get this done by myself," I replied, seething under my forced smile and casual air.

First off, if I was completely out of my depth, of course I would call Larry. I knew why he wanted me to do the phoning; he wanted Larry to remember my name and voice with the call for help. As if I would never mention the fact that Jeff himself was topping up his tan while the office was working on a huge contract. Men can be very silly sometimes – they don't think beyond the next sentence. Jeff was a prime example of this type of male.

Secondly, I was indeed going to call Larry for back-up, but only when Jeff Almighty was safely speeding along, three miles above our heads on his way to Majorca. I didn't want to admit I was out of my depth in front of Jeff, regardless of whether I was or not.

"Could you bring in your entire file on this contract? I want to see it all before I leave, I don't want any surprises when I get back," he said as I was leaving the office.

"You're not leaving for over four weeks, Jeff."

"I still want to see it. Leave it on my desk before you knock off today, unless you have a problem with that?"

"No, none at all," I replied, rolling my eyes as I left the room.

That was the start of it. Jeff was antsy about the fact

that I was looking after the contract alone and wanted to rubber-stamp every move I made and phone call I received. He watched out the office door each time my phone rang and if he left one yellow sticky on my desk he left a hundred. Weekly updates became daily updates and then hourly updates. I was to leave the file on his desk before I left every night and he went through it every morning, then called me in and we "discussed" it at length. There was very little to say about it after the third meeting, things didn't move quickly enough to necessitate an hourly meeting. I was to talk to him about every letter I received and every page that appeared on my desk. It was bordering on harassment, I'm sure of it. He never left me alone.

The weeks ticked by and a fortnight before he left for his sun holiday he came over to my desk. He grabbed an empty seat from the desk beside me. He spun it around so that he was sitting on it backwards, David Brent style.

"Give the guys in Dame Street a call. I think we need a few heads on this one. They'll need a few days to get a team together and, don't take this personally, but maybe a few men on the team would look a bit more professional?"

"What do you mean 'more professional'?" I asked, bristling.

"You know, just in case they need to talk tough. Sorting out contracts isn't really the time for polite chit chat. That is most definitely not the face we want to put forward."

"I completely agree. Chat like that should not and

does not happen during meetings. When have you ever heard any girl in this office discuss make up or periods?" I seethed.

"Look, I said it was nothing personal. I don't want you getting all defensive on me as usual. It was a comment. Most places where women congregate you can usually hear the chat about 'girls' stuff'." He held his finger up and made inverted comma signs as he said the words "girls' stuff".

"Jeffrey, if you are going to continually make comments about 'girls' stuff', please have the balls to use the correct word. The word in question is 'period', not time of the month stuff or blobbing, and what you have referred to on several occasions as being in the blobs is in fact PMT, and people who get it bad have been known to commit murder during these few days. So watch it," I smiled menacingly at him.

"I must check if veiled threats to kill your manager are acceptable under the Personnel Handbook."

"I know that repeated sexist comments are most certainly not acceptable."

"Amelia, I am the boss in this office. I think I asked you to make a phone call. Just make it," he sniffed.

"Fine, I'll call Dame Street and see who they want to send over. They may not feel it's necessary to send anyone over. They may send a group of women. Don't forget, sometimes you men like to hear what strong arms you've all got and how us little girlies couldn't possibly do all the brave things you big boys do! In short you guys like to have your egos massaged. No man can lay on the bullshit or flirt like a girl. It's a gene we're born with and you lot have to sit and watch."

"Fine, whatever you think yourself, missy."

He stayed where he was. I looked at him.

"Are we finished?" I asked.

"No, you have to make a phone call."

"You're going to sit there and listen?"

"Yes, put it on loudspeaker. I need to hear this."

"I'm not making a call out here on loudspeaker with you sitting looking at me," I said.

"Then make it in my office. Either way, I've asked you to do something and you have to do it." He stood up and pointed to his office door.

"I will make the call, but I really would rather you didn't listen into it, pretending you weren't involved. If 'we' make this call then it's a conference call and you do some of the talking yourself."

Finally the call was made. I spoke to Larry at my own desk and with no intervention from Jeff. I told Larry I was holding the fort the following week alone and that it coincided with the Australian contract. He knew what I wanted without me asking and told me that he'd send a group out on Wednesday morning and we would deal with it together. He said that he'd send out Stephen, Louise and Brian from the office and they would take instruction from me.

I told Jeff and he was pleased to hear that some men were coming over, to lend the "professional touch" to the team.

I went home to my mother's house that night all ready to complain bitterly about my day in the office. I was rehearsing the story as I walked up the road towards the house. Then as I got closer, I saw Jenny's car in the driveway.

Great, I thought to myself. She was like an Antichrist lately.

She had finally realised at seven months that she had stretch marks. She made the discovery at some point in the last two weeks. She rang Mum in tears one night, Mum nearly had forty fits and then forty more when she realised the drama was nothing more than a few stretch marks. I didn't want to say anything but I'd seen stretch marks on her side at Christmas but, thanks be to God, I never bothered to say anything about them. She would most likely have shot me at thirty paces if I had. Now that would have been a Christmas to remember for all the family.

Anyway, here she was and no doubt she was complaining again. I walked into the hall and right enough, her voice was to be heard complaining about aches and swollen legs. Mum and Mike were making soothing noises at her and I wondered about turning on my heel and leaving again. In fact, I did more than think about it; I had the door open to go back out when Mum appeared at the kitchen door.

"Amelia, I thought I heard the front door. You gave me a fright."

"Sorry," I replied, shutting the door behind me and coming into the hall.

"Jenny and Mike are here. They just had their first antenatal class. Mike was telling me all about it."

"Really, anything exciting?" I wasn't too keen on hearing all about it. Some things I firmly believe should be on a need-to-know basis. All aspects of childbirth come under this heading.

"Come on in. They went through the whole delivery in this class. It's very interesting. It's completely different from when I had you children."

She makes me laugh the way she still refers to all of us, a thirty-one-year-old, a thirty-year-old and a twenty-five-year-old as children.

"We're not children, Mum," Jenny complained.

I could feel my blood pressure rise as I headed toward the kitchen door. Mum flinched just a touch and rallied.

"Jenny is a bit upset," she mouthed at me as I walked in.

"Hi, Jenny!" I smiled as I rounded the kitchen door.

"Hi," Jenny moaned, looking at her legs that were considerably thicker than they had been. "My legs are like tree-trunks – will they go down after the baby is born, Mum?"

"Yes, all these aches and pains will disappear when the baby arrives."

I pulled out a chair and sat beside Jenny. Not by choice – it was the only seat left.

"How many weeks now?" I asked, putting my hand out to feel her tummy. "Has Bert or Helga been kicking?"

"Stop calling it Bert or Helga! I am not calling it either Bert or Helga, and I'm thirty-two weeks." She got all hot and bothered when she was annoyed.

"It's a joke; I just think Bert and Helga are funny names!" I laughed. "Can I feel your tummy?"

"No, you can't. Why do people think it's all right to just come up and grab my tummy?"

"Oh, get lost! I didn't grab your tummy. I asked if I could touch it!" I attacked, a little too vigorously in hindsight. "Jenny, get a grip. This is a new baby and we're all excited even if you're not!"

Mum and Mike stared open-mouthed and Jenny's face went a really deep crimson.

"Who says I have to be excited? I'm having this baby, isn't that enough for you all?" Jenny blurted before she started to cry.

Mike leaned over the table and held her hand. "She's a bit emotional. It's been very tough on her. She's had every problem under the sun. Piles, swelling, the lot. And now she doesn't want to go through the labour – people shit on the table, did you know that?"

"Shut up Mike! They don't all need to know everything!" Jenny cried.

"People poo on the table, in front of the doctor?" I asked. This was not a need-to-know item, but now that I'd heard I was eager to know the facts.

"They do, just sometimes, not always, but that was the last straw for Jenny. She wants a section and they won't do it without a medical reason."

"I don't blame her. And you have piles, Jenny? How did they diagnose that?" I asked, sympathy and disgust in equal measures.

"Shut up, Amelia. This is not funny," Jenny wailed and for the first time in months I was on her side.

This was awful. Piles and poo, and that's the mother not the baby! "I'm just asking. I'm not laughing at you at all," I assured her.

"Well, stop asking," Jenny turned her attention to Mike. "Mike, I'm going to kill you for telling them all that. I hate you!"

Mum took the situation in hand. "All right, I think we've all had enough of this conversation. Mike say no more. Jenny come inside and put your feet up."

She took Jenny into the sitting-room and set her up on the couch.

While Mike and I were alone in the kitchen I asked him about the antenatal class. He said it was all very interesting and, of course, made the obligatory comment about thanking God he's a boy. Why do men all think this is news to us girls? And why are they surprised when we thank God that we're girls when it comes to asking people out and asking people to marry them?

Mum returned to say Jenny was asking for Mike, so he went in. No doubt to be murdered for telling us all that she had piles. Mum gave out to me in turn for bitching at Jenny.

"Mum, she will not be jumping for joy when that baby is born," I said.

"No mother ever is jumping about after giving birth."

"Mum, you know I was speaking figuratively. She is having serious problems with the baby. I think something should be said."

"I have spoken to her about it," Mum confided. "She is aware of it, and she has been talking to her obstetrician about it. They're dealing with it. But please say nothing to her."

"Mum!" I gasped. "You should have told me that and I would never have said anything!"

"I didn't know you were going to attack her right here!"

"I was defending myself. She attacked me," I complained.

"Look I don't care who bothered who first, just stop having a go at her," Mum stood up. "I presume you're staying for dinner?"

"What are you having?"

"Spaghetti Bolognese is easy."

"All right, I'll stay."

46

Things in work were at fever pitch. It was Friday, Jeff was finishing up and I was officially taking charge of the office. He was terrified; it was as if I was liable to blow the office up if I was left alone with it for over an hour.

He handed me the file for the Australian contract and told me to put it somewhere safe. I contemplated putting it in the bin just for show but he would never have seen the joke. I put it in the filing cabinet, locked it and put the key on a chain around my neck. He told me that I was not as funny as I thought I was. I told him I was; he just didn't understand my wit. He headed back to his office. I believe I won that particular battle. I would be back later to erect a flag just beside the cabinet.

During the weeks prior to Jeff's holiday we'd had two meetings with Stephen, Louise and Brian and we all seemed content enough to let the contract meeting run its course. We were happy that the Australians would be pleased with the progress and the recruits already lined up for interview. I was happy with the team and content that we all knew what was expected of us in during the meeting.

Five o'clock came and Jeff left the building. That was it. He was gone. We could all rest easy on Monday when we came in. He was not going to be waiting, watching and commenting throughout the day. The office belonged to the ordinary people now.

Monday rolled around with alarming speed. I arrived in to find a yellow sticky on my computer screen; it advised me that our entire office hung on the coming meeting. Big as it was, I was not completely sure this meeting was in fact that big.

The week raced by; the atmosphere in the office helped that. Thursday dawned and with it the Big Meeting. I was happy that we were all fully prepared for the meeting, but I couldn't help feeling worried about the whole thing.

I got to the office and checked my suit. I'd had the foresight to bring a fresh shirt with me, so I hung that on the back of Jeff's office door. At 9:30 the call came through. Brian was down with a bug of some kind and there'd only be Louise and Stephen coming over for the meeting. That was a blow. Stephen was not the most eager worker in the world and I had relied on Brian to listen and do a lot of talking in the previous meetings. Without him I figured there'd just be me to talk up the company and field most of the questions. I was not overly pleased with the news but tried to sound professional.

"We'll see if we can do anything this end, but I think you should be fine with Stephen and Louise," Larry said.

"That's fine. We should be all right," I smiled, sick at the thought of this going belly-up through no fault of my own. I could just hear Jeff laughing and telling everyone at the Christmas Party about this cock-up.

The meeting was scheduled for eleven and we were taking them all out to lunch after it was wrapped up. At ten, taking advantage of the fact that I was in charge and therefore allowed to take my time in these things, I went to the toilets and tried to make myself presentable. Twenty minutes later, with a new shirt, new tights, layer of make-up and hair tidied, I looked like a new girl. Would I have handed over a major contract to the girl in the mirror? I just might!

I went outside, put my phone on forward and walked into the meeting-room. The bottled water was cold and all the glasses were sparkling clean. Every seat had a pen and a notepad provided and the room was cool enough without being like a fridge. For one moment I wished Jeff was here to see how well organised I was.

There was a knock on the door and Jeff's secretary poked her head in.

"The Dame Street gang's all here," she smiled.

"Great, I'll be right there."

I followed her back out to the office and greeted them. We didn't have much time so I brought them straight into the meeting room. I showed them the layout and we ironed out last-minute details, like who would answer various questions. I would take all the questions with

411

regard to staffing and interviews. Stephen would talk money and on-going contracts. Louise would deal with talking up the agency, and any history they wanted to know about us.

Another knock on the door. Could this be the Australians? We all stared at each other for a second.

"Oh God!" I mouthed at Stephen and he looked just as concerned.

The door opened and we all stood up. It was Jack. What was Jack doing here? I could feel my cheeks flush under my layers of make-up.

"Jack! What are you doing here?"

"Larry sent me to take Brian's place. He was worried that he was leaving you in the lurch," Jack grinned.

"But why didn't he say it to you before we left?" Stephen asked.

"I dunno. He just came out of his office, told me to grab a taxi and get over here. I'm to take your orders, Amelia. So what do you want me to do?"

I looked at my watch: 10:45. We didn't have much time.

"How much do you know about this case?" I asked.

"I looked at the letters in the taxi, seems straightforward enough. Big company, big contract, rubber seal today. Kiss ass and smile a lot, right?"

I looked at Stephen. He was laughing.

"That's about the speed of it," I smiled, my cheeks beginning to cool down.

"Great, where will I sit?" Jack pulled out a chair. "Also, did I hear we were getting a free lunch after this?"

We were all laughing about that comment when there was a final knock on the door and that was it. The Australians were in the building and all joking was set aside.

They came in, sat down and got to work. They drove a hard bargain. They were not a bit like the casual, relaxed crowd we all know from *Neighbours*. We talked business and nothing else. They listened and questioned and finally two long hours later we all signed on the dotted lines and shook hands.

A quick breather and we headed for lunch.

We were booked into a restaurant around the corner opposite Fairview Park, so we walked. Jack walked ahead with Louise and one of the Australians called Alan. I didn't want to but I found myself watching his every move. He was lovely but I couldn't help wishing he wasn't here. He was out of reach and I had been so busy with work that I was managing to put some space between us. Now here he was and I was right back to square one. My heart fluttered when he spoke and I found myself watching him as he talked, walked, chatted and for the most part completely ignored me. I knew the drill. I'd go home tonight and dream about him, and then wake up in the morning with my giant-sized crush on him alive and well. Back to square one all right.

Lunch was a success, the food was delicious and no one sent anything back. We ordered wine and everyone seemed completely happy with how things had worked out. I sat back and relaxed. I have to admit I thanked God for the Dame Street gang as I was now referring to them. They had helped a lot and, for all his joking beforehand, Jack had really given some show-stopping answers to some gruelling questions.

The Australians went off just after three and we were left to congratulate each other on a job well done. Which we did, again and again. It was decided that we might go for a quick drink after work to celebrate, I had been left with the company credit card and I was happy to use it for such an occasion.

We all headed straight to the pub at five. We found a corner seat in a surprisingly busy pub. The place was jammers with students. It was only when I got to the bar that I saw the big banner: it was their Rag Week, and the Ball was tonight. One plus was that the bar would empty at some point in the night and they would not be returning. I got back to the seat and explained the situation. They decided to wait around, as long as the free drink kept flowing. I looked at the credit card and confirmed that we might be able to organise that. It had been so stressful over the last three weeks in the office that now the meeting was over and contract signed I could finally relax. It was a bit like finishing my Leaving Cert. For the first time in months I had no work to do. I could actually relax, not sit here thinking that there was something else I should be doing.

It was great how quickly we all relaxed into the casual chat again. We discussed all the office gossip, and Ray figured in the conversation again and again. It appeared he was busy "socialising" to his heart's content. There was not a living thing in the office that was not falling victim.

414

If it had a heartbeat it was open season. Mairead had not been back but was still on payroll – Jack had seen her payslip. No one knew exactly what was going on there but they were all watching with bated breath. Ray had bounced back and was not the least bit bothered by any mention of her or her allegations.

"Is she right? Has he reason to worry?" Louise asked.

Every head turned to me. I'm quite sure I went crimson.

"I really can't remember," I lied.

"Then he wasn't awful," Stephen commented. "If he was dreadful you would have remembered. I certainly remember dreadful nights, in that department, much longer than I ever remember fantastic ones."

"True, the cringe factor on a bad night is a huge problem – it can go on for hours!" Jack laughed.

"I thought you guys never gave us a second thought?" said Louise.

"It's true – we don't think about you at all, especially if it's a disaster," Jack grinned. "It's completely personal. If we don't perform well, then we think about that. You really don't figure in it!"

"Oh my God! Straight from the horse's mouth!" Louise spluttered. "You men are so full of your own importance!"

"Well, it's true!" Jack defended himself laughing. "Don't tell me you think only about us if a night of passion goes horribly wrong? You have to worry about your performance!"

"No, usually if a night of passion, as you call it, goes wrong it's something you lot have done!" I said.

"What, you think no girl ever just lies there and thinks of Ireland?" Stephen laughed.

"Yes, I'm sure some do, but it's usually because you lot are so completely boring, she's thinking of her shopping list as she waits for you to finish!" I said, a little surprised at the level the conversation had dropped to.

"You think of shopping lists?" Jack and Stephen asked in unison.

"No, not necessarily," I laughed, "and may I say this conversation has gone completely downhill!"

"It's true – this is a fairly lowlife conversation," Louise added. "We should really stop before we drink much more and someone thinks it's a plan to give some sort of demonstration!"

At that we all sobered up a bit and changed the subject.

We had another few drinks before people began to fade. The thing about going to the pub straight from the office is that you fade some time around eight or nine and usually about ten o'clock you fall into a drunken sleep. You forget that by ten you have been drinking for up to five hours already and you shouldn't. It's really bad for you.

Stephen was the first to make moves towards leaving. He finished his pint and looked around for his jacket.

"Is anyone else ready for bed?" he asked.

"Not just yet, but I won't be far behind you," I replied.

"I might go with you – are you getting a taxi?" Louise asked, draining the last of her drink.

"Yeah, come on."

They left very quickly and Jack and I were left alone. Jack had about three quarters of a pint left and I was working very hard at finishing a large glass of red wine.

We sat quiet for a moment. I wondered how long it would take Jack to finish his drink and make for the door. Sure enough he was downing the pint very fast. All but a mouthful was left when he put the glass back down.

He turned around to face me.

"We're still friends after our night out, aren't we?" he asked.

"I hope so. I really just want to say –"

"No, stop – let's not get into it again. There's no need to rehash the whole thing."

"I just want you to know I would never have said it if I thought you were going out with someone," I cringed. "I really am sorry,"

"No need to apologise. These things happen from time to time." He smiled at me and I was left just a little weak at the knees. Why was he so bloody nice?

"Still going strong with Brenda?" I asked, being the glutton for punishment that I am.

Jack finished his pint. "Yes, we're fine."

"Would you like another?" I asked, pointing at his glass.

"No, I'd better not. I should head soon."

"Right." I picked up my drink and tried to finish it.

He waited patiently while I drank a little more of the wine. Finally I had to give up, pretending I was not going to finish the glass. The atmosphere was too much and we both wanted out.

We walked up the road in silence and hailed the first taxi that passed. They dropped me off first and Jack went on home.

Inside, I took off my make-up and got into my pajamas. I sat on the couch flicking stations before I went to bed. Right enough I woke up the next morning with my massive crush on Jack reawakened and no way of ever seeing him again.

The next day, I was only in the door to the office when Ruth rang me. She was dying to hear about how things had gone the night before. She was very disappointed to hear Jack had dropped me home in virtual silence and was still going strong with Brenda.

"Well, that's that, I suppose," I told her. "I really should start looking further afield."

"Maybe you should," Ruth replied, sounding almost as miserable as I did.

"I might take you up on that offer you made about Chris's friends!" I laughed half-heartedly.

"Don't knock it – they might be just what you need. Mister Right-Now and all that!"

"Well, don't go setting me up just yet," I said as I watched a few staff members walk in the door ten minutes late. "Listen I'd better go – I want to catch a few eyes here and make people feel bad!"

I hung up and gave various people "the look"; they smiled sheepishly and gave various excuses as to why they were late.

I spent the day making sure all 'i's' were dotted and

't's'were crossed for his nibs' return on Monday. I was not going to be complained at if things weren't perfect.

At 5:30 I turned off my computer and walked out.

The week had been a success, the office hadn't blown up and a few of the people on our books had managed to secure jobs while he was away. All in all I was very proud of myself. He would never know that I was completely terrified for the first forty-eight hours. I would never tell him that I had spent an hour in the toilets on Monday morning sick with nerves, convinced that the entire staff would either call in sick or hand in their resignations.

Neither of which had happened, you'll be pleased to hear.

47

The weeks passed by quite uneventfully. Jeff returned and drove us all mad for a while, then we got used to him again and managed to ignore him.

Jenny had four weeks to go and we were all waiting with bated breath. I know that most women and pretty much every first-time mother goes over her due date. But as the weeks went by we were getting very excited in the house. Jenny was huge, seriously, the size of a house, and I'm not talking about those two-bed "starter homes" that they charge the earth for, I'm talking a monster five-bed detached on its own grounds, perhaps with a lake and a wooded area within the grounds and a herd of deer grazing on the grass. She was enormous. Luke had a book open as to what size the baby would be, but it was all top secret – Mum would have killed him if she'd known and Jenny might have actually exploded, thus ending the book I suppose. Dad, Luke, Luke's girlfriend Susan, Ruth and myself were changing our bets as the days went by. I had five euro on it being a girl, going a full week over and weighing about eight pounds – I figured no more than eight, maybe seven nine or so. Luke was sure it was going to be a boy, and he'd weigh in at just over ten pounds and that Jenny would be carting around a ten-pounder for an extra fortnight – that thought alone brought tears to my eyes. I went straight to the kitchen and made her a cup of tea.

Jenny would call in to Mum in the afternoon and we'd ask her pertinent questions.

Any backache?

Any stomach pains?

Cramps?

Any new pains?

Any bursts of energy?

Any nesting?

We'd then all rush upstairs and re-adjust our bets.

We heard that last Thursday she's had a false start and when the doctor examined her he confirmed that although it was a false start they should have the baby-bag at the door, as there was very little chance of her going much over her due date.

This news changed all bets and we were eager to get up the stairs before Luke "closed the book". He had developed this habit in the last few days that after a bet was placed he'd announce that he was "closed for all further bets" and make a show of closing his notebook. Dad had words with him and he opened the book again.

That Friday night Luke and I were in his room

discussing the betting situation and counting the money laid down already, when Mum arrived in on top of us. She must have tiptoed up the stairs in an attempt to take us by surprise. She did. We dived to cover the money and close the box it was being held in.

"I know what you're up to," she tutted. "Jennifer and I want to place a bet."

"What?" I replied, considering feigning innocence.

"How much is it? Is there a minimum bet you have to place?" Mum asked, ignoring the look on my face.

"No, but we're not taking any more bets on a baby girl being born on her due date, the day before or the day after," Luke said, reopening the book.

"Right, I say a baby boy, a week early. Are we betting on weight?" Mum asked unflinching.

"A boy!" I laughed. "Mum, don't let her hear you bet on a boy. She'll go mad!"

"I think it's a big bruiser of a boy she's having," Mum said.

"Hang on a minute!" Luke smelled a rat. "Does Jenny know the sex already?"

"No, she does not," Mum was indignant. "She doesn't want to either. There are few enough true surprises in this life."

"Did she do the wedding-ring-over-the-tummy thing?" Luke's eyes narrowed.

"Not that she told me. Are you taking the bet or not?" Mum waved a fifty euro impatiently at us.

"Fine." Luke took the money and wrote down the details of her bet. "And what about Jenny?"

"She wants to bet on a girl, two weeks early," Mum handed over another fifty euro.

"Wishful thinking on the two weeks early thing," I sniggered, making a mental note to change my bet in line with Jenny's one.

Luke must have read my mind. No sooner was the bet taken than he announced that there were no further bets being taken on Jenny's betted dates.

Mum looked at the book and read the bets that had already been laid and how they were changing almost daily.

The date Jenny herself had betted on came and went. I sat up until midnight just to be sure I'd be ready for the off, just in case I got that call. I watched Sky News as they changed over from Wednesday April 21st to Thursday April 22nd. I listened to the headlines and then went to bed. So Jenny had just lost fifty euro, I thought to myself as I brushed my teeth and turned out the light. Nothing happened the following week either. Again we waited, breath bated and hearts pounding every time the phone rang. Noone's phone rang for more than three rings – we were falling over furniture and breaking family heirlooms in order to get to the phone.

Each time we were disappointed: some relation would ask if there was any news and we'd have to say no. They'd try to engage us in conversation about the weather or some tribunal or other. We were having none of it. They'd be cut short and told that we were trying to keep the phone line open for any news from Mike. Some would get the hint and go away; others would not. The ones who didn't get the hint will not be getting a Christmas card from the Slaters this Christmas. They have no one to blame but themselves. Mum is adamant about it.

Suddenly we were in March. No baby and Jenny was becoming somewhat unhinged. She would come in and announce: "Do not adjust your set – I'm still nine months pregnant."

Then she'd settle down in her chair and whine about the pains and aches and the fact that she had put on almost three stone and that most of the weight was on her ass not the baby.

Maybe we'd be waiting the full two weeks past her due date. I didn't know what effect that would have on Jenny – she was bad enough all ready. It would kill us though. Mum would have to be hospitalised. She'd be frantic.

I know we'd been waiting for the news for almost a month now, but when the call finally came from Mike it was a complete and utter shock.

The phone rang at about 8:20 on Wednesday the 5th of May.

Mum had just sat down and she asked me to go and get it, her feet were swollen and she was not getting back up again. I leaned over, stretching as far as is humanly possible because I didn't feel like getting up from the couch.

"Hello?"

"Amelia?"

"Mike!" I sat up,

Mum threw her mug of tea back on to the table beside

her and was on her feet in about .02 of second.

"I'm a Dad! I'm a Dad!" he shouted down the phone, his voice cracking. "Jenny had a boy! I have a son!"

"A boy!" I shouted and Mum actually knocked me over grabbing for the phone.

"Mike, a boy? How are they? What weight is he? Why didn't you call us as soon as she went in?" Mum asked, tears falling down her face.

I ran upstairs shouting to Luke and Dad.

"It's a boy! It's a boy!" I yelled.

Luke came out of his room and we jumped around hugging on the landing we were so happy. We have not hugged like that since we were tiny children. Dad appeared from the kitchen and went into the sitting-room.

Mum came tearing up the stairs. "Get your coats on – we can go in and see them for a few minutes if we hurry. Amelia, Jenny wants some Clinique package or other. Can you bring it with you?"

I had bought her a big basket of Clinique moisturisers with skin creams, tinted moisturiser and lip-balm as a present, but it was back in the apartment.

"It's in the apartment," I said.

"Well, we'll go and get it. She wants it; apparently her face is a mess, so she says. We'll swing by the apartment."

"All right."

Luke and I had our coats on in no time and were waiting by the door, another thing we rarely did nowadays. Coats on and queuing by the front door was a regular sight when we were teenagers but not so much now for some reason.

Mum tidied herself up and reappeared with a huge teddy bear from somewhere in her room. Dad appeared, coat on and car keys in his hand. We filed out and jumped in the car.

"We have to call in to Clontarf on the way," I told Dad.

"On the way to Holles Street?" Dad said.

"Yes, I have to pick up a few things for Jenny. She asked for them." I knew that was the winning card. If Jenny wanted us to swing by Belfast on our way in, we'd have done it.

We pulled into the carpark in Clontarf and I was given strict instructions not to be more than three minutes.

I ran up to the apartment and grabbed her gifts; I also had bought a floppy giraffe for the baby, in the neutral tones of lemon and cream. I shoved them in a bag and raced out, avoiding the mirror and the temptation to change my clothes and fix my make-up. I was on a timer here and I really wanted us to get to the hospital as soon as we possibly could. Tomorrow I would call in looking drop-dead gorgeous; tonight I was in an oversized grey tracksuit and pink hoody.

I raced down the stairs and was just opening the main door of the block when a man stepped to the side and held the door open for me. I flashed him a smile and raced by. Then I screeched to a halt. I turned back towards him just as he turned to me.

"Jack?"

"Amelia," Jack smiled."Where are you off to?"

"My sister just had her baby. I'm running to the hospital."

I was truly caught in a Catch 22: I wanted Jack to stay but there was no way I was missing the baby.

"Shit," Jack muttered, then stopped. "Sorry, not about the baby, that's fantastic about the baby. Was it a boy or a girl?

"A boy, we're racing in to see him. Mum and Dad are waiting for me," I pointed at the car and Dad started the engine. I could see Mum gesturing frantically at me.

"I'll drop you in," Jack announced.

"What?"

"Yeah, I'll drop you in. I'll wait outside. I need to talk to you."

Dad beeped at me.

"You might not be able to get into the hospital, and I might be a while," I said.

"No matter – can I drop you in?"

"Fine, just hang on."

I ran over to Mum and explained that Jack was bringing me in and to tell them we were right behind in the car.

"Who's he? Tell him you're in a hurry," Mum complained.

"It's Jack. He'll drop me in to the hospital."

"Who's Jack when he's at home? Is he a neighbour?" Mum was taking him off her Christmas-card list as we spoke.

"Dad, will you explain at the hospital and make sure they let us in?" I asked around Mum's frowning profile.

"Will do."

They drove off at high speed.

I turned back to Jack who was standing by his car a few feet away. I went over and Jack took the Clinique basket from me and opened the car. He put the basket on the back seat and I got in the front. Now that we were in the car I was suddenly very aware of the "newness" of this situation. I was suddenly shy and more than a little self-conscious sitting there. Jack looked like he felt the same way.

"So, a boy," he said as he started the car and we drove out. "And did you say she's in Holles Street?"

"Yeah," I smiled.

"Well, that'll teach me to ring before I call to someone's house late at night," Jack smiled. "I really walked in on a family moment. Sorry about that."

"No, it's not your fault. You weren't to know – it doesn't happen every day that my sister has a baby."

"No, they say it happens every second of every day, but it rarely enough happens to anyone we know!" Jack laughed, and it was true.

Babies are born all day every day, something like eight thousand of the tiny dots in each Dublin maternity hospital each year, but it's rare enough that any of us know the baby in question. And tonight, for the first time in my life, I'm an aunt and there's a baby just been born that I'm related to. This baby will like me, and I'll love it and we'll be connected. I got a hot gush of love through my entire body. I checked my watch not wanting to waste any more time in the car than was entirely necessary.

"We're nearly there," Jack smiled as he caught my eye. He was right. One set of traffic lights later we were circling Merrion Square looking for a parking space. We pulled in and grabbed the presents from the back of the car.

I rushed into the hospital, and looked blindly around for directions. Jack took over: he went straight over to reception and gave them Jenny's name. The girl smiled and told us she was expecting us. We were directed to the Merrion wing and we raced through the corridors. Finally we located the room and rushed in. Mum, Dad, Mike's parents, Mike and Luke were sitting around the room looking subdued and loved up.

"Jenny!" I grinned, hugging her close. "Where is he?"

"Right here," Jenny smiled down at this tiny baby wrapped in a blue blanket. "This is Conor Michael Elliott."

He was fast asleep and completely unaware of the fuss his arrival had caused.

"What happened? Why didn't you tell us you were here?" I asked.

Jack walked around the back of me and looked at the baby, then went over to Mike and shook hands. I was vaguely aware of his movements but I was more interested in Jenny and baby Conor. How long would it take before I got used to calling him by his name? Suddenly there was a person called Conor in our family, and I couldn't get my head around it.

"I went into labour last night and we came in this morning, but it was going so slowly that I asked Mike not to call anyone. I was sure it'd last forever and we didn't want everyone ringing for updates. Then suddenly I went from four centimetres to nine centimetres in about twenty minutes and then everything went so fast. It was actually quite quick – once I got to that point there was no looking back."

"Did you get an epidural?" I asked.

"Yes, I'd just got it in time, a few minutes later and they said I'd have been too far gone," Jenny laughed.

"And did you poo?" I asked in a hushed whisper.

"No, I don't think I did," Jenny whispered.

"Think? You have to be sure on that one. How can you not be sure?"

"I'm almost certain – there really is no way of knowing for sure. You can't see down there and they keep changing these pad things from under you."

"Ask the midwife," I advised. "That kind of information is very important."

"No, it's not," Jenny smiled. "Not any more. Once Conor was born and he was healthy I could have danced naked up Grafton Street. And you know I'm not that kind of girl!"

We sat staring at the tiny bundle for a further half-hour before Dad suggested that we allow Jenny get some rest. The disappointment at leaving the baby behind was tangible.

Mum finally pulled rank and insisted that she be allowed hold him.

"I must hold my grandson before I leave," she announced and, of course, Jenny let her.

Well, that was it: we all queued up and held him. He slept through it all, completely exhausted by the day's events. We left the hospital grinning at each other and hugging on the steps.

"Oh shit!" I announced and everyone looked around.

"My bag, I left it upstairs."

I turned and ran back up to the room. I knocked and went in only to find Jenny sitting alone – the baby had been taken back to the nursery and Mike had left with the rest of us. Jenny was sitting crying by herself.

"What's wrong?" I asked, suddenly afraid that the smiles of ten minutes ago were a show and in fact she was still having a hard time coming to terms with motherhood. I went over and sat beside her on the bed. She tried to stop crying, shuddering with sniffs and sobs.

"Is it because it's a boy?" I asked tentatively.

"No," she cried, blowing her nose and shivering. "He's gone back to the nursery and I miss him. Already, I miss him."

"That's all right. That's normal I'm sure," I smiled, hugging her around the shoulders.

"But I was such a bitch all through the pregnancy! I never stopped bitching about everything. When he kicked I complained. What kind of a person complains about that?" Jenny cried.

I didn't know what to say about it. I'd never been pregnant so how could I advise her?

"It was the hormones," I assured her. "I'm sure loads of women complain all through the whole nine months."

"Not about the kicking, that's meant to be a wonderful feeling. I never stopped complaining and now he's here I love him so much. I don't deserve him – he's perfect and I don't deserve it – I'm a bad mother!"

"You're not a bad mother! You are a cranky patient, you don't suffer pregnancy gladly, but you said yourself, you love Conor. That's what counts!"

"I do love him, I absolutely love him!" Jenny turned towards me. "Please, never let him know I was such a bitch about him before he was born. I have no idea why I was such a tyrant."

"It was hormones, and the main thing is you love him now. He's perfectly healthy and you love him. Forget about the last nine months and enjoy your maternity leave," I smiled. "Now I better go. Jack's waiting for me."

Jenny smiled at me and I left.

Talk about your hormones being all over the place! But I was glad she acknowledged she had been such a bitch.

I got down to the main door and everyone was gone – just Jack was left sitting on the steps outside. I opened the door and went out to him. He heard the door opening and stood up.

"Thanks for waiting. I was longer than I expected. Jenny was having a moment and I had to reassure her that she's a wonderful mother," I said, hopping down the steps.

"No bother. It's a lovely night. I didn't mind waiting."

We walked in companionable silence across the road and by Merrion Square to Jack's car.

Although it was after ten the sky wasn't completely dark and the air was warm after the sunny day. We walked and I absent-mindedly watched the bushes on the other side of the railings. Suddenly one of them moved and we heard the unmistakable sound of "love-making" coming from the other side of the bush.

"Oh my God!" I laughed, half amused and half appalled. "Are there people in the park?"

"Yeah, leave them to it!" Jack laughed. "Amelia, come away from there!"

Despite myself I had moved toward the railings and was peering in.

"You don't want to disturb them," he said, from behind me.

I stepped back too far and bumped into him, then twirled around to apologise.

"Sorry!" I said.

I was very close to him, almost touching. Then he leaned forward. I didn't move. He leaned closer and we kissed. His lips were warm and soft and there was the old familiar smell of freshly ironed clothes. I put my hand up to the back of his neck and he leaned his body closer. We leaned close and his arms enfolded me. All I kept thinking was: I'm kissing Jack!

Then very suddenly a new thought struck me. I pulled away.

"Your girlfriend! Jesus, sorry, Jack!" I stepped back, out of his embrace.

"She's gone. That's why I was coming over. That's why I didn't want to leave."

"Really?" I said. It all sounded a little convenient to me.

"Yes, things were going downhill. We probably could have sorted it out, but neither of us wanted to. She went back to her ex and I hung around for a fortnight wondering if I should call you or just knock on your door."

"So you picked tonight of all nights to knock on my door?"

"And it was a good thing I did. Another two minutes and I'd have missed you!"

"You have no idea how close you came to missing me. I was only running in to get a present. I'd been in my mother's all day."

We walked up to his car and he drove me home. Then he came up to the apartment for a cup of tea as we both needed to wind down a little after all the happenings of the night.

Of course, once we got into the apartment winding down was the last thing on our minds. Trying to keep some lid on things, I put on the kettle and was standing in the kitchen waiting for it to boil when Jack came in. He came up behind me and put his arms around me. I turned around and we stood face to face for a moment before he kissed me. I put my hand up to his face and felt his cheek, noticing he was beginning to need a shave. Then he put his hands on my waist and lifted me up on to the counter-top. He kissed me deeper and ran his fingers through my hair. His hands wandered towards the zipper on my hoody. I had no top on underneath and I felt we were moving too fast.

"Stop," I whispered.

His hand was removed in heartbeat, and he breathed, "Sorry!"

We kissed for a few minutes until the kettle boiled. I pulled away.

"Still want a cup of tea?"

"Not really," he smiled and took my hand, leading me back to the sitting-room.

Once on the couch it was hard to keep things from moving very fast. He moved down to my neck and kissed very lightly, making my stomach flip with anticipation. His hand hovered close to my top but he didn't touch it.

Jack was a complete gentleman. I had made it clear under the top was out of bounds and he never went near it, at least not until I gave him the come on! He glanced at me, that glance you get at moments like these, full of meaning, and suddenly the slightest shake of your head can put an end to the night. Needless to say, I didn't shake my head. I went the other way, and Jack didn't need to be told twice.

Having said that, I was still determined to keep some kind of hold on my self-respect and not allow things to move any further.

But Jack was good and my resolve was weakening with every second that passed. For such an unassuming guy, he certainly must have listened in his biology classes. As I say my resolve was weakening, but not enough. I pulled away from him and suggested that we leave it there for the first night.

"Sorry, you're right," Jack leaned back and sat up.

"Would you like a cup of tea now?" I asked.

"I suppose I'd better. I can't leave just at the moment," Jack replied, rearranging himself with an embarrassed grin.

"I see," I smiled and went to the kitchen.

I returned with two mugs of tea. I placed one on the coffee table, noting as I did that Jack was beginning to

435

calm down a little. He saw me look and blushed.

"Stop that!" he smiled, then picking up his mug he held it high. "So cheers to the new auntie!"

"Yea, cheers indeed!" I raised my mug and grinned.

"God, he's fabulous, isn't he?"

"Very cute, from what I saw of him anyway."

"He's so small! My God, I really had no idea he was going to be that tiny. You should have seen her – she was huge!"

"That's a charming thing to say about your sister," Jack laughed.

"It's true, she was a monster, and he was only seven pounds three, after all that."

"Hey, seven three is a good weight. Wait till you have to pass a 'tiny' baby of just seven pounds three!" Jack pointed out.

Again, tears sprang to my eyes. "Dear God, how do we do it?" I asked in all seriousness.

"I have no idea. I just thank God I'm a man and will never have to find out!"

"I might never have any," I said, not totally unhappily. "I mean, why do we all presume we'll have millions of kids?"

"Oh, I think some people are just destined to be mammies and daddies," Jack said. "You are definitely destined to be a mammy."

"Do you think so?" I brightened up a little. "Sometimes I can be very impatient with kids."

"Everyone's impatient with other people's kids – we all hate them if we were completely honest."

Jack and I sniggered the snigger of two people who were in the know. We knew this was true; we could think of kids we hated and pretended to like. We didn't name names, but we knew, and it was one of those bonding moments that come along every now and then.

Jack glanced at the clock, the one on my video. It was a quarter to twelve.

"I'd better be off," he said, leaning forward and putting his mug back on the coffee table. "Work tomorrow."

I watched him get up off the couch and stretch. He turned to me and held out his hand. I took it and he pulled me up to standing.

"Will I call you tomorrow night?" he asked.

"You'd better call me tomorrow," I smiled, stretching as I spoke.

I followed him out to the front door and kissed him goodbye.

"I'll call you tomorrow," he said, smiling down at me as he left.

He walked down the hall, turned the corner and was out of sight. I shut the door and began to clear up. I would watch a little television before I went to bed; there was no point in trying to sleep now. I was too worked up; too much had happened all at once tonight. I put the mugs in the dishwasher and tidied up the sitting-room. I turned up the TV which had been muted earlier on. I watched a re-run of *Cheers* and marvelled at Kirsty Allie's puffed sleeves. I picked up my mobile phone, wondering about the hour and whether I should ring Ruth. I decided to text her instead.

It said: *Baby Boy, Conor Michael, 7lbs 3oz. Jack and I got it 2gether. Big news! Ring asap!"*

No sooner was the text sent than my phone rang. I began to tell about all about the comings and goings of the night.

I finished the story, answered all of her questions and took a breather while we both digested the news. It was at this point that I realised I was exhausted. I yawned so wide I made my eyes water. We said goodbye, I turned off the lights and headed straight to bed.

Even though I'd been really excited I fell into a deep sleep. Maybe for the first time in months I was truly relaxed and happy as I drifted off.

The following morning I went into Jeff's office and booked a week off work. He tried to complain but I pointed out that I'd told him about my plan to take the time off last January.

"And Jeff, you might think about watching what you say to me in general, around the office. Some of your comments are quite sexist. Don't force my hand – I will take it to Personnel if I have to," I told him.

His mouth opened and shut like a goldfish. I stood up and left his office.

I had a week off starting Monday, Jeff was beginning to run scared of me, Conor was here, full of health and energy, and I had Jack.

All in all the tables were turning, and March was shaping up to be a fantastic month.

Maybe this was the start of something really good; maybe I was getting my life together. Finally!

Six months later . . .

Just to keep you all posted.

It's now November. Conor is a happy, healthy and very loud six-month-old. I can't remember what the house was like before he arrived. He is such a tiny person and yet his presence is felt in every square inch of the house – perhaps that's because he brings such an entourage everywhere he goes. They fill every square inch. His toys, bottles, nappies and soothers can be found in all kinds of places. We found one of his soothers in the drinks cabinet last week; no one knows quite how it got there. I know he shares some of my family genes but there's no way he's drinking already!

Work is going well. Jeff's still there and still making dreadful remarks all the time. He doesn't say too much to me though; he's still a bit scared of me. Which suits me just fine.

Jack and I are still together. Still going strong, as they say.

I met Ray the other day. I hadn't seen him in a few months and although he's still gorgeous I was not overly impressed. Jack has that something, the "it" factor that cannot be bought or learned – you either have it or you don't. I now realise that Ray never had it. Jack, on the other hand, has it in spades. It's lots of little things really: respect, manners, loyalty, a quiet strength, a fantastic smile and a great body. If on top of all of the above he manages to make you laugh regularly, you know you've hit the jackpot. If you find a guy like this, and he's not already married, of course, you really should think about marking your territory fast.

We all know the type. You didn't even realise you fancied him until one day you wake up and there he is, all around you and you're in love. That's the best way to describe Jack. One day he was there and I'm hoping he never goes away.

I don't know if Jack and I will ever get around to having any "little Jacks" of our own, but it's a lot of fun practising. We practise all the time and you know what they say . . . practice makes perfect. So if we ever get around to it, our kids will be bloody well amazing!

The End